TRAILBLAZERS

FEATURING

HARRIET TUBMAN

AND OTHER CHRISTIAN HEROES

DAVE & NETA JACKSON

TRAILBLAZERS

FEATURING

HARRIET TUBMAN

AND OTHER CHRISTIAN HEROES

BETHANY HOUSE PUBLISHERS
Minneapolis, Minnesota

Trailblazers: Featuring Harriet Tubman and Other Christian Heroes

Previously published in five separate volumes:
Listen for the Whippoorwill Copyright © 1993
Kidnapped by River Rats Copyright © 1991
Quest for the Lost Prince Copyright © 1996
Exiled to the Red River Copyright © 2003
Assassins in the Cathedral Copyright © 1999

Cover design by Lookout Design, Inc.

Scripture quotations are from the King James Version of the Bible.

Published by Bethany House Publishers
11400 Hampshire Avenue South
Bloomington, Minnesota 55438

Bethany House Publishers is a division of
Baker Publishing Group, Grand Rapids, Michigan.

Printed in the United States of America

ISBN 978-0-7642-0666-5

DAVE and NETA JACKSON are an award-winning husband-and-wife writing team, the authors or coauthors of more than a hundred books. They are most well-known for the TRAILBLAZERS, a forty-book series of historical fiction about great Christian heroes for young readers (with sales topping 1.7 million), and Neta's popular YADA YADA PRAYER GROUP novels for women.

Dave and Neta also brought their love for historical research to the four-volume series of HERO TALES. Each book features fifteen Christian heroes, highlighting important character qualities through forty-five nonfiction stories from their lives.

The Jacksons make their home in the Chicago metropolitan area, where they are active in cross-cultural ministry and enjoy their grandchildren.

Books by
Dave & Neta Jackson

Heroes in Black History

Hero Tales Volume I

Hero Tales Volume II

Hero Tales Volume III

Hero Tales Volume IV

Trailblazers: Featuring Harriet Tubman and Other Christian Heroes

Trailblazers: Featuring Amy Carmichael and Other Christian Heroes

LISTEN FOR THE WHIPPOORWILL

HARRIET TUBMAN

Authors' Note

All the historical facts and information about Harriet Tubman in this story are true. Rosebud and her family, the little band of runaways, and the Quaker family depicted in this story, while not actual people, are based on typical people and events that happened while Harriet Tubman was a "conductor" on the Underground Railroad. Thomas Garrett, the Quaker abolitionist, and William Still, secretary for the Vigilance Committee in Philadelphia, were also real people who aided Harriet Tubman and the slaves' journey to freedom on the Underground Railroad.

CONTENTS

CHAPTER 1

THE STRANGER

Leaning over the edge of the rain barrel, Rosebud plunged the wooden bucket into the water. Hauling with all her strength, the girl then heaved the heavy bucket over the edge, spilling half of the water in the process—most of it on herself.

Rosebud cussed under her breath, then looked quickly around to see if Mammy had heard. But she could still hear her mother singing inside the cookhouse:

Climbin' up the mountain, children.
Didn't come here for to stay,
If ah nevermore see you again,
Gonna meet you at de judgment day.

Sarah Jackson was cook for the Big House on the old Powers Plantation, and twelve-year-old Rosebud had been helping her mother as long as she could remember. Today was bread-baking day, and Rosebud's job was to scrub out the big pots that the dough had been mixed in.

Sloshing water over her bare feet with every step, the girl carried the bucket over to the pots lying on the grass. April clouds hid the sun and she shivered in the cool Maryland air. Rosebud hated baking day, and she especially hated scrubbing out the dough pots. Gooey flour clung in great clumps to the sides, and scrub as she might, it never seemed to come off.

Rosebud was working on her second pot when she heard hoofbeats. Even though the cookhouse stood behind the Big House, from where Rosebud was working she could just see the long, tree-lined lane leading up to the Big House. A lone horseman was riding up the lane. She didn't recognize the man or the horse.

"Isaac!" she yelled. "Isaac! You better make tracks. Horseman comin'!"

Fifteen-year-old Isaac appeared from behind the cookhouse. "I seed him," he hissed at her as he trotted past. "Don't be telling me my business." Then he disappeared around the front of the house to hold the stranger's horse while the man dismounted.

Isaac was stable boy for the Powers Plantation. Rosebud knew her older brother liked taking care of the riding horses, but he had a bad habit of sneaking off to catch crawdads in the creek below the stable. Once Mr. Powers couldn't find Isaac when he wanted his horse; Isaac had been given a terrible whipping when he was found asleep in the straw. "Fool boy gonna get us all on the auction block," Rosebud's pappy had muttered. Abe Jackson was Mr. Powers' top field hand, but he didn't mess with "Massa Powers." Frightened, Rosebud had taken it upon herself after that to be Isaac's eyes and ears and let him know when he was wanted.

A few minutes later she saw Isaac run back toward the stable. Curious, Rosebud dropped her scrub brush and walked cautiously along the side of the Big House, being careful to keep out of sight. The stranger talking to Mr. Powers was square-jawed and stocky, with a full head of white hair. From behind the bushes she could just make out what he was saying.

"President Fillmore is finally enforcing the Fugitive Slave Law—which makes my job easier." The man spit out a stream of tobacco juice, threw back his head, and laughed. "But it makes them Nigra-lovers up north crazy mad."

"I don't need a slave catcher." Mr. Powers sounded annoyed. "My slaves are very loyal."

Rosebud saw the stranger take a long, critical survey of the buildings on the plantation. The cookhouse, stable, tobacco barns, weaving shed, and the rows of tiny cabins hidden among the trees in the slave quarters all looked tired and weather-beaten. Even the Big House needed a coat of paint.

"Waal," the man drawled, spitting again, "I'm buyin' slaves, too—need 'em for a chain gang down South, clearin' forest land for crops. I can pay a good price."

"I'm not eager to sell any of my slaves if I can help it," said Mr. Powers curtly. "But if cotton and tobacco prices keep falling . . . I may be forced to do something." He shrugged. Just then Isaac reappeared with Mr. Powers' big bay horse, all saddled and bridled. "Ah! Here's my horse. We can take a look at some of the slaves if you like, but I'm not making any promises."

But as Mr. Powers put his boot in the left stirrup and started to swing into his saddle, the saddle slipped.

Before Rosebud knew what was happening, Mr. Powers had whirled angrily on Isaac. "You good-for-nothing boy!" he yelled, striking her brother about the head again and again with his riding crop. "Are you trying to break my neck? Maybe you'd rather work a chain gang down South, eh?"

With an angry jerk, Mr. Powers tightened the saddle girth and rode off with the stranger toward the tobacco fields. Rosebud could see Isaac fighting back angry tears. Looking around, the boy saw his sister watching from the corner of the Big House. Upset that someone had witnessed his humiliation, Isaac ran around the Big House and took off through the trees toward the creek.

Rosebud was scared and raced back to the cookhouse. "Mammy!" she cried, trembling. Sarah Jackson was just sliding a long wooden paddle out of the oven with four loaves of golden bread, steaming and fragrant. The older woman straightened. Her black face, framed with a blue bandana tied around her head, shone with sweat. It was obvious that she was heavy with child, soon to give birth.

Words tumbled out in a rush as Rosebud told what had just happened. "Is Massa Powers gonna sell Isaac to a chain gang?" the girl cried, fear in her eyes.

Sarah wiped her face with the bottom of her apron. "Hush, now, girl. Massa Powers was just embarrassed to be made a fool of in front of a stranger," she said. "He prob'ly didn't mean nothin' by it." But she went to the door of the cookhouse and looked anxiously in the direction of the creek.

Rosebud pleaded to go look for Isaac, but Sarah ordered her to finish cleaning the dough pots. Rosebud could hardly keep her mind on her work. What if Isaac had run away? What if he wasn't there to unsaddle Mr. Powers' horse when he came back? She'd heard tales whispered fearfully among the slaves about the dogs sent after a runaway. She had to find Isaac!

But when the pots were finally drying on the grass, it was time for Rosebud, along with Phoebe—a young slave woman whom Sarah was training to be a cook—to help prepare supper for the folks in the Big House.

By the time the last steaming pot of oyster stew and fresh bread had been delivered to the serving maids at the back door of the Big House, daylight was almost gone. With heart thumping, Rosebud ran to the stable. Mr. Powers' horse was in its stall munching the hay in the manger . . . and there was Isaac, cleaning Mr. Powers' saddle with oil. But even in the half-light, Rosebud could see an angry welt from the riding whip alongside Isaac's eye.

Isaac refused to look at her. With exaggerated slowness, he put away the oil and cleaning rag and hung up the saddle. He closed the stable door, slid the latch, then sauntered carelessly toward the creek. Without a word, Rosebud followed two steps behind.

This was a familiar ritual. Around the cookhouse and stable and yard—and especially around the white folks—Isaac wore an invisible mask, and even ignored his younger sister. But almost every evening, Isaac and Rosebud waded in the creek or walked noiselessly—like Indians—in the woods. Then Isaac would talk, pointing out which berries were poisonous, showing her how to catch crawdads without getting pinched, how to tell direction by the moss growing on the north side of the big oak trees.

Walking behind Isaac, Rosebud let out a sigh. Her brother hadn't run away. They were walking to the creek as usual. Maybe everything was going to be all right.

But Isaac was quieter tonight. He just sat on the bank of the creek and watched it flowing west, gurgling its way toward Chesapeake Bay, which neither of them had ever seen even though it was only ten miles away. Like many slaves on the Eastern Shore of Maryland, the Jackson family had rarely been off the plantation, and then only to go into town on an errand.

As twilight deepened, Rosebud heard a friendly bird call. It sounded like, *Whip-poor-will. Whip-poor-will.* "The whip-poorwill's back!" She grinned. The little brown-speckled bird hid quietly among the dead leaves on the ground during the day, and only woke up as night approached. This was the first one she'd heard this spring.

The stars started coming out. Pointing a finger at the sky, Isaac finally spoke. "See the Big Dipper there?"

Rosebud looked through the bare branches of the trees, which hadn't started to leaf yet, and nodded.

"If you follow the two stars that make the drinkin' edge of the Dipper, they point straight at the North Star . . . see?"

Rosebud nodded again as she picked out the bright star.

" 'Follow the North Star' . . . that's what they say," Isaac murmured. " 'Follow the North Star to freedom.' "

Rosebud didn't like the tone of Isaac's voice—wishful and stubborn at the same time. She hoped he wasn't thinking what she thought he was thinking.

When the two children finally crept into the log cabin in the slave quarters, Sarah and Abe Jackson were sitting by the smoky fireplace talking in low voices. " . . . saw Massa and that slave trader from Charleston looking over the field hands," Abe was saying.

"I know Massa's worried about money, but you don't think he'd start selling off slaves, do you? How's he gonna get the crops in?"

"I dunno. In these bad times, some slave owners raise slaves to sell just like another cash crop. And Massa Powers—he sho' is wound up tight these days. Ain't like it used to be."

"Hush," warned Sarah, glancing at the children. Rising

awkwardly, one hand on her swollen belly, Sarah fished out two tin plates, which she had kept warm in the ashes, and handed them to Isaac and Rosebud. Hungrily, the two children sucked the meat off the small smoked fish and stuffed corn bread into their mouths. As they lay down on the straw-stuffed mattresses on the floor and pulled up the thin blankets, Sarah began to sing softly:

Hush. Hush. Somebody's callin' mah name.
Sounds like Jesus. Somebody's callin' mah name.

The last thing Rosebud remembered was her mammy's soothing voice . . .

I'm so glad. Trouble don't last always.
Oh, mah Lawd, what shall I do?

Rosebud woke with a start. The cabin was empty and sunlight was streaming through the chinks in the logs. Grabbing a piece of cold corn bread, the girl ran through the trees to the cookhouse. She saw Mr. Powers riding down the front lane on his big bay. Her mother and Phoebe already had the fire built in the oven and were mixing biscuit dough.

"Where's Isaac?" Rosebud asked.

"In the stable where he belongs, doin' chores," said her mother. "Now wash your hands and face and fry up that piece of side meat. Miz Powers be wantin' her breakfast soon . . . Phoebe! Don't stir those biscuits so hard. Gotta do it gentle-like."

Rosebud smirked. Phoebe was twenty years old and had been working with the field hands until last week. But Mr.

Powers' overseer thought the attractive young black woman distracted the male slaves from their work, so he moved her to the cookhouse—much to Sarah Jackson's dismay. "Rosebud is a better cook than that hussy," she had complained to her husband.

Later that morning, while Rosebud was plucking feathers from a freshly butchered chicken, she heard childish laughter. The Powers' children, two girls about four and six, were playing tag in back of the Big House. Nanny Sue, one of the house slaves, was watching over them. Rosebud wondered what it would be like to wear ribbons in her hair and dress in a fine cotton dress with a ruffled petticoat. She had never talked to the two little girls. Only the housemaids and Old Jim, the butler, were allowed to associate with the Powers family or to enter the Big House.

Just then Rosebud saw Isaac ride by the cookhouse on a young chestnut horse he'd been breaking in for Mrs. Powers. "Isaac!" she called, but he continued at an easy trot down the wide front lane.

"Where's Isaac goin', Mammy?"

"Now, how would I know?" Sarah said impatiently. "Miz Powers prob'ly sendin' him on an errand. You stick to your pluckin'—Massa Powers bringin' guests home tonight and we got two more chickens to do."

When Mr. Powers arrived in late afternoon, accompanied by two men on horseback and two ladies in an open carriage, three fried chickens were crisp and golden on a platter warming by the stove and a pot of black-eyed peas and rice—known as Hoppin' John—was bubbling over the fire.

"Isaac!" yelled Mr. Powers. Rosebud saw her mother go to the cookhouse door and glance anxiously toward the stable. They hadn't seen Isaac return on the chestnut horse.

Just then they heard Old Jim's voice. "I seed the boy go off on the Missus' horse, Massa Powers," said the aging butler, out of earshot of the guests who were dismounting and going into the house. "Thought you'd sent him off on an errand."

"No . . ." Mr. Powers' voice was irritated. "But maybe Mrs. Powers did. Will you ask her please, Jim, when she expects him to return? I need him to rub down these horses for our guests."

Old Jim returned a moment later and shook his head silently. Mr. Powers' face went dark. He held an angry conference in a low voice with Old Jim, then stomped furiously into the house. Another slave soon appeared to take care of the horses and carriage, and yet another was sent into town on horseback, riding at breakneck speed.

By the time the sun had set, there wasn't a slave on the Powers Plantation who didn't know that young Isaac Jackson had run away, riding off on his mistress's horse in broad daylight.

CHAPTER 2

RUNAWAY!

Abe Jackson, bone-tired from plowing the winter-hard soil, ran immediately to the cookhouse when he heard the news. Sarah was rocking herself on a stool in silent distress. Rosebud, curled unhappily in a corner, saw her pappy pat his wife awkwardly on the shoulder.

"That Isaac's a fool!" he spat out, shaking his head. "He's tryin' to cross the Red Sea all by hisself. He shoulda waited." Abe's voice lowered to a whisper. " 'Cause I been hearing that there's someone they call Moses, leadin' our people to the Promised Land up north on some kind o' railroad that goes underground."

"Don't talk 'bout any Moses!" moaned Sarah. "Ol' Nat Turner thought he was Moses, and it weren't long till he got hisself killed."

"Huh!" snorted Phoebe with a wicked grin. "Not afore he done killed a lot of white folks first!"

"What do you know about it?" Sarah snapped at the young

woman. "Happened a year or two afore you were even born. Lots o' things changed after Nat Turner tried to get the slaves stirred up. Black folks ain't allowed to go to church together or teach their kids the Bible. Can't teach the younguns to read or write. Can't even sing 'bout Moses! White folks is scared."

Rosebud strained to hear the low talk of the grown-ups. She never realized what a risk her mother was taking when, night after night, she told Bible stories about Moses and King David and Jesus after Rosebud and Isaac had lain down on their mats. She always thought the reason Mammy whispered was to help them go to sleep.

But . . . did Pappy mean there was a new Moses? And what kind of railroad went underground?

Rosebud's thoughts were interrupted by a commotion outside. Opening the cookhouse door a crack, the Jacksons and Phoebe could see three men on horseback—Mr. Powers and the two gentlemen who came for supper—trying to control their excited horses. Old Jim was holding a flaming torch, which cast dancing shadows all about the stable yard.

Rosebud's heart pounded as another figure rode into the torchlight. A shout went up. "Here he is! We can go after the runaway now."

The white-haired slave catcher had returned.

The ground seemed to shake as the little band kicked their horses into a gallop past the cookhouse and down the front lane. Old Jim disappeared with the torch, and all of a sudden a quiet darkness fell over the yard and buildings of the Powers Plantation. Not a slave was to be seen.

Back in their tiny cabin, Rosebud lay stiffly on her mat, ears straining to catch any sound from outside. *Run, Isaac, run!* she thought. *Don't let them catch you!* Then the other part of her heart cried silently, *Come home, Isaac. Don't go away. Who will go walking with me down by the creek? Who will be my friend?*

Sometime during the night, she heard a muffled sound. Her mother was crying. "Lord, Lord," she heard Mammy moan, "what's goin' to happen to my boy?"

Rosebud drifted off to sleep, but she awoke with a jerk. Hoofbeats were coming down the lane. Shouts. Rough laughter. Her parents heard it, too, and leaped up from their straw mattress.

The sun wasn't up yet, but the April sky was yellow and pink with first light. Abe and Sarah, still in their nightclothes, went running hand in hand through the hickory and ash trees, past the other slave cabins toward the Big House, with Rosebud at their heels. As they reached the stable yard, the slave family stopped and froze.

Mr. Powers and the other two horsemen were dismounting. Bringing up the rear was the white-haired slave catcher holding a rope; at the end of the rope was Isaac, arms tightly bound. The boy's ankles were chained with iron fetters. But Isaac's face was a mask, showing no emotion.

Sarah gave a little cry, and Abe reached out a big arm to steady her. A few other slaves, mostly field hands heading out for work, had also appeared silently in the yard.

Mr. Powers noticed the bystanders. "Abe, get your woman and girl outta here!" he ordered. "You—" Mr. Powers pointed at one of the young field hands. "Take care of these horses. The rest of you get to work—*now*!"

As Abe drew Sarah away, Rosebud hung back, hiding in the shadow of a large hickory tree. What was going to happen to Isaac? She saw Mr. Powers turn to the slave catcher. "Give him a whippin' he won't forget!" the plantation owner said harshly. "Then chain him in the stable. I'll decide what to do with him later."

The slave catcher reached in his pocket for a fresh chew of tobacco. "This one's a troublemaker, Mr. Powers. You'd be better off without him. Just want to remind you that I'm leaving for Charleston tomorrow morning. And I pay top price for young bloods like this. A couple years on the chain gang will calm him down."

With that, the slave catcher jerked the rope, nearly pulling Isaac off his feet, then headed for the stable, chuckling to himself. The two guests slapped Mr. Powers on the back and the three men went inside the Big House.

Rosebud felt rooted to the hickory tree, not knowing what to do. A few minutes later she heard the stinging snap of a rawhide whip and an agonized scream inside the stable. It was Isaac! Putting her hands over her ears, Rosebud ran for the slave cabins.

Her parents hardly noticed as Rosebud threw herself down on the straw mat and pulled the blanket over her head. Abe was holding his wife in his big arms. "Oh, Jesus, help my boy . . . help my boy," Sarah cried.

Oh, Jesus, Jesus, Rosebud echoed silently, *stop that bad man from whipping Isaac!* Then an awful thought crept into her head. *Mammy is always talking to Jesus and askin' for help . . . but why doesn't Jesus ever do anything?*

She felt her father shaking her. "Come on, now, Rosebud. You gotta help your mammy. It's near her time, you know, and she's upset. But there ain't nothin' we can do for Isaac right now. Go on . . . take your mammy up to the cookhouse. The Big House will be expectin' breakfast, same as always."

Abe pulled on his overalls and started out for the fields.

Then he called back, "Rosebud! You stay away from that stable, you hear?"

The day dragged by slowly in the cookhouse. As soon as one meal was done, it was time to start the next one. Sarah was lost in her own thoughts and hardly seemed to notice Phoebe's irritating chatter. But when Phoebe returned from taking the noon meal to the Big House, she had news.

"I heard how they caught Isaac," she said smugly.

Sarah stopped cracking the shells of the boiled crabs for the crab cakes she was making. "Go on," she said, looking Phoebe in the eye.

"He musta rode that chestnut horse hard, 'cause it went lame up by Hurlock—"

"Hurlock!" said Sarah. "Why, that's only fifteen miles north o' here."

"Well, a white man saw him walkin' the horse and demanded to see his travel pass. 'Course Isaac didn't have no pass, so the man hauled him into town. He figured somebody would turn up soon to claim him—and sho' enough, along comes the slave catcher and Mr. Powers in the middle of the night, and there's Isaac, all tied up waitin' for 'em. Huh!" Phoebe snorted. "Don't know why Isaac didn't hide in the woods and wait till dark."

Rosebud felt like hitting Phoebe, but her mother gave her a warning look that said, *Be careful. Don't start no trouble. Keep your feelings to yourself.*

Finally the crab cakes and baked corn had been sent up to the Big House for supper. The last of the baking pans had been washed and the cookhouse floor swept. But the field hands hadn't come in yet. Phoebe had an opinion about that: "Mr. Powers prob'ly told the overseer to work the field hands extra today, get 'em good and tired so no one else wanna run away."

As her mother and Phoebe headed back toward the slave cabins to get their own supper, Rosebud saw her opportunity. Pappy wasn't home yet, even though it was getting dark. Keeping to the shadows, the girl ducked behind the stable. She listened, but all she heard was the sound of horses munching hay. Taking a chance, she pulled open the back door of the stable and slipped inside.

It took a few minutes for her eyes to adjust to the darkness inside the stable. Then she saw Isaac, half lying on the ground, his hands and feet chained to a post.

Rosebud stifled the cry that rose to her lips. Instead she called softly, "Isaac. It's me, Rosebud. I have supper for you."

Moving swiftly toward her brother, Rosebud reached out to help him sit up. But when she touched his back, he cried out and cringed. Rosebud pulled her hand away; it was wet and sticky with Isaac's blood.

Tears sprang to her eyes, but she brushed them away and quickly undid the knot in her apron. Carefully she held a stolen crab cake to Isaac's lips. She half smiled in the darkness. If the Powerses only knew their supper was being fed to the runaway!

Isaac ate hungrily as she held the crab cake to his mouth. When he'd swallowed the last bite, he whispered hoarsely, "Don't you cry 'bout me, Rosebud. I don't care what they do. . . . I'm gonna be free."

"But why, Isaac!" Rosebud cried. "Things ain't so bad if you don't get Mr. Powers all riled up. Why, we got Pappy and Mammy, and she gonna have a baby soon. . . . Just be a good boy and ever'thing gonna be okay."

Isaac shook his head. "Bein' a slave ain't never okay. Now go on, git . . . don't let 'em catch you here."

Reluctantly, Rosebud stood up. As she silently let herself out the back door of the stable, Isaac's hoarse voice floated toward her in the dark: "Just remember what I said: Someday I'm gonna be free!"

CHAPTER 3

TWO GRAVES

Rosebud was dreaming about catching crawdads in the creek with Isaac when her father shook her awake the next morning. Stumbling sleepily behind her mother toward the cookhouse, Rosebud wondered why she had a heavy feeling that something was wrong. Then she remembered: Isaac.

What's going to happen to him? she worried. *Will Mr. Powers keep him chained in the stable another whole day? Will he still let him be stable boy, or make him go out with the field hands? What if . . . ?* She shook the last thought out of her head. But as she lit the fire and helped her mother mix up the hasty pudding, Phoebe burst in the cookhouse door.

"That slave catcher's back—and he's got a chain gang!"

Dropping her spoon, Sarah Jackson ran out of the cookhouse door as fast as her pregnant body would move. Rosebud grabbed her skirt and dashed after her. There, coming up the lane like a king, was the slave catcher on his horse. Trailing behind him were five black slaves chained to each other by iron rings around their necks, their hands and feet also shackled with iron fetters and chains.

Rosebud whirled around and her mouth went dry. Mr. Powers was leading Isaac out of the stable and coming toward the chain gang.

The field hands, who had been walking with their hoes toward the fields, stopped and stared. Rosebud saw her pappy drop his hoe and walk unsteadily back toward the Big House. The white overseer didn't stop him.

Without a word Mr. Powers handed Isaac over to the slave catcher. Rosebud watched in shock as the man locked an iron ring around her brother's neck and chained him to the last slave in the gang. Then, with a grin, the slave catcher counted out several bills and handed them to Mr. Powers.

"You won't regret it," the stocky man beamed as he swung back up on his horse. "I'll be back. Remember what I said." He spit out a stream of brown tobacco juice and started back down the lane, the line of slaves shuffling in their chains behind him.

"No!" screamed Rosebud. "Don't take Isaac! No! No!" She would have run after him, but Phoebe grabbed her and held her fast.

Just then Rosebud's mother let out a high-pitched cry and sank to the ground in a dead faint. Abe ran over to his wife and barked at Rosebud, "Get some water." Wrenching herself out of Phoebe's grip, Rosebud ran to the rain barrel and was back in a moment with a dipper of water, hiccupping with sobs.

As Abe held the dipper to Sarah's lips, Mr. Powers walked over. "I'm sorry about this, Abe," he said. "I didn't want to do it. But I can't have mutiny among my slaves." Mr. Powers looked around at the other slaves, who stood frozen in little groups and staring at the chain gang as it disappeared down the lane.

"Let this be a warning to you!" the plantation owner shouted. "Do your work as you're told, and we'll get this plantation back on its feet again. Now, get on about your business!"

Mr. Powers turned back to the Jackson family, knelt down, and helped Abe get Sarah back on her feet. "Take care of your woman, Abe," he said. "You lost one child; let's not lose the new one." Then the white man walked back into the Big House.

As Abe and Rosebud helped Sarah back to the cookhouse, Rosebud heard her pappy mutter something sarcastic under his breath. She wasn't sure, but it sounded like, " 'Course not, Massa. Gotta raise one more slave baby to line your pockets with money."

———

For days Rosebud cried whenever she thought about Isaac. His straw mattress lay empty in their little cabin in the slave quarters; now there was no one to walk with her down by the creek after the day's work was done. One of the older slaves who was worn out with field work was brought in to be the "stable boy."

Nights were the worst. In the stillness she could almost hear the rawhide whip snapping in the air and feel the wet, sticky blood on Isaac's back. Again and again he marched through her dreams, chained by his neck to the chain gang.

She wanted to tell her parents about what Isaac had said that last night, but she was afraid to admit that she had disobeyed by going to the stable. So she kept her brother's words locked in her heart: "I don't care what they do. . . . I'm gonna be free!"

Rosebud was also worried about her mother. Mammy rarely talked or smiled now while working in the cookhouse. She moved slowly and heavily, as if the burden she carried was sapping all her strength. And now and then Rosebud heard her singing mournfully in a low tone:

Sometimes I feel like a motherless chile
Sometimes I feel like a motherless chile
A long ways from home.

About a week after Isaac had been taken away, the two women and Rosebud were working in the cookhouse when Sarah suddenly stopped in the middle of grinding dried corn into cornmeal and gave a loud groan. Gripping the edge of the wooden table, she lowered her bulky body onto a stool.

Phoebe took one look at the older woman and said, "Get the midwife, Rosebud. Hurry!"

For a moment Rosebud couldn't think. Midwife? Who was the midwife? Then she remembered: Nanny Sue, the nanny for the Powers children, was the one they always called for slave babies.

Her heart pounding, Rosebud hurried to the back door of the Big House and pulled the bell string. It seemed a long time before anyone answered, and Rosebud frantically rang the bell again. One of the housemaids finally opened the door.

"Quick, missy!" Rosebud said anxiously. "Get Nanny Sue to the cookhouse right away. My mammy gonna have her baby!"

Nanny Sue, a plump, middle-aged house slave with a golden-brown face, soon appeared and followed Rosebud to the cookhouse. She took one look at Sarah and helped the groaning woman lie down on the floor. With experienced hands, she felt Sarah's rigid stomach.

"This baby ain't right," she murmured. "It ain't turned around yet."

Frightened, Rosebud watched as the midwife massaged her mother's tummy, trying to coax the unborn child to turn around so that it could be born headfirst. The minutes dragged. From time to time Sarah gave a loud groan from the floor.

"What's the trouble here? Is this going to take long?" said a new voice. With a start, Rosebud looked up and saw Mrs. Powers standing at the doorway of the cookhouse.

"It's Sarah Jackson, Miz Powers," said Nanny Sue, still bending over the laboring woman. "It's her time, but the baby ain't right. Can't get it turned around."

"Oh dear . . ." Mrs. Powers looked flustered. "And I'm expecting the banker's wife for lunch. Do you think . . . could we move her back to her cabin? Really, the cookhouse is no place to have a baby."

Without waiting for an answer, Mrs. Powers motioned at Rosebud. "You, girl, go to the stable and ask the man to bring the wagon. He can take your mammy back to her cabin."

Reluctantly, Rosebud did as she was told. In a short while, the wagon pulled up by the cookhouse door. Nanny Sue was shaking her head and muttering, "Shouldn't move this woman." Nonetheless, she and Phoebe helped Sarah get up and somehow got her into the back of the wagon.

Rosebud was about to hop on, too, when Mrs. Powers caught her arm. "No, girl. You need to stay here. Nanny Sue can take care of your mammy. You and Phoebe need to finish making the noon meal. Now hurry up. I'm expecting company."

Rosebud felt like jerking away and running after the wagon, but Phoebe gave her a warning look. *Do as you're told. Don't start no trouble.*

Everything seemed to take longer without Mammy. The clam chowder smelled a little scorched and the corn bread looked a little lumpy, but Rosebud hoped that Mrs. Powers wouldn't notice. Phoebe and Rosebud worked all day in the hot cookhouse. As they scrubbed the cooking pots, then started supper, Rosebud wondered anxiously if Mammy had had the baby yet and if it was all right.

Finally, at twilight, the supper dishes of fried catfish, boiled potatoes, and steamed carrots had been delivered to the back door of the Big House. Without a word, Rosebud took off running for the slave cabins, leaving Phoebe to clean up the supper pots. She had to find out what was happening!

A small crowd of slave women were gathered around the outside of the Jackson's cabin. They parted silently and let Rosebud step into the dark doorway. Her heart thumped fearfully. Was something wrong? As her eyes adjusted to the dim light, she saw Nanny Sue sitting beside her mother on the straw mattress, wiping her face with a wet cloth. Then someone else caught her eye; it was her pappy, sitting on a stool by the fireplace with a wrapped bundle in his lap.

Rosebud looked anxiously at Nanny Sue. *The baby . . . ?*

Nanny Sue shook her head. "Baby was born dead, child. A big healthy boy, but the cord was around his neck. He never made it to the light of day." She handed Rosebud the wet cloth. "Now we gotta help your mammy. She ain't doin' too good. It was a hard birth."

The next morning at daybreak, a procession of slaves wound its way through the slave cabins to a little clearing in the woods down by the creek. Abe Jackson walked at the head of the line, holding his dead baby boy wrapped in a thin cotton blanket. Rosebud followed at her father's elbow, shivering in the cool spring morning. Only Sarah was missing; she was still too weak to get up.

A small hole had been dug in the graveyard among the simple wooden crosses. As Abe laid the little body in the bottom of the grave, Old Jim began reciting the Twenty-third Psalm in a quavering voice: " 'The Lord is my shepherd. I shall not want . . .' "

One by one the other voices joined in. " 'He maketh me to lie down in green pastures: he leadeth me beside the still waters. He restoreth my soul . . .' " Tears ran down Rosebud's face as the familiar words her mother had taught her filled the little clearing. " ' . . . Surely goodness and mercy shall follow me all the days of my life: and I will dwell in the house of the Lord for ever. Amen.' "

Then Abe spoke for the first time. "The baby's name is Matthew. It means 'Gift of God.' God gave me a son to replace the son I lost . . . and then God took him back again. Isaac wanted to be free. But Matthew is already free. He will never be a slave."

"Praise God Almighty!" a voice shouted from the crowd. Another voice burst into a song:

Thank God a'mighty, I'm free at last.
Surely been 'buked, and surely been scorned,
Thank God a'mighty, I'm free at last.
But still my soul is-a heaven born,
Thank God a'mighty, I'm free at last.

As they sang, several field hands shoveled dirt into the little grave and patted it into a smooth mound. Then the group of slaves quietly broke up and disappeared through the trees, back to the day's work.

Rosebud went to work in the cookhouse with Phoebe,

aching inside. If only Mammy would get better! Mammy would make everything all right again.

But Sarah did not get better. Abe and Rosebud had to hold up her head to feed her warm broth several times a day. Sometimes she tossed feverishly on the bed and called out, "Where's my baby?" Then Abe would gently remind her that the baby was home in heaven with Jesus.

Even Mr. Powers stopped by the little cabin to see how Sarah was doing. He stood awkwardly on the dirt floor, turning his hat in his hands. That same day he rode down the lane on his big bay horse and returned with the doctor from town.

The doctor shook his head. "This woman's got a fever—an infection from childbirth. She might make it, she might not. We'll have to just wait and see."

The first day of May was "issue day," when all the slaves lined up after work to get their monthly ration of basic foodstuffs: flour, cornmeal, dried pork rinds, salted fish, salt. Rosebud was so worried about her mammy she barely noticed that the rations were skimpier than usual. Of course without Isaac their family was smaller; but the overseer barked at the complaining slaves, "Got bad times ahead; everybody gotta tighten their belts."

Work in the cookhouse was hard without her mother. Mrs. Powers frequently sent complaints about food that wasn't properly cooked or didn't taste right. "Oh, please, Mammy, get well," Rosebud whispered as she stumbled home at night, dead tired. "I need you."

But less than two weeks after they buried baby Matthew, another sad procession wound its way through the woods to the little clearing. A larger hole had been dug beside the tiny grave; this time, four men lowered Sarah's body into the ground. This time, Abe did not say anything; he just stared mutely as the men shoveled dirt into the grave.

Grief seemed to stick in Rosebud's throat; her eyes were bright with hot, unshed tears. Isaac was gone . . . the new baby was dead . . . and now her mother, too. It was too much. Her feelings seemed frozen inside of her. She heard the mournful voices singing, "Deep river, my home is over Jordan . . ." as if they were far away.

As Abe and Rosebud turned away from the grave, they saw Mr. Powers watching from the edge of the clearing. He cleared his throat as they approached.

"I'm mighty sorry, Abe," he said, twisting his hat in his hands. "Your Sarah was a good woman. We will miss her." Then Mr. Powers put on his hat and walked off.

"Miss her cookin', you mean," Rosebud hissed when he was out of hearing.

To her surprise, her pappy didn't scold her. Abe had a strange, hard look on his face.

"You gonna pay for this, Massa Powers, *sir*," he said in a low voice. "Because you done broke my Sarah's heart when you sold Isaac to the chain gang."

CHAPTER 4

MOSES IS BACK!

Rosebud and Phoebe tried to keep up with the cooking for the Big House, but it was too much. The cookhouse had to turn out three meals a day for Mr. and Mrs. Powers and their two children, Old Jim the butler, Nanny Sue, four housemaids, and any guests.

One of the housemaids told Phoebe, who told Rosebud, that Mrs. Powers had thrown a fit when she heard that Sarah had died. "We train a good cook and take care of her and let her raise a family, and then she abandons us!" the white woman had stormed to her husband. "The least she could have done was produce a live brat. Now we've lost three slaves in three weeks—all named *Jackson*!"

"Now, Martha—" Mr. Powers had tried to interrupt. But Mrs. Powers was on the warpath.

"And what do we have left? A skinny child and a field hand cooking for the Powerses! We'll be the laughingstock of the Eastern Shore."

"Who's doing the cooking is the least of our worries," Mr. Powers had snapped (according to the maid). "The bank is leaning on me to repay the loan we took out for the south quarter. If tobacco prices don't turn around this year, I may have to sell off some land . . . or some of the slaves."

Rosebud didn't tell her pappy what Mrs. Powers had said about her mammy, but she did tell him what Mr. Powers said about the bank.

Danger of frost was past and it was seedtime. Abe Jackson and the other field hands worked from sunup to sundown putting in tobacco, cotton, and corn. It was also time for the slaves to plant the little vegetable gardens around the cabins and in the sunny patches between the trees for their own food: collard greens and sweet potatoes, squash and carrots, peas and string beans. There was no time during seedtime for walking by the creek after work, but that was just as well for Rosebud. Walking in the woods reminded her too much of Isaac.

Then, a week after her mother had been buried, Mr. Powers hired a white woman from town to come help with the cooking. Mrs. Bumper, the new cook, had her own way of cooking. When Phoebe or Rosebud tried to do things the way Rosebud's mammy had taught them, Mrs. Bumper yelled at them. She seemed offended to be working with slave girls and made it very clear that she was the boss. "I may be hired out," she sniffed the first day, "but don't you nigger girls forget who your betters are."

The second day Mrs. Bumper was on the job, she slapped Rosebud across the face for spilling some flour on the floor. After that, Rosebud tried to keep out of her reach. But Mrs. Bumper wasn't about to be outsmarted by a snippy black girl; she came armed with a long, green switch from an ash tree. Any time Mrs. Bumper thought Rosebud was working too slow or being too messy, she switched her across her bare legs, bringing quick tears to Rosebud's eyes.

Rosebud tried not to complain to her pappy, who seemed moody and sad. They talked little at night, too tired to do much else except lie down on their straw mattresses and stare into the shadows. But one night, aching with loneliness for Isaac and her mammy, Rosebud spoke in the darkness.

"Pappy, I disobeyed you the night Isaac was tied up in the stable . . ."

"I know you did, Rosey."

What? Pappy knew?

"It was wrong to disobey me . . . but I didn't have the heart to scold you, knowing you were a comfort to Isaac."

Rosebud's courage rose. "He said something, Pappy. He said, 'Don't worry 'bout me. I don't care what they do. . . . Someday I'm gonna be free.' "

There was silence in the cabin. When Abe finally spoke, his voice was choked. "The boy's right. Someday he's gonna be free; I know it." Then her pappy's voice became almost fierce. "And me . . . and you, too. I ain't gonna rest until every Jackson is free."

Abe's words frightened Rosebud. Was her pappy going to run away, too? The thought was terrifying. She didn't want to see her pappy whipped and sold to the chain gang, too.

As the May days got longer, the field hands stayed out in the fields later and later. One evening after work, while waiting for her pappy to come home for supper, Rosebud was pulling weeds in the little garden plot behind the cabin. Her legs still stung from the switching Mrs. Bumper had given her for spilling the chicken gumbo she'd been carrying to the Big House. As she jerked a stubborn weed out by its roots, she muttered,

"Why'd you have to run away and get caught, Isaac? Nothin's right anymore, an' it's all your fault!"

As she worked alone in the sweet-smelling earth, she became aware of the voices of two slave women who were also waiting for their men, working in a garden plot just around the corner of the Jackson cabin.

"Some say it's 'bout time for Moses to show up again," said one voice.

"What d'you mean?"

"Ain't you heard? Last couple years, right around seedtime and again around harvest, a few slaves here, a few slaves there, just up and disappear. Ain't never heard from again."

"So? Maybe they got caught and sent down South in a chain gang, just like Abe's boy, Isaac."

"Nah. You always hear about the ones that get caught. Massa Powers makes sure o' that!" The two women laughed. "But the ones that don't get caught . . . they say it's this new Moses who gets 'em out."

"What Moses? Nat Turner's ghost?" Another chuckle.

"Nah. Nobody knows who he is. He ain't violent. But white folks are scared of him just the same—with good reason. They say he can see in the dark like a mule and smell danger downwind like a fox. No one ever hears him comin' 'cause he can move through the underbrush without making a sound—like a tiny field mouse. And when he comes, slaves disappear, and no one ever finds 'em."

"True enough?"

Rosebud wanted to hear more, but the field hands were coming back, their weary voices singing to keep their spirits up: "Keep yo' han' on the plow, hold on! . . . If you wanna get to Heaven, let me tell you how . . . Jus' keep yo' han' on de gospel plow . . ."

A short while later Abe watched his daughter in tired silence as she prepared their late supper. Rosebud still wore a tow-linen shirt that hung straight from her shoulders, the same as worn by all slave children. But at age twelve, it only hung to her thighs, showing her long, bare legs.

As she bent over in the dim firelight, Abe suddenly spoke. "Rosebud . . . what are those bruises on your legs?"

Rosebud was startled. "Uh . . . ain't nothing, Pappy."

But Abe got up and turned his daughter so he could see her legs in the flickering firelight. Dozens of switch marks laced the backs of her legs.

"Who's been whippin' you?" he demanded. "That Bumper woman?"

Rosebud nodded, afraid she was going to cry.

Abe swore and slammed a fist into his other hand. Then he sank down on a stool and put his head in his hands. "Sorry, Rosey," he groaned. "Your mammy would roll over in her grave if she heard me talk like that. But I get so mad . . . can't even protect my own children."

Rosebud quickly served up the beans flavored with smoked pork neck bones. She even had a surprise: a couple pieces of sweet potato pie one of the other slave families had given them. But Abe didn't seem to notice.

"Pappy?" Rosebud said, trying to be cheerful. "Tomorrow's Sunday. Ain't no work till Monday. You can rest all day."

"What about you?" he sighed. "They got you up in the cookhouse on Sunday, too?"

"Well . . . just for a while. We made all the food today, but Phoebe and I gotta bring it up to the house for the noon meal when the massa and mistress get back from church goin'. Oughta be okay—Mrs. Bumper's stayin' home tomorrow." Rosebud managed a grin.

Suddenly Abe grabbed Rosebud in a big bear hug. "I'm so sorry, baby," he said. "Life is tough for you right now. An' I don't know when it's gonna get better. But hang on . . . hang on. One o' these days Moses is gonna come, and then we gonna be free . . ."

"Hush, Pappy," Rosebud shushed him, just like her mother used to do. "You know Mammy didn't like you talkin' 'bout Moses; it's too dangerous. Ever'thing gonna be okay. We got each other."

When Rosebud finally lay down on her straw mattress, she could almost still feel her pappy's arms around her. She felt comforted. At least they had each other. . . .

Rosebud awoke with a start. It was still pitch black inside the cabin. What had awakened her?

Then she heard a strange sound . . . like someone singing right on the other side of the cabin wall. She strained her ears . . . there it was again. The voice was husky and low, one she'd never heard before. Now she could even make out the words.

Go down . . . Moses,
Way down in Egypt land!
Tell old . . . Pharaoh,
Let my people go!

That was the song the slaves weren't supposed to sing! Who was singing it? And why was he singing in the middle of the night?

Then Rosebud realized that her pappy had heard the sound,

too. He bolted out of bed and stood, half-awake and swaying, in the middle of the dirt floor.

"He's come!" Abe whispered. "Moses has come. We gotta go! We gotta go *now*!"

"What are you sayin', Pappy?" Rosebud cried. "We can't go nowhere! The slave catcher will find us . . . and then . . . and then . . ."

By now Abe was wide awake. "No, don't you see? Tomorrow's Sunday. Ain't nobody gonna miss us for a whole day! And by that time, we will be long gone. 'Cause Moses knows the way, knows where that underground railroad is."

Rosebud watched, frightened, as Abe stole quietly over to the door and opened it a crack. "Come on, now, Rosey. Time has come to go."

Obediently, Rosebud got up, quickly pulled on a loose jumper over the tow-linen shirt she'd slept in, and started for the door. Then she had a horrible thought.

"Pappy! I can't go. I gotta bring the Powers' dinner to the Big House by midday. If I don't show up, they're gonna know we're gone . . ."

Just then they heard the low, husky voice behind the cabin once more:

Tell old . . . Pharaoh,
Let my people go!

Abe seemed frozen to the spot, anguish on his face.

Almost without thinking, Rosebud whispered desperately, "You gotta go, Pappy! You gotta go without me. It's the only way."

Her words shook Abe out of his daze. He grabbed her by the shoulders and looked intensely into her face.

"I'm a-goin', Rosebud. But when I know the way, when I find that underground railroad, I'm comin' back for you. Be ready when harvest is over. Just listen for the whippoorwill."

"Pappy—wait! What do you mean? Whippoorwills call all the time!"

"No, listen for a code: one time . . . then two times together."

"One time . . . then two times together," Rosebud repeated numbly.

Abe slipped into the night and Rosebud stood trembling in the darkness. Her pappy was gone.

She was all alone.

CHAPTER 5

LISTEN FOR THE WHIPPOORWILL

Rosebud could hardly keep her hands from shaking as she and Phoebe carried the cold fried chicken, pickled beets, and a tart made from dried fruit to the back door of the Big House for their Sunday dinner.

"I *said* . . . we forgot the biscuits," repeated Phoebe impatiently. "What's the matter with you? Do I have to say everything twice?"

"Sorry," Rosebud mumbled, and ran back to the cookhouse to get the pan of biscuits. She felt like everyone could tell just by looking at her that her pappy had run away, as if it were written all over her face.

But no one paid any attention to Rosebud. She stayed inside the cabin most of the afternoon, even though the May sunshine was warm and inviting. But that night she hardly slept at all. *Massa gonna find out tomorrow that Pappy is gone,* she thought, her teeth chattering.

Rosebud was at the cookhouse early Monday morning. By the time Mrs. Bumper and Phoebe arrived, she had the fire going in the fireplace and a pot of grits was bubbling gently on an iron hook. Mrs. Bumper looked at her suspiciously, tied on her apron, and set to work.

The women were just getting ready to take breakfast up to the Big House when they heard a horse gallop furiously into the stable yard, then excited voices.

"What's that overseer all hot about?" Phoebe wondered aloud, peeking out the door. "Hey! He's comin' this way!"

The overseer of the field hands, a burly, ugly man with tiny eyes, burst into the cookhouse. "Where is she—Abe Jackson's brat?" he demanded. Then he saw Rosebud. "There you are, you snake!" He grabbed her by the arm, pulled her roughly outside the cookhouse, and pushed her down in the dirt. Then he stood over her threateningly.

"Where's your pappy?" he growled. "Tell me now!"

Rosebud was so frightened that she couldn't speak.

"Ain't gonna talk, eh? I'll loosen your tongue!" With that, the overseer pulled a short leather whip out of his belt and drew back his arm. Instinctively Rosebud put her arms over her head and cringed on the ground, so that the blows fell once, twice on her back.

"What's going on here!" It was Mr. Powers' voice.

The overseer stepped back, his face red and puffing. "It's Abe Jackson, Mr. Powers—he's missing. Didn't turn up at the field this mornin'. Then I found out none of the slaves have seen him since Saturday night. Checked his cabin—it's empty. Thought his kid could tell us somethin'."

Mr. Powers yanked Rosebud to her feet and held her arm tightly. Tears traced small muddy lines down the girl's face and her chest was heaving; she looked down at her bare toes, not daring to look at his face.

"Where's your pappy, girl? Tell me what you know!" her master demanded.

Rosebud shook her head. "I don't know where he is! When I woke up Sunday mornin', he was just gone."

Mr. Powers swore under his breath. "I never thought Abe Jackson would betray me . . . and leave his kid an orphan, to boot." He let go of Rosebud's arm and she stumbled backward.

Mr. Powers whirled on the overseer. "Ride into town. Get as many men to ride with me as possible—tell them there's a reward," he ordered. "Get the sheriff's dogs if you can and meet me back here in an hour. Abe's already got a day's start—but no runaway slave is going to make a fool out of me!" He turned to the white cook who was standing, hands on hips, in the cookhouse doorway. "You—Mrs. Bumper—pack some food for the saddlebags. And don't let this girl out of your sight."

Within an hour the overseer had returned with three men on horseback and two fierce, slobbering dogs. They took the dogs to the Jackson cabin and let them sniff around, and immediately the dogs took off baying, following the day-old scent into the woods. Mr. Powers and the small posse followed, leaving the overseer in charge of the plantation.

Mrs. Bumper seemed to take an evil pleasure in being given charge of Rosebud. She used the green switch frequently, as if Abe's running away and Mr. Powers' absence gave her permission to punish the girl whenever she wanted.

By day's end, the men and dogs had not returned. When Mrs. Bumper left for the night, the overseer locked Rosebud in her cabin, then let her out the next morning.

Tuesday passed; still no word. Rosebud was so anxious

she could hardly eat and only slept out of exhaustion. Then Wednesday a rider came up the front lane toward the Big House. Rosebud's heart beat hopefully. It was Mr. Powers . . . alone.

Without a word the master dismounted and handed the reins of his horse to the stable man, who led the tired animal into the stable. Later that evening Old Jim the butler told a housemaid—who told Phoebe, who whispered to Rosebud—that he overheard Mr. Powers say that the dogs had tracked Abe all the way to the Choptank River, and then all traces of him had disappeared. The dogs went up one side of the river and down the other, and still couldn't find a scent.

"But Massa's gonna put out a Wanted poster with a reward," Phoebe reported, shaking her head. "Even if Abe makes it up North, the Fugitive Slave Law makes it possible for someone to catch him and send him back."

Rosebud's hopes sank. Would she ever know if her pappy had made it to freedom?

Gradually the stabs of fear and loneliness that marked Rosebud's days and nights settled into a dull ache. Mr. Powers moved Phoebe into the Jackson cabin with Rosebud, the overseer stopped locking the door at night, and life on the plantation returned to its normal hum of summer work.

Mrs. Bumper was still grouchy and used a switch on Rosebud's legs from time to time, though Rosebud—who was learning to work fast and rarely spilled or made a mess—gave her little reason. But one night after a painful switching, as Rosebud lay on her straw mattress in the hot cabin, straining to hear the night birds over Phoebe's heavy breathing, the girl realized her birthday must have passed. Her mammy had told her she was born in early summer in the prettiest time of the year, when the rosebuds were popping out on the wild rose bushes that splashed color along the edges of the woods.

I'm thirteen years old now, thought Rosebud. *Ain't got no mammy . . . ain't got no pappy. That means I'm the woman of the family now. It's time that Mrs. Bumper woman stopped treating me like a naughty child.*

Early the next morning before work, Rosebud hurried to the weaving shop with a cloth bundle under her arm. Using a pair of scissors, she cut a few inches off the bottom of her mother's old dress, which Rosebud had washed and put away, then quickly stitched a hem. The dress was still pretty roomy on the slender girl, so she tied it around her waist with the strip of material she had cut off.

When she arrived at the cookhouse, Rosebud had tucked every piece of her hair under the blue bandana her mother used to wear, just like Phoebe and all the other slave women, and her bare legs were covered to the ankle.

Mrs. Bumper sneered. "Well, ain't you puttin' on airs."

"Ain't puttin' on airs, Miz Bumper," Rosebud said. "But I'm doin' a grown woman's work, and I aim to be treated like one."

Phoebe giggled and, when Mrs. Bumper wasn't looking, winked her approval at Rosebud.

Mrs. Bumper still yelled at Phoebe and Rosebud, just to make herself feel superior, but she no longer tried to switch Rosebud's legs through the long, heavy skirt, knowing it would be useless.

One day in early August, just before the field hands started the first harvest, Mr. Powers called Rosebud to come out of the cookhouse. She went outside, heart thumping. Was it something to do with Pappy? A white man she didn't know was standing with Mr. Powers, dressed in a plain black coat and trousers tucked into riding boots.

"Rosebud, Mr. Jenkins is the blacksmith in town and his wife is about to have another baby. He wants to hire a young girl for a while to do some cooking and cleaning. I'm hiring you out for a spell."

Rosebud almost smiled. Well! She wouldn't mind getting away from Mrs. Bumper. Then, just as suddenly, her spirits fell. What if Pappy came back for her while she was gone? He wouldn't know where she was! He would go away without her!

But Mr. Powers gave her no time to think. "Get your things. You're leaving with Mr. Jenkins right now."

A short time later, Rosebud was sitting on the back of Mr. Jenkins' wagon as it rumbled down the lane. She held a change of clothes and watched the Big House disappear behind the trees.

Rosebud had never been anywhere except the Powers Plantation, and most of that had been spent in the cookhouse. It was hard to get used to a house on the edge of town, with only one hired man helping Mr. Jenkins in the blacksmith shop. She slept on a pallet in the corner of the kitchen and cooked for the first time in her life on a new-fangled black iron stove.

Mrs. Jenkins seemed frazzled taking care of her two little ones, with another due in a matter of days. She basically left Rosebud to figure out what to do with the cooking, and seemed almost grateful to have something—anything—on the table at mealtime.

The baby was born in the middle of the night. Mr. Jenkins went for the doctor, and Rosebud, lying on her pallet in the kitchen, soon heard a lusty cry from the Jenkins' bedroom.

Suddenly, a big dam of sorrow and loneliness seemed to burst inside Rosebud.

If only baby Matthew had lived! How she would have loved to help take care of a new little brother, carting him around on her hip, letting him suck a piece of pork rind when his teeth came in.

If only her mammy hadn't died! Now she had no one to sing the sweet Jesus songs at night, or tell her Bible stories, or just be there with her comforting presence.

If only Isaac hadn't been sold down South in a chain gang! Now she had no friend to catch crawdads in the creek with, or show her how to creep through the woods without frightening the woodland animals. She didn't even have the comfort of her memories, because thinking about Isaac brought looming fears of what his life might be like on the chain gang.

If only Pappy hadn't left her! Now she was alone . . . so alone, with no one who really loved her or cared about her. And now, if he came back, she wouldn't be there, and she'd be alone forever.

The sobs that welled up from deep inside seemed like they were going to tear her apart. Rosebud stuffed a wad of her nightdress into her mouth and cried silently until, exhausted, she fell asleep.

Rosebud had been with the Jenkinses only three weeks when a messenger came from the Powers Plantation: Mrs. Powers wanted Rosebud to return. Bewildered, Rosebud gathered up her little bundle and climbed up on the wagon seat beside the old slave who had been sent to fetch her.

"Heh, heh," the man chuckled as they drove out of town. "Miz Powers ain't happy with Mrs. Bumper's cookin' after all. Once you left, she realized you're the only one who really knows how to cook like your mammy."

Rosebud let herself smile real big. She was going home—home where Pappy could find her.

The hot, steamy days of August on the Eastern Shore of Maryland melted into a hot September. All the days seemed alike: sweating in the cookhouse all day long, coming back to the slave quarters to pick vegetables from the little garden plots as twilight fell, then lying in the dark, airless cabin, listening to Phoebe's gentle snores, straining to hear the whippoorwill.

Rosebud heard whippoorwills, all right, along with the *gobble, gobble* of wild turkeys, the twittering of songbirds getting up before sunrise, and the *cut-cut-cut* of the woodcocks. But never anything that sounded like the code her father had given her. As the days gradually turned cooler, Rosebud began to worry. Had she heard it and not recognized it? Had her pappy come and gone?

The harvest was in and corn shucking had begun. On the first day of October, "issue day," Mr. Powers and the overseer handed out new clothes for the coming year. The slave children each received two tow-linen shirts, which they changed once a week. The women were given one dress (to add to last year's), two sets of underthings, and a shawl. The men were given two pairs of trousers, two shirts, and a wool jacket. Everyone was given one pair of shoes, one pair of stockings, and one blanket.

Rosebud felt a sense of pride as she took her things into the cabin. It was the first time she'd been given a dress on issue day, one that fit her a little better than the one she'd cut down from her mammy. She tried on the shoes, but they hurt so bad she took them off again.

Instead of spreading out the new blanket over her straw

mattress, Rosebud rolled up her new dress and shawl in the blanket and tied it with the strip of cloth she'd cut off her mother's old dress—just in case. She wanted to have her best clothing ready to go if the signal came in the night. Then, using the blanket roll as a pillow, Rosebud fell into a contented sleep.

She awoke with a start. What had awakened her? She listened. But all she heard was Phoebe's steady breathing and an occasional snore.

Then suddenly she heard it. *Whip-poor-will* . . . Silence. Then, *whip-poor-will, whip-poor-will.*

Rosebud's heart seemed to beat in her throat. One time, then two times together. That was it! The code!

She scrambled to her feet and grabbed the bedroll she'd been using for a pillow. Creeping over to the fireplace, she felt around until she found last night's pan of cold corn bread and smoked fish, rolled them in one of her mother's old bandanas, and tucked it in her belt.

She listened. All was silent. Had she heard right? What if it wasn't Pappy after all? What if it was just an old whippoorwill grubbing for insects . . . ?

Whip-poor-will . . . Silence. *Whip-poor-will, whip-poor-will.*

There it was again! Now she had no doubts. Holding her breath, she quietly opened the cabin door and slipped into the night.

CHAPTER 6

A FRIEND WITH FRIENDS

As she shut the door of the cabin behind her, Rosebud stopped. Which direction had the sound come from? *Oh, Jesus . . . let it come again.* She waited, hardly daring to breathe.

Then she heard it once more. One bird call . . . then two, coming from the direction of the creek. Quickly Rosebud ran through the trees, swinging wide so that she didn't come too close to the stable, hardly noticing the rocks and sticks she stepped on with her bare feet in the dark.

As she came near to the creek, Rosebud slowed to a walk. Where was Pappy? She kept walking, looking this way and that in the darkness, but seeing nothing.

Then suddenly a low, husky voice called quietly: "Over here." Slowly Rosebud followed the voice behind a thick clump of ash trees. She could see a shadow, a shape . . . who was it? The girl stood still.

"Pappy?" she whispered.

"Shhh," said the husky voice. "Come."

It wasn't her father's voice! For a panicked moment, Rosebud wondered whether to run back to the safety of the cabin. But her feet started to walk after the dark shape ahead of her. As her eyes adjusted to the moonless night, hidden beneath low October clouds, Rosebud realized that the person in front of her was not wearing trousers, but a skirt.

Was this woman taking her to her pappy? There was only one way to find out. Rosebud kept walking, clutching her bundle close to her chest.

They'd been walking through the woods about half an hour without speaking a word, when a small clearing suddenly opened up in front of them. Other dark shapes moved . . . more people. Her eyes made out two men and two more women.

One of the men moved toward Rosebud and her guide. She knew immediately it wasn't her pappy; his shape was too tall, too skinny.

"Who you got with you?" the man demanded in a whisper. He peered closely at Rosebud. "What? This ain't nothing but a young'un—a girl at that!" The man swore. "How she gonna keep up? An' we already have a babe in arms. . . . How we gonna keep it from cryin' and givin' us all away?"

Rosebud's heart beat faster. Was this the man they called Moses? What if he wouldn't let her go with them?

"Where's my pappy . . . Abe Jackson?" she managed to ask, pushing the words past the lump in her throat.

"Your pappy ain't here," whispered the woman who had guided her through the woods. "He wanted to come for you, but it wasn't safe. We gonna take you to him if we can."

Conflicting emotions collided inside Rosebud. She wanted to cry with disappointment that her pappy hadn't come. But . . . he must be alive! She wanted to cry out, *Is he well? Is he free?*

But the low, husky voice commanded: "Come on, now. We gotta make tracks before mornin' light."

The woman took off quickly through the woods, with the little group keeping up as best they could. Rosebud, not wanting to get lost, followed close to their guide. Behind her came the other two women; one was carrying a bundle that might be the baby the man mentioned. The two men brought up the rear.

Rosebud was bewildered. *What is going on here? Is that tall, skinny man the "Moses" that Pappy had talked about? But why is the woman leading the way?*

After a while Rosebud noticed something else. The woman in front of her moved almost silently through the woods, while the group behind her crashed and stumbled in the dark. Rosebud tried to remember what Isaac had said about walking quietly in the woods: avoid stepping on dry leaves and sticks that might snap . . . walk on spongy moss or hard dirt to avoid leaving a trail . . . don't make any sudden movements. But he hadn't told her how to do that in the dark!

The blanket roll she carried seemed to get heavier and heavier. A couple of times Rosebud's eyes flew open and her head jerked as if she'd fallen asleep for a few seconds while plodding through the night.

Then suddenly, the woman stopped and held up her hand. The followers listened. All Rosebud could hear was the gentle sound of water swishing and splashing, like the creek behind the stable back home.

"Into the water," the woman commanded. "Best way to cover our scent. Follow exactly where I go." Before anyone could protest, she pulled up the bottom of her skirt, tucked it in her belt, and stepped down a small, muddy bank into the dark water.

Following her example, Rosebud tucked the bottom of her dress into her belt. The mud squished between Rosebud's toes and felt soothing to her sore feet. The water was cold but only came up to her knees, and she soon got used to it.

Rosebud couldn't tell how long they walked in the creek. It was slow going. The creek's bottom was full of smooth, slippery rocks, and it took all her concentration not to fall into the water. Then she became aware of a new sound: the muffled cries of a baby waking from sleep.

Finally, their guide climbed out of the water and sat down on the ground. Gratefully Rosebud sank down on the grassy bank and leaned against a tree. The woman with the baby sat down close-by, unbuttoned the top of her dress, and put the fussing baby to nurse. The second man touched her gently on the shoulder before sitting down and resting his arms and his head on his knees.

That's when Rosebud realized the people around her were no longer just dark shapes, but she could make out their features and clothes. She looked up through the trees; the sky was getting lighter in the east.

The woman with the baby looked just a little older than Phoebe. Was the young man who touched her, her husband? The other woman was a little older and stouter, but not fat. Then there was the tall, skinny man who seemed to have a permanent scowl on his face.

After a curious glance around the little group, Rosebud's gaze rested on the woman who had guided them through the night. She had a plain face, framed by a bandana tied neatly around her head. The most outstanding thing about her was an ugly scar, right in the middle of her forehead.

The woman stood up. For the first time, Rosebud realized

how short she was. With no trouble at all, Rosebud could look her right in the eye.

"It's time to go," the woman said in her peculiar, husky voice. "Everyone must be very quiet and move slowly. We are almost to our first station."

Station? Rosebud thought, as the little group got up wearily and began to move again. *Does she mean a train station?* Her heartbeat quickened. Maybe they were going to ride on the strange railroad her pappy had told her about, the one that went underground.

As dawn approached, the trees began to thin out. They were coming to the edge of the woods. The short woman stopped and held up her hand for absolute silence. Then Rosebud saw something strange through the bushes: a lantern, burning brightly, was hanging from a fence-post. And beyond the lantern stood a small white farmhouse.

Whose farm is this? Rosebud wondered. It didn't look anything like the Powers Plantation! Maybe it belonged to some free Negroes, farming for themselves. *Oh, how Pappy would love to have a little farm for himself and his own family. . . .*

Her thoughts were interrupted as their guide motioned the little group to follow her quickly through the gate and up the wide path to the farmhouse door. The woman's eyes darted to the right and to the left, watching, listening.

At the door the woman gave a knock. Two knocks, then three together. It seemed like an eternity before a muffled voice on the other side of the door said, "Who's there?"

"A friend with friends," said the husky voice softly.

The door opened a crack, then wider.

Rosebud's eyes widened. It was a white woman! They'd been tricked!

CHAPTER 7

FOLLOW THE RIVER

Rosebud was terrified. They were all going to get caught—just like Isaac had been! She turned to run but the little black woman with the scar grabbed her wrist in a steel-like grip and pulled her into the doorway.

"Come in quickly," whispered the white woman, who was wearing a long nightdress, her hair tucked up under a ruffled nightcap. "One, two, three . . . six passengers," she counted. "And a baby . . . my, my." She led the way down a short hall to a door, which she opened.

Steep, narrow stairs led down to a cellar. With her wrist still held in the steel-like grip, Rosebud felt herself being pulled down the stairs, the others following close behind. It was dark in the cellar, but soon a lantern was handed down the stairs. Then Rosebud heard the sound of a key turning in a lock.

"Oh no!" Rosebud cried in a panic. "We're prisoners now!

The slave catcher's gonna get us! Mr. Powers's gonna sell me to the chain gang for sure—"

"Hush, girl!" commanded the husky voice. "We're safe here—if you don't make a racket and wake up the whole countryside."

Rosebud choked off her words, but her heart was still racing. What was happening? Who were these white people? Why had they been locked in the cellar?

The stout woman came over to Rosebud and wrapped her big arms around the girl. "There, there, child. Don't be frightened. It's been a hard night. Sure you're scared—we all are. But it's all right. There, there . . ."

Gradually Rosebud relaxed in the woman's warm embrace. For just a moment, it felt like she was safe in her mammy's arms again.

Then the woman nodded her head in the direction of the woman with the scar. "Don't you know who this is, honey?" she whispered.

Rosebud shook her head.

"Why, this here is the one black folks call Moses, 'cause she's been leadin' folks like us out of slavery to freedom . . . but most white people call her a slave stealer." The stout woman chuckled. "Whatever they call her, I heard that she can put a hex on a mad dog, an'—"

"—see in the dark like a mule, and creep silently through the forest like a field mouse," giggled Rosebud.

"Nonsense!" the husky voice snorted, overhearing their whispered conversation. "I'm only a woman who listens to the good Lord and lets Him lead me wherever He wants me to go. My name is Harriet Tubman, child. You can call me Harriet—I was named after my mammy."

So Moses was a woman, not a man! Rosebud felt ashamed

of her fears. This small woman, no bigger than she was, had braved the dangers of being a runaway—not once, but again and again! "But . . . if you're the one they call Moses," Rosebud stammered, "did you take my pappy on the . . . the . . ."

"Underground railroad?" Harriet Tubman smiled. "Yes, I did. Abe Jackson traveled with me last spring."

"Where is he? Is he all right? Is he free? When can I . . . ?" The words tumbled out in a rush.

But Harriet signaled with her hand for silence. The key was turning in the lock at the top of the cellar stairs. Then a white man came down the stairs.

Rosebud instinctively lowered her eyes as she'd been taught to do in the presence of a white man. Then she heard the man say, "I brought you breakfast. Eat all you want. You're going to need your strength."

Rosebud lifted her head. The man was setting down a bucket of fresh, warm milk with a dipper in it and a basket with rolls, butter, and cold sausage.

Hands reached for the food, but Harriet stopped them. "Lord God Almighty," she prayed, her eyes squeezed tight and her hands raised toward heaven, "thank you for your bountiful blessing—"

"Amen!" the tall, skinny man interrupted and grabbed a sausage.

While they ate, Rosebud found out the names of the others. The stout woman was Mary Tucker, and the young woman with the baby was her sister Sally. The young man was Sally's husband, Tobias Brown, and their baby boy was named Toby after his pappy. Mary, Sally, and Tobias were from a plantation near Bucktown. The tall, skinny man's name was Charles Walker, and he had run away from a plantation over by Church Creek.

"Who are these white folks?" asked Charles nervously, jerking his head toward the footsteps overhead. "An' when are we gonna get on that train that travels underground?"

Harriet Tubman shook her head. "Don't ask names. If any of us get caught, they can't make us tell somethin' we don't know." Then her eyes twinkled. "But just to set your mind at ease, I've stopped at this station on the 'underground railroad' more times than I can count—and I ain't never lost a passenger yet."

Rosebud was puzzled. If this farmhouse was a station on the underground railroad, where was the train? She was just about to ask when Harriet lay down on the cellar floor, using a sack of potatoes for a pillow.

"Better get some sleep," grunted the small woman. "We won't be movin' before nightfall."

Rosebud yawned. She *was* tired from all that walking, and her tummy was full. Rosebud laid her head on her bedroll, listening to the contented gurgles of baby Toby . . .

"Wake up, girl!"

Rosebud opened her eyes. The room was dark. What was that strange voice? Where was she?

Then it all came back to her in a rush: She had run away, and she had no idea where she was.

"It's our turn to use the privy." The voice belonged to Mary Tucker. "Then the white lady says we gotta be ready to go."

Groggily, Rosebud followed Mary up the cellar steps, then out the back door of the farmhouse to a small outhouse. It was already dark, but there were no clouds. A few stars were starting to twinkle.

When they arrived back in the cellar, a lantern had been lit. Mary and Rosebud joined the others, who were dipping something hot and steaming out of a big bowl onto pretty plates with blue flowers. Rosebud stared. Whoever heard of a white woman letting slaves eat off her china plates! She took a bite of the strange food—sliced potatoes in some kind of creamy sauce. Rosebud thought she had never tasted anything so good.

Then it was time to go. The farm lady gave each person a roll left over from breakfast and a hunk of cheese to take along. One by one the runaways slipped out the back door to the barn. Two farm horses were harnessed to a wagon inside. Without a word, the farmer helped each person lie down in the wagon bed and covered them with rough potato sacks. Rosebud heard a gentle sucking sound and realized that Sally Brown must be trying to nurse the baby to sleep so it wouldn't make any noise.

With a jerk, the wagon rolled out of the barn. The wagon bed was hard and uncomfortable, and the potato sacks made Rosebud itch. The road was bumpy, jostling the bodies under the sacks back and forth. Rosebud lost all track of time, but at one point it sounded like the wagon rolled over a bridge.

After a long time—was it one hour? two hours?—they heard the farmer say, "Whoa . . . whoa." The wagon stopped. Then they heard, "It's all right; you can get out now."

Gratefully, Rosebud pushed off the potato sacks and crawled stiffly out of the wagon. She saw the farmer talking to Harriet Tubman.

"Head straight through those woods, Mrs. Tubman, and you'll get to the Choptank River. Just follow the river—it'll eventually take you to Camden, Delaware. From there . . . well, you know the way to Philadelphia from Camden."

Mrs. Tubman? What a strange white man. Rosebud had never heard white people call black people by anything but their first name—or "girl," or "boy," or "hey, you."

The little black woman and the burly white farmer shook hands, then the little group headed into the woods. Behind them they heard the farmer say quietly: "God go with you."

Once again the little group walked all through the night. Rosebud could see the Choptank River through the trees. It was a big river—nothing like the little creek running through the Powers Plantation. From time to time, Harriet waded into the river and walked along the shallow water next to the shore to hide their scent just in case someone sent dogs after them.

As the night wore on, Rosebud began to tire and dropped back little by little. Once she looked up, and the others had disappeared. Frightened she started to run, but the others were just beyond the next clump of trees.

"See?" grumbled Charles. "The young'un won't be able to keep up; gonna slow us all down."

"You walk first, Mr. Walker," said Harriet. "Just keep the river in sight. We'll all be right behind."

Charles Walker grunted in agreement and moved on, his long legs setting a faster pace. Tobias put his arm around his wife's waist and helped her along. Mary was taking a turn carrying the sleeping baby. Harriet brought up the rear with Rosebud. To Rosebud's surprise, the woman began to talk to her.

"How old are you, Rosebud . . . thirteen? I remember when I was thirteen. Can't never forget, 'cause that year changed my whole life."

Rosebud forgot about being tired. She could hardly imagine

that this daring woman had ever been a young girl like herself.

"It was corn husking time on the Brodas Plantation—that's where I grew up, down near Bucktown. We were workin' fast, people were singin' and havin' a good time. But I saw one of the field hands who was keepin' to himself, lookin' around now and then. So I watched him. Suddenly, when the overseer wasn't lookin', he up and starts runnin'. Well, it didn't take long for the overseer to realize he was missin' and go off after him. I was a curious child, so I followed along behind to see what was gonna happen.

"Well, the slave had snuck into a store, hoping to hide. But the overseer went into the store and I followed, lookin' in the doorway. Just then the slave made a run for it. The overseer was standin' by the counter, askin' the storekeeper if he'd seen his slave, when he heard the commotion. Seeing his slave just about to get away, he grabbed a heavy weight from the counter and threw it with all his might toward the door. I saw it comin' but I just stood there . . . and that's the last thing I remembered for weeks on end."

"Is that how you got that scar?"

"Sure enough. I nearly died, and it took months before I could get out of bed and able to work again. I often heard my mammy prayin', 'Lord, I'm holdin' steady on to you and you've got to see us through.' And sure enough, He did. And," the woman chuckled softly, "as far as I know, that slave got clean away. God sure works in mysterious ways."

Mysterious ways is right, thought Rosebud. Sometimes she couldn't figure out if God was for her or against her. Her brother didn't get away . . . and her mammy and baby brother died. Rosebud shook those upsetting thoughts out of her head. Right now she could at least be thankful that her pappy had gotten to freedom, and that she had heard the "whippoorwill" and found Harriet Tubman.

As the sky began to lighten, Harriet called the group to a stop. "There's no station near here—we're goin' to have to lie low during the day. Can't risk walkin'." With that, Harriet plunged deeper into the woods, away from the river. She halted where the underbrush was thick, almost impassable.

"Find yourself a thicket to hide in. Try to get some sleep if possible. We'll walk again when darkness can cover us."

Walking had kept Rosebud fairly warm during the cool night, but once they stopped she began to shiver. Then she remembered her new shawl. Unrolling her bundle, she put on her new dress over the old one, wrapped herself in her shawl, and lay down on the blanket. Within moments she was fast asleep.

That night the little group set out again, following the same pattern: walking in the woods for a while, then wading in the river. Rosebud ate the corn bread and smoked fish she'd brought from home. Afterwards she was still hungry and was tempted to eat the bread and cheese, but decided to wait.

About midnight, Rosebud noticed that Harriet was leading them away from the river. Soon they came to a road. Harriet still kept to the woods, keeping the road in sight, until they saw the few scattered buildings of a small town.

"What's this?" demanded Charles.

"Our next station," said Harriet. Walking swiftly, she approached the back door of a house that was a little separated from the others and knocked.

There was no answer.

Harriet knocked again and waited. Finally a muffled voice said, "Who is it?"

"A friend with friends."

The door cracked open an inch. "Go away! Go now!" The man's voice was urgent. "The slave catchers were here today . . . they searched the entire house. It isn't safe! Go away!" And the door shut in their faces.

CHAPTER 8

"MOVE ON—OR DIE!"

Without a moment's hesitation, Harriet plunged back into the woods, the others right at her heels. Rosebud was so tired that she stumbled several times. She felt like she couldn't walk another whole night! But she kept going, putting one foot in front of the other.

"Faster," Harriet urged. Then Rosebud heard her mumble under her breath, "Lord, I'm goin' to hold steady on to you, and you've got to see us through."

The little group headed back toward the Choptank River, but soon the ground began to feel mushy and soft underfoot. The Choptank had large swampy areas spreading out from its banks. Harriet tried to avoid them while staying as far from the road as possible, but the going was slow.

As a new October day began to dawn, baby Toby started to fret. His mother tried to nurse him as she walked, but Toby would have none of it. Soon his fretting had become a loud cry.

"Make that baby shut up!" hissed Charles angrily.

Harriet stopped, fished in the big pockets of her skirt, and pulled out a brown medicine bottle. "Didn't want to use this unless necessary," she said, "but this will help keep the baby quiet."

Sally looked worried, but tried to hold Toby still as Harriet poured some liquid from the brown bottle down his throat.

"What is it?" Rosebud whispered to Mary. She took advantage of the brief stop to unwrap the bread and cheese still in her bandana, then stuff as much as she could into her mouth.

"Probably tincture of opium—a drug that will put him to sleep for a few hours."

"Shh!" Harriet said, holding up her hand for silence. They listened. A dog was barking in the distance. Then it was joined by another . . . and another.

"Into the swamp—*now*!" Harriet commanded, and plunged right into the mud and marshy grasses. Gulping the food in her mouth and clutching her bundle, Rosebud tried to hurry, but the mud seemed to pull at her ankles and hold her back. As she struggled on, the mud turned to swampy water and got deeper. It crept up to her knees, then her thighs, and the bottom of her dress was soaked. But ahead of her, Harriet kept right on pushing. Behind them, the barking dogs seemed to be closing in.

As the swamp got deeper, a layer of fog seemed to be sitting on the surface. Soon Rosebud was chest deep in the marshy water; even the men were wet to the waist. Only little Toby was dry, slung over his pappy's shoulder, fast asleep.

Holding her bundle on her head with one hand, Rosebud pushed aside the tangle of water lilies, floating mossy beds, and tall grasses. Little green frogs leaped for their lives as the two-legged creatures invaded their home.

The barking of the dogs seemed to change to a frenzied hunting bay. Then they heard shouts: "The dogs have picked up a trail! This way!"

Harriet Tubman was pushing through the water lilies toward a little grove of skinny trees sticking up out of the fog. "Get down—as far as you can get," she hissed as they all squeezed in among the trees and grasses.

Rosebud lowered herself in the marshy water up to her neck, knowing it was useless trying to keep her bundle dry now. Her heart was pounding and her mouth was dry. *Oh, Jesus, Jesus, don't let them find us!*

Somewhere through the fog they could hear the men and dogs crashing through the woods. Then more shouts: "They've gone into the swamp!"

"You're crazy—they can't hide in the swamp."

"Look at the dogs. They have lost the trail right here at the edge of the swamp."

"Well, they gotta come out somewhere. Come on."

The noises headed upriver and soon faded away. Charles started to rise out of the water, but Harriet put her finger to her lips, frowned, and gave a slight shake of her head. Her meaning was clear: it might be a trick; the slave catchers could have left someone behind.

The sun crept higher in the sky and burned off the layer of fog on the swamp. Flies and other insects started buzzing around their heads. *If only I could have a drink!* Rosebud thought, licking her dry lips. Once she felt a snake slither between her ankles under water, and she had to stifle a scream.

A couple of times Rosebud looked at Harriet and saw that her eyes were closed and her mouth was moving. She could barely hear the almost silent whisper: "Lord, I'm holdin' steady on to you, and you've got to see us through."

Then baby Toby started to stir on his pappy's shoulder. "I need to feed him," whispered Sally, tears in her eyes.

Harriet shook her head. "Can't risk it," she whispered back. Feeling under the water for her pocket, Harriet brought out the brown bottle and gave Toby another dose of the tincture of opium. Soon the baby fell back into his drugged sleep.

Then they heard voices again.

"Hear anything?" said one voice.

"Nah. I don't think they're in there. And I'm getting tired sitting here waiting."

So! The slave catchers *had* left someone behind!

Rosebud wanted to cry. Would they ever get out of the swamp? What if those men and dogs stayed there all day and all night?

The voices and noises faded away once more. But Harriet shook her head: it still wasn't safe.

Soon the sun was high overhead and the biting insects seemed unbearable. But after a while a shadow passed over the swamp. Clouds were gathering swiftly and Rosebud could feel a breeze off the river. And then it began to rain, an autumn downpour.

Finally Harriet left the little grove of trees and waded back through the swamp under cover of the heavy rain. Gratefully, the others followed, thoroughly soaked to the skin. Rosebud tilted her head up and let the cool, clean rain run into her dry mouth.

Harriet led them back downriver before they came out of the swamp. Rosebud thought she had never in her life been so wet and smelly and miserable. The little group made a camp of sorts in the woods, and when the rain stopped, they stripped off their outer clothing and spread it on the bushes to dry.

Rosebud undid her bundle, wrung out her shawl and

blanket, then wrapped them around her. "M-M-Miz Harriet," she said, her teeth chattering, "ain't we ever goin' to ride that underground train?"

Harriet didn't answer. Instead she got a faraway look in her eyes. "Did you ever hear the story of Tice Davids?" She didn't wait for an answer. "Ol' Tice was born a slave, just like you an' me. But one day he sees his chance to run and heads for Ohio—that's a free state out West, you know. Trouble is, his master found out quick-like and was after him like greased lightning. Oh, man, he was hot on Tice Davids' tail, couldn't have been more than five minutes behind.

"Then Ol' Tice comes to the Ohio River; in he goes and swims across. Master comes along behind, sees Tice climbing out the other side, and calls someone to row him across. But when that master got to the other side, he couldn't find a trace of Tice Davids nowhere! He went up the river; he went down the river. 'It's just like he disappeared on an underground road!' the master said when he came back empty-handed." Harriet's eyes were wide and mysterious.

"Well, about that time . . . this was around 1831—I was younger than you, 'bout ten years old—ever'body was talking about them new-fangled steam engine trains. An' pretty soon folks were saying that Tice Davids had disappeared on an *underground railroad*. Well, this gave the abolitionists an idea . . ."

"Abo . . . aboli—what?" said Rosebud.

"Abolitionists. That's what they call folks who think slavery is wrong, and not only think it, but do something about it!"

By this time, Mary, Sally, and Tobias had moved closer so they could hear the story. Even Charles, though his back was turned, seemed to be listening.

"Anyway," Harriet continued, "this gave the abolitionists

an idea. The folks who were willing to help runaway slaves started using railroad code words to talk about escape routes. Me, I'm a 'conductor'; you're my 'passengers.' Or sometimes runaways are called 'parcels' or 'bales of black cotton.' Safe houses with secret rooms or haylofts are called 'stations' and the people who run them . . ."

Harriet's eyelids started to sag, and her words suddenly started to slur.

" . . . are called . . . 'station masters' . . ."

Without further warning, Harriet just toppled over and lay crumpled on the ground.

"Oh, Lordy . . ." Mary said, moving swiftly to the small woman's side. Rosebud stared. What was happening?

Tobias knelt down and checked Harriet's pulse. Then he looked at the others.

"I think she's all right; she's just sleeping . . ."

"Sleeping!" snorted Charles. "People don't fall asleep like that!"

"What I mean is," said Tobias patiently, "I heard that sometimes Miz Tubman has sleeping spells—on account of that head injury she had as a young girl. Sometimes she sleeps a couple hours, sometimes a whole day, but she wakes up again, and then she's fine."

Sure enough, Harriet was breathing long, slow breaths, as if she was in a deep sleep.

"You mean we have to wait here till she wakes up?" said Charles. "It's almost nightfall—time to be movin' on. What if those slave catchers come back?"

Tobias stood up and glared at Charles. "Yes, we wait. She's been riskin' her life to help us. The least we can do is stick by her during this spell."

Charles grumbled but sat down again. Rosebud shivered

as she pulled the damp shawl and blanket tighter around her against the cool night air. Because of hiding in the swamp all day, she had not slept for twenty-four hours. Even though she was worried about Harriet Tubman, she was grateful to lie down and close her eyes.

"Rosebud. Wake up."

Rosebud sat up with a start. It was Harriet, shaking her, then shaking each of the others in turn. "Come on, it's time to go," the woman whispered huskily.

The night was pitch black; clouds still covered the moon. Rosebud smiled to herself; she was glad Harriet was all right. But . . . her throat hurt. If only she could get a drink!

As the little group got up stiffly and gathered their still damp clothes from the bushes, Harriet said, "I'm sorry my sleeping spell has set us back. I should've warned you, but it's been half a year since I last had a spell. But now we got some fast walkin' to do to make up for lost—"

"Count me out."

It was Charles's voice. All eyes turned and stared at him.

"What do you mean, man?" said Tobias.

"I mean I ain't goin' on. Some 'underground railroad' this is! We ain't got no food . . . we've been sittin' all day in the swamp like drowned rats . . . an' now we find out this little woman here has sleepin' spells. Some Moses you are!"

Charles snatched his damp clothes from the bushes and tied them into a bundle with a piece of rope he wore around his waist. "At least back on the plantation, I had two meals a day and a roof over my head," he muttered, slinging the bundle over his shoulder. "If I turn up on my own account, maybe my master won't take it so hard that I been gone a few days."

In the stillness of the woods, everyone heard the metal click, and then Harriet's low, husky voice: "*No one goes back.*"

All eyes turned toward Harriet Tubman. She was standing with her feet apart, arm outstretched, pointing a pistol at Charles's chest.

"I'm not afraid to use this, Charles Walker. You move on with us—or you die!"

CHAPTER 9

THE FUNNY PARSON

There was a shocked silence. Then Charles slowly grinned. "You wouldn't shoot me . . . a little woman like you."

The pistol never wavered. "If you try to leave, you're a dead man."

"But why?" Tobias protested. "Let him go. We'll be better off without him. Rosebud, here, complains less than he does."

Harriet kept the pistol pointed at Charles. "A runaway who turns back is dangerous," she said quietly. "His master or the slave catchers will force him to tell what route we've taken . . . who has helped us along the way . . . where the stations on the underground railroad are. I'll kill one cowardly slave before I'll let him endanger the lives of hundreds of innocent people."

For half a minute, everyone stood frozen. Then Charles set his bundle down. "All right, all right. I'll go on with you. You womenfolk need another man to protect you, anyhow."

Rosebud was tempted to giggle—if her throat hadn't hurt so much. She suspected that in a tight spot, Charles would look out for himself. But Harriet slowly lowered the pistol and said, "That's right. We all need to help each other."

Within a few minutes they were once again moving through the night. Rosebud kept close to Mary, but they walked silently. Her throat hurt too much to talk. As the night wore on, the young girl also realized how hungry she was. She reached for the bandana tucked in her waist with the last of the bread and cheese—it was gone. It must have fallen out in the swamp.

As the birds began greeting the first rays of daylight, Harriet pointed out berries that were safe to eat. Rosebud eagerly picked a handful of huckleberries and put them in her mouth all at once. They were past their prime and had lost their juiciness, but at least they were something to eat. But she had difficulty swallowing them.

As the sky got brighter, the little group hid themselves among the thick underbrush and dropped off to sleep quickly from exhaustion.

In her sleep, Rosebud dreamed that someone was standing with a heavy boot on her chest. She could hardly breathe. Had the slave catcher caught her? What was going to happen to her? Why did he keep standing on her chest? Why couldn't she breathe?

A coughing fit woke her, and she realized she'd been dreaming. There was no one standing on her chest, but it hurt and she found that it was hard to get a deep breath. She squinted at the sun; by its position, Rosebud figured it must be midafternoon—too early to continue their journey along the river. She coughed a couple more times, then lay back on her bed of moss and leaves with her eyes closed, listening to the *chit-chit-chit* of the squirrels and the honking of geese flying south, high overhead. It was so peaceful, it was almost easy to forget that she was hiding in the woods as a runaway.

Suddenly Rosebud had the distinct impression that someone was watching her. Her eyes flew open . . . and she found herself staring into the face of a white boy a little older than herself standing about five feet away.

Immediately the boy put a finger to his lips. "Wake up the others," he whispered. "Thee must come with me—quickly."

Rosebud blinked. It wasn't a dream. The boy was still there, wearing a funny black hat with a flat brim. Again he whispered, "Quickly! Wake up the others."

Frightened, Rosebud scrambled to her feet and woke up Harriet Tubman first, then Mary and the others. Harriet immediately stood up and went over to the boy, who looked about fifteen.

"I have been looking for thee," he said. "Thee must all come with me quickly."

With that the boy turned and started through the woods, heading away from the river.

"Do you know who that boy is?" hissed Charles Walker, frowning suspiciously.

"No, I don't," Harriet admitted. "But he has the speech of the Quakers, many of whom have been our friends. I think we should trust him. But," she looked at each of them, "be watchful."

Rosebud brushed bits of dried leaves and moss from her dress, then had to run to catch up with the others. The boy was walking swiftly and the fast pace made it hard for Rosebud to muffle the coughing that pushed up from her chest. If only she could get a good, deep breath!

They must have walked about half an hour before the boy finally slowed and stopped. The woods opened up onto a small meadow, and in the middle sat a plain, white, one-story building. It did not look like a house or a barn. Four wooden steps led to a door in the front of the building, and four steps led out the back. Along the side were five windows in a row.

The boy stepped into the clearing and looked around the meadow carefully. Then he motioned for the others to follow as he strode quickly toward the building and led them inside.

Just inside the front door Rosebud sank down on a bench and looked around. All she saw were two rows of wooden benches on either side of a large room. What was this—a church? Rosebud had never been inside one before . . . though her mammy used to tell her about the log cabin churches the slaves had, before the white people passed a law saying slaves couldn't go to church or learn to read. Mammy said white folks thought black folks got too many strange ideas from the Bible about being free like everyone else.

"Wait here," said the boy quietly. "Don't stand near the windows. I'll be back." Then he was gone.

"Are we gonna stay here?" said Charles. "This could be a trap."

Harriet was thoughtful. "Tobias, you watch near the windows on that side, and Charles, you watch on the other. Stand so you can't be seen from outside, but be alert."

Sally was stripping off baby Toby's soiled, damp clothes and putting on some fresh ones that she had tucked inside her dress. By now the baby was wide awake and whimpering for his breakfast.

Rosebud's head was pounding so hard that she hardly noticed when Mary sat down on the bench beside her. Mary pulled Rosebud close, so that her head could rest on Mary's big shoulder.

"Someone's comin'," said Tobias in a quiet voice. "It's the boy, and he's got a white man with him."

"Just one?" asked Harriet. Tobias nodded.

The little group stood and faced the back door as the boy came in with the man right behind him. The middle-aged man was dressed similarly to the boy: black trousers and a plain black coat over a white shirt, and a funny looking black hat with a flat brim.

The man looked around from person to person.

"Well, well, well, Isaac," he said, "who has thee found?"

Rosebud's head jerked up. The boy's name was *Isaac*? Just like her brother!

"Who is the leader of this group?" asked the man politely.

Harriet stepped forward. "My name is Harriet Tubman. My friends and I are seeking safe passage to Pennsylvania."

"Harriet Tubman?" asked the man. He stroked his beard thoughtfully. "I have heard of Harriet Tubman—'the Moses of her people,' they say—but I never thought I would have the honor of meeting thee." He held out his hand. "I am Benjamin Woodhouse. My family and I are Quakers. This is our meetinghouse."

"Are you a preacher then?" Mary spoke up.

"No, friend. Quakers don't have preachers. I am the clerk of our meeting, which . . . never mind. That's not really important right now. Art thou hungry?"

Everyone just stared at him.

"What a foolish question," the man chided himself. "Of course thou art hungry. We will bring something to thee shortly. Isaac, run tell thy mother we need food—lots of food." As Isaac ran off, the man then turned back to Harriet. "Friend Harriet, I am afraid this meetinghouse is somewhat bare with only hard benches for thy comfort. But thee must stay here until nightfall. Then thee can come to the house under cover of darkness."

Harriet drew herself up to her full height, which was only five feet. "Sir, are you a station master?"

"A . . . what?"

Rosebud saw the alarm in the others' faces. This man didn't know anything about the "underground railroad." It could be a trap after all!

But the man caught their looks. "Wait," he said. "I think I know what thou art asking. No, I am not a station master on . . . what did Friend Thomas call it? . . . the 'underground railroad,' yes. But Friend Thomas—that's Thomas Garret in Philadelphia . . ."

A broad smile broke out on Harriet's plain face. "You know Thomas Garret, the man who makes shoes?"

"Yes, indeed," smiled Benjamin Woodhouse. "It is he who hast told me of you. We—my wife Maggie and I—have been troubled in our spirit for some time because of slavery in the land. But we have felt helpless, not knowing what one small family could do. But I was in Philadelphia on business and stopped to see Friend Thomas, a fellow Quaker, and he—"

"I am sorry I doubted you," Harriet Tubman interrupted. "Thomas Garret is a great friend of the abolitionists, black and white alike. He has risked his life and reputation many times—and his money, too, I understand."

"Yes, yes, thou art quite right," Benjamin chuckled. "He was fined a goodly amount for aiding runaways and breaking the Fugitive Slave Law—an evil law in the sight of God! God help us all."

The small black woman and the Quaker man with the strange speech sat down on a bench and talked on as the others listened or nodded off in sleep. Between coughs, Rosebud heard Harriet say, "Your boy said, 'I've been lookin' for thee.' What did he mean?"

Benjamin shook his head. "Well, that is the strange thing. He was telling me—ah! Here is Isaac now, and his mother, with thy food."

A pretty, middle-aged white woman in a plain black dress and white cap came in the back door of the Quaker meetinghouse with Isaac, both of them carrying baskets and a steaming iron kettle.

"Maggie, this is Harriet Tubman, of whom Friend Thomas told us so much, and these are . . . these are . . ." Benjamin Woodhouse looked perplexed.

Harriet came to his rescue and briefly introduced each of her "passengers" by name. Rosebud thought the boy Isaac looked at her funny when Mrs. Tubman said her name was Rosebud Jackson. But she soon forgot about it as the iron kettle was placed on a wooden bench, and Maggie Woodhouse got busy ladling out a delicious-smelling chicken soup into six fat mugs.

The Quaker woman handed a mug of soup and a slice of bread to each person, stopping to admire baby Toby who was contentedly sucking his fingers. When she came to Rosebud, who was trying to keep from coughing long enough to sip the hot soup, the woman looked at her closely and put her hand on the girl's forehead.

"This child is not well!" she said, looking up at the others with alarm. "Her clothes are damp and she's shivering. We must get her to bed right away, or we will have a case of pneumonia on our hands!"

CHAPTER 10

SLAVE CATCHER!

Maggie Woodhouse wanted to take Rosebud to the house immediately, but her husband insisted that they wait until dark. "We must be very careful," he said. "Go ahead, Isaac, tell your mother and Mrs. Tubman what you told me."

Rosebud, who was trying to swallow the hot soup in spite of her sore throat, jumped at the sound of the boy's name. She didn't like this white boy having the same name as her brother. Every time someone said "Isaac," she expected her brother to suddenly appear.

"Well, Ma'am," the boy was saying to Harriet, "I took one of Papa's horses into Petersburg to the blacksmith this morning—"

"Petersburg!" exclaimed Harriet Tubman. "Have we crossed the state line into Delaware?"

"Yes, ma'am. Anyway, there was a stranger there having his horse shod. I heard him tell the blacksmith that he was looking for some slaves who'd run away from the Tidewater Flats down near Bucktown in Maryland . . ."

Sally gave a frightened cry and pulled the baby closer.

" . . . but they'd given him the slip in the swamp ten miles downriver," Isaac went on. "And then it rained very hard, he said, which made tracking with dogs nearly impossible. But he was sure the runaways were following the river and coming this way. He said there was a big reward . . ."

At the mention of a reward, the runaways shifted uneasily. "I knew all this sweetness and light had a stinkin' center," Charles muttered under his breath, and began edging slowly toward the door. But Benjamin Woodhouse's eye caught his movement.

"No, no, Mr. Walker," he said. "I assure thee, young Isaac is only telling what the stranger *said*. A Quaker would never betray a fellow human being for a reward, or we would be as guilty as Judas Iscariot who betrayed our Lord in Gethsemane for thirty pieces of silver!"

Isaac looked bewildered by the effect of his words on the anxious runaways. He looked at his father. "Go on, Isaac," Benjamin encouraged him.

"Well, I—I was afraid that the runaway slaves were going to be caught unless someone helped them. Friend Thomas had told Papa that runaways often hide in the woods during the day, so I decided to go looking for thee."

"Glory to God that you found us instead of the slave catchers!" said Harriet.

"But . . . if the dogs pick up our trail, that trail is going to lead right here," said Tobias soberly.

The room was silent except for Rosebud's coughing as everyone realized the truth of what he'd said.

Then Benjamin Woodhouse spoke. "Maybe, maybe not. I have an idea. . . ."

Rosebud snuggled under the duck-down comforter in the little attic room. She had never been in such a soft, warm bed! It would be so pleasant . . . if only she didn't feel so sick.

They had waited in the Quaker meetinghouse until dark, and then Mr. Woodhouse had told them to walk back down the road, the way they had come. Rosebud had stumbled along, leaning on Mary, wondering what was happening and wishing she could go to sleep, when along came a wagon behind them with Mr. Woodhouse driving a team of horses! The Quaker man picked them up, and by taking the long way around, drove the wagon back to the Woodhouse farm. Mary whispered in her ear that he was doing it to fool the slave catcher's dogs.

At the house, Mary and Mrs. Woodhouse had stripped off Rosebud's damp underclothes, pulled one of Mrs. Woodhouse's flannel night dresses over her head, and tucked her in this bed. It had taken a long time to stop shivering, but now she was warm and drowsy.

Rosebud slept fitfully the rest of that night and all the next day, waking from time to time with a terrible coughing fit that seemed like it was going to rip out her insides.

As the room began to get dark again, Harriet Tubman came into the little attic room and sat on the bed.

"Rosebud? Are you awake?"

The girl nodded miserably.

"There's something I want to tell you. When I first ran away to freedom, the way sometimes got hard. But deep down in my soul, I knew there was one of two things I had a right to: liberty or death. If I could not have one, I would have the other. I was determined that no slave catcher should take me alive; I would fight for my liberty as long as my strength lasted, and when the time came for me to go, the Lord would let them take me."

Just then Rosebud had a coughing fit and Harriet helped her with a drink of water. Then Rosebud sank back onto the soft pillow. Why was Harriet telling her this? The Woodhouses seemed like nice white folks; they were safe now, weren't they? Besides, Rosebud always felt safe with Harriet. She always seemed to know what to do.

"Now you listen to me," Harriet said, gripping the girl's shoulders. "When things get tough, I want you to say this prayer: 'Lord, I'm goin' to hold steady on to you, and you've got to see me through.' Can you say that?"

Rosebud nodded. "Lord, I'm a-goin' to hold steady on to you, and you've got to see me through," she repeated hoarsely.

"Good girl. Now, you sleep. You need to get better."

It wasn't until the next morning that Rosebud learned that Harriet Tubman and the rest of her fellow runaways had headed north once more under cover of darkness and left her behind.

Rosebud pulled away from Maggie Woodhouse's hand and turned her face to the wall, sobbing into the pillow.

"Don't cry so, child," said the motherly woman. "Thou art too sick to continue the journey. They had no choice but to go without thee."

"Th—th—they could've waited t—t—till I'm better," Rosebud hiccuped in a muffled voice.

"Humph. It's much harder hiding seven black souls than one, in a small white family. Nay, I agree with Mrs. Tubman;

they needed to push on to the next station. They will wait for thee in Philadelphia."

Philadelphia! That was another fifty miles—Mary had told her that much. She was only halfway to freedom. But she could never make it alone. She didn't know the way! An overwhelming feeling of despair set off new sobs into the pillow.

Later that afternoon, it was Isaac who came up to the little attic room with some hot broth for their patient. "What day is it?" Rosebud asked hoarsely.

"Why, it's Sixth Day," said Isaac.

Sixth day? What a funny way of talking these Quakers had! But Rosebud was too proud to ask what he meant. She thought a moment; if Sunday was the first day of the week, then sixth day would be Friday. "Issue Day" at the Powers Plantation had been the first Saturday of October, and she had run away that night . . . which meant she'd been gone six days already. Only six days? It felt like a lifetime!

She realized Isaac was staring at her. "Thee has been crying," he said finally.

Rosebud looked away.

"Don't worry," Isaac said. "My mother will take good care of thee. And thee can use my room as long as thee likes."

Startled, Rosebud turned her head back and stared at the boy. *His room?* It had never occurred to her that he had given up his room for her. She just thought all white people had extra rooms in their houses.

That day and all the next, Rosebud worried. The Woodhouses were being very nice to her, true, but she didn't want to stay here any longer. She wanted to be with Harriet Tubman and the others. She wanted to find her pappy. But how? She felt so alone—more alone than she'd felt since her mammy died and her pappy had run away.

By the next day, Rosebud was feeling much better, even though she was still coughing. "That's good, that's good," Mrs. Woodhouse said. "Thee has to get all that stuff out of thy chest. Now here . . . put these on and come down to supper tonight. Thee must get thy strength back." And she laid Rosebud's dresses, bandana, and shawl on the bed, freshly washed and dried.

At suppertime, Rosebud got dressed and timidly made her way down the narrow stairs. Maggie Woodhouse was setting supper on a plain wooden table, nicely crafted, with four straight-backed chairs around it. Benjamin Woodhouse smiled at Rosebud and held a chair for her. Then the rest of the family sat and bowed their heads while Benjamin said a blessing.

As the food was served, Maggie chatted away, asking Rosebud questions about her family, but Rosebud was so nervous sitting at the same table with a white family, that she could only nod yes or no. Finally Benjamin saw her distress and guided the conversation away from the girl.

"Tomorrow is First Day, Papa," said Isaac. "Can Rosebud come with us to Worship Meeting?"

Rosebud looked startled. She'd never been to church before. But a *white* church?

"No, I'm afraid not," said Benjamin, shaking his head.

"But, Papa!" Isaac protested.

Rosebud didn't know whether to be disappointed or relieved. But it was just as she thought. White folks—even Quakers—didn't want black folks in their church.

"Don't forget that Rosebud, young as she is, is a runaway," Benjamin explained. "We are *hiding* her. No one must know she is here."

"Well, then, in that case, I will stay home to keep her company," said Isaac.

Again his father shook his head. "Then people will wonder where thou art, and we don't want to tell a lie. We must do everything just as we always do. We will go to Meeting tomorrow, and Rosebud must stay here."

The next morning the Woodhouse family walked through the woods to the Quaker meetinghouse, leaving Rosebud at home. As the hours ticked away on the wall clock in the front hall, Rosebud thought, *This is my chance. I could leave now, and no one would stop me.* But then she realized she did not know how to find her friends. She could go back and follow the Choptank River, but Harriet had said that it soon dwindled to a creek in Delaware. Where would she go then? And she didn't have a travel pass. Any white person could stop any black person at any time and demand to see a pass from his or her master; it was the law.

With a sinking feeling, Rosebud realized she was trapped, just as much as if she were tied up in the stable, as her brother Isaac had been.

The next morning, Rosebud got dressed and came down to the kitchen, where Mrs. Woodhouse was bustling about.

"Mrs. Woodhouse . . . ma'am," Rosebud ventured. "When will I be able to leave and join my friends in Philadelphia?"

"Soon, dear, soon," said Mrs. Woodhouse, fanning the wood in the cast-iron stove and tucking a stray wisp of brown hair under her starched white cap. "We must be sure that thou art completely well . . . oh, here." She handed Rosebud a basket. "Will thee go out to the barn and gather some eggs for our breakfast? I cannot make this fire burn right!"

With a sigh, Rosebud took the basket and let herself out the back door of the house. As she rounded the corner and started down the path to the barn, she was startled to see Isaac talking to a strange man in the barnyard. She stopped and stood uncertainly, not sure what to do. Then her mouth went completely dry.

The man talking to Isaac Woodhouse was the white-haired slave catcher that had taken her brother away on the chain gang!

At just that moment, Isaac looked up and saw her. In a flash his face contorted into an angry scowl. "You lazy, good-for-nothing girl!" he shouted. "Get that broom and sweep the path like Mama told thee to!"

Rosebud was shocked. She started to protest, to tell Isaac that his mama wanted her to gather eggs, but he came toward her with his hand raised as if to strike her. She looked around frantically and saw an old broom leaning against the house. Dropping the basket, she started sweeping the path furiously, sending bits of dried leaves and grass flying.

Isaac went back to talking to the slave catcher. Rosebud's heart was beating wildly. Would the man remember her? He didn't seem to; maybe because she was wearing a bandana and a woman's dress now, instead of the tow-linen shirt she'd worn as a child last spring. But what could explain Isaac's sudden change in behavior? Unless . . . unless she'd been tricked. The Woodhouses had let the other runaways go, but maybe they had kept her behind to make her their slave!

After a few minutes Isaac yelled at her again. "All right, that's enough. Now pick up that basket and get those eggs. Hurry! Don't keep Mama waiting all day!"

Bewildered, Rosebud picked up the basket she'd dropped and ran to the barn, ducking inside its huge doors into the cool, dark interior. She could hear the man laughing behind her. The sweeping and running made her start to cough again, causing tears to well up in her eyes. What was happening? Why was Isaac talking to that evil man?

She peeked out the door into the barnyard. She could see some big papers rolled up under the man's arm. As she watched, he took one out and unrolled it for Isaac to see. Rosebud squinted hard and then gasped. It was a drawing of Harriet Tubman, she was sure of it!

Just then Isaac looked up and yelled, "What are thee lookin' at, girl? Get back in there and fetch those eggs!"

As Rosebud turned away, she heard the man continue, "There's a big fat reward for anyone who catches this she-devil," he said, grinning. "*And* for the niggers she's got with her. Slave owners are tired of their slaves disappearing when she comes around."

"I don't blame them." Isaac nodded. "That's some reward—twenty thousand dollars!"

"Yep. Well, you take this here poster and put it on your fence, like you said. Somebody somewhere is gonna git her. Maybe it'll be you!" And he laughed again. "Meantime, you're doin' a pretty good job keepin' Sassy there in line—heh, heh."

Rosebud saw Isaac take the poster and wave as the man mounted his horse and start back down the road.

With a sinking heart, Rosebud shrank back against the inside of the barn door. Now she knew the truth. It was a trap. Either they would let her go, and follow her, so that she would lead them to Harriet Tubman . . . or they would keep her here, hoping Harriet would come back for her.

Either way, freedom seemed to be slipping from her grasp.

CHAPTER 11

I AM ROSALIE! I AM FREE!

Rosebud realized that Isaac Woodhouse was heading for the barn. She quickly scurried toward the sound of cackling chickens and discovered a row of neat wooden boxes along the back wall.

"Scat!" she hissed to a fat hen on one of the nests. The hen protested loudly. Thrusting her shaking hand into the straw, Rosebud pulled out a smooth, warm egg.

"Rosebud?"

Isaac's voice startled her. She slowly put the egg in her basket but did not turn around.

"Rosebud, I'm sorry for how I spoke to thee out there! But that was a slave catcher! He was looking for Harriet Tubman and the rest of you. When thee came out of the house, I had to make him think that thee . . . uh, that thee . . . well, I didn't want him to get suspicious!"

Rosebud was silent.

Isaac's voice sounded miserable. "Rosebud, thou must

believe me! I did it to fool him. But . . . but I know it hurt thee badly."

Rosebud squeezed her eyes shut and two tears ran down her cheeks. She felt so confused. One minute this white boy was yelling at her and treating her just like a slave; the next he was apologizing and talking to her in a kind way. *Oh, Lord,* she cried inside, *I'm tryin' to hold steady on to you . . . but I'm all mixed up and don't know what to do!*

Ignoring Isaac, Rosebud finished gathering nine brown eggs and walked back to the house, fighting back the tears. Without a word she set the egg basket on the kitchen table and walked up the narrow stairs to the attic room. Below her she could hear Mrs. Woodhouse's anxious voice. "Rosebud? Is something wrong? . . . Isaac! What happened?"

Alone at last, Rosebud let the tears come, wave after wave of fear and loneliness and confusion. Exhausted from crying, Rosebud finally slept.

When she awoke in late afternoon, her stomach hurt with hunger. She hadn't had anything to eat all day. But as she crept down the attic stairs, she heard voices arguing in the dining room.

The stairs creaked and the voices stopped. Mrs. Woodhouse came to the open doorway. "Why, hello, Rosebud. Did you have a good sleep? You must be hungry, poor child!" The Quaker woman steered the girl into the kitchen and within minutes set a plate in front of her with two lovely fried eggs, two large muffins, a slice of fried ham, and a mug of cool milk.

Rosebud's mouth watered. As she ate, Benjamin Woodhouse also came into the kitchen, followed by Isaac. "Isaac told us about the slave catcher that came to the farm today," he said. "I am proud that he acted so quickly to keep that evil man from suspecting that thou art a runaway. But we know it was very upsetting. We are all sorry. Thee must forgive him."

Rosebud stared at her plate. Forgive Isaac? Did that mean telling him it was all right to call her "lazy" and "good-for-nothing"? She couldn't!

Mr. Woodhouse cleared his throat. "This incident has forced us to come to a decision. Thee must leave, Rosebud. It is no longer safe here. If the slave catcher asked around, our neighbors would tell him that we have no slaves."

His wife started to protest, but Mr. Woodhouse held up his hand. "Mrs. Woodhouse thinks thou art not yet well enough, but we must take that chance. Thee must leave tonight. Now . . . we must get ready."

Rosebud tried not to show her dismay. Tonight? Were they just turning her loose? But she didn't know where to go! If the slave catcher found her alone on the road or in the woods, he would surely know she was a runaway! But she obediently went upstairs and rolled her extra dress and blanket into a bundle. She retied her mammy's bandana neatly around her head, put on her shawl, and waited for it to get dark.

Finally she heard Mrs. Woodhouse call her.

"Oh, Lord, I'm tryin' to hold steady on to you . . ." she breathed as she walked down the narrow stairs for the last time.

Mrs. Woodhouse handed her a bundle of food and gave her a motherly hug. "Go quickly, child. They're waiting for you in the barn."

Rosebud walked uncertainly to the barn. Who was waiting—Mr. Woodhouse? Was he going to tell her where to go? There was no light inside, but as she pulled the door open, she heard Mr. Woodhouse's voice. "Ah, there you are, young lady. Now up you go." The next thing she knew, he was helping her climb into the seat of the farm wagon. And from the wagon seat, Isaac held out a hand and pulled her up beside him.

"Isaac is going to drive thee to find thy friends—all the way to Philadelphia, if need be," said Mr. Woodhouse. "Now, go and Godspeed."

———

Rosebud rode silently beside Isaac as the team of horses headed north. She felt ashamed. The Woodhouses had been very kind to her since Isaac had found them out in the woods. And Isaac's upsetting behavior that morning had kept the slave catcher from knowing she was a runaway. And yet . . . doubts still nagged at her. What about all that reward money? Could Isaac be using her to get to Harriet Tubman?

It was so hard to know whom to trust! No white person had ever been her friend in all her thirteen years. And yet, if she was wrong about Isaac, she was being very ungrateful.

"Art thou cold?" Isaac asked, finally breaking the silence.

"No. My shawl is warm."

They rode on in silence once more. It was Isaac who again spoke first. "Is Rosebud thy real name?"

She hesitated. Many slaves were given nicknames by their masters, who might not bother to know a slave's full name. But Rosebud was the only name she had ever known. "My mammy said I was born when the rosebuds came out."

"What about the rest of your family? Do they have unusual names like you?"

Before Rosebud realized what was happening, she was telling Isaac about Abe and Sarah Jackson, and her brother Isaac, and about Isaac running away and getting caught and being dragged away on the chain gang. As she talked, all the loneliness of the last days and weeks and months seemed to come spilling out in words.

She told about burying baby Matthew and her mammy, and how one night her pappy had heard someone singing, "Go down, Moses," outside the cabin, and that was the last time she saw him. But he had told her to "listen for the whippoorwill" after harvest . . . and that's how she ended up with Harriet Tubman and the others, running north to freedom. "But most of all," Rosebud said, "I just want to find my pappy again."

Isaac was thoughtful for several minutes. "Abe . . . Sarah . . . Isaac. Did you know thy family is named after one of the most famous families in the Bible?"

Rosebud shook her head.

"Abraham loved God, and God promised that he would be the father of a great nation. The only problem was, Abraham and Sarah were very old and didn't have any children. It looked impossible! But they believed God's promise, and sure enough, they finally had a baby and named him Isaac."

Isaac laughed. "That's why my parents named me Isaac," he confided. "They waited a long time for me, too. Anyway," he went on, "after many years, Abraham's family became so big, no one could even count them. They became God's chosen people, the Jews—the same people Moses led out of slavery."

Rosebud was astonished. Why hadn't she ever heard this story before? Think of it! Her pappy and mammy and her brother were named after a famous family in the Bible.

They had been traveling along the road for hours and the sky was starting to get light. Rosebud thought about what Isaac had said.

"Do you think that promise could be true for my family?" she ventured. "About becoming a family—again—even though it looks impossible?"

"Sure. Why not? In the Bible God was always doing impossible things."

"Even finding my brother Isaac?"

Isaac Woodhouse grinned. "Especially thy brother Isaac. After all, he is Abraham and Sarah's son, right?"

Isaac pulled off the road at daybreak to give the horses a rest and let them munch on the grass. After eating some of the food that Maggie Woodhouse had packed, Rosebud fell asleep under a tree. But a few hours later they were on their way again.

"When we go through a town, thee must sit in the back of the wagon," Isaac said. "I am sorry. But Delaware is still a slave state; we must not make anyone suspicious."

Rosebud meekly submitted to this indignity. She realized that Isaac was doing it for her good.

They rested the horses again in late afternoon, then started again at twilight. "We are coming near to Wilmington," Isaac told Rosebud. "That is where Friend Thomas Garrett lives. That was where Mrs. Tubman was heading—he will know what has happened to thy friends."

But as they drew near the city, they saw first one, then another, then *another* poster with the picture of Harriet Tubman on it.

"We may have trouble here," Isaac murmured. "Wilmington is so close to the state line that the slave catchers and bounty hunters will be on the alert, trying to stop any runaways from getting into Pennsylvania."

Rosebud was scared. She was so close to freedom! What if she got caught now?

Isaac had an idea. "Rosebud, wrap thy blanket around thee

and lie under the wagon seat. Try not to move—and don't cough! It's dark enough, no one will see thee." Rosebud did as she was told, and at the last minute Isaac took off his flat-brimmed Quaker hat and stuffed it under the wagon seat as well.

Inside the blanket under the wagon seat, Rosebud could feel every rock and rut in the road. Gradually there were more noises, too—horses and carts rumbling along the road, people hailing each other, laughter from the inns along the road.

"Be very quiet," Isaac murmured. "We are coming to a bridge and there are people about."

"Hey, you, boy! Stop!" said a gruff voice.

Under the blanket, Rosebud held her breath.

"Have you seen any runaway slaves?" said the voice. It came from someone standing right beside the wagon wheel. "We're lookin' for a certain group o' darkies—tall, skinny man . . . young wench with a baby . . . 'nother young man . . . young girl 'bout ten or twelve . . ."

"Don't fergit the fox!" yelled another voice, laughing.

"You mean this one?" said Isaac. Rosebud heard the rustle of paper. Then she realized he had said "you" instead of "thee."

"I see you got one o' them posters," chuckled the first voice.

"Yep," said Isaac. "With the kind of money being offered for that Tubman woman, I plan to start hunting as soon as I get home—right after supper."

"Well, get along with you, then. But don't be pickin' up no strangers."

The wagon lurched forward and made a terrible racket as the horses clomped over the wooden bridge that led into Wilmington, Delaware. It seemed a long time before Isaac finally said, "Whoa!" and then, "Thee can come out now. We are here."

Rosebud crawled stiffly out from under the wagon seat. The wagon was pulled into a narrow alley beside what looked like a shoe shop. Isaac helped her down, and they knocked softly on a door in the back.

"Who's there?"

"Uh . . . I have a small package for thee," said Isaac. He'd obviously been instructed by Harriet Tubman in "underground railroad" language.

The door was unlatched and the two young people were quickly pulled in. Rosebud saw an elderly white gentleman with a round clean-shaven face and plump jowls. "Harriet! Harriet Tubman!" he called happily. "Your package has arrived."

Rosebud was amazed to discover that Harriet and the others had only arrived at Thomas Garrett's "station" the night before. She and Isaac had covered as many miles by wagon in twenty-four hours as the others had in five nights of walking. "Don't worry none, child," Mary assured her. "Ain't no way all of us could've come by wagon without getting stopped by slave catchers."

The next morning Isaac prepared to head home. But first he took Rosebud aside. "I've been thinking," he said. "Thy brother has the same name as I do. That makes us spiritual kinsfolk in a way . . . and, well, I've been thinking about the promise God made to Abraham. And I want to make a promise to thee."

A promise? What was Isaac talking about?

Isaac took a big breath. "I'm fifteen now; soon I'll be a man. But as soon as father can spare me from the farm, I am going to find thy brother, and I will help him run away—or . . . or

I will buy him and set him free! That is my promise. But . . . thee must realize, it might take a long time."

Rosebud was speechless. No one had ever made her a promise before. But she believed Isaac. Someday . . . someday, he would help her brother be free.

"Thank you, Isaac," she whispered. Tears blurred her eyes.

"Oh! And something else!" Isaac looked a little embarrassed. "May I call thee Rosalie? Rosebud is nice—but it seems to me the rosebud has grown up and become a flower. In fact," Isaac twisted his hat in his hands, "you are the bravest girl I have ever met."

Again Rosebud didn't know what to say. She tried the word in her mind: *Rosalie*. It had a nice sound—a new sound.

Isaac seemed to read her mind. "You used to be Rosebud, the slave. But now you could be Rosalie, the free woman."

Rosebud nodded. She tried it out. "I am Rosalie. I am free."

Then she laughed aloud. What a wonderful sound!

I am Rosalie! I am free!

CHAPTER 12

THE FREEDOM TRAIN

"Where are thy shoes, young lady?" questioned Thomas Garrett gravely, when Rosalie joined the others for breakfast in a small secret room at the back of Garrett's shoe shop.

Rosalie looked down at her bare feet and shook her head. "I got my first pair on Issue Day—the day I ran away—but they pinched my toes and I didn't think I could run very far."

Garrett chuckled. "Well, let's see what we can do for thee. Stockings would help."

Sure enough, after breakfast the old gentleman brought a pair of stockings and a pair of shoes for Rosalie to try on. They felt funny, but the leather was soft and the shoes laced firmly up to her ankles.

"Wear them around the house—thee will get used to them. And thee will need shoes up north in the winter!" said Mr. Garrett.

The kindly gentleman also gave new shoes from his shop

to the other runaways, whose old shoes were falling apart from the long trek through the woods and water.

Rosalie was glad to be back with Harriet and the others—even the sour-faced Charles Walker. They hid all day in Garrett's secret room, and that evening he came and outlined the plan for the next day.

"Philadelphia is only twenty miles across the border, but it is probably the most dangerous part of thy trip," he told them. "I have arranged for a bricklayer who is sympathetic to our cause to drive thee into Philadelphia—but thee must go in daytime, just like any other load of bricks."

Even Harriet looked puzzled.

"The bricklayer has built a false floor in the bottom of the wagon; that is where thee will lie. Then the wagon will be loaded with bricks. No slave-catcher wants to unload a wagonful of bricks! It is a trick we have used before, and it has worked well . . . although not very comfortable for the passengers, I admit. As for the baby . . . Harriet, does thee have thy—?"

Harriet held up the brown bottle from her pocket.

"Good," said Garrett. "Thee will need to keep the baby quiet until thee gets to Philadelphia. There William Still, a free black man with the Vigilance Committee, is expecting thee."

"Will we be free then?" asked Rosalie eagerly.

"Yes . . . and no. Pennsylvania is a free state. But under the accursed Fugitive Slave Law"—Garrett's forehead knitted angrily—"a slave catcher can follow a runaway slave into a free state and still drag him back to his former master. I urge thee all to keep going!"

"But where?" several voices chorused.

"To Canada."

Rosalie would never forget the ride from Wilmington to Philadelphia under the load of bricks. Before sunup the next morning, they all lay down head to toe in the bottom of the bricklayer's wagon, and a false floor was laid over them. Rosalie could hear the thump, thump, thump as the heavy bricks were stacked on top.

She wanted to scream. It felt like being buried alive! But Harriet patted her comfortingly. "Shh, shh. It'll be all right, child. Say the prayer."

Oh, Lord, I'm goin' to hold steady on to you, and you've got to see me through . . .

The wagon rattled and shook mile after mile. Every now and then they heard the driver say, "Whoa!" and voices would demand to know what kind of load he carried. But one look at the bricks and they were always waved on.

Late that afternoon the wagon was unloaded in the heart of the city of Philadelphia, behind a brick building that housed the Vigilance Committee—a group of black and white abolitionists whose sole purpose was to help runaway slaves. William Still, the secretary, ushered the weary group into the committee's office and took down all their names in a record book. He was the first black man Rosalie had ever seen wearing a suit, starched white shirt, and tie.

"Rosalie Jackson," Rosalie said when it was her turn to give her name.

Harriet and the others looked at her in surprise.

"My name is Rosalie. I am free!" the girl said firmly.

At that everyone broke into grins and cheers.

"You got that right, young lady," said Mr. Still. "Now we are going to try to keep you that way."

To Rosalie's amazement, they were given train tickets and transported the next day in two buggies to the Philadelphia train station. There they climbed into a real passenger coach and sat in real seats at the back of the train car with several other black folks. As Mr. Still handed Harriet a large hamper of food, he said, "You better lie low for a while, Harriet. They've got a price on your head now."

The small woman nodded. "I know. But it ain't ever stopped me before, and it ain't goin' to stop me now. I still got family back in the Tidewater Flats—especially my pappy Ben and my mammy Old 'Rit. I want them to die free."

Mr. Still shrugged, as if he knew it was useless to argue, and got off the train just as the whistle blew.

Rosalie couldn't get over riding in an actual train behind a real steam engine. "Is this the *real* underground railroad?" she asked Harriet curiously.

"No, Rosalie," Harriet smiled. "If you have money for a ticket, anyone can ride this train."

As the miles clicked away outside the train windows, Rosalie realized she was going farther and farther from home. She heard the conductor call out the names of the stations: Allentown . . . Scranton . . . Binghamton.

"We're in New York state now," Harriet told her.

Rosalie held baby Toby up to the window, pointing out the cows and horses grazing in the bright October sunlight. As she watched whole forests of trees march past—all gold and red and yellow and green—a tight lump formed in her throat. How would she ever find her pappy now? She was going so far away! And how would her brother ever find her, if Isaac Woodhouse kept his promise? She wanted to be free; she didn't ever want to be a slave again! But . . . would she ever see her family?

The steam engine pulling their train chugged through the countryside all that day and all through the night. The hard benches were uncomfortable, but snuggled against Mary's shoulder, Rosalie somehow fell asleep, jolted awake from time to time when the train pulled into yet another station.

"Rosalie. Rosalie, wake up." Mary was shaking her. "If you're gonna have a big name like Rosalie," her friend complained good-naturedly, pushing Rosalie's head off her lap, "you're gonna have to sleep on your own. My leg is asleep!"

Rosalie stretched. Sunlight was pouring into the train windows, and passengers were getting their bags together.

"We're coming into Niagara," Harriet informed them. "This is where we get off."

When the weary travelers got off the train, Rosalie could hear an immense roar. She wanted to ask what it was, but Harriet was already heading out of the train station and down the street. The others hustled to keep up. Between the neat wooden buildings lining the street—a ladies dress shop, hotel, saddle shop, and blacksmith—Rosalie caught glimpses of a big gorge with trees on the other side, and the roar was getting louder.

Harriet turned at a break in the buildings and walked toward the sound. As they turned another corner, Rosalie saw a sight she had never dreamed of in her whole life.

In front of them stood a deep gorge. To their left, a river poured over a wide, steep cliff into the gorge in a massive waterfall, thundering loudly and sending a cloud of white spray into the air. But beyond the first waterfall, another arm of the river was pouring into the gorge, three times larger and shaped like a big horseshoe. The roar was deafening.

"Niagara Falls!" Harriet shouted over the thundering sound. "That's Ontario, Canada, on the other side. And freedom!"

The little group stood in speechless wonder for several minutes before Harriet hurried them on. They followed the road along the gorge away from the falls, walking about two miles north, until they came to a bridge over the river. "The Niagara River flows north from Lake Erie into Lake Ontario and finally into the ocean," Harriet explained as the little group stood staring at the narrow suspension bridge hanging over the deepest part of the gorge. The water was far below.

Since the bridge was only one lane wide, the little group had to wait their turn while a farmer's wagon rumbled across from the other side. In spite of herself, Rosebud's knees shook at the thought of walking over the deep chasm on that wobbly bridge.

"William Still gave us papers to help us get into Canada," Harriet assured the others as they waited. They were standing off to the side, hoping to not attract attention.

Rosalie didn't say much. Freedom—real freedom—lay just across the river on the other side. The slave catchers couldn't take a runaway slave back from Canada. William Still had told them that Canada didn't have to obey the Fugitive Slave Law.

Finally it was their turn to cross the bridge. Harriet gave them each a coin, donated by the Vigilance Committee back in Philadelphia, to pay the bridge toll. Dutifully, Rosalie paid her toll and stepped onto the bridge. She did not dare look down. But halfway across, Rosalie stopped and stared back at the United States—the country where she had been born and raised a slave. *Good-bye. Good-bye to slavery!* But at the same time Rosalie felt sad. Somehow the thought of freedom didn't feel so wonderful without her family.

As they stepped off the bridge on the other side, Rosalie held back a little behind Harriet, Charles, Mary, Tobias and Sally, and little Toby. Their journey was over. But what would they do now?

Rosalie waited numbly while a customs agent checked

their papers that Harriet handed him. Then suddenly she heard her name.

"Rosebud! Rosebud Jackson!"

Her head jerked up. Who was calling her name?

She saw a black man running toward her, dodging people who were milling about with bags and boxes. The man looked familiar, big and square and handsome—

"Pappy!" she screamed. And the next moment she was being caught up into Abe Jackson's strong arms and kissed all over her face.

Rosalie could hardly breathe for happiness. Over Pappy's shoulder she saw Harriet Tubman laughing. Harriet had known all the time, known that she was bringing her home—home to her pappy!

"Oh, baby," Abe murmured as he finally set her down. "I've been watching the bridge for days, knowin' you were comin'. Miz Tubman said she would bring you . . . and she did, she did." And he caught her up again in a big bear hug.

"Pappy," Rosalie whispered in his ear. "I've got something to tell you. My name isn't Rosebud anymore. *I am Rosalie. And I am free!*"

MORE ABOUT HARRIET TUBMAN

Around 1820, a slave baby was born to Ben and Harriet ("Old 'Rit") Ross in the slave quarter of a tobacco plantation situated in the Tidewater Flats of Maryland, along the Eastern Shore of Chesapeake Bay. The little girl was named Araminta ("Minty" for short) and, like the rest of her brothers and sisters, was enthralled by the Bible stories, songs, and spirituals taught by their deeply religious mother.

Edward Brodas, the plantation owner, was not a cruel master, but times were hard and sometimes he had to "hire out" his slaves to make ends meet. When Minty was six years old, she was hired out to Mrs. Cook, a weaver, who needed a girl to help her wind yarn. But Minty was stubborn and did not want to learn to weave. In frustration, Mrs. Cook sent her off with Mr. Cook to help him set muskrat traps, which Minty liked better. But the constant damp and cold brought on a severe case of measles, after which Minty always had a husky voice.

At age seven, Minty was again hired out to a "Miss Susan" to help care for her baby. Minty's job was to keep the baby from crying and waking Miss Susan at night—leaving the young girl exhausted. After Miss Susan beat her for taking some sugar, Minty ran away and spent five days hiding in a pigpen.

By now the Brodas Plantation was in serious financial trouble. Edward Brodas did not like separating families, but two of Minty's older sisters had been sold "down South" to one of the slave traders who came through Maryland regularly. Being sold "down South" struck terror in the hearts of the slaves and was used as a threat to keep them from running away. It meant never seeing family and home again, with the probability of being sold to a cruel master.

Fear was stalking the land. Denmark Vesey, a free Negro, and 130 slaves were executed for plotting a violent slave insurrection. After that, slaves were not permitted to be out at night or gather in groups (even for worship) or sing the comforting Negro spirituals, such as "Go down, Moses . . . Tell old Pharaoh, Let my people go!"

In the meantime, realizing young Minty was hopeless at domestic work, Brodas hired her out as a field hand. It was hard work, but Minty liked being outdoors, and by age eleven she had a strong, erect body and calloused hands. She had taken to wearing a woman's bandana around her head and had shed the pet name of Minty. Folks called her Harriet, now, after her mother.

When Harriet was thirteen, one of the field slaves tried to run away during corn husking time. In an effort to stop him, the overseer threw a two-pound weight at him, but Harriet stood in his way and the missile hit the young girl in the forehead instead. She was unconscious for days, then slipped in and out of a stupor for months. As Harriet slowly recovered, a constant prayer was on her lips—for her master: "Change his heart, Lord, convert him."

Even though Harriet recovered, she suffered severe

headaches and peculiar sleeping fits for the rest of her life. As winter turned to spring, the rumor being whispered in the slave quarter was that Harriet and her brothers would be sold to the next slave trader. Rebellion surged in her heart, and her prayer changed. "Lord, if you're never going to change Massa Brodas' heart—then kill him Lord! Take him out of the way."

Within weeks Edward Brodas became ill . . . and died even before the new tobacco crop had been planted. Conscience-stricken, Harriet thought she had killed him! "Oh, Lord," she cried out, "I would give the world full of silver and gold to bring that poor soul back. . . . I would give myself. I would give everything!"

Edward Brodas had promised Ben and Old 'Rit that they would have their freedom when he died. But all his will stated was that none of his slaves could be sold outside the state of Maryland. Brodas' heir was very young, so his guardian, a Dr. Anthony Thompson from nearby Bucktown, administered the plantation.

Soon Ben Ross and his daughter were hired out to a Mr. Stewart, a builder. Harriet asked Mr. Stewart if she could work in the woods with her father instead of being a housekeeper, and was granted permission. Soon she was swinging a broad-axe, cutting timber, hauling logs, plowing fields, and driving an oxcart. At the same time she was learning woodlore from her father: how to tell direction by the moss growing on the north side of the trees and the north star at night; how to walk quietly through the woods like the Indians so as not to disturb the woodland creatures; and how to make bird calls.

In 1844, at the age of twenty-four, Harriet married a free Negro named John Tubman, bringing a handmade patchwork quilt as part of her trousseau. But she was still a slave, working as a field hand for Doc Thompson. She talked to her husband about running away, but he said it was foolishness; in fact, he would tell her master if she tried it! That hurt her deeply. After that, she stopped talking about running away, but she thought about it all the time.

In 1849, the young Brodas heir died, and Doc Thompson began making plans to sell slaves "down South." This time Harriet's mind was made up: "There was one of two things I had a right to, liberty or death. If I could not have one, I would have the other, for no man should take me alive. I would fight for my liberty as long as my strength lasted, and when the time came for me to go, the Lord would let them take me."

Now Harriet's daily prayer became, "Lord, I'm going to hold steady on to you, and you've got to see me through." She had heard about an "underground railroad" that took slaves to freedom in the northern states. One night she took her patchwork quilt and silently made her way through the woods to Bucktown. She knew a white Quaker lady there who had once said, "If you ever need help, come to me." There she learned that the Underground Railroad was not a railroad at all, but a network of "stations" (sympathetic farmers and townspeople) who would hide slaves and help them reach freedom.

Leaving her quilt with the Quaker lady as a gift, Harriet set off on her long journey on foot. She traveled only at night, using all the woodlore she knew to make her way north. At each friendly "station," she was told where to go next. Along the way she traveled in a wagon under a load of vegetables, was rowed up the Choptank River by a man she had never seen before, was concealed in a haystack, spent a week hidden in a potato hole in a cabin that belonged to a family of free Negroes, was hidden in the attic of a Quaker family, and was befriended by stout German farmers. Still afflicted with her head injury, she sometimes fell asleep right on the road, but somehow managed to escape detection.

Approaching Wilmington, Delaware, Harriet had been instructed to hide in a graveyard. A man came wandering through muttering, "I have a ticket for the railroad." This man disguised Harriet in workmen's clothes and took her to Thomas Garrett's house, a famous Quaker abolitionist. Garrett, who had a shoe shop, gave her new shoes and fancy women's clothes and drove her in his buggy north of Wilmington. Before she went on he gave Harriet, who couldn't read or write, a paper with the word *PENNSYLVANIA* written on it so she could recognize when she crossed the state line.

When Harriet finally crossed into Pennsylvania, she had traveled ninety miles. "I looked at my hands to see if I was the same person, now I was free," she said later. "There was such a glory over everything. The sun came like gold through the trees, and over the fields, and I felt like I was in heaven."

But freedom wasn't heaven. The very next year Congress passed the Fugitive Slave Law of 1850, making it a crime for anyone to help a runaway slave and stating that runaway slaves, if found, could be returned to their masters in the South. Harriet couldn't sit back and enjoy freedom for herself. She had to go back and get her family.

In December of 1850, Harriet went back the way she had come and safely brought her sister Mary and Mary's husband and two children to freedom. The following spring, Harriet went back and led her brother and two other men to safety. That fall she went back a third time, disguised as a man, to get her husband—only to discover that John Tubman had taken another wife! Deeply hurt, she nonetheless gathered together a small group of slaves and led them north.

Now Harriet's motives changed. Before she had come back

only to lead her family to freedom; now she took anyone who wanted to flee. She became a legend, both feared and admired. Who was this mysterious person the slaves called "Moses," who spirited away the slaves? Many thought she was a man.

During her lifetime Harriet Tubman led at least three hundred men, women, and children to safety over the Underground Railroad, including her aging parents, Ben and Old 'Rit. The trips got longer and more dangerous because of the numerous slave catchers out looking for runaways. Now she had to lead her small bands all the way to Canada. "But I never lost a passenger," she said proudly. By 1860, the reward for her capture had reached a staggering $60,000.

In November 1860, Abraham Lincoln was elected president of the United States. Within a year, eleven southern states had seceded and formed a new union: the Confederate States of America. Soon Harriet, who had settled in Auburn, New York, had a new role as scout, spy, and even "nurse" (making use of her woodlore knowledge of healing herbs) for the Union Army. But even though Harriet Tubman was highly respected and given many privileges during the war, she never received any of the back pay due her for her services to the Union Army.

The Civil War ended on April 9, 1865. Abraham Lincoln was assassinated six nights later. In December 1865, the Thirteenth Amendment was ratified. At last a dream had come true: slavery was dead.

Two years after the war ended, Harriet learned that her former husband, John Tubman, had been murdered. Even though she was only forty-seven years old, she felt old and lonely for the family life she never had. But two years later she married a black war veteran named Nelson Davis, who was twenty years younger than Harriet. Davis had tuberculosis and was virtually an invalid; he died at the age of forty-four after nineteen years of marriage.

During this time, Mrs. Sarah Hopkins Bradford, an Auburn schoolteacher, wrote and published two books about Harriet Tubman: *Scenes in the Life of Harriet Tubman* (1868) and *Harriet, the Moses of Her People* (1886). Mrs. Bradford donated the royalties from the books to Harriet, who used the money to establish a home for the sick, poor, and homeless. Harriet also earned money by raising and selling vegetables house to house in Auburn. Sometimes she didn't get much selling done, because each customer wanted to give her a cup of buttered tea and hear stories of her adventures on the Underground Railroad.

In 1903, Harriet donated her home and twenty-five acres of land to the African Methodist Episcopal (AME) Church of Auburn, though she continued to live there herself. Against her wishes, the AME Church began to charge a fee to the Home's residents.

On March 10, 1913, Harriet Tubman died at the age of ninety-three. The citizens of Auburn, New York, erected a bronze tablet outside the courthouse, which reads:

IN MEMORY OF HARRIET TUBMAN.
BORN A SLAVE IN MARYLAND ABOUT 1821.
DIED IN AUBURN, N.Y., MARCH 10TH, 1913.
CALLED THE MOSES OF HER PEOPLE,
DURING THE CIVIL WAR. WITH RARE
COURAGE SHE LED OVER THREE HUNDRED
NEGROES UP FROM SLAVERY TO FREEDOM,
AND RENDERED INVALUABLE SERVICE
AS NURSE AND SPY.
WITH IMPLICIT TRUST IN GOD

SHE BRAVED EVERY DANGER AND
OVERCAME EVERY OBSTACLE. WITHAL
SHE POSSESSED EXTRAORDINARY
FORESIGHT AND JUDGMENT SO THAT
SHE TRUTHFULLY SAID
"ON MY UNDERGROUND RAILROAD
I NEBBER RUN MY TRAIN OFF DE TRACK
AN' I NEBBER LOS' A PASSENGER."
THIS TABLET IS ERECTED
BY THE CITIZENS OF AUBURN.

FOR FURTHER READING

Bains, Rae. *Harriet Tubman: The Road to Freedom.* Mahwah, NJ: Troll Associates, 1982.

Burns, Bree. *Harriet Tubman.* [New York]: Chelsea Juniors, 1992. Part of the Junior World Biographies. Includes bibliographical references and index.

Elish, Dan. *Harriet Tubman and the Underground Railroad.* Brookfield, CT: Millbrook Press, 1993. Gateway Civil Rights series. Includes bibliographical references and index.

Ferris, Jeri. *Go Free or Die: A Story About Harriet Tubman.* Minneapolis: Carolrhoda House, 1988. A Carolrhoda Creative Minds book.

Humphreville, Frances T. *Harriet Tubman: Flame of Freedom.* Boston: Houghton Mifflin, 1967. Piper Books series.

McGovern, Ann. *"Wanted Dead or Alive": The True Story of Harriet Tubman.* New York: Scholastic Book Services, 1965. (Also published under the title: *Runaway Slave, the Story of Harriet Tubman.* New York: Four Winds Press, 1965.)

McMullan, Kate. *The Story of Harriet Tubman: Conductor of the Underground Railroad.* New York: Dell Publishing, 1991. A Dell Yearling biography.

KIDNAPPED BY RIVER RATS

WILLIAM & CATHERINE BOOTH

Authors' Note

William and Catherine Booth, Charlie Fry and his Hallelujah Band, and George Scott Railton and the seven Hallelujah Lasses commissioned to "invade" New York were real people. All other characters are fictional. However, the situations presented in this story accurately portray the conditions of many children in London in the 1880s as well as the life and ministry of the Salvation Army.

CONTENTS

CHAPTER 1

ATTACK ON THE CATHEDRAL STEPS

The great hound nosed its way through the dense, sour fog that swirled in the narrow alleys of London's east side. Somewhere ahead it smelled human, maybe still alive or maybe food in the gutter. It was hungry enough to eat anything.

A growl rumbled deep in its throat as it rounded the corner and surveyed the cobblestone street ahead. Its huge head hung low to the ground, a torn lip revealing a sharp fang. Coarse, gray hair spiked along the ridge of its back. The lone gas light in front of Saint Paul's Cathedral cast a greenish glow through the mist. No one there.

Or was there? Deep in the shadows of the side door to the cathedral lay a black heap. The dog approached quietly, sniffing the heavy air. No death here . . . but maybe there would be something to eat just the same.

Jack Crumpton came awake slowly. Why was Mama pulling on his night shirt? Why was his bed so hard? Why was he so cold?

And then it all came back to him. He wasn't in bed . . . Mama was dead, and he and Amy were homeless on the streets of London.

He rolled over with a start. There, snarling and pulling on the sleeve of his coat, stood the biggest wolf-dog he'd ever seen. Jack grabbed for his stick. It was caught under Amy. He pulled it free and swung it at the beast's immense head. The creature ducked the blow without loosening his bite on the coat.

Just then Amy sat up and screamed, "Don't let him have it, Jack! The biscuits in your pocket are our last food."

With one hand Jack pulled with all his might on his coat. With the other he swung his stick toward the dog's nose. This time the stout stick landed with a sharp whack. The brute yelped and made one more desperate lunge backwards, its ugly fangs still embedded in the sleeve of Jack's old coat. The strength of the beast pulled Jack over and he rolled down the steps. But he wouldn't give up his coat.

And then with a sickening rip, the sleeve tore free, and the dog made off into the gloom with Jack's sleeve flapping around its head like a neck scarf in a winter blow.

Jack rose slowly to his knees on the grimy street and tried to inspect his coat by the dim glow of the nearby street light. Safely in its pocket there remained two small hunks of bread no bigger than his fists.

"You all right?" asked Amy as she came down to help him up.

"Yeah, but he got me sleeve. Guess I'll have one cold arm come winter."

"Don't worry, Jack. By then we'll find Uncle Sedgwick, and he'll surely take us in."

"I hope so," Jack said as he followed his older sister back up the steps to huddle in the skimpy shelter of the doorway to the great cathedral. Amy shared her shawl with him, wrapping the garment that their mother had knitted around the both of them. In the dim light its beautiful light and dark greens looked like gray and black, but it was still just as warm.

London had been strange and unfriendly to the two children. They had come to the city a few weeks earlier with their mother after their father had died in a coal mine accident. Mama hoped to find her brother, Sedgwick Masters, a successful tailor. But in London in the fall of 1881, it wasn't so easy to track someone down if you weren't sure of his address. Mama's cough seemed worse after the damp, two-day journey to London, so they found lodging where the landlady charged two shillings per night for an unheated gable room at the back of a dreary house.

The next day, Mother was too ill to look for Uncle Sedgwick. She soon got so sick that the children didn't dare leave her side. They took turns going out to find a penny's worth of bread or some vegetables or broth and bringing it back to Mama. And each day Mrs. Witherspoon, the landlady, came pounding on the door demanding the rent until in one week's time almost all their money was gone.

"You can't stay here without paying your rent," the old landlady had said gruffly. Jack thought her face looked like a prune.

"We'll pay," promised Mother, and then fell into a great fit of coughing that brought up more blood. When she finally got her breath back, she said, "Just give me a chance to get well and find my brother, Sedgwick Masters, the tailor."

"I've never heard of any tailor by that name. Besides, you got consumption, woman. You ain't never gonna get well."

The old woman had been right. Four days later Mother Crumpton died in her sleep.

When Witherspoon came for the rent the next morning, she started shrieking twice as loud as the children had cried during the night. "I told you! I told you she'd never make it. Now what am I going to do? What am I going to do? You two young'uns get out of here. I should never have let this room out to you in the first place." She paced back and forth wringing her hands. "What am I ever going to do?" Then she looked at the children again: "Get out! Get out, I told you."

"But we can't go—that's our mama," protested Amy.

"Was . . . was. She *was* your mama. She ain't no more. This here's just a body that I'm going to have to pay to have taken away. And this room ain't yours anymore, so get out!"

Fighting back the tears, Jack went over and struggled with the trunk that held all their belongings. He was strong for twelve years of age, and Amy, who was just two years older, could put in a full day's work. But they would have done well to get the trunk down the stairs, let alone carry it any distance through London's narrow, busy streets.

"You can just leave that right there," growled old lady Witherspoon. "I'll hold it as collateral till you pay up. You owe me five days' rent plus whatever it costs to have this body taken away. Until you pay up, you can just leave that trunk right here. Now go find that rich uncle of yours, if you got one."

The two children, numb with grief, had wandered aimlessly around London's lower east side until they fell asleep in the doorway of the great cathedral. Now wide awake, their hearts beating loudly as they peered into the darkness, fearful that the beast would return, Amy resolved, "Tomorrow, Jack. Tomorrow we'll go find Uncle Sedgwick."

They arranged their coats over themselves as they cuddled together. Jack listened to the night as the distant wail of a baby's cry drifted through the dense fog.

Yes, tomorrow they had to find Uncle Sedgwick.

CHAPTER 2

BLOOD AND FIRE

When Jack awoke in the morning, his sister was already sitting up watching the hustle and bustle of the street. Jack rubbed his eyes and turned over to see what drew her attention.

They had slept late. The sun had already burned off most of the fog, leaving a bright haze overhead. Jack looked up. There was a hazy circle around the sun; must mean rain.

The street was full of people. A fat woman waddled by carrying a large basket of laundry. She was so fat that she seemed to have to work very hard just to get where she was going. "Hold on ta me skirts," she barked at three apple-faced children coming on behind her, each one a smaller copy of the mother.

A man pulled a creaking two-wheeled cart piled high with lumps of coal. "I miss Pa," Jack said as tears came to his eyes. He pulled his cap lower. Straight brown hair poked out all around. His hair was the same color as his mother's had been. Amy, however, had her father's hair—red and curly, but not so red as to look orange and not so curly as to be frizzy. For a sister, she could look very pretty, Jack sometimes thought. Today, however, smears of dirt trailed across her forehead and down one cheek. Her hair was tousled, her clothes a mess. Mother would never have let Amy go out looking like that. But now she was gone, and they were alone, so alone.

"What you lookin' at?" Amy asked. "Give me one of those biscuits."

Jack dug in his pocket and took out the hunks of stale bread. He handed one to Amy and stuck the other in his teeth as he examined his coat with its missing sleeve. He ought to go search for it. There was a good chance the dog dropped it once it realized it held nothing to eat.

"You think that dog would have eaten us last night?" he asked Amy.

"I doubt it. Who ever heard of a dog eating a person? It's not like we were sheep and it was a wolf."

"Dogs go bad and kill sheep sometimes," said Jack. "Besides, that one last night looked half-wolf."

"That it did. I've never seen such an ugly thing. I did once hear of dogs eating dead people during a famine."

Just then Jack heard the most peculiar sound. It was the high pitched sound of a flute and the deep thump, thump, thump of a drum. He stuffed the rest of the biscuit in his mouth and looked down the street. Coming around the corner about one street away was a small parade. Each person was in a uniform; most carried some kind of a band instrument, and one held high a brightly colored flag, but it was not the familiar British Union Jack.

"You think they're bobbies?" asked Jack, ready to run.

"Policemen don't march around with a band," said Amy. "Otherwise how would they ever catch any crooks?"

The troop continued marching up the narrow street beside the cathedral. Small children, chickens, and cats scampered to the side to get out of the way. Then, right at the bottom of the steps, a tall, wiry-haired man with a bushy, gray beard and a black top hat shouted a command, and the troop stopped and turned like a machine toward Amy and Jack.

"They *are* bobbies," yelled Jack as he grabbed his sister's hand and tried to make a break for it.

"Hold on there, lad," said the man with the big beard as he easily reached out and caught Jack's arm. "Where are you off to so fast?"

"We ain't done nothin'," stammered Jack. "We just . . . I mean, sir, we are just looking for our uncle." Jack squirmed to get free.

"Listen, lad, we're not the police, and we're not after anything more than your soul. But I do want to talk to you. So will you hold still a minute?"

After my soul? thought Jack. *Who could be after my soul other than God or the devil?* Jack had only occasionally gone to church, but he wasn't about to let anyone get his soul. On the other hand, you can't just grab a body's soul, or could you? Jack stood still, and the man's iron grip loosened on his arm.

The man took off his top hat and stooped down with his hands on his knees until he was on eye level with Jack. The man's nose was large and somewhat hooked. His gray eyes shone like polished steel, deep-set under two eyebrows that were not shaped the same. The right one arched high while the left one sloped, giving him a skeptical expression.

"So, where do you two live?" he commanded. His wiry beard jutted out and bobbed with each word, carefully pronounced with military precision.

"We live . . ." began Jack.

"We live with our Uncle Sedgwick," finished Amy with authority.

"I see." The man cocked his head and examined Amy. "But you don't know where he is . . . and so you must 'look' for him. Is that it?" Both children nodded. "A likely story, indeed," said the man.

"General, come now," interrupted a woman who stepped forward. "Can't you see that these children are scared to death? I'm Catherine Booth, children," beamed the woman with a warm smile. She wore a dark blue bonnet tied under her chin by a broad red ribbon. "And this man, who would love to take you captive, is none other than my husband, General William Booth of the Salvation Army."

It was only then that Jack realized that the troop was made up almost equally by men and women. While the women wore long dresses, their uniform was very military looking. And as for the men, they did look like soldiers on dress parade with sharply cut, dark blue uniforms and small brimmed caps with shiny metal crests on the front. The general was dressed the same except for his top hat and slightly different insignia on his uniform. Then Jack noticed that on the collar of each person there was a highly polished, brass letter S.

While Mrs. Booth talked, the other members of the troop set up the flag and the drum and prepared to play right on the steps of Saint Paul's Cathedral. A chill ran through Jack's body as a slight breeze waved the flag. He didn't read too well, but he easily made out the words "Blood and Fire" inscribed above a cross, two crossed swords, and again the letter S. "Blood and Fire" . . . "Blood and Fire" . . . what could it mean?

Mrs. Booth concluded her introduction by inviting the children to stay and listen to the music. Her face was solemn but her eyes were smiling.

"I think we'd better be going," said Amy as she pulled Jack down the steps and away from this strange army. "Jack, she *said* that the general wants to take us captive," whispered Amy when Jack tried to squirm away.

The children spent all that morning walking the streets of East London looking for their uncle. Time and again they would race forward when they saw a sign indicating a tailor's shop. But when they got close, it always had someone else's name on it.

Once when they were getting a drink of water from a public fountain, Amy said, "Maybe we ought to be going inside and asking, even though his name's not on the sign. Maybe his shop is in someone else's name."

"That means we have to go back and check each one we've been to," moaned Jack.

"But it might speed up our search," said Amy. "One tailor ought to know the others. If they are in the same business, someone is bound to know him and can direct us to the right shop."

In the third shop they entered, a skinny old man as crooked as a dried-out oak limb glanced up over the top of his spectacles and said, "Sedgwick Masters, eh? Whatcha want him for?"

"He's our uncle,. and we're trying to find him," said Amy.

"Well, I don't know where he is," said the old man, returning to his sewing, "and I don't care to know, either."

"Why not?" asked Jack.

"'Cause the last time I heard of him was when he stole two of my best customers."

The children stared as the man put a handful of pins in his mouth. Finally Amy said, "But you *have* seen him, then?"

"Didn't say I'd seen him," mumbled the tailor as he took one pin after another from his mouth as fast as a dog scratches fleas and stuck them in the garment he was sewing. "Actually, I never laid eyes on the man."

"But you gotta know where he is if your customers went to him," persisted Amy.

"Listen here, young lady, I don't gotta know nothin'. When one of my customers came back to me, I was grateful. I didn't pry into why he had left or why he came back."

Jack and Amy walked to the door in despair. Then suddenly Jack turned back. "Wait," he said. "Who were those people, the customers of yours who went to our Uncle Sedgwick? Where are they now? Maybe they know where our uncle is."

"Like I said, only one came back. He was that dandy, Filbert. Wanted me to make him three new suits so he could impress the ladies of Europe. Last I heard, he'd set sail for France. Was going to tour the Continent for 'his cultural enrichment,' he said. I haven't seen him since."

"Who was the other person," said Jack, "the one who didn't come back?"

"Well, now, I *do* know that she's still around. But she's never come back to me, so maybe she's still using Masters. Who knows?"

"But who was she?" persisted Jack.

"Oh, she's the wife of that general, or so-called general. Booth, Catherine Booth, was her name. They're the ones who started that Salvation Army. They march around here all the time." The tailor looked up at Jack and added, "Say, boy, you better get your jacket fixed. You're missing a sleeve there."

CHAPTER 3

CAUGHT FOR A THIEF

Amy and Jack left the tailor's shop in high spirits. Their uncle couldn't be far, and now they knew someone who could lead them to him.

"But, Amy," said Jack, "that woman said the general wanted to take us captive. What if he does?"

"We can't let him," said Amy. "We'll have to find them when they're not together and ask her then."

They headed back toward the cathedral. It was a long walk, and it was getting late in the afternoon. As they hiked along, Jack noticed a most wonderful smell. He looked up, and there in the window of a building that was built right out to the street sat two steaming pies. Jack stopped, and that caused Amy to stop and look up, too. "They're chicken pies, just like Mom makes," said Amy.

Jack's stomach growled and suddenly ached. The children were getting very hungry, not having had anything to eat all day except one hard biscuit early that morning, but Jack's stomach hurt from more than hunger. "They're just like Mom *made. Made*, Amy, not *'makes.'* Mother can't make pies anymore. Remember? It's just like old lady Witherspoon said, Mom's dead." He stomped off down the street, keeping his head turned away so Amy wouldn't see the tears that swam in his eyes.

"Jack, wait." Amy caught up to him. "I didn't mean anything. Those pies just made me think about Mom; that's all. I miss her, too, you know."

"Yeah, I know," he mumbled. "It's just that I wish she hadn't left us. It ain't fair; now we're all alone, and I'm starving."

"Don't be angry, Jack. It wasn't her fault. We just gotta hang together and find Uncle Sedgwick. Then we can get something to eat."

"But what if we never find him?"

"We will; we will."

They rounded a corner and came to a street market. Jack's mouth watered when he looked at the bright red apples in a grocery stall. *Just one bite, just one bite would taste so good,* he thought. The grocer was looking the other way, helping a customer. Suddenly Jack grabbed two apples, one for himself and one for Amy, and tried to put them into his pockets. But the apples were so big that they wouldn't fit. While he was struggling, the grocer turned around and saw him.

"Hey, you little brat," he yelled. "Put them back."

In fright Jack turned and started to run. "Amy, come on."

For a moment Amy was confused, but when she saw the grocer lunge around the end of his table with his cane raised high, she started running after Jack fast enough.

"Stop, thief! Stop, thief!" yelled the grocer as they dodged between the other stalls in the street market. Jack turned down an alley, an apple clutched in each hand, and Amy was right behind him. The cobblestones of the alley were rough, and garbage and puddles of sewage made it slick. Jack looked back to see the grocer hot on their heels.

Suddenly Amy screamed, and Jack heard a loud crash. When he looked back, a rain barrel had tipped over into the center of the alley and had broken open. Water was flooding everywhere. Amy was on the ground in the middle of it. Just then the grocer skidded to a stop above her and grabbed her by her hair. He raised his cane.

"No," yelled Jack and raised his two apples high so the man could see them. "Don't hit my sister."

"You bring them apples back to me, then, you little tea-leaf."

Jack approached the grocer. The man's face was purple, and he was breathing hard, but he hadn't let go of Amy's hair. Jack put both apples in one hand—they were almost too big to hold that way—and came closer, holding them out to the man. Suddenly the cane whistled through the air and came crashing down on Jack's hand and wrist. One apple exploded; the other went flying across the alley. Jack felt more pain shoot up his arm than he had ever known in his life. "That'll teach you ta thieve from me, you little brats. Every day, robbing me blind. It's got so a man can't make a livin' any more." And with that the man turned and lumbered back up the alley.

Jack realized that he was crying. He didn't want to cry; he wanted to be brave for Amy. But he couldn't help it. A great red welt was growing across his wrist, and his hand felt like he'd never use it again. Then Jack noticed that Amy was crying, too. Her clothes were wet, and she was holding her ankle. "What's wrong," said Jack through his sobs.

"I think I hurt my ankle," she said.

"Can you stand up?" Jack asked.

"I don't know. I think it's really hurt. But what about your hand?"

Jack held it out and tried to move his fingers. At least they did move, but the pain throbbed harder than ever. "I think it's okay," he said, not at all sure that was so.

"Here, help me up," said Amy.

Jack offered his other hand to help her. Amy stood up using Jack for balance, keeping her right foot off the ground. Slowly she put it down and tried one feeble step, but the moment she put weight on it, she gave a little cry and almost fell again. "I think it's really hurt, Jack."

"What're we gonna do?"

"I don't know. Maybe it's just twisted. Here, let me lean on you."

The two hobbled back down the alley as evening turned the shadows to blue, purple, then gray. "Wait a minute," said Jack. "Grab hold of the corner of the building." Then he ran back down the alley, searching for something.

In a few minutes he returned. "Here," he said as he held out the badly bruised apple that had not been totally smashed by the grocer's cane. "I know it isn't ours, and I shouldn't have taken it. I'm sorry about that, 'specially because of your foot. But I guess the grocer didn't want it. At least he didn't take it back, and we need something to eat. Want a bite?" He rubbed it on his pants to wipe off the alley's grime.

Amy took a bite, then held on to Jack's shoulder as they limped off down the street, sharing the apple.

CHAPTER 4

THE CAVE IN THE CITY

It was nearly dark. The lamplighter was lighting the lamps on each post.

"Jack, I don't know where we are. I don't know where the cathedral is anymore."

"Neither do I," said Jack. "But there's something different up ahead. It looks like the street ends. But then there's nothing."

As they approached, they found that the street butted into another one that went along the side of a great river. On the river moved large barges, barely visible in the dark except that some had a lantern on deck. On the other side of the river down farther were three ships tied up. The tall masts and rigging of these sailing ships made a lacy silhouette against the last pale light in the sky.

"I don't think I can walk any more," said Amy. "My foot's hurtin' something fierce. I wish Mother were here. She would know what to do." The two made their way out of the street just as a coach and four horses raced past, the wheels and hooves clattering on the rough cobblestones. Amy leaned on the wall for support. Jack gazed at the shiny black water below.

"There's something down there," Jack muttered almost to himself. "I'm climbing down."

"Wait," said Amy as she reached for her brother, but he was already scrambling over the wall, lowering himself to the river. Then she, too, noticed it. Right below them the water did not come all the way to the wall. There was a little sandy beach not much wider than what a person could walk on.

Jack walked along it toward a nearby bridge. At the base of the pillar supporting the end of the bridge the little stretch of sand was replaced by large rough rocks. Jack's fingers found small handholds in the cracks between the stones of the pillar, and he hung on as he carefully inched his way around the pillar, stepping from one slippery rock to the next. There, under the end of the bridge, was a small cave. It actually extended ten or twelve feet back under the street above. The floor of the cave was sandy, and when one got away from the river a ways, it was pretty dry. A large limb of a tree and other pieces of driftwood had piled up along one side. There was even a packing box and a broken bucket.

Something scurried across the sand and into the pile of driftwood. Maybe it was a cat . . . or a rat. But if it was a rat, it was the biggest rat Jack had ever seen. Jack reached down and picked up a stone. "Show your head just one time," Jack threatened. When nothing moved, he cut loose with a wicked sling anyway and the stone cracked against the old bucket. Still nothing came out. Jack picked up a second stone and moved toward the back of the cave, ever watchful of the pile of trash. But the back of the cave was so dark that he could only sense its general location. He didn't *think* there was anything else lurking back there, but he wasn't going back there by himself to find out.

"Jack! Jack! What are you doing?"

Jack could just hear his sister's voice. He climbed back around the pillar and looked up at her. The evening gloom made her face barely visible. "There's a cave down here!" Jack said.

"So?"

"This is great! Come on down."

"Jack, why would I want to climb down there to explore an old cave? We don't even have a place to sleep tonight."

"Why not in this cave? At least if it rained, we wouldn't get wet. There's some wood down here. We could even light a fire."

Amy groaned. "Jack, sometimes I don't know what to do with you. Don't you realize that my ankle is hurt? I could never climb down there."

"Yes you could. It's not far."

Amy stood there looking at him, then out across the river, then back across the street into the part of London where they'd spent the day looking without luck for their uncle. Finally she turned back to Jack. "Okay. But you've got to help me get down. My ankle is swelling up bigger and bigger."

In a few minutes both children were standing together on the narrow strip of sand at the river's edge. The night sounds of the big city were cut off from them, and all they could hear was the gentle ding, ding, ding of the bell from the river buoy up near where the ships were docked.

Jack held Amy's arm as she inched herself around the pillar. Once, her foot slipped on the rough rocks below and she turned her ankle again. She cried out, then caught her breath. He could see pain etched on her face.

"Here we are," Jack said encouragingly.

Amy hobbled across the sand toward the back of the cave. "It's dry now. But what happens if it rains and the river level rises. We'd be flooded out. In fact, how would we even get out?"

Jack shrugged, then realized that it was too dark in the cave for Amy to see his gesture. "Here, let's make a fire," he said as he drew a few of the smaller sticks from the pile of driftwood and trash. He tried not to think of the animal that had so recently run into that pile.

"How are we going to light a fire, Jack? We don't have any matches. There's no way we can light a fire down here."

"Maybe we could go borrow some coals from someone's hearth," offered Jack.

"Sure, just walk up to one of those pubs along the riverfront and say, 'Could we please have some live coals? We ain't got no place to live and we're camping under the bridge.' If we did that, one of those drunken sailors would throw us in the river."

Jack continued breaking sticks and laying them for a fire. There had to be a way; there just had to be.

"Jack! I know. Take a little stick and climb up one of the street light poles. Stick it in there just like the lamplighter does. But instead of lighting the lamp, you can light your stick to bring back for some fire."

It was a great idea. Jack found a small, dry stick in the pile of trash and left the little cave. He climbed the wall and ran down the street to the nearest lamp. But climbing the pole wasn't as easy as it looked. It took him three tries before he made it. Then clinging carefully to the pole, he put his stick into the little hole and touched the flame. It flared brightly, and he slid down the pole.

The stick was burning fast. Jack ran down the dark street

and scrambled over the wall and dropped to the sand below. But the fall through the air blew out the flame. He stood there by the black river with only a glowing ember in his hand. Carefully he blew on it to get a weak flame to return. It glowed brightly for a moment, but then went out completely.

"Amy, get me another stick—a little longer, and make sure it's dry. This one went out."

In a few moments Amy handed another stick around the pillar so that neither child had to navigate the slippery rocks. Jack climbed back up the wall. He was getting to know where the good hand and foot holds were now, even in the dark.

This time when he returned with the burning stick he was careful not to shake his hand as he dropped the last few feet to the ground. The flame held.

Back in the cave he held it to the little pile of wood he had made. Some of the smallest splinters lit easily, but they also burned down quickly. As the little flames on the sticks grew smaller and smaller, both children huddled close and blew gently, adding one twig at a time. Finally, when they thought they were going to be plunged back into darkness, some new sticks caught and the fire began to grow.

They fed it with new wood and smiled as it crackled cheerily. At last they began to feel warm as they cuddled together on the sand at the back of the river cave.

CHAPTER 5

RIVER RATS

It was drizzling when the children awoke in the morning. They sat up and looked out into the river. A riverboat was pulling slowly upstream; two men worked steadily on the oars to move it against the current. The open boat was piled high with potatoes and cabbages—going to market, no doubt.

"Wish I could have one of them," said Jack. "I'm starving."

In the distance they could see several other boats on the water—people starting their day to the sour smell of coal smoke in the London air.

"Oh no. Our fire's gone out," moaned Amy as she pulled her shawl around her shoulders. "And the street lamps will have been put out by now. We can't even get another light until tonight."

"It's not my fault," said Jack. "You could have gotten up in the night and put on more wood yourself. There's plenty of it."

"I didn't say it was your fault. I just said we don't have a fire."

"It sounded like you were blaming me," complained Jack.

"Well, I wasn't. So what's the matter with you this morning?"

"I'm just hungry," said Jack. Tears came to his eyes. "And I want Mama. Why'd she have to die?"

Amy put her arms around him, and together the two children cried. Finally Amy sniffed and wiped her face with her shawl. "But we can't give up, Jack. We just can't."

"But what are we going to do?"

"This morning you have to go find that Salvation Army woman. What was her name?"

"You mean the one the tailor said was Uncle Sedgwick's customer? Booth something, wasn't it?"

"Yes. Booth, Catherine Booth. You have to go find her, Jack. Catherine Booth, don't forget that name."

"But why not you?"

In answer, Amy stuck out her foot and pointed to her ankle. "I really can't walk, Jack. There's no way I can wander around the city until I get better."

"What about the river?" said Jack. "What if this rain makes it rise and floods you out like you said?"

"It's not rising yet. Look at those rocks, the water's even lower." She nodded over to the piling around which they had to climb every time they came into the cave. "You know, unless there is a real big rain or spring floods, I think the only thing that changes the water level in this river is the tide."

Jack looked suspiciously at the pile of trash. "The tide? But that comes from the sea every day, twice a day. We've already been here one whole night, and there hasn't been any high tide."

"No. I'm talking about big tides, the kind that come once a month. Maybe they come up the river this far. I don't know."

"Yeah, maybe that's how all this junk got here. It floated here sometime when the river was high, high enough to come up into this very cave. And we don't know when that's going to happen."

"Well, it's not going to happen today," said Amy. "I'll tell you what, you go looking for Catherine Booth, and if it starts raining hard, you can come back here and help me out."

That seemed to satisfy Jack, and he got up to leave.

Part way out into the river there was another set of pillars holding up the huge bridge. Up near the top in the shadows of the beams Jack noticed movement. He looked closely and then realized what it was. A rat was crawling along the beam, possibly the very one that had hid in their pile of driftwood the night before. Jack stooped down and found three stones in the sand. Carefully he eased over to the side of the cave to get a better angle. The rat was in full view now, stopping every few moments and looking around.

Suddenly Jack let fly with a rough, oblong stone. It was a long throw, but Jack was a good shot. The stone whizzed just over the rat's head. The ugly creature bounded forward a few feet, then stopped and looked around, its round rump high and its beady eyes shining. Apparently the rat was uncertain what had happened or where its enemy was. That moment of hesitation was all Jack needed. He took aim and flung a second stone with all his might. It sailed through the air and found its mark, hitting with a thud that knocked the rat off the beam and into the river.

"You got him, Jack."

"Yeah." Jack stared at the place where the rat had splashed into the water. In a few moments something floated to the surface and drifted lifelessly down stream. "Yeah, I got him good." In his excitement, Jack flung his third rock out over the river in the general direction of where the rat had been. But because he hadn't aimed, the stone flew beyond the pillar and landed on the front of a boat that had just nosed out from behind the pillar.

"Hey, what's the big idea?" yelled a burly voice as a huge sailor stood up in the boat. His partner continued rowing. "What you brats trying to do? You want to kill someone? I've a mind to come in there and thrash the both of you."

"We didn't mean to," answered Amy.

"Hey, Rodney," said the one still at the oars. "It's a girl."

"Yeah, and just about the right age, too. But we got to get back to the ship. We'll take care of this later." Then he yelled again at Amy and Jack, "You throw any more rocks at us, and I'll bust your heads."

"We won't," said Jack.

"You bet you won't, and we'll be back to see that you don't, too." They laughed with a roar as the big man sat down clumsily and took up his oars. Soon they were far down the river.

"That was a close one," said Jack. "I almost got two river rats." And he laughed.

"Don't joke about it, Jack. Those were evil men."

"You don't think they will be back, do you Amy?"

"Who knows. They probably go back and forth from their ship every day when they are in port. We'll just have to attract no more attention. Now you go on, Jack. See if you can find that Booth lady."

"But I'm starving, Amy. When are we going to get something to eat?"

"I don't know. I'm hungry, too. Maybe you can ask someone to give you some bread when you are out."

"Yeah, maybe so. I'll bring you back something," said Jack as he worked his way around the rocks at the bottom of the piling. "I promise that I'll get you something."

CHAPTER 6

THREE GOOD HITS

By the time Jack had climbed up to the street, the drizzle had stopped, for which he was very grateful. The streets were full of people, and no one seemed to pay any attention to the young boy climbing over the wall along the edge of the River Thames.

Jack looked all morning for the Salvation Army. He found the church where he and Amy had spent the night, but they weren't there. He asked people on the street where they were. "Oh, they're around; they're around here every day somewhere," a boy about Jack's age told him. "Why, you looking to throw a little mud?" the boy asked.

"No. Why would I throw mud?" Jack said.

"Beats selling papers," the boy shrugged as he ran off.

Jack didn't understand what he was talking about. Why would throwing mud beat selling papers?

The smell of baking bread caught Jack's attention. It was coming from a bakery with rolls and loaves of bread in every shape and size in the window. There was black bread, brown bread, and even white bread. His mouth watered as he looked through the window, and he remembered his promise to bring Amy something to eat.

An idea struck him, and he ran down the street to the next corner. He turned and ran on until he found a little alley that led him to the back of the bakery shop. He pounded on the door until a bald man with bushy black eyebrows opened the door.

"Yeah, whatcha want?"

"Sorry to bother you, sir. But I was wonderin' if I could earn a loaf of bread?"

"Away with you. We got too many beggars around here already."

"I ain't no beggar, sir. I was wantin' to work for it. Any old job will do."

"Ain't got any. Come back when you can pay a copper. Then I'll be glad to *sell* you a loaf of bread," and he slammed the door.

Jack turned away and kicked at a cat in the alley. The thing hissed at him and jumped to the top of a rain barrel. Jack had a mind to grab it, lift the lid, and give the ugly creature a good dunking. But he knew his problems weren't the cat's fault. Instead, he hissed back at it until the cat scampered up on a shed roof out of his reach.

Jack was so discouraged when he came out of the alley that he was tempted to return to the river and tell Amy it was no use. But just then his ears caught the deep thump, thump, thump he'd heard the other morning on the cathedral steps. It had to be the Salvation Army band, but where was it?

He turned right and ran down the street, but the sound didn't get louder. Between the close buildings, the sound echoed so much that it was hard to tell from which way it came. Jack decided that it must be on the next street. He turned the corner and ran up to the next street. The band wasn't there, but the sound was louder. Now he could hear the flute and the horns. It sounded as good as a circus. He ran faster, and when he came around the next corner he was rewarded. There, halfway down the street, was the Salvation Army band playing a song so joyful that it made Jack want to dance.

The band was on a loading platform for a warehouse. The platform was about the height of Jack's head. This put them up so everyone could see and hear them. But getting close was a different matter. The narrow street was jammed with people. Some were singing, some just standing there. Some were yelling, but Jack couldn't make out what they were saying.

He worked his way through the crowd until he was directly across the street from the band. Behind him was the open door to a pub. From there he could see the band clearly. Unfortunately, the general and the lady he had seen on the cathedral steps weren't among them. But he decided to listen to the singing and the band. Maybe afterwards he could ask them where Catherine Booth was. The song boomed out:

We're bound for the land
of the pure and the holy.
The home of the happy, the Kingdom of love;
Ye wanderers from God
in the broad road of folly,
O say, will you go to the Eden above?

Jack wasn't sure what it all meant, but he liked the tune, and he sure would like to go to some land where there weren't so many troubles. The chorus asked, "Will you go? Will you go?" over and over again with such earnestness that Jack almost shouted, "Yes!"

Just then something went flying through the air and landed right in the bell of one of the horns. It jammed the horn into the player's mouth so hard that his lips began to bleed. Jack could see that the thing thrown was a dead cat.

A tremendous roar went up from the crowd. Some were cheering. Some were yelling to leave the band alone. "They're doing no harm."

More things went flying through the air: rocks, bottles, and mud that splattered on the band players, turning their uniforms into an ugly mess.

The throwing seemed to be coming from a group of boys just about Jack's age, and most of them were right around him. As the fray continued, one after another yelled, "There, I got a hit!" "Count one for me." "Bull's-eye; that's a halfpenny for me."

The riot calmed down when the Salvation Army people got down from the loading platform.

"Hey, boy. Come here."

Jack looked around and through the doorway into the dark interior of a pub. A man stood there behind the bar wiping the counter, a pint of beer in his hand. His hair was cut short, but he had a huge walrus moustache, the ends of which drooped nearly to the bottom of his strong, square jaw. "Yeah, you," the man said, nodding to Jack.

Jack stepped through the open door. It was an ordinary enough pub with a bar down one side and a big barrel on the end of the bar. It would hold beer. On the wall behind were several smaller barrels on their sides with taps in the ends. They would hold whiskey, rum, and gin of the cheaper variety. Above them were bottles of the expensive stuff. Around the dark room were a few tables with chairs and a big old stove with a bucket full of coal beside it.

Jack approached slowly. The man just stood there, sipping from time to time from the pint in his hand. He wore the faded red top of long-handled underwear frayed at the sleeves and around the neck. His black working pants were held up with wide braces, and his heavy boots were worn and scuffed. "You seen them Salvationists before?" he asked, pointing out the door.

"Yes, sir. I seen 'em once before," answered Jack.

"You live around here?"

"Sorta." Jack squirmed.

"Well, listen here. That Salvation Army intends to ruin my business. They want to shut down every gin house in London, and quite a few of my regulars have already converted. It's hittin' me where it hurts. You know what I mean? Right in my money pouch. But I'm a fair business man, and I'm willin' to pay for what I need. You seen them boys out there?"

"Yes, sir," Jack said, not exactly sure who the man meant but certain he'd find out soon enough.

"I pay each and every one of those boys a halfpenny every time they make a hit that counts. You know what I mean?"

Jack shook his head no. He actually did have an idea what the man was saying, but he could hardly believe his ears.

"What I'm sayin' is, when they throw somethin' and they make a good hit, I keep score and pay a halfpenny each hit. The way I figure it, pretty soon those Salvationists will give up and find better things to do than trouble a legitimate business man. I got a legal license to run this pub, you know."

"Yes, sir," Jack said, not quite sure what he was agreeing with but feeling he ought to say something.

"So, what do you say? I'll pay you the same?"

"I got no cause to bother those people," Jack protested.

"No cause," the man growled through clenched teeth. "I just told you the cause, you little brat." And he made as if to lunge after Jack.

Jack turned to run out the door when the man changed the tone of his voice. "Wait. I didn't mean nothin' against you, boy. Look here. Come on back in here. You look like you could use a job. Am I right?"

"Yes, sir," said Jack. "Me and Amy, well, we need some . . ." Jack stopped, thinking it best to keep his troubles private.

"Okay, then. You need some money; I got a job for you to do. That's cause enough, wouldn't you say?"

Jack thought about it a moment. The hunger pains in his stomach were getting unbearable, and he'd promised to bring Amy something to eat. He could find that Mrs. Booth tomorrow. If they didn't get something to eat soon, neither of them would be strong enough to search the city for their uncle.

"All right. How do I get paid?"

"I'll be watching. You come back here after it's all over."

When Jack left the pub he expected that the Salvation Army would have packed up and left for some place safer. But instead one of the men was standing up on the platform speaking:

> "A lot of you don't have jobs, some of you lack a place to live, and maybe you are even hungry. When Jesus saw people just like you, He cared. He cared enough to do something.

There were five thousand men plus women and children in that crowd. That's a lot more than there are of you gathered here today on East Tenter Street.

"But Jesus asked a small boy to share what he had, and Jesus multiplied it. The Bible says that He 'took the five loaves, and the two fishes, and looking up to heaven, he blessed, and brake, and gave the loaves to his disciples, and the disciples to the multitude. And they did all eat, and were filled: and they took up of the fragments that remained twelve baskets full.'

"Jesus said, 'Come unto me, all ye that labour and are heavy laden, and I will give you rest.' But so many of you try to find your rest in gin and beer. You think you can drink your troubles away, but the Bible says, 'There is a way which seemeth right unto a man, but the end thereof are the ways of death.' "

Just then a howl went up from several people in the crowd, and a very ripe tomato landed right at the feet of the speaker, splattering red juice all over his legs. Another tomato just missed the flag that flew above them.

"Down with the Salvationists," yelled someone. "They just want to shut down our pubs." And several more things flew through the air.

Jack looked around and saw that some of the boys he had noticed before were again throwing things, so he, too, reached down and picked up a small pebble and gave it a gentle toss toward the speaker. He really didn't want to hurt anyone. The pebble flew through the air in a high arch and bounced harmlessly off the speaker's cap.

Jack glanced toward the pub. The owner was leaning casually in his doorway, his muscled arms crossed on his chest. He looked at Jack, scowled, and shook his head. Jack got the message: no halfpennies for little pebbles, even if he did score a bull's-eye. With a raised eyebrow the pub owner pointed to the street not far from Jack's feet. His hand barely moved as his finger made a sharp jab toward the spot on the ground and then another jab toward the speaker. Then the man looked away, ignoring Jack.

Jack looked down. There was a pile of fresh horse droppings. The man wanted him to throw those round, green "balls." Jack hesitated to pick them up. How could he? On the other hand, they wouldn't hurt anyone, and he was so hungry.

Tentatively Jack picked one up and gave it a toss. It went wide of its mark. Jack looked over to the pub owner. He shrugged slightly and looked away. Just then someone else's old shoe hit the speaker as he was repeating the verse about there being a way that *seems* right but leads to death. The crowd roared. Earlier—during the music—many people had seemed with the Salvation Army, even singing along. Now they had turned against them. They had become an ugly mob, enjoying being mean to the speaker.

Jack reached down and got another handful. This time he let fly. His aim was true, and the pub owner gave a slight nod. Jack threw again and again. Each time it was easier, almost like sport. He cheered when he got a second good hit and then a third.

Suddenly whistles began blowing and several police came down the street yelling, "Break it up! Break it up! That's enough now. Everyone go on home."

Jack ducked back into the pub. The owner was already behind the bar wiping glasses as though nothing had happened. When he saw Jack, he said, "Get out of here. I don't want those cops finding one of you boys in here."

"But my money," protested Jack. "You saw me get three good hits. You owe me a penny and a half."

The man flipped Jack the money and then snarled, "Now beat it."

CHAPTER 7

BREAD AND WATER

Jack ran back to the river with a loaf of bread under one arm and a halfpenny still in his pocket. He hadn't found Mrs. Booth, but he was able to keep his promise to get something for Amy and him to eat.

He'd gone back to the same bakery where the man had turned him away when he'd asked for a job. At first he thought that he'd never give that man his business. But the more he thought about it, it made him feel good to imagine slapping down his penny on the counter and demanding the biggest loaf of that good-looking white bread that he could see. He'd show that bakerman that he wasn't a beggar.

But when he got to the bakery, the man wasn't anywhere around. There was only a girl just a little older than Amy minding the shop. He bought the loaf and soon forgot about the ornery baker as he ran to the river.

He scrambled over the wall and dropped to the narrow

strip of sand below. "Amy, Amy. Look here," he called as he worked his way over the rocks and around the pillar.

"Jack," Amy said as she got up from the sand and came toward him. "Where have you been? You've been away 'most all day. What you been up to?" Then she saw the loaf he was holding out. "Jack, where did you get that bread? You didn't steal it, did you?"

"No. I didn't steal it, and I didn't beg for it, either. I earned some money, and I *bought* it. What's more, I still got a halfpenny left, right here in my pocket." Jack pulled out the little copper and held it in the palm of his hand for Amy to inspect.

"Oh, Jack. I'm so hungry. I'm glad you got something to eat." She broke off a hunk of bread and began eating it. Jack grinned and did the same.

Then Jack realized that in spite of how hungry he had been, he had come all the way back home to share the bread with Amy before taking any himself. *It wouldn't have been right to eat it by myself,* he thought. *Whatever we've got is for sharing.* What was even stranger, he was thinking of this damp cave as "home." He looked around as he chewed. The place really was terrible.

"Did you find Mrs. Booth, Jack?"

"No. But I'll look some more tomorrow. She's bound to turn up soon." He didn't want to tell Amy that even though he hadn't found Catherine Booth, he had found the Salvation Army. Then she'd want to know why he hadn't asked the Army where Mrs. Booth was. That might lead to telling her how he'd earned the money, and he knew she'd be angry. But she sure was enjoying the bread, and so was he.

"Look, Jack," Amy said after taking a few bites, "I appreciate the bread, but finding Mrs. Booth is more important than wasting time earning money."

"Well, I tried to find her."

"Trying's not good enough. We've *got* to find her."

"Well, we gotta eat, too, don't we?" Jack said angrily.

"But we can't keep staying in this old cave. We *have* to find Uncle Sedgwick. And Mrs. Booth is our only hope."

Amy fell silent, and Jack didn't try to answer her. What could he say without giving himself away? Besides, when Amy got silent like that, Jack knew she was angry. He decided to be silent, too, hoping that pretty soon the whole thing would blow over. Jack knew it wasn't the best way to work out problems, but he was a little bit mad at himself, and he didn't want to admit to what he had done.

Sure enough, in a few moments Amy grabbed the old bucket and said, "I've been working on this broken bucket. I got the slats fitted back together, and I scrubbed it out with sand. Then all day I've been soaking it so the wood will swell. I put some rocks in it and held it under water. Now it doesn't leak. At least it holds water all the way up to where this one slat is broken. You could take it up and get some fresh water from the fountain up the street. Then we'd have drinking water."

"That'd be awful heavy to carry," said Jack looking at the bucket. It wasn't such a big bucket, but it didn't have a handle. And with the broken slat, he'd have to carry it tipped part way over to carry enough water to make it worth his trip. That could be heavy and hard to carry.

"But Jack, I haven't had anything to drink since we came down here last night. I was afraid to drink the river water. It's so dirty, I'm sure it would give a person the fever."

Her idea made sense, but he answered, "Let me just sit here and rest awhile. I been running all over town."

"Jack, I really am very thirsty."

"All right, all right. Just let me finish my piece of bread."

When Jack finally got back with the water, Amy had another fire laid. It was getting near dusk, and the lamplighter would be along soon. "I found a couple more sticks to use as matches," she said. "You know, if you were up there when the lamplighter came along, he'd probably just give you a light."

He probably would, but Jack didn't want to ask him. It would look so dumb asking for a light. Why would a boy on the street need to light a little stick? What would he tell the man, Jack wondered. "I'll just climb up the pole after he's gone," said Jack irritably. "Besides, since I fetched this water, I need a drink."

He started to reach his hands into their water bucket to scoop up a drink when Amy shouted, "Don't put your dirty hands in our drinking water. Go wash 'em first."

"I thought you said the river was dirty."

"So it is, too dirty to drink. But it's cleaner than your hands. It looks like you been playing in mud pies. And they stink, too. What'd you do today to earn that money?"

"All right, give me that stick," Jack said, not wanting to answer Amy about his earnings. "I'll go up and get the stupid light, and wash my hands when I get back."

When the fire was blazing and the children were sitting around it eating some more bread, Amy bent her hurt foot back and forth, testing her ankle. "It's a bit better, but I still don't think I should walk around town tomorrow. Would you mind going out by yourself again, Jack, to look for Mrs. Booth? We've got to find her! She's our only hope. We can't stay down here much longer."

Jack grunted but didn't feel like talking. What if he found Mrs. Booth and one of the Salvationists recognized him and told her he was one of the boys throwing things at the band? Maybe he'd just go looking for Uncle Sedgwick himself.

Later, when Amy was curled up sleeping by the fire with her green shawl thrown over her, he sat staring into the little flames. The song that the Salvationists were singing kept playing in his mind: "We're bound for the land of the pure and the holy," and then that haunting chorus: "Will you go? Will you go?"

The music had sounded pretty . . . he especially liked that horn. Thinking about it now made him feel bad that he had thrown stuff at them. Back and forth he argued with himself:

It wasn't that bad. I didn't really hurt anyone.

But, I must admit, they didn't do nothin' to deserve it. And even if they had, throwing horse manure is pretty mean.

But we needed the money.

Finally he drifted off into a fitful sleep filled with dreams of the Salvationists climbing on a train and singing. But every time Jack tried to get on the train with them, they would sadly shake their heads and say, "Sorry, we're bound for the land of the pure and the holy, and pure and holy you're certainly not."

CHAPTER 8

ROCKETS AWAY

The next morning Jack split the remaining bread with Amy and climbed up to the street. It was later than he'd started out the day before, and the morning was already sunny and warm. The air had the memory of summer to it, maybe one last time before the chill of autumn.

At home he had liked the autumn. The trees turned such beautiful colors, and the apples got shiny and juicy. Mama sure could make the best apple pies. But in the city there were no trees to fill one's eye with flaming reds and yellows. In the city it was just gray and chilly, not the kind of crispness that made you want to take a deep breath and run and play. Autumn in the city just reminded him that he had no mother to bake apple pies, and he had no home to keep warm in during the cold, wet winter. And winter was surely coming.

But today *was* sunny, and Jack felt better than he had last night. Maybe those Salvationists wouldn't recognize him. Maybe finding Mrs. Booth was the best way to find Uncle

Sedgwick. That was what Amy expected him to do; his sister had made it very clear. "It's the most important thing," she'd said. "We can't stay down here in this cave." When Jack pointed out that he had brought her some bread, she'd said, "What's a hunk of bread, Jack? We don't have a home, and winter's coming. You've got to find Mrs. Booth. Don't be doin' anything else today." Now as Jack trudged along, he knew Amy was right, but he was feeling pretty hungry again.

But where should he look? Finally he ended up on the street with the pub where the man had paid him the day before. Maybe the owner would know where the Salvationists were, and . . . maybe he could use some more "help." Just once more; then he could get something to eat. *Then* he would talk to Mrs. Booth.

When he got there and peeked through the door, the owner said, "You, boy, come in here. Don't stand there in the doorway. I don't want people seeing you hangin' 'round here."

As Jack walked up to the bar, he noticed three little stools on the floor in front of it. "What are these stools for?" he asked.

"Them's for children, of course. Where you from, anyway? You ain't from around here, or you'd for sure know what a children's stool was. Beside, you got a country accent to your talk."

"So what if I ain't from around here? Why do children need stools in here?" Jack insisted.

"It's so the little ones can reach the bar so's they can get themselves something to drink. What else?"

"You mean you serve beer to little children?"

"Ha! Only if they can't afford something stronger. It's good for business to get your customers started young. They develop a bigger thirst that way." The man polished the bar with his dirty apron for a few moments, then said, "So what you want? You thirsty or something?"

"No," Jack said. "I was just wonderin' if . . . well, if you needed any more help with those Salvationists."

"Ah. So you want to earn some more money, do you?"

Jack nodded.

"Well, you go over on Queen Victoria Street, 'bout five streets down. Can't miss it—big building with a sign calling it 'The Christian Mission.' You hang 'round there, but not too close, mind you. You'll see some of the other boys about. Sooner or later a bunch of them Salvationists will come marching out. You follow them at a distance until they set up for their show. Then let 'em have it. You got it? You were a pretty good shot yesterday. Just keep it up."

"But how will you know how many hits I get so's to pay me?"

"I got someone watchin'—name's Jed. He'll keep track and report to me. You come by later and I'll pay you. But don't you come straight back here. I don't want no trouble. Understand?"

Jack headed toward Queen Victoria Street, but it was well into the afternoon before he found the building. As he approached, he debated with himself whether to try and earn some more money or go up to the door and see if Mrs. Booth was there. *Maybe*, he thought, *they've already gone*.

But the question was decided for him when one of the other boys noticed him looking at the place and called him to come around the corner. "What you doin' getting so close, mate?"

"I thought they might've gone out already," said Jack.

"Not yet, but you're going to give us all away, dummy,"

hissed the boy. "If they know we're waitin' for them, they might not come out at all."

"Forget him," said an older boy standing near. "He don't know nothin'. I'm Jed, Winslow's man. You heard of me, boy?"

Jack nodded.

Jed snorted. "Those Salvationists go out every day, rain or shine, whether we throw stuff at them or not. They believe it's their God-given duty to save the world."

"Save the world?" asked Jack. "But I thought they were just trying to ruin people's business."

"Oh, yeah. They got it in for people in the sin business," Jed smirked.

"What's a sin business?" asked Jack.

"Gin houses, white slavers, and the like," said Jed. "Tell ya the truth, I'd just as soon they shut down the gin houses. My old man's a drunk, and he beats me every night he comes home drunk, which is nearly every night. So I say good riddance."

"Then how come you workin' for Winslow?" piped up one of the younger boys.

"It's a way to get a few coins," Jed shrugged.

Jack persisted. "But what are white slavers?"

"Don't you know what white slavers are?" The younger boy leaned close to Jack's ear. "They steal young girls."

"Yeah," said Jed, "*kidnap*'s the word for it. Sometimes they even sell the girls to rich men over in France or Holland or Germany who want to buy a mistress."

A kind of dread made Jack's stomach tighten. "Isn't there some kind of a law against kidnapping girls? And how do they get them over to Europe, anyway? Somebody would see 'em."

"Law? There ain't no law that sticks. That's one of the things the Salvation Army is always yellin' about—tryin' to get the government to stop the slavin'. As for gettin' the girls over to Europe, that's easy." Jed was clearly enjoying his role of dispensing worldly wisdom. He lowered his voice. "They drug 'em. When the girls are unconscious they nail 'em in coffins with air holes drilled in 'em and ship 'em over. Ain't nobody ever asks to see a dead body inside a coffin, so no one ever knows that it's a live girl inside. 'Cept . . . they ain't always alive."

The knot in Jack's stomach got tighter. "What do you mean?" he demanded.

"Sometimes they drug the girls too much and they die," Jed said matter-of-factly. "And *sometimes* they don't give 'em enough, and they wake up 'fore they get there." He paused for effect. "What would *you* do if you woke up and found yourself nailed inside a dark coffin? Why, some of them girls go screamin' crazy, and some just plain die trying to scratch their way out."

All the boys were silent as they considered such a horrible fate. Finally one of the younger boys said, "My cousin was kidnapped by a white slaver, and ain't no one ever heard from her since."

"Your cousin?" asked Jack. "How old was your cousin?"

"Thirteen, but she looked older."

"Thirteen, fourteen, it don't make no difference," snorted Jed. "Those slavers will take any girl about that age."

Just then they heard a familiar boom, boom, boom. The Salvation Army band was coming out.

The boys stayed hidden until the band went marching down the street, then they followed just out of sight. Along the way they gathered things to throw. Jed picked up some stinking old bones that the dogs hadn't eaten. The other boys found some rotten tomatoes in a pile of garbage, which they loaded into a rag, gathering up the four corners to make a bag in which to carry them.

Jack looked but didn't see Mrs. Booth with the band. Good. After he got his money from Winslow, he could go back to The Christian Mission and ask for Mrs. Booth. But Jack was thinking hard. If the Salvation Army was against those white slavers, wasn't it better to help them instead of fight them? But his growling stomach kept him following the band with the other boys.

This time the Army went down near the docks where the ships loaded and unloaded. The docks were wide and stuck out into the water like big fingers. Warehouses were built on some of the docks. Others were just flat platforms to receive goods from the ships that would tie up between them.

The boys stayed back while the Salvationists set up right at the beginning of one dock, with their backs to its warehouse. There was no ship tied up at that dock. The next dock was the flat type. On the other side of it was a huge, square-rigged merchant ship. Dozens of sailors and dock workers were preparing it to set sail. It was to these men—across the narrow slip of water between the docks—that the Salvationists planned to sing and preach. Of course, there were plenty of people going back and forth along the street at the foot of the docks who would hear them, too. And that's where the boys stood behind several bales of cotton waiting for their chance to pelt the Salvationists.

When the group was ready, one of the Salvationists picked up a megaphone to speak. It was General Booth himself. Somehow, as the boys had followed along, Jack hadn't seen Booth in the group. But there he was. Quickly Jack looked to see if Mrs. Booth was also there, but he didn't see her. Then the general began speaking.

"Many people wonder why we call ourselves the Salvation Army. We're an army because we fight. We fight for the souls of men and women and boys and girls. We fight to release them from the shackles of sin and bring them to Jesus. We fight to bring them to that land of the pure and the holy.

"Listen to me all you brothers who sail the seven seas and work these docks. While women weep, as they do now, I'll fight; while little children go hungry, I'll fight; while men go to prison, in and out, in and out, as they do now—yes, I can see some of you know what I'm talking about—well, I'll fight. While there is a drunkard left, while there is a poor lost girl upon the streets, where there remains one dark soul without the light of God—I'll fight! I'll fight to the very end!

"That's why we're called the Salvation Army. But before I tell you about Jesus Christ and how He can free you from sin, listen to this beautiful song, sung by our three Hallelujah Lasses and accompanied by Charlie Fry and his Hallelujah Band."

As the band was getting tuned up, Jack's attention was distracted by a couple of sailors on the dock across from the Salvationists. One was holding a small torch as the other tipped over a crate and then wrestled it around. The first one bent down and was doing something with the torch. Then he stood up, threw the torch into the water, and both men started running. It was then that Jack recognized one of the sailors as the "river rat" he'd almost hit in the boat on the river the morning before.

Suddenly from the crate on the dock there came a cloud of white smoke and a loud *hissst* as something rocketed out of the crate, across the water, and landed among the Salvationists.

Before the Salvation Army people could jump back, several more rockets flew into their midst. They were signal flares, shooting right at the Hallelujah Lasses. As Jack watched, two of the women were hit directly by the flaming torpedoes while other Salvationists jumped around dodging the flares as they landed among them. Soon there was thick smoke everywhere. The last thing Jack saw was the two women who had been hit trying to put out their flaming clothes.

Everyone on the street began to run. Jack and the other boys were running with them. People scattered in every direction, and Jack found himself alone. When he had no more breath to run farther, he slowed to a walk. He was heading back toward the river cave. Why would those sailors do such a thing? Yesterday Jack and the other boys had been throwing trash. It made a mess and might have left a few bruises, but those flares could have killed people. What was going on?

As Jack climbed over the rail beside the river, he felt dejected. The afternoon would soon be over and he still had not contacted Mrs. Booth. And today he had no money and couldn't bring back anything for Amy to eat. As he thought about it, Jack dreaded facing her. How could he tell her about what had happened?

He didn't call out to her when he climbed around the pillar, but even if he had, it would have done no good. She wasn't there. All that was left in the cave was her green shawl and a strange deep gouge in the sand by the river.

CHAPTER 9

KIDNAPPED

"Amy! Amy!" Jack called. She must be nearby somewhere. But there was no answer. He kicked around amongst the trash at the back of the cave. He didn't know what he was looking for . . . maybe she'd left a note.

Nothing.

Jack picked up Amy's shawl. What now? Maybe she'd gotten tired of staying in the cave and had climbed up to the street to walk around. Should he look for her or just wait? As he stood uncertainly at the cave opening, his eyes were drawn again to the deep gouge in the sand at the river's edge. He inspected it more carefully. It was about four feet long, coming right out of the river. In fact, at the water's edge, where the water was no more than an inch deep, Jack could see that the groove extended into the river. Something had been dragged up out of the river, something heavy like a boat.

Of course! That was it. Someone had beached a boat in the cave. As he looked more closely, Jack could see large boot prints in the sand. Then, right next to the water, where the sand was damp and firm, Jack saw Amy's footprint on top of one of the boot prints.

The clues were clear: A boat had stopped, and Amy had gone away in it. But who could have been in the boat, and where could Amy have gone? Jack looked out over the river in the late afternoon sun. There were several boats on the river, but none small enough to be beached in the cave.

"Amy! Amy!" Jack yelled with all his might out over the water. His voice echoed in the hollow confines of the cave and off the stone bridge above. But there was no answer from his sister.

"Amy, Amy, Amy," muttered Jack as he stumbled around inside the cave, kicking the sand with his feet. "Don't leave me, Amy. Papa's dead, and Mama's gone . . ." He still didn't like saying the words out loud that admitted his mother was dead. Jack kicked angrily at the charred sticks in the fire pit. "And now you've run off! How will we ever find Uncle Sedgwick?"

That's when Jack noticed the water bucket. It had been tipped over. He felt the sand around it. Wet. *Strange,* thought Jack. *Amy wouldn't dump out our water.* But someone had, and not very long ago, either, because the sand was more than damp. It was wet, very wet, like someone had just poured out the water ten or fifteen minutes ago. One of Amy's footprints was planted squarely in this wet sand, too. But it was also pulled off to the side as though her foot had been dragged away.

A terrible realization began to sweep over Jack. Amy hadn't gone off on some errand, and she hadn't gone off willingly with someone in a boat. She had fought. She had struggled, and then she had been taken away against her will.

Amy had been kidnapped.

That's why the water bucket was tipped over; that's why

her shawl had been left behind, and that's what all the tracks in the sand indicated. Someone had grabbed her and pulled her into that boat. She had been kidnapped. There was no getting around it.

As soon as Jack realized what had happened, he felt certain he knew who had done it. It had to be those two men who had fired the flares at the Salvationists, the ones Jack almost hit when he was throwing rocks at the river rat. Yeah, those river rats were the only people who knew anyone was staying in this cave. And they would have had time. If they had come on the river instead of running all around through the streets of London as Jack had done, they could easily have been here and gone before Jack arrived. But why? Why would they have wanted to kidnap Amy?

Somewhere in the back of Jack's mind there was a clue. They had been angry at Jack for throwing rocks and had threatened him if he ever did it again. But there was something else, something they had said—not to him, but—about . . . about what? And then Jack remembered. It was what they'd said about Amy. The one rowing had said something like, "Hey, Rodney, it's a girl." And the other one, the big burly one who had been standing up yelling at Jack, had said, "Yeah, and just about the right age, too."

"The right age for what?" wondered Jack aloud, and the moment he said it a cold chill ran down his spine. Those men where white slavers. And they'd taken Amy.

Jack fought back the wave of panic that swept over him. He had to find his sister. He had to get her back.

Out of the cave Jack ran, almost slipping on the rocks as he scrambled around the pillar. In a moment he had scampered up the wall and was on the street. Where would he go? Whom could he ask? How could he find her? He ran along the river's edge, looking at all the boats going peacefully back and forth below. Amy had to be in one of them. But what if he were going the wrong direction? While he ran himself breathless going up the river, what if the kidnappers were rowing as fast as they could down the river with Amy tied up under an old blanket in the bottom of the boat so no one could see her? Jack's mind ran wild as he tried to imagine what could be happening to her. Would she be nailed in a coffin and thrown down into the dark, damp hold of a ship? Would she die from too much of the drug? Or would she wake up and go crazy trying to scratch her way out? Would she be sold to someone who would beat her? And then he sucked in his breath with a start—whether the person who bought her beat her or not, she wouldn't be free. He might not ever see her again.

Jack ran all the faster. He dodged through day merchants pushing their carts back from the market. He pushed aside groups of other children in his way. He tripped over the bucket of a fisherman who stood with a pole and line at the wall by the river's edge.

But he never saw Amy. In fact, he didn't see even one boat that looked like the one the sailors had been in.

Finally, Jack fell to the cobblestone street exhausted and crying in great sobs as he tried to catch his breath. It was useless. He could never find his sister this way. He could run up and down the Thames River and all over London for days without ever seeing her. By then she might be shipped off to face some horrible life. . . . He didn't want to think about it.

Slowly he picked himself up and walked back toward the cave. Maybe he was wrong. Maybe he was imagining all this. Yeah, that had to be it. Amy wasn't really kidnapped. She had just gone out to get some fresh air and would be back in their cave by the time he got there. He should just settle down and quit imagining the worst.

He took a deep breath and thought about the Salvationists. If there was a God like they said there was, He certainly wouldn't let such a terrible thing happen to his sister. After all, she had never done anything so bad. She hadn't even thrown stuff at the Salvationists.

And then another thought crossed Jack's mind. What if God was punishing her because of the bad things he had done? "Oh, God," he found himself saying, "please don't. Don't let her be kidnapped. I won't throw any more stuff at that Salvation Army, and I won't steal any more apples or anything."

But when he got to the cave, it was just as he had left it. Amy was not there.

CHAPTER 10

THE DEVIL'S MILE

When Jack got back up to the street, the lamp-lighter was coming along, but Jack didn't care. Unless he could find Amy, he wouldn't need a fire tonight.

What was he going to do? Somehow he had to get help. He thought of trying to find a bobby, but then he remembered what Jed had said: there were no laws the policemen could enforce to stop the slave trade. The Salvation Army was fighting to get such laws passed, but so far there was very little the police could do. Besides, why would a bobby believe a wild story like his?

No, the police weren't likely to search the city for his sister on the mere word of a boy, who had no home and no parents to back up his story. But if he could just find out where they were holding Amy . . . then maybe someone would believe him and help.

Slowly an idea began to form in Jack's mind. Maybe Winslow, the pub owner, would know about the slave trade. At least he was dead set against the Salvation Army and their attempts to change things, and he wasn't against doing some shady deals on the side.

It wasn't much of an idea, but it was the only one he had. Jack set off through the darkening streets at a jog.

When Jack got to the pub, Winslow was busy with customers. In fact, the popular bar was full of loud-talking workmen who probably should have been home with their families. A woman played a piano as several men around her sang songs. The bright flames in the fireplace reflected off the bright copper pots hanging from pegs on the wall. Candles sat in the windows and elsewhere to light the room.

Jack stepped up to the bar and tried to get Winslow's attention. When the pub owner saw Jack, he scowled and kept on filling pints with beer. When he finally came Jack's way, he was obviously irritated. "Whatcha want? Don't go tellin' me I owe ya some ha'pennies. I heard what happened down at the dock today, and I don't pay boys who run off."

"I didn't come to collect," Jack said anxiously. "I just wanna ask if you know a big sailor named Rodney?"

"Maybe I do, and maybe I don't. Rodney's a mighty common name. What's it to you?"

"He kidnapped my sister, and I got to find her," Jack pleaded.

Winslow's scowl deepened. "Listen, boy. I don't have nothin' to do with kidnappin' girls. Never have, never will. I just run a legal pub."

"Yeah, but both you and Rodney don't like the Salvation Army."

"How do you know that?"

"'Cause it was Rodney and another guy with him that fired

those flare rockets at the Salvation Army this afternoon. I saw 'em do it," said Jack.

"So what?" said Winslow. "Rodney's got his reasons for not liking the Army, and I got mine. That doesn't mean we work together."

"But you do know him, then?"

"I know who he is, nothin' more," said the pub owner as he walked back down the bar to serve a new customer.

When he returned, Jack persisted. "All I want to know is where he took my sister. Do you know where Rodney might be?"

"I don't know nothin'. Understand? I don't want anyone thinkin' that I'm tied in with Rodney and his kind. It's a dirty business they're into." Winslow turned away to draw a pint of beer for a customer. In a few minutes he came back over to Jack. "You say he took your sister? Hmmm. Come to think of it, I have seen Rodney hanging out with Mary Jaffries. She runs at least a dozen bawdyhouses. There's four of 'em over on Church Street in Chelsea, and another just over on Gray's Inn Road. But there's one I've heard tell where Rodney hangs out. Up on Devil's Mile. You might try there for your sister."

"Where's the Devil's Mile?" said Jack.

"Ain't the real name. That's just what they call it. Uh . . . what's the name of that street? Hey, Peter," Winslow called to a customer across the room. "What's the name of that street they call the Devil's Mile?"

"You mean Islington?"

"Yeah, that's it, Islington High Street. But it ain't a mile long; it's just a little short street."

"But where is it?" asked Jack.

"Stubborn boy, ain't you! Drivin' me crazy." He stared at

Jack for a few moments. Then he said, "All right. Here's what you do. Go up Aldersgate. It turns into Goswell. Soon's you cross Pentonville Road, you're right there. 'Bout a mile and a half from here. Can't miss it. Now beat it. Go on; get out of here."

Jack discovered that you *could* miss the street, and rather easily, too, especially at night. But once he found it, he knew it was the "Devil's Mile." Every other door seemed to be a pub that was open and noisy, even this late in the evening. Many people were out on the street, some well-dressed and businesslike and others dirty and drunk. Jack even had to walk around three men sleeping on the sidewalk, or maybe they were passed-out drunk.

But how was he going to find Amy? She wasn't likely to be in one of the pubs, or she could have just walked out. Winslow had mentioned a "house" operated by some woman. But how would he know which one? There were several houses along this street . . . at least between the pubs. Jack wandered along the street, looking in the door of every pub and studying every house hoping to find some clue.

Then from across the street Jack heard a familiar voice. A huge man came out of a pub and yelled back to someone inside: "You don't need to worry. I always deliver my merchandise." It was Rodney, and he was coming across the street right toward Jack! If Rodney hadn't seen him yet, he soon would. There was nowhere to hide. Suddenly a horse and carriage came clattering down the street at a fast trot. It was a fancy four-wheeler with two little lanterns twinkling brightly.

Yelling at the driver, Rodney jumped back out of the street to avoid being run over. The driver swerved toward Jack and tried to slow down as he cursed back at Rodney. "Look before you stagger across the street, you fat lout, or you'll end up greasing my wheels."

It was Jack's chance. As the carriage swung past, he jumped on the back step where a coachmen sometimes stood. He held on with all his might and crouched down in the shadows as the carriage whisked him down the street away from Rodney. When he looked back, Rodney had crossed the street and was entering the house right by where Jack had been standing.

That must be where he's hiding Amy, thought Jack.

He dropped off the carriage and ran back up the street, weaving between the night revelers and jumping over the drunks until he got to the house into which Rodney had disappeared.

But how could he find out whether his sister was inside? Lights glowed dimly in the windows behind heavy red drapes, and piano music tinkled softly through the night air. From time to time, Jack could hear laughter within the house.

Finally, Jack could wait no longer. He had to do something, so he dashed up the steps and pounded on the door. Immediately the door opened, and a pinched-faced little doorman leaned out. "What do you want?"

"I'm looking for my sister, Amy," Jack said. "Is she here?"

The man sneered. "I don't know you, so how could I know who your sister is? Now be gone with ya." And he started to close the door.

"Wait," said Jack. "Maybe you've seen her. She's a little taller than me, and she has dark red hair. It's curly, and she's very pretty. Have you seen her? She's been kidnapped by a man named Rodney. He just came in . . ."

At the mention of Rodney's name, the man slammed the door before Jack could say more.

Jack stood on the steps wondering what to do until he saw another horse-drawn cab approaching. The cab stopped, and a finely dressed man opened the door, stepped out, and approached the house. Jack was feeling desperate. "Excuse me, sir," he said, "my sister has been kidnapped, and I think she's being held inside this house by some very bad people."

The man reacted as if he had seen a ghost. He stared wide-eyed at Jack for a moment, then raised his cane in a threatening manner. "You haven't seen me here," he commanded. Then he turned and ran after the cab that was just starting to pull away. He caught the driver's attention and got him to stop. Then the man rode off without looking back.

Jack realized that if he was going to free his sister he wasn't likely to get any help from anyone on the street. He would have to find some other way to get Amy.

Most of the buildings and houses on Devil's Mile were built side by side with no space between them. But three houses down, Jack found a little passage between two buildings that allowed him to walk back to the alley behind the house. The passageway was even too narrow to drive a cart through. Jack turned and walked up the alley, counting three houses to the building he thought Amy was in. Maybe, he thought, he could find a way inside through a back entrance.

The only light was from a half moon that shown through a hazy sky. Laundry hung like dancing ghosts from clotheslines strung across the alley. When Jack was sure he had located the correct building, he was disappointed to find the back door securely locked. The door actually led into a low lean-to shed that was built onto the back of the house. Above the shed were two windows leading directly into the house. They were both shuttered. But through the cracks in the shutters on one of the windows, Jack made out the dim shine of a light. *Could Amy be in there?* Jack wondered.

A little farther down the alley, he found some old boxes. He brought them back to the shed and piled one on top of the other. Then he climbed up. It gave him just enough height that he was able to pull himself up onto the roof of the shed. From there he crept toward the window with the light. He tapped on the shutter softly, but there was no response. He tapped again harder and called out, "Amy! Amy! Are you in there?"

In the quiet evening, he was certain that everyone in the neighborhood could hear him. But still there was no answer.

Jack waited a moment, adjusting his weight so as not to slip down the shed's roof. Finally, he decided he had to try for all he was worth. What difference would it make if he was careful not to get caught but never found Amy? So he beat on the shutter with his fists and yelled with all his might.

The shutters flung open, knocking him down the roof where he fell to the ground just as a man leaned out and bellowed, "What do you want out here, anyway? Get out of here or I'll beat the daylights out of you!" Then the shutters closed.

Jack picked himself up and started to run when he heard another voice. It was a girl's voice coming from behind the dark window, the one with the shutters still locked. "Jack! Jack! Is that you?"

It was Amy!

"Amy!" Jack called back in relief. "I came to get you. Let's get out of here."

"I can't. I'm locked in this little room."

"Are you okay? Have they hurt you?"

"No. No one's hurt me yet." And then Jack could hear her start to cry. "But Jack," Amy sobbed, "you gotta get me out of here. I'm scared. This is an awful place, and I think they are going to take me away tomorrow."

Just then someone came running out of the little passage between the buildings and into the alley. In the dim light Jack could see that he was big, and he was headed right for Jack.

CHAPTER 11

MIDNIGHT RAID

Jack had only a glimpse of the man running down the alley toward him, but he was sure it was Rodney. He took off the other way, not knowing if he could get out of the alley in that direction. He stumbled over trash and fell two or three times, but finally he came out into another street where the glow of a distant street lamp gave him some hope. He ran faster, and after he had crossed a couple other streets, he was convinced he was no longer being chased.

He slowed to a walk, keeping to the shadows where he couldn't be seen, but his heart went on racing for quite some time.

He had found Amy; that was good. But finding her confirmed all his worst fears. If he couldn't get her out of that place, she would soon be shipped away, and he might never see her again.

He had to get some help! But who could help him? Who would believe him? Who would even care? And what could one or even two people do. What he needed was an army to raid that place and rescue his sister. . . .

Jack stopped in his tracks. That was *it*—an army! What was it General Booth had said down by the docks? "While there is a poor lost girl upon the streets . . . I'll fight! I'll fight to the very end!" Jack needed the *Salvation Army*. Maybe they would help him save his sister.

It was nearly midnight when Jack found the Salvation Army headquarters again on Queen Victoria Street, not far from the river. Everything looked so different at night that he almost didn't recognize it. Inside all the lights were out. But Jack was determined. He pounded on the door until a young man in his nightshirt and looking very tired answered. A candle flickered weakly in the room behind him.

"I have to speak to General Booth," Jack said urgently.

"He's not available right now," the man said. "He's trying to sleep. Look, son. If you need something to eat, come back tomorrow morning. We'll serve you breakfast."

"That's not it! I have to talk to the general."

"I'm sorry. He can't be disturbed. He's very tired."

Jack was close to tears. "But he said he would fight! And I need him to fight for my sister right now. Tomorrow may be too late!"

The young man opened the door a little wider. "What do you mean, 'fight for your sister'?"

"She's been kidnapped," said Jack, fighting back the tears. "Rodney took her—that, that sailor down at the docks, the one who fired those flare rockets at you today! Now she's locked up in a house on the Devil's Mile. They're going to ship her out tomorrow!"

The young man reached out and pulled Jack through the doorway. "I see. That's different. Come on in, son." He led Jack through a long hall to a huge kitchen, where he lit a lamp and put it on a small table. "Wait here," he said. "Oh, if you want something to eat, help yourself to those bran muffins on the counter."

Jack thought that muffins had never tasted so good. In his fear for Amy he had forgotten he hadn't eaten anything all day. He was licking his fingers when the general himself came into the kitchen, his steely gray hair sticking almost straight up and his shirt buttoned crooked.

"What's this about your sister being kidnapped?" he boomed. His eyes looked like a storm about to strike.

So Jack told him, and the general kept asking questions, his voice getting more gentle as he talked. Soon the whole story came out . . . including Jack throwing stuff at the Salvation Army to earn some money for bread and the fact that he and Amy had been living in a cave under a bridge since their mother died.

"This is terrible," thundered the general. He stalked back and forth in the kitchen, tugging on his beard. Then he asked Jack to describe again very carefully where Amy was being held. When he had asked a few more questions about the shed on which Jack had climbed, the general mused, "Hmmm. If they haven't moved her to a different room, there's a chance we could climb up there with a bar and pry open those shutters. We just might be able to have her out of there before they even notice. But son, I need to know whether you are telling me the whole truth, and that you're not leaving anything out. Because if we make a mistake, we could be in very big trouble for breaking into some citizen's home. Now, are you completely sure your sister is being held there against her will?"

"Yes, sir!" said Jack. "She talked to me through the shutters. She said, 'I got to get out of here,' and I know it was Amy."

"All right," said the general. "Philip," he turned to the young man in the nightshirt, "get a couple of the other officers, and let's go see what we can do."

When Jack and the four Salvation Army men got back to the Devil's Mile, a cab was just pulling away from the front of the house. "Is that the house?" asked General Booth in a low voice.

"That's it," said Jack. "And the way to get around back is through that little passage between those two buildings up there. Come on; I'll show you."

"Not yet," said the general. "First we ask God's help."

They all stood in a little circle in the shadows across the street a little way down from their objective, and the general's gentle voice spoke quietly. "Lord, you know of the great sins that plague this city and the terrible suffering it brings to so many people. Now we ask your help and protection as we try to free one of your little ones. Give us success, and protect her from any harm. Amen." The general straightened.

"All right, son. Lead the way."

When Jack and the men got to the shed behind the house, the boxes he had piled up were still there. It gave him hope that Rodney and his gang had not done too much to secure Amy.

The boxes, however, weren't strong enough to hold the bigger men, so they gave a boost to young Philip. From the top of the shed, Philip pulled one of the other men up.

"Now you listen to me, Jack," whispered the general. "If we get your sister out, but someone discovers us in the process, grab her and take off running back to headquarters. We'll try to delay them to give you some time. Think you can find headquarters again?"

"I think so," said Jack. He was trying not to shiver in the cold night air.

Just then Jack looked up to see the two Salvation Army officers getting ready to pry open the shutters over one of the windows with the iron bar they had brought with them. "No!" said Jack in a desperate whisper. "Not that window. The other one." He'd almost been too late.

The men moved like cats across the shed roof to the other window. In the near black night, they looked at Jack. "Yeah, that one," he whispered.

The men put their bar between the two shutters and gave a pull. There was a creak, but nothing happened. Again they pulled. This time there was a loud snap and a splintering sound as the shutters swung open. Both men hung on to the swinging shutters so as not to lose their balance on the steep roof.

From inside the room there came a scream.

"Amy!" Jack called. "Amy, open the window."

Amy's scream had come only from the fright of waking up in the middle of the night to see a couple dark shapes outside her window. Now Jack could just barely see Amy standing inside the window working frantically to get the window open. But just as the latch came free and Amy was raising the window, a light appeared in the room behind her.

"Hey, what are you doing there?" came a woman's angry voice. "You get back in here. You can't leave."

Amy was climbing out the window just as the woman caught her and tried to drag her back inside. "Help her!" screamed Jack to the two men on the shed roof.

They grabbed on to Amy's arms while the woman inside

held fast to one of her legs, but it wasn't much of a tug-of-war. In just moments the men had pulled her free, and Amy was standing on the roof holding tightly to her rescuers.

The woman inside was screaming for help as the two men on the roof lowered Amy to the general and the other man in the alley below. As soon as Amy was safe on the ground, the general said to Jack, "Don't wait for us. Get her out of here. We'll see you later."

Jack and Amy ran for all they were worth. They were three streets away before Jack even dared to look back. No one seemed to be following. "Let's slow down," he gasped. "We've got a long way to go." But Amy kept running, her arms swinging like windmills, and her hair flying back.

When Jack caught up to her side again, he noticed in the dim light of a street lamp that tears were streaming across her cheeks. "Amy, what's the matter? Come on; slow down." He reached out and put his hand on her shoulder. She jerked away, but she did slow down. As soon as she was walking, great sobs began to shake her body, and she buried her face in her hands.

"Hey, Amy, what's the matter? Are you hurt?" Jack awkwardly patted her shoulder, while he tried to catch his breath.

She shook her head wildly. "No," she sobbed. "I'm just so glad we're back together." She stopped and threw her arms around her brother. Jack looked around, but there was no one on the street to notice. He wrapped his arms around his sister and hugged her close. In a few moments they continued on toward the Salvation Army headquarters.

Within an hour, the strange little group was all together again, being served hot tea in headquarters' kitchen by none other than Mrs. Catherine Booth. As the men told their story with big gestures and Mrs. Booth murmured sympathetically, Jack and Amy looked at each other. Finally, they could ask the lady with the smiling eyes about their Uncle Sedgwick, the tailor.

CHAPTER 12

ESCAPE TO AMERICA

When the story was told and second cups of tea had been poured, Amy spoke up. "Mrs. Booth," she said, "one day when we were looking for our uncle, we asked another tailor about him. He said you did business with our uncle for a while. Do you remember him?"

Mrs. Booth knit her forehead. "Well, it's been almost two years since I've used any tailor. We sew all our uniforms ourselves these days. It helps teach the new recruits a useful trade."

"But when you did use a tailor," said Jack, "you used to go to one over on . . . oh, I can't remember the name of the street. Anyway, he was an old man, and he said you had been his regular customer until you switched to our uncle, Sedgwick Masters. Don't you remember?"

"Why yes, Sedgwick Masters the tailor. Now I remember. I used him for only a few months. Actually, he was the one who suggested that we sew our own uniforms."

"But where is he now?" asked Amy. "You see, he's our only living relative. We don't have any other family. We've got to find him so we can have some place to live. Mother said he had some money, so he could take us in."

The lines on Mrs. Booth's forehead deepened. "I don't know where he is anymore. But I don't think he's in London. At least the other day I noticed that his old shop was empty. Come to think of it, he used to talk a lot about the great opportunities overseas—in India, Canada, even Australia. Maybe he finally packed up and left. I just don't know."

Both children sat in stunned silence. Their last hope for finding their uncle had evaporated. Amy blinked away the hot tears that sprang to her eyes. It was a terrible lost feeling not to have any home. The cave wasn't comfortable, but they'd made the best of it—even pretended it was an adventure—because there had always been hope, the hope that they would soon find their uncle and have a home and family again. Now that hope was gone. She had been rescued, but now what were they going to do?

Jack looked down at the floor, hoping the hair that fell over his eyes would hide the fact that he was crying. But looking down made him feel all the more hopeless. The sole of his right shoe was tearing loose from the uppers, and they had no money to buy new ones, or even to get it fixed. And they couldn't go back to the cave—it was too dangerous. What would they do?

Mrs. Booth stepped between the children and put a hand on each of their shoulders. "There, there," she said, "remember what our Lord Jesus said: 'Are not two sparrows sold for a farthing? and one of them shall not fall on the ground without your Father knowing.' So, 'Fear ye not therefore, ye are of more value than many sparrows.' God will not forget you, my young friends. Besides, for now you can stay here with us. And now it's very, very late. Let's get to bed."

The cots were plain, but they were the first warm beds that Jack and Amy had slept in for many nights. A feather bed in a palace couldn't have felt better.

Three days later the children were enjoying their life at the Salvation Army headquarters. They had received a bath, clean clothes, and were eating three good meals a day. Jack even had a different pair of shoes. They weren't new, but at least they weren't falling apart. The children had also been given chores to do, but Jack and Amy didn't mind; it made them feel useful. Philip Barker, the young man who had met Jack at the door the night he came for help, and his wife, Martha, had taken special responsibility for the children. They assigned chores for the children to do and found clothes for them.

One day the Barkers took Jack and Amy to Mrs. Witherspoon's. There they paid the debt for the rent that the children had been unable to pay when their mother had been so sick. "I ought to charge interest, it's gone unpaid for so long," grumbled Mrs. Witherspoon.

"Well, it's only been a few days. That hardly seems appropriate . . ." began Philip.

"We'd be glad to add whatever you think's fair," broke in Martha, "provided you tell us where their mother was buried. I'm sure the children would want to visit her grave. And, of course, you will be returning their trunk now, won't you?"

"You can have that old trunk, but you'll have to go upstairs and get it yourself. I'm not going to carry the thing down for you."

"And where was Mrs. Crumpton buried?"

"How should I know? I'm not the mortician."

"But you would have a receipt. It's the law," said Philip, holding a small coin out toward Mrs. Witherspoon.

"Oh, all right. It's probably around here somewhere."

The Barkers took the children that very afternoon to the cemetery and found the pauper's grave where their mother was registered as having been buried. They stood there a long time and cried as they thought about her and the ways their life had changed in the last few days.

That evening they cried again as they went through their belongings from the old trunk. Jack and Amy had never prayed much before, but every evening before bedtime, the Barkers asked them to come to their room for family prayers. There Philip read a few verses from the Bible, and both he and Martha prayed. This evening the prayers were for the children's loss of their mother and that God would comfort them. "Would either of you like to pray, too?" Martha asked. Jack liked the way she smiled at them—but he wasn't sure about praying, not even at a time like this. But Amy prayed, and afterward, Jack wished he had, too.

The Barkers prayed like Jesus was a friend sitting right there in the room with them. It made Jack feel like the Barkers really cared about them and that God cared about them, too. It was almost like being part of the family.

But the children were afraid that this good arrangement couldn't last. And sure enough, one afternoon about a week later, General Booth called them into his office. When they entered the small room, the general was sitting behind his large desk and Catherine Booth was sitting in a large straight-backed chair to his side. Standing with their backs to the tall bookcase were also Philip and Martha Barker.

Oh no. This is it, thought Jack. *They're going to tell us we have to go. Or maybe the general remembers what I told him about throwing stuff at the Salvation Army, and he's going to punish us.*

After the general cleared his throat, he spoke as though he were addressing a crowd of people on the streets. "Miss Amy Crumpton and Master Jack Crumpton," he began, "you may not realize it, but Officers Philip and Martha Barker, here, have been commissioned for a very important mission.

"You see, a year and a half ago we dispatched Commissioner George Scott Railton and seven hallelujah lasses to establish a beachhead for the Gospel of our Lord Jesus Christ in New York City in the United States of America. They have been very successful in the fight and are now asking for reinforcements. The Barkers have volunteered as brave soldiers of the Cross, along with another family. Soon they will be leaving and will no longer be able to care for you here."

Just as I thought, worried Jack. *It's all over.*

"However," continued the general, "we'd like to give you a choice. If you choose, you can stay here working in the headquarters, doing the kinds of jobs you have been doing for the last few days. Maybe in time you'll be able to track down your uncle, but I can't make any promises in that regard. Actually, Philip has been doing some investigation around town, and there doesn't seem to be a trace of Sedgwick Masters anywhere. He seems to have disappeared. We're very sorry about that; I'm sure it brings you great sorrow to be without family. But you are welcome to stay here if you choose."

Jack looked at Amy. The relief that showed on her face was exactly what he felt. At least they would have a place to stay. Jack already knew what his choice would be. He wasn't about to go back to that cave under the bridge with no food and no bed except the cold hard sand.

But the general was continuing: "But there is another choice.

As you know, the Barkers here have no children of their own—as much as they have wanted them. And they would like to invite you to be their adopted children and go with them to America. This is your other option. We don't want to put any pressure on you, so you choose freely to go or to stay."

Both Amy and Jack turned in astonishment to the Barkers. The Barkers were smiling. "We would like to have you," said Martha gently. "We've already come to care about you very much."

Jack just stared. Go to America? Be adopted? He opened his mouth but no words came out. To his relief he heard Amy stutter beside him, "Th-thank you, ma'am. Thank you, General, sir. We . . . uh . . . Jack? Do you want to go?"

Jack nodded dumbly. Then a big grin spread over his face. They were going to America!

Just two weeks later Jack and Amy stood on the deck of a great ship. "There's our trunk," said Jack, as they watched the last of the crates and luggage being loaded into the hold. The morning fog was lifting and London's towers were coming into view. Jack looked over the ship's side. The dockmen had loosened the great ropes that held the ship, and the sailors were hauling them on board.

"Jack, look!" Amy said, tugging on his sleeve. Jack looked up. A couple of the smaller sails had been loosened and were slowly filling with air. The ship edged away from the docks into the River Thames on its way to the sea.

The children looked around for Philip and Martha. The Barkers were standing near a pile of their belongings talking to another man and woman. A small child clung to the other woman's skirts. An older boy—maybe fifteen—and a girl about Jack's age completed the group.

"That must be the other Salvation Army family who's also going to America," Amy whispered.

"At least there's some other children on this ship. I wonder if they'll be friendly—us being adopted and all."

The word felt funny to Jack. *Adopted*. They had gone with the Barkers to the magistrate, who had asked them a lot of questions about their parents, their Uncle Sedgwick, where they had lived before and what they were doing in London. Then Philip had talked a long time with the magistrate, and Jack overheard words like, "highly irregular," and "you do-gooding Salvationists."

Then, abruptly, the magistrate motioned to Jack and Amy once more. "Do you children desire to be adopted by Philip and Martha Barker, and do you choose to go to America of your own free will?" Both children nodded firmly.

"So be it, then," the magistrate had growled, scrawled his signature on some papers and pushed them forward for the Barkers to sign.

Now as they stood on the deck of the ship, their new father interrupted Jack's thoughts. "Come on, then," Philip motioned to Jack and Amy. "Let's take our satchels to the cabin and get settled for the voyage. Martha needs some help."

The ship had moved out into the Straits of Dover by the time the new little family had made up their bunks and unpacked their things in the cramped cabin. They hadn't talked to the children from the other family yet, but the boy had nodded friendly-like at Jack and stood back so Jack could go down the narrow steps to the lower deck with his bundles.

Now he and Amy were back up on deck as the sea breeze tugged at the large white sails above them, causing the rigging to creak. In the distance the White Cliffs of Dover seemed to wink and wave in the sunshine. Martha Barker stood beside them humming a tune that Jack recognized, but he couldn't remember the words. Finally he said, "Ma'am, excuse me for interrupting, but what's that song you're humming?"

"Oh that?" she said, and she began to sing:

"We're bound for the land
of the pure and the holy.
The home of the happy, the Kingdom of love."

"Is that where we're headed, Mrs. Barker?" asked Jack.

Martha smiled. "It sure is, but not on this ship. That song speaks of God's Kingdom. It is Jesus, alone, who can take us there. But we're on our way, sure enough. And just like you and Amy chose to be adopted into our earthly family, you can choose to be adopted into Jesus' family, too. Then we'll be bound for that other Kingdom together."

Mrs. Barker rested her hand lightly on Jack's shoulder. He let it stay there as he looked out over the choppy blue waters. Amy caught his eye and smiled. They were heading for a new life, and, yes, he wanted to know more about that Kingdom of love.

MORE ABOUT WILLIAM AND CATHERINE BOOTH

Born in Nottingham, England, on April 10, 1829, William Booth grew up learning the trade of a pawnbroker. His father died when William was just fourteen, and life got harder for the poor family. But the next year William became a Christian and soon committed his life to telling others the Gospel. William was especially influenced by the methods of the great evangelist, Charles G. Finney.

Catherine Mumford was also born in 1829, on January 17, in the English town of Derbyshire. Her parents were Methodists and took great care to give Catherine a good education. Catherine was a good student and is said to have read through the Bible by the age of twelve. She gave her life to the Lord at home at the age of seventeen.

As young people, both William and Catherine were very concerned about how much damage drinking could do to people and families. In fact they first met each other at a friend's house when William quoted a poem about the evils of alcohol. Their relationship grew over four years until they married on June 16, 1855, in South London.

Together they forged a great partnership in a traveling evangelistic ministry. Most remarkable was the fact that Catherine, in addition to William, became a powerful preacher, something women didn't do in that day.

They became particularly concerned for the poor people of England. To minister to them, they opened the East London Christian Mission in 1865. In a short time, William Booth began calling the mission the "Salvation Army." This name reflected his and Catherine's sense that in order to save people from evil and bring them to Christ, Christians needed to organize and behave like an army, the Lord's army, going into spiritual battle. Their newspaper was called *The War Cry,* leaders in their mission were "officers," converts were called "captives," and people began calling William "General." Outreaches of their mission into new cities (and later other countries) became known as "invasions."

In 1881 the Salvation Army moved its headquarters to a former billiards club at 101 Queen Victoria Street, just a block away from Saint Paul's Cathedral.

The enthusiasm of this movement not only brought the Gospel to people, it gave poor people something new to live for. Even though the characters of Jack and Amy in this book are fictional, their situation was very real. The slums of East London were said to have a "gin shop" every fifth house with special steps to help even the tiniest children reach the counter. By five years of age many children were severe alcoholics, and some even died.

But the street corner preaching of the Salvation Army was so effective in converting people and influencing them to stop drinking and gambling that business began to drop off at the pubs and gin shops. In response, the owners encouraged ruffians to attack the Salvationists. In the town of Sheffield in

1882, an organized street gang—a thousand strong and known as the "Blades"—attacked a Salvation Army procession. Later that day, General Booth reviewed his "troops" all covered with blood, mud, and eggs, with their brass band instruments bent and battered, and said, "Now is the time to have your photographs taken!" It showed how hard they were fighting for the Gospel. There were many such mob attacks. The incident referred to in this story about sailors firing rockets at point-blank range into a group of singing Hallelujah Lasses happened at Gravesend, on the River Thames. In 1882 alone, 669 Salvationists were assaulted and sixty of the Army's buildings were wrecked by mobs. Over the years, in many outposts around the world, Salvation Army members were actually killed by violent attacks.

As this story shows, prostitution was also a severe problem in London. The city was said to have eighty thousand prostitutes in the early 1880s. Over a third of these girls had been forced by white slavers into prostitution when they were between thirteen to sixteen years old. Kidnapping and shipping the youngest, most innocent girls to Europe was very common.

The Salvation Army confronted this problem head on. They staged "rescues" (as in the case of Amy). They set up shelter homes for the girls coming out of prostitution. One home, operated by a Salvation Army sergeant, Mrs. Elizabeth Cottrill, redeemed eight hundred girls in three years. Finally, seeing that a main problem was that there were no laws protecting young girls, General Booth staged seventeen days of nonstop protest meetings in London and gathered 393,000 signatures on a petition that measured two-and-a-half miles long. The Salvation Army soldiers grimly marched to Parliament and demanded that the government pass and enforce new laws. This the government did on August 14, 1885.

Hunger was an equally severe problem in the slums of London. Because of the poor health conditions, orphans were everywhere. By 1872, the Salvation Army had opened five lunch rooms where—night or day—the poor could buy a cup of soup for a quarter of a penny or a complete meal for six cents. Thousands of meals were given away free.

In time, Booth realized that what the poor needed was training in new job skills and relocation out of the city. This the Salvation Army attempted in the 1890s. Urban workshops (initially safety-match factories) were set up to get homeless and jobless people employed and off the street. The next stage was to move them to colonies in the country where they could learn farming skills. Finally they were given the opportunity to move to new settlements overseas where they could get a new start on life. While this grand plan did not last past 1906, the Salvation Army still provides effective urban workshops to help homeless and jobless people. Today the Salvation Army helps 2.5 million families around the world each year. Also, their program to help people stop drinking is the largest in the world.

William Booth used to say that he liked his religion the same way he liked his tea—"H-O-T!" By this he meant that he did not like the dull and boring kind of services that took place in most churches. The Army's banner that announces "Blood and Fire" refers to the saving blood of Jesus Christ and the fiery power of the Holy Spirit. This "hot" Gospel was one key to the Salvation Army's effectiveness. Not only did the Salvationists employ a kind of street evangelism that was more like a modern-day protest march, but Booth used music to attract people. It wasn't the somber kind heard in most cathedrals;

it was lively music that stirred people up. He encouraged his musicians to write Christian words to the popular tunes of the day. And it worked. People soon began singing along, and the message got through. Even today, Salvation Army bands play on street corners at Christmas time, inviting people to contribute money for the poor.

The Booths had eight children of their own and adopted a ninth. Seven of the Booth's children became well-known preachers and leaders—two as generals of the Salvation Army. But on October 4, 1890, Catherine Booth, who had never been strong physically, died of cancer at the age of sixty-one.

William Booth continued in the ministry, traveling worldwide and preaching 60,000 sermons before he finally died on August 20, 1912, at the age of eighty-three.

Joining the Salvation Army with its challenge to take the world for Christ provided excitement and direction that attracted many of the otherwise purposeless and hopeless youth a century ago. And the Army's dramatic social work truly transformed several aspects of bleak urban life. But the heart of the Gospel as preached by the Booths called people first to repent of their sins and then surrender to Jesus Christ as Lord and Savior.

And that solid foundation has lasted. Today the Salvation Army's three million members minister in ninety-one countries of the world.

FOR FURTHER READING

Bramwell-Booth, Catherine. *Catherine Booth*. London: Hodder and Stoughton, 1970.

Collier, Richard. *The General Next to God*. New York: E.P. Dutton & Co., Inc., 1965.

Ervine, S. J. *God's Soldier: General William Booth*, 2 vols. London: Heineman, 1934.

Gariepy, Henry. *Christianity in Action*. Wheaton, IL: Victor Books, 1990.

Ludwig, Charles. *Mother of an Army*. Minneapolis: Bethany House Publishers, 1987.

"William and Catherine Booth" in *Christian History*, Issue 26 (Vol. IX, No. 2), 1990. (The whole issue of this periodical is devoted to the Booths and the Salvation Army.)

QUEST FOR THE LOST PRINCE

SAMUEL MORRIS

Authors' Note

As amazing as it is, all the information in this story about Prince Kaboo (later called Samuel Morris) is true. In several respects, the character of Jova coincides with that of a Kru boy who was given the Christian name of Henry O'Neil or Henry O. Neil. As a slave of the Grebos at the same time as Kaboo's imprisonment, he witnessed Kaboo's final torture, the flash, the voice from heaven, and Kaboo's mysterious escape. Henry also escaped at the same time and found his way to Monrovia, where he confirmed Kaboo's story, became a Christian, and was baptized.

Later, Samuel Morris (Prince Kaboo) arranged for Henry to come to the United States to be educated. The real Henry O'Neil did not, however, wait six years before going to Monrovia, or make the journey as a quest to bring Kaboo back to the throne. The assassins and the final meeting between Kaboo and Jova are fictional. But Samuel Morris's witness did inspire many to become missionaries to Africa and elsewhere.

CONTENTS

CHAPTER 1

THE KING'S RANSOM

Fourteen-year-old Jova gathered with the other Kru people in the village square in front of the king's great house. He lifted first one bare foot and then the other to get relief from the burning heat of the packed earth. It was a particularly hot day, and the silvery sun high overhead drew beads of sweat from his dark forehead.

There was a rustling in the leaves of the soap trees that towered above the thatched roof of the king's house as two monkeys jumped from limb to limb. *I wouldn't mind being a monkey sometimes*, Jova thought. *All they do is play up there where the cool breezes blow.*

Just then, the reed mat moved aside from the door on the king's house, and two servants came out onto the porch carrying ostrich-feather fans. Jova stood as tall as he could, nearly as tall as the men around him. This was no time for playing like a monkey; he wanted to be counted among the warriors. Jova had a strong, handsome face with large, clear eyes that did not shy from looking others in the eye. He kept his close-cropped hair neatly free from nappy tangles.

Jova had already gone through the dreaded "bush-devil" initiation school. Supposedly it had made a man of him, so now he must act like one. He waited quietly for the king to come out and speak.

Everyone waited, but the king did not appear.

While Jova watched the door of the king's house, he thought about the bush-devil school. Around the age of twelve, every boy in the village was taken out into the jungle to a fenced-in stockade made of tightly woven palm fronds and thorn branches. It was impossible to escape. There, for many months, a "devil" taught the boys the customs of the Kru people and how to be a man, even the art of war. It had been a terrifying experience for Jova. Sometimes he thought the figure that looked like a walking bush was a man in a bushlike costume, but other times Jova believed that he was indeed a devil. Whatever he was, he had remarkable, magical powers enabling him to hypnotize a chicken, cause a tree to die, or put a curse on an enemy.

Jova's hand drifted to his forehead, where a small blue tattoo and scar extended from between his eyebrows down to the bridge of his nose. It was the Kru tribal mark and proved that he had gone through the bush-devil school. When he and his friends had finally graduated, they had been permitted to come home, where a great celebration awaited them. All of Jova's relatives had honored him. His father, of course, was not there. He had been killed in the last war. But his mother, uncle, and aunts had made a magnificent feast.

However, in spite of the initiation, Jova knew that he would not really be accepted as a man among his people until he proved himself with some heroic deed—maybe killing a leopard or fighting bravely in battle or bringing back some treasure to his people—the honey from a hive of bees, an elephant tusk, or some iron for knives and spears.

A fly buzzing around Jova's head brought his mind back to the present. He brushed it away with the back of his hand, and then noticed the reed mat on the king's door move.

When the king finally emerged from the dark interior of his mud-walled house, he did not walk proudly in his flowing brown-and-white striped robe. Instead, four of his personal guards carried him out on a wooden chair. As soon as they set him down, the two servants stepped forward to wave their ostrich-feather fans to cool him.

When the people saw their king, they gasped. His head hung slightly to one side, and his eyelids drooped until they nearly closed over bloodshot, watery eyes. His kinky gray hair was matted and dull. It was obvious that the old man was very sick.

When the murmuring finally became silent, the king spoke in a breathy, weak voice. "My people," he said, and then coughed as he drew in another breath. "I am dying."

The men shuffled nervously, and some women around the edge of the group began a moan that rose to the high-pitched trill of grief. But when the king held out a thin, shaky arm from which leathery folds of skin hung like rags, silence returned.

"You must not grieve for me," he said. "There will be time enough for that later. Pray now that when I die you will have no cause to grieve for yourselves."

He wheezed again, trying to catch his breath, and a whisper skittered among the people as they turned from one to another asking what he meant. The king was quick to explain. "When I die, there will be no one to take my place, and without a strong king on the throne, our enemies—the bloodthirsty

Grebos—will see our weakness, and they are likely to attack us again."

Another murmur went through the crowd. Memories of long, vicious battles, of lost brothers and fathers, of burned crops and destroyed houses, and women and children taken captive were still fresh in the minds of all the Kru people. For they had suffered a bitter defeat at the hands of the cruel Grebos only a few years before.

The Kru people could not survive another war. They were just beginning to recover from the last one. As the king's dreadful words began to sink in, the high-pitched trilling wail of some of the women could again be heard around the edge of the crowd.

Finally the old man raised his hand once more to call for quiet. Then he continued, "There is only one hope. My son, Kaboo, must be found and brought back to rule in my place. Without him, we are doomed. But with a new young king on the throne, we would be safe because the Grebos would know we are strong."

A coughing fit silenced the king, and the crowd held its breath until the spasm stopped. The king sat with his eyes closed as he gulped in air like a fish out of water. When he seemed out of danger, quiet whispering spread among the Kru people.

It had been six years since there had been any news of Prince Kaboo, and most people considered him dead. But there had been reports that he had escaped safely from his Grebo captors and had fled into the forest. Many doubted it, and even those who believed the story had given up hope of him returning safely. Probably, they speculated, he had been attacked by the fierce "leopard men," those cannibals who roamed the jungle at night killing and eating fellow humans who ventured too far away from their village in the dark. Or maybe he had been bitten by a poisonous snake, or pulled into a river by a giant crocodile. Anything could have happened; the jungle was a dangerous place. So, whether he had not escaped, or had escaped but met tragedy in the jungle, most people believed Prince Kaboo was dead.

But the king believed otherwise. His confidence that his son was alive set everyone talking. Where could Kaboo be? How could anyone find him this long after he had disappeared?

"Silence!" shouted one of the king's guards. "Your king addresses you."

"My good people," continued the king when quiet had returned, "to the brave warrior who finds and returns Prince Kaboo to sit on this throne, I offer a king's ransom—five balls of rubber the size of a man's head, twenty goats and twenty pigs, four elephant tusks as tall as a man, plus all the rice one man can haul in a day." He wheezed a great breath and then said, "Only find my son! Find my son!" And he raised both hands as though giving his tribe a blessing.

With that the king's guards carried him back into his house, and the people broke into an uproar of cheers, arguments, and general confusion as they speculated on whether Prince Kaboo was dead or alive and whether anyone could find him.

"Such a fortune!" said a muscular warrior standing near Jova. "Anyone who wins a king's ransom would be the richest man in the village."

"How can the king offer that much wealth?" said another. "I know he has that many goats and pigs, and maybe he has the rice. But the rubber and the elephant tusks—they must be hidden somewhere. I've never seen them."

"If the Grebos hear he has rubber and ivory, they will attack us for that alone, king or no king," said the first man.

"I don't think the prince is alive. How could he be after this long?"

But Jova did not cheer or argue or talk to anyone. His mind was racing. He would go on a quest that everyone would consider brave. He would prove he was a man. He would bring home to his people a great treasure and get a king's ransom in return.

These thoughts raced through Jova's mind because . . . he knew where Kaboo had gone, and, as far as he could tell, he was the only person who knew!

CHAPTER 2

A PRINCE AT PAWN

It had happened six years before when Jova was only seven, but he had seen it all . . .

Day after day, the Grebo warriors had attacked their village. Brave Kru men had fought them off, several falling under the spears of the Grebo warriors. Their small fields of rice and sugarcane around the village were burned; the only crop that survived was the roots of the cassava plant. All the goats, pigs, and chickens had been scared into the jungle, and the village was low on food.

One day when it seemed that the Grebos had withdrawn, Jova's father and several other men went hunting for food. Possibly they would come across some of their livestock roaming in the forest, or maybe they could find some other food—small game or edible roots and tubers.

But they never came back. The little expedition was attacked at the river when they were out in the water checking their traps.

The next day, while the Kru village was having a funeral for the men of the food expedition, the Grebos attacked again. This time guards were not on duty, and the Grebos ran through the village burning houses and capturing women and children before the remaining men could mount a defense. That raid was the beginning of the end. There had been so much death and destruction that the people felt like giving up.

For as long as anyone could remember, there had been trouble between the Krus and the Grebos. It had usually amounted to brief raids on each others' villages. Sometimes it involved the "leopard men" from one tribe or the other who caught an enemy tribal member alone in the forest at night. But these disputes usually ended when "sufficient" revenge had been taken, and there would be a year or two of peace before another incident broke out. It was like an ongoing feud.

But this time the Grebos were waging an all-out war on the Kru. "Maybe we should just surrender," suggested some of the Kru elders to their king that night around the fire. "Surrender certainly can't be worse than this destruction. Soon there will be nothing left of us."

But the proud king resisted. To him, it was hard to think of anything worse than surrender. It might even mean his death. He just shook his head and walked slowly back to his house.

The next morning, just as the light began to turn the sky from a deep violet to greenish gray, terrible screams broke out from the jungle all around the village. Seven-year-old Jova peeked outside in time to see hundreds of Grebo warriors running between the houses. He was just pulling back when strong arms grabbed him and pulled him out. He fought to free himself, but the powerful warrior tripped Jova, then sat on him while he tied his hands and feet with cords. Then he picked the boy up and carried him like a sack of rice over his shoulder.

Jova kicked and squirmed until he almost made the man lose his balance. Angry and yelling at his uncooperative captive, the Grebo threw Jova to the ground and hit Jova so hard that all the breath was knocked out of him. The boy lay stunned as he stared up into his captor's face.

Three parallel lines on the man's right cheek marked him as Grebo. His nostrils flared, and his eyes flashed. "Be still, or I will crush you!"

The words sounded strange with their thick, Grebo accent, but Jova understood them because both the Grebos and the Krus used the Kruan language.

The blow and the warning were enough of a shock that when the Grebo picked him up again, Jova did not kick and struggle but allowed the man to carry him into the jungle.

When they arrived at a small clearing a mile or so from the Kru village, the Grebo warrior put him down alongside other prisoners. The captives were herded into a small group surrounded by a few warriors, all of whom wore the three-lined tribal mark on their right cheeks. Their ready spears prevented any escape. After a whispered consultation, the Grebos cut the cords that bound the prisoners' feet and forced them to walk ahead of them down the narrow trail.

They marched for a day and a half until they came to the main Grebo village. There the prisoners were shoved into a stockade and guarded day and night.

As the Kru prisoners watched and listened from behind the prison fence, it became clear why the Grebos had been attacking them so fiercely. They had a new war chief who had decided that the way to end the ongoing feud with the Kru was to wipe them out completely—or at least reduce them to such a weak nation that they would never rise again.

A few days later, young Jova and the other Krus were drawn to the wall of their stockade by a great commotion outside. From all the noise, Jova thought another large group of prisoners must be arriving. But when he looked through the closely spaced bamboo poles that formed his prison, he saw only three captives; two women and . . . Prince Kaboo, the king's fourteen-year-old son!

The Grebos were dancing around the prince and yelling that the war was over. The Kru people had been defeated.

Within the stockade, the prisoners began talking among themselves, wondering what it all meant. Would they be allowed to go home?

When Prince Kaboo and the two women were thrown into the stockade, the other prisoners ran to their aid, but their attention was mainly on the young prince. They picked him up from the dust where he had fallen, brushed the dirt off him, and offered him what little water they'd been given.

"What has happened to our village?" cried first one voice, then another. Slowly, the story came out as Prince Kaboo and the two frightened women helped one another tell the tale.

The last battle had overrun the town. Those who had not been captured or killed had fled into the jungle. This time, *all* the remaining houses had been burned. Everything of value was stolen, and still the Grebo chased the fleeing Kru people, killing anyone they caught. Finally, to end the slaughter, the king sent a messenger to the Grebo war chief offering a full surrender.

The Grebos agreed to stop chasing and killing the Krus if the king and all his people would return to the site of their former village and surrender in person.

The next morning, the Kru people came out of the jungle in twos and threes to stand among the smoldering ruins of their houses and give themselves up to the Grebo war chief and his army of fierce warriors. They were a sad remnant—dirty, exhausted, and weeping. Many were wounded.

In exchange for their lives, the Grebo war chief said that each year the Kru people would have to pay a tax of twenty baskets of rice, fifty cassava roots, ten bundles of sugarcane, and ten goats. Furthermore, the first payment was due immediately.

"But," protested the Kru king, "you have destroyed everything. We cannot possibly pay such a big tax."

"Either pay the tax or die." The war chief shrugged as though he did not care what they chose.

"Give us time," begged the king, "and we will pay all you ask."

"How do I know this? Maybe you will all run away into the jungle. Or maybe you'll try to regain your strength and wage a war of revenge on us," objected the war chief. "Isn't that what has happened for years?"

"Us take revenge?" said the Kru king angrily. "It is you who always starts something new."

"Silence! We are the victors, and you are worth nothing more than a chicken feather blown by the breeze. You will do as I say!"

Remembering his circumstance, the king bowed and said

humbly, "Then I give you my word. We will not retaliate. We will pay your tax—only give us time."

"You are our slaves now," sneered the war chief. "Your word means nothing. Give us something in pawn to prove that you will pay your tax. Then we will spare your lives. When you pay your debt, we will return your pawn."

The king looked hopelessly around at the ruins of his town. "I have nothing left," he said.

"Who is that beside you?" said the war chief, pointing to the handsome boy standing beside the king. It was Kaboo.

"Oh! Just a lowly boy of the village," said the king, hoping to protect his son.

"Do not try to fool us, you dog!" spat the war chief. "We can see that he wears a gold ring. He must be your son."

"No, no. He is just a worthless village boy." This time the king pushed Kaboo away from him so hard that the boy tripped and fell into the ashes of a nearby house.

"Worthless, is he?" said the war chief. "Then bring him here, and I shall kill him this instant." He raised his machete as he nodded to one of his warriors.

"Have mercy!" pleaded the king. "You are right. He is my son. Only do not harm him."

The war chief looked scornfully at the Kru king groveling before him. "Yes, I think you do value him. We will take him in pawn. When you pay your tax debt, you may have him back."

With that, the Grebo warriors had left the burned-out Kru town and brought away Prince Kaboo as their prisoner.

Within a week, most of the Kru captives were distributed among various Grebo families as slaves. Seven-year-old Jova went to live with one of the elders of the village who had four wives. Each of the wives and even the family's children had the authority to boss him around from dawn to dark: "Fetch some wood for the fire." "Clean up this mess!" "What are you standing there for? I need some water. Hurry up!"

He had never worked so hard in all his life. There was not a moment to rest, let alone play. He looked for a chance to escape, but someone was always watching him. And even if Jova had gotten away from the elder's wives, whom he called the "fearsome foursome," he was in a village with hundreds of Grebo around, all of whom knew he was a slave.

One day when Jova was going to fetch water from the stream that ran through the center of the village, he heard a jangling sound coming from within the stockade prison where he and the other captives had been held. He looked through the narrow gaps between the bamboo poles and was shocked to see Prince Kaboo making his way across the small enclosure. The noise came from a log that was attached to the older boy's foot. The log was about two feet long and was as large as a man's leg. On one side of the log, at about the halfway point, a deep notch had been cut, large enough to fit around Kaboo's ankle. Then an iron strap had been nailed across the open side to keep his leg within the notch.

A chain was attached to each end of the log. It was long enough to create a loop that served as a handle. By lifting the log by the chain, Kaboo could support it so it didn't drag on the ground or trip his other foot. Jova watched in horror as Kaboo made a great effort to swing his logged leg forward to take one faltering step. Jova could see that despite the lifting chain, the heavy hobble had gouged sores into Kaboo's ankle.

Walking was slow going, and obviously painful.

"Kaboo," called Jova softly. "Prince Kaboo."

The prince looked over toward the fence. When he finally spotted Jova's dark eyes, he looked around frantically to see if anyone was watching, then waved furtively with his other hand. "Go away," whispered Kaboo just loudly enough to be heard across the yard. "You will be caught."

"Why are you still here? Why haven't they made you a slave to some family?" asked Jova, ignoring the warning.

Kaboo made a few painful steps toward the fence. "They are afraid that I might escape. Your worth is only that of a slave, but I am the pawn for the whole war debt. There is a guard here with me at all times." He glanced behind Jova, and a frightened look came to his face. The prince waved his hand as though to shoo Jova away and then quickly turned away from the fence.

Suddenly a great pain stung Jova's shoulders, and a voice behind him shouted, "What are you doing here, dog? Get out of here! Do not bother the prisoner."

Jova turned just in time to dodge another swing of the guard's short whip. Quick as a greased pig, he ran toward the stream to fetch water for his master's household.

CHAPTER 3

THE WHIPPING CROSS

Each day when Jova passed the stockade, he strained to see through the fence and catch a glimpse of Kaboo. Was the prince still there? Was he well? Did the Grebos feed him enough?

But always the guard seemed to be within sight, so Jova walked on without stopping and without seeing Kaboo.

Days stretched into weeks, and then one day there was a great commotion in the village. Word spread rapidly: The Kru king was coming to pay the war tax. All the village turned out, and Jova managed to escape his duties long enough to see the spectacle.

The rumor was correct. His king came leading a procession of several Kru men into the Grebo village. Wisely, they were not carrying any weapons that might infuriate their victorious enemies. And the Grebos, not taking any chance that this was a trick, stationed their well-armed warriors along the pathway.

The Kru were burdened down with heavy baskets of rice and bundles of cassava roots and sugarcane. Behind them came a small herd of goats. They walked slowly, as though they were a funeral procession. On they came until the king stopped before the Grebo war chief. With a bowed head, the king said, "Here is the tax you demanded; now release my son." Slowly the other Kru men set their loads of rice, cassava, and sugarcane before the Grebos and brought forward the goats.

With his head held high—in obvious contrast to the sad king's bowed head—the war chief looked down his nose and counted the riches set before him. "Where is the rest of it?" he demanded in a why-are-you-bothering-me voice.

The king's head snapped up, and his eyes flashed. Suddenly suspicious, he said, "What do you mean?"

"This is only half of your debt. Why have you taken so long to pay your debt when you bring me only half of what you owe?"

"You said the yearly tax was to be twenty baskets of rice, fifty cassava roots, ten bundles of sugarcane, and ten goats—and that is what I have brought at great hardship to me and my people."

The war chief sighed and rolled his eyes. "I demanded *forty* baskets of rice, *one hundred* cassava roots, *twenty* bundles of sugarcane, and *twenty* goats. Do not try to fool me."

The king's nostrils flared. His mouth became a straight, hard line, and he took several breaths before he got himself sufficiently under control to speak. "Must the Grebos add to their treachery with deceit? We did not wage all-out war on you, but you on us! In defeat, we have acted honorably in bringing this unjust war tax to you. My people have emptied their houses and have borrowed from their relatives in distant villages. We have nothing to eat and will have to search day and night for grubs and roots in order to survive until the crops you burned can be replanted and grow up to harvest. Why do you lie about the amount of the tax?"

Four Grebo warriors stepped forward with raised machetes, as if to attack the king, but the war chief halted them by raising his hand. Then he continued addressing the Kru leader. "As you can see, your head remains connected to your body only by my grace. We are the victors, so we can set the tax at whatever amount we please. See? Now I set it at *three* times what you have brought! What do you think of that?"

Before the stunned Kru villagers could react, he sneered, "Besides, it is good if you Kru must scrounge and scrape to stay alive. That way you will not have time to make war, and we will be safe from your revenge. What do I care whether you live or die? But if you live, I intend to make sure that you never regain your power, that you never rise again to threaten us. We intend to keep you as lowly as the chickens that scurry to move out of our path."

He turned to go back into his house when the Kru king cried out, "Wait! What about my son?"

The war chief paused but turned back only halfway. "Your what?"

"My son, the prince."

"Oh . . . oh yes. You did leave a pawn with me, didn't you? I forgot. I don't know what's become of him, but one thing is certain: If you do not bring the remaining tax you owe, he will not have anything to eat." With that, he marched briskly into his house.

The king and the Kru delegation turned, and with bowed heads headed out of the village. But they had not taken more than a few steps before someone threw several rotten monkey plums at them. The plums splattered near the king's feet, and his men quickly gathered around him to shield him. The rotten fruit was soon followed by rocks and even handfuls of goat droppings as someone yelled, "Here's some Kru food. Eat that, you pigs!"—making a direct hit on the shoulder of the king's robe.

The king and his men pulled closer together and started to trot, trying to escape the village before they were injured.

Jova raced through the mob, too, attempting to keep up. He had to dodge between the people as they yelled and jeered. "Your Majesty!" Jova shouted. "I have seen Prince Kaboo. He is well."

The king kept running but looked over his shoulder and called back, "Watch out for him! Whatever you do, watch out for him."

Someone grabbed Jova by the arm and yanked him to a stop. He looked up into the angry face of his master's second wife. She put out her foot and gave Jova a shove, tripping him to the ground. "Where do you think you are going?" she sneered. "Get back to the house!"

Two months went by, and Jova spent his eighth birthday with no celebration, no recognition. He worked just as hard and didn't get even an hour off.

From time to time, he managed to see Prince Kaboo briefly through the stockade fence as he went on errands. The prince remained brave, but Jova noticed that he was getting thinner. His cheeks were hollow, and his eyes peered from deep, dark sockets.

Jova began saving bits of his own food, wrapping them in leaves, and sneaking them to the prince whenever he could.

Then one day a delegation from the Kru village came bringing several baskets of rice, bundles of withered cassava roots, and a few thin goats. "This is all we have," said the man in charge as he placed the payment before the Grebo war chief. "There is no more rice, no more food in our village."

"I demand full payment!" roared the war chief as he pointed at the delegates. "Full payment must be made immediately. For each day that payment does not come, your prince will receive a public beating right here in our town square. That should inspire your lazy king to gather the taxes he owes. Now, get out of here and deliver that message to him!"

The delegation was driven out of town, and the next day at noon, Prince Kaboo was brought out of the stockade into the public square, where many people had gathered. There in the center were two logs protruding at an angle from the hard-packed ground. They were about five feet tall and crossed in the middle so that they made an X. Kaboo was brought to this cross and one hand was tied to the top of each log. His bare back was then beaten mercilessly with a whip made of poisonous vines.

Even before the beating ended, Jova could see great welts rising where the whip had struck. The poison in the vines was inflaming the skin even more than the strength of the blows. But Prince Kaboo did not cry out. He bravely suffered the whipping and was led back to the stockade, swinging his hobbled foot along in a shuffling stagger.

The next day the same thing happened, though this time there were welts on Kaboo's back even before the whipping.

That night as Jova was out feeding his master's goats, another Kru prisoner called to him quietly. "Did you hear what happened this afternoon?"

Jova shook his head.

"Wuledi escaped."

Jova's eyes widened. Wuledi was one of the Kru girls who had been taken captive. "How?"

"I'm not sure, but she was taken into the jungle with two other Kru girls to gather palm fronds. Just before they were to return, the Grebo who was in charge sent her off to get another armload. Then he brought the other two Kru girls back to town and left Wuledi out there. Everyone presumes she ran off through the forest for home."

Jova frowned. It did not sound like an escape; rather, it sounded as if she was *allowed* to run away. The next day after Prince Kaboo's whipping, Chiedi, another Kru slave, "escaped," though no one knew the details of how it happened.

After a week, there had been one escape per day, and Jova had an idea what was happening. The Grebo war chief was allowing one Kru at a time to escape to take a report back to the king concerning how his son was suffering. It was a cruel but powerful way to put pressure on their leader. The longer he delayed in paying the full tax, the more his son suffered.

Jova vowed that if the occasion arose, he would not go. He would stay and keep smuggling bits of food to his prince. Kaboo's health was failing rapidly. His back was a mass of open and infected sores. He was thinner and weaker than ever. The only good thing was that, in becoming so weak, he no longer seemed like an escape risk to the Grebos. They had at last removed the log-hobble from his foot.

Just before noon the next day, the Kru king and two assistants came to the Grebo village. This time, they brought only two baskets of rice, a bundle of immature sugarcane, and seven dead monkeys on a pole. But there was a fourth person with them, the king's only daughter, Mona, who was a couple years younger than Kaboo.

"You are a mighty warrior, one to be feared above all other

Grebos," said the king as he knelt before the Grebo war chief. "We have brought you what we could."

The war chief looked over the offering with a sneer on his face. "You bring me monkeys when I demand goats? Who do you think I am? Only poor people eat monkeys."

"We *are* a poor people, O chief," said the king, lowering his head even farther. "We did not mean to insult you, but this is all we have. Have mercy on us and accept these articles in payment of our debt. Please, release my son."

"Bring him out," commanded the war chief.

Moments later, with one warrior on each side to support his arms, Prince Kaboo was dragged out. He was too weak to stand or even to hold his head up. When the warriors released him, he fell to the ground in a heap. In horror, the king started to go to him but was halted when Grebo spears touched his chest. He reached his hand out toward his son and pleaded, "May I take him home now?" Then, unable to control his agony at seeing his child's sad condition, the king began to weep.

"You may take him when you have paid your full debt!" snapped the war chief.

As tears streamed down his face, the Kru king said, "I have one further offer. Please allow my daughter to be pawn in place of my son. He cannot endure more. She, at least, is healthy and strong and could take his place for a while."

The Grebo war chief took a deep breath and looked from side to side at some of his advisers as he considered the offer, but before he could answer, there was a stirring from the crumpled body on the ground.

Prince Kaboo raised his head and in a faint voice said, "No. My sister must not take my place. Mona is younger and could not stand these beatings. Someday I am to be king. I am brave enough. I will endure the suffering."

Then he rose shakily to his hands and knees and began to crawl. The crowd that had gathered around parted to let him through, and then Jova saw where he was going. Prince Kaboo was heading toward the whipping cross! Slowly, step after step he advanced, his head hanging so low that his matted hair almost raked the dust.

When he reached the cross, he pulled himself up and flopped his broken and tortured body over the X, and there he waited.

Seeing his opportunity to put more pressure on the Kru king, the Grebo war chief nodded to one of his assistants, and the man quickly retrieved the whip. Everyone stepped back as he whirled it around his head and laid it with a resounding crack across Kaboo's ribboned back. Again and again the whip whistled through the air, finding its mark on the boy's deformed body.

It was the worst beating Jova had ever witnessed. A half hour later, the shaken Kru king was led weeping out of the town, and the people began to return to their activities. But Jova felt frozen to the spot. The little boy knew that Prince Kaboo could not take much more of this punishment. He would soon die.

CHAPTER 4

ESCAPE INTO THE JUNGLE

Two days later, as Jova walked toward the stockade with a small ball of cassava mush for Prince Kaboo hidden in his hand, he noticed that the prison gate was wide open. He paused and approached cautiously. What was happening? Where was the guard? Jova couldn't see anyone.

He peeked in and warily entered the stockade. No one seemed to be present. Then, in the dark doorway of one of the huts, he spotted a small mound. After looking around to be sure no one was watching, Jova approached. It was a ragged, old blanket covered with stains and dirt. But when he got close, he could see that sticking out from under it, back into the dark interior of the hut, were two thin legs. One had the obvious wounds of the hobble log around the ankle.

"Kaboo? Prince Kaboo," Jova whispered. "Is that you? Are you all right?"

After a moment, he rallied the courage to step forward

and pick up the edge of the dusty blanket. Kaboo lay staring up at him with an open mouth and wide, gaping eyes that did not seem to see anything. Jova jumped back in horror. His prince was dead!

But no, the staring, unblinking eyes moved just a little to follow Jova's movement. And then the mouth was moving, too, trying to say something.

Jova dropped to his knees and held his ear close as he strained to hear what his prince was saying. "What?" he urged. "Say it again."

"Water" came the faint whisper through a mouth so cracked and dry that it still hadn't closed.

Jova ran to find a drinking gourd, but it was dry. He grabbed it and raced out of the stockade and down to the stream. He pulled the plug and waited as the cool water gurgled in. "Faster, faster," he urged as he jerked the gourd back and forth under water.

When it was finally full, he raced back to the stockade. This time he took no precautions to avoid being seen. Carefully, he dribbled some of the water into Kaboo's mouth. The first mouthful made the prince choke, and Jova worried that he had done something dangerous, but at last Kaboo managed to swallow.

For an hour or more, Jova stayed with his prince, feeding him tiny bits of cassava mush and getting him to drink more water. He found a rag and used some of the water to wash the sores on Kaboo's back.

Finally, when Kaboo could sit up, he noticed the open gate and whispered painfully, "Looks like . . . they're not worried . . . about me escaping . . . anymore . . . can't even crawl . . ."

When Jova had done all he could, he promised to bring food and water to Kaboo every day, and then he left. If he was going to serve his prince, he could not anger his master too much or there would be no freedom to sneak off to the stockade.

Apparently, the Grebos also realized that Prince Kaboo was near death, and they knew that a dead pawn wasn't worth anything. If the king's son was dead, the Kru people would have no incentive to try to gather more taxes.

So the Grebos decided that they would stage one last display. The next morning, they herded all the Kru prisoners to a clearing near the edge of the village. After allowing so many prisoners to escape to take word back to the king about how his son was suffering, only eight prisoners remained.

In the middle of the clearing, there was a large ant hill, and the prisoners were put to the task of digging a pit just a few feet from it. The digging was not hard, but the ants were disturbed, and frequently a few angry ones stung the diggers. When Jova took his turn, he was stung three times on his left foot. In a matter of minutes, his foot was swollen and burning with such fire that he had to be replaced by another digger.

When the pit was as deep as Jova was tall, the Grebo warriors who were guarding them told them to stop and listen to what the war chief had ordered.

"This pit is for your prince," one of the warriors began. "Tomorrow's beating will be delayed until sundown. If your king has not brought the full payment by then, his son will be buried in this pit with only his head sticking out. Then we will prop his mouth open with a stick and put honey on his face. First the stinging ants will do their work, and then the driver ants will come and eat his flesh, bite by little bite. Before the next morning, nothing but a white skull will be left here in this field."

Several of the slave prisoners began to wail, and the guards got angry. "Save your wailing," the head guard said. "There will be time enough for that if your king fails to rescue his son. Silence!" he shouted as he walked among them looking from one to the other.

"There is still one thing that *you* can do that might save your prince," he shouted—and this succeeded, as his yelling had not, to stop the loud wails. "Your prince needs a runner, the fastest one among you, to take this message back to his father. Who will it be?"

No one spoke. They were all staring at the ground.

"Come on now. Step forward. It means your freedom. And, if you are fast enough, maybe you can get the message to the king in time for him to gather the required rice and other items in time to save his son."

Still no one moved. All the slaves appeared to be busy counting their toes.

Suddenly, a rough hand hit the bottom of Jova's chin and jerked his face up to confront the angry warrior. "You!" he demanded. "Who is the fastest one here?"

Jova's eyes rolled from side to side as he tried to look around. His jaw was held so tightly in the warrior's grip that he could not turn his head. Finally, in a weak voice he replied, "She is." He pointed to Gami, a tall girl of about sixteen. Jova recalled the happy festivals the Kru people had enjoyed in former years. There had been games and races, and Gami had won every foot race.

"Then be off with you!" shouted the Grebo, raising his hand as though to strike the girl. "And tell your king the message."

All the next day, Jova listened for the arrival of the king, but he did not come. In the afternoon, Jova sneaked away from his job of splitting palm fronds for a new roof thatch on his master's house. He ran to the stockade to visit Kaboo, taking a little food and water. His gifts during the last couple of days had kept the prince alive, but Kaboo was still growing weaker and sicker. He could not even sit up.

"Why hasn't your father come?" asked Jova frantically. He knew it was a foolish question.

The prince was struggling to draw a breath. "Do not blame him," he wheezed. "He would . . . come if he had . . . anything to bring." He stopped again to catch his breath. "Our people are ruined . . . broken. They have nothing left to pay. . . . That is why my father cannot come."

Jova stayed with the prince as the afternoon passed, not caring whether he got in trouble or not. Then, when the sun was dropping below the trees that surrounded the village, two guards entered the stockade. They ignored Jova but picked up the weak prince by his arms, just under the shoulders. Again, the prince was so weak that his feet dragged on the ground; his head flopped down on his chest as though it were barely attached.

Jova followed them out to the whipping cross where they draped Kaboo's battered body across the logs without bothering to tie his hands. Soon a crowd began to gather. Everyone knew that this would be the last whipping, and for some ghastly reason, they gathered to watch.

When the war chief arrived, he looked around, saw Jova trying to hide behind some of the Grebos, and said, "Where are the other Kru slaves? I want all the prisoners here to witness this last punishment. I want all the Kru snakes to know how fierce we Grebos are. Never defy us, or this will be your fate. Resisting our rule is useless."

The Kru prisoners, Jova along with the others, were pushed to the front to watch. A huge Grebo warrior stepped forward with a newly woven whip of poisonous vines. His muscles bulged, and an angry scowl contorted his face. He swung the whip around, making it whistle through the air.

And then, just as the whip was about to fall on Prince Kaboo's raw back, there was a blinding flash in the sky—brighter than the noonday sun—and a loud voice that said, "Rise up and flee! Rise up and flee!"

The man with the whip fell to the ground without having even touched the prince.

Everyone saw the flash and heard the words, but only Kaboo responded. His body peeled up off the whipping cross like bark being stripped from a tree. Slowly, he stood up straight and looked around. He took one tentative step, looking down as though he didn't know whether his feet would work or not. And then, to the utter amazement of everyone who watched, he ran at full speed across the open space toward the edge of the circle of those who had come to watch.

The crowd of Grebos parted as if they were water through which a swift canoe passed. Everyone stepped aside and allowed the prince to run through their midst unhindered. Kaboo dashed down the town's street and into the jungle.

For a few minutes, everyone stared with wide eyes, unable to believe what they had just witnessed. Then total chaos broke out, and the crowd began to flow down the same street through which Kaboo had run. Jova ran with them, but when they got to the forest's edge, everyone held back. Within an hour it would be dark, and no one wanted to be in the jungle after dark. Not only were there wild animals to be concerned about, but the leopard men might appear and attack them.

In a few moments, however, the war chief began organizing

his men, ordering them to collect torches and weapons to pursue the fugitive.

Suddenly, Jova realized no one was standing between him and the jungle trail. In fact, no one was watching him at all. Almost without thinking, he took off and ran down the same trail Kaboo had taken. Shouts and threats echoed behind him, but he kept running.

The mud of the trail felt cool beneath his feet. Vines caught his toes and nearly tripped him, but he carried on. Leaves slapped his face as the welcome gloom of the jungle closed around him. Far behind him came the sound of the Grebo warriors as they, too, set off down the jungle trail.

But somewhere up ahead of Jova was his prince.

CHAPTER 5

LEAD, KINDLY LIGHT

Jova ran hard. He had to catch up with Kaboo. Kaboo was older and would know what to do.

Thorns stung Jova's legs, and he was getting winded from running so hard. But he and Kaboo were free! The last few slivers of afternoon sunshine pierced through the thick cover of leaves, turning the jungle into a shimmering Eden of greens and golds and browns and blacks with a bright ivory or lavender flower here and there.

If Jova could only catch Kaboo, all would be well.

But several minutes passed, and Jova had run a mile or more, and still he saw no sign of Prince Kaboo. *How can such a weak person run so fast and so far?* he wondered.

The trail took a sharp turn and then descended toward the river. With his heart pounding from exhaustion, Jova welcomed the easier, downhill path and let his legs stretch out to full stride. Then he tripped over a root, and before he could recover his balance, he went flying off the trail, through the foliage, and crashed headfirst into the trunk of a tall oil palm tree.

Everything went black.

How long Jova lay there, he never knew, but when he came to, the small patches of sky between the high branches of the trees were identifiable only by occasional stars. He sat up and was so dizzy that he lay back down and tried to think about his situation.

He could not hear any Grebo warriors, but he was alone in the jungle, and night had arrived. Back up the trail somewhere were the dreaded Grebos. Or maybe they had passed him while he was unconscious among the ferns. He did not know which way to go.

Even if Jova managed to avoid the searching warriors, he was far from home and alone in the jungle at night. There would be many poisonous snakes and rivers thick with crocodiles. He thought of elephants. They, too, could be dangerous, but they seldom bothered someone who was not bothering them, and they made a lot of noise. He could get out of their way in time.

But he could not escape the leopard. The big cats hunted at night and would attack if they were hungry and thought their prey was weak.

Worse still were the leopard men. No one seemed to know whether they were men possessed by the spirit of the leopard or leopards who took on the form of men. The few people who had survived an attack by the leopard men claimed that leopard men sometimes walked on two feet like men and sometimes on all fours like an animal. They spoke to one another like men but also screamed and snarled in the night like the great cats. They had spotted fur and terrible claws and ate human beings.

But if they were men, that would make them cannibals! Jova shivered at the thought.

One thing was sure: No one walked safely in the jungle alone at night where the leopard men roamed.

Jova sat up again—more slowly this time—and this time his head did not spin. Slowly, he rose to his feet. There was a big knot on his head just above his left eye, but apparently nothing was broken, only sore and achy.

He took a couple steps in the direction he thought the trail lay, then looked around and tried to get his bearings. Far off between the trees, down near where Jova imagined the river ran, he saw a light. His first impulse was to run in the opposite direction, but it was not the flickering yellow flame of a torch that warriors might carry. Instead, a gentle white glow illuminated a small area as though a tiny bit of daylight was leaking into the dark forest.

Jova crept closer and peeked around a tree. What he saw amazed him even more.

In the strange, glowing light on the forest floor rested a large old log, and out of its hollow end crawled Prince Kaboo. Once Kaboo stood up and brushed himself off, the light began to move, and Kaboo followed. To Jova, his prince appeared completely healed of his wounds. He did not limp from the injuries of the hobble log, nor did he stagger as one who had been starved and beaten nearly to death. His steps were sure and easy.

With a start, Jova realized he was about to be left alone, so he moved forward. Once his feet assured him that he was on the path, he began to follow the light. Travel was not so easy for him as for Kaboo, however. The distant light gave him a direction, but it did not illuminate his way. Huge tree roots crisscrossed the forest floor above ground. Some extended out from the base of trees so high that they looked more like props than roots. Jova tripped and stumbled and crashed along, making so much noise that he was certain Kaboo would hear him following and run off in fear.

But Kaboo continued steadily along, sometimes stopping briefly to pick berries or fruit.

Keeping his distance, Jova continued to follow. When Jova came to the same places where Kaboo had found fruit, he felt around in the dark, also hoping to find something to eat. More often than not, he failed. But he did gather a few sweet morsels.

Through all this, Jova was uncertain what was happening. Was he dreaming? Had the knock on the head caused him to see strange visions? Or was this really happening?

In his mind, he reviewed what had occurred from the moment he first came to after his fall. It looked as though Kaboo had hidden in the hollow log to allow the Grebo warriors to pass by. Now that it was night, another strange light—though not so blinding as the one that had flashed at Kaboo's escape—was leading the prince through the jungle.

The scene was so astounding, Jova could not understand it. He considered calling out and making himself known to Kaboo and asking him what was happening. But he feared doing so in case the prince would run. Even worse, the whole scene might disappear, and he would find himself back on the jungle floor in the dark of the jungle night. So Jova kept silent, or as silent as he could as he stumbled along. In that fashion, he continued to follow the strange circle of light that dodged between the trees ahead.

Jova traveled that way all night, staying back just far enough that he would not lose sight of the prince or be seen himself.

As morning came, the light slowly faded—or, rather, it was

swallowed up by the natural daylight that filtered through the trees into the jungle. As the jungle once again took on its familiar appearance, Jova became more convinced that he was not dreaming or seeing visions . . . at least not any longer. There was Prince Kaboo up ahead of him, walking along through the jungle as if nothing unusual had happened. He disappeared behind one tree, only to appear a moment later from the other side. Everything seemed completely natural.

The only explanation Jova had for how he had gotten from knocking himself out with a fall the evening before to following the prince in the morning light was the mysterious event he had witnessed during the night. He had to accept it as true!

Working up his courage, Jova was about to call out or run ahead to catch Kaboo when he saw the prince turn off the trail. Kaboo pushed through the undergrowth until he stood between two fallen logs. There he lay down and pulled some large leaves over himself. He was hidden, just as he had been in the log the night before.

Jova crept closer. But at the distance of a stone's throw, he stopped. Something inside him prevented him from going closer. He decided to settle down and watch to see what would happen next. He found a large tree with high, exposed roots. Down between two of them, he crouched and made himself comfortable and completely hidden in every direction except facing Kaboo's hiding place. There he sat, intending to keep watch, but he was so tired that before long he fell asleep.

For the first time in months, his dreams were not filled with the frightening images of warfare and slavery among the Grebos. Instead, he dreamed of his home and the stream near his village where it went over a cliff and created a beautiful pool below. When the sun shone through the forest leaves, the watery playground was filled with spray and the joy of children's laughter as they frolicked in the water. Jova was a good swimmer, but he had been afraid to jump off the cliff into the pool like the older boys. And then one day, Prince Kaboo had led him to the edge and urged him to take the leap. It was such a long way down, but his prince went first and yelled for him to follow. Finally, Jova had jumped down into the rainbow mists.

He awoke with a start, remembering his dream and the reality. Life in the village had been good. He had made that jump not once but hundreds of times after getting over his initial fear. On that day, he had begun to play with the big boys.

By now it was night again. Jova had slept the whole day away wedged between the winged roots of the tree. He stood up and began to crash through the undergrowth toward the trail, but in only a few moments he was hopelessly tangled in vines. He fought and pulled and struggled until, by the time he was free, he had completely lost all sense of direction. He was exhausted, and the panic that had grown almost familiar to him started bubbling up within him again. He tried to control it and keep it from driving him to run blindly into the dark. He must not do that. If he didn't crash headlong into a tree, he could get caught again in the bramble patch.

Finally he calmed himself and looked around, trying to decide which way to go—when he saw the light again. This time, it seemed much farther away, almost out of sight. *Kaboo must have left before I awoke!* Jova thought. *I must hurry!* Now he had a direction, but keeping free of the vines slowed him down, and before he felt the familiar path beneath his feet, he had lost sight of the light.

CHAPTER 6

A COWARD TURNS BACK

Jova hurried as fast as he could through the gloom of the forest. But without the distant light to provide direction and help him see the silhouette of what was before him, the going was hard. Still he kept at it, sometimes stumbling or running into low-hanging limbs and vines, sometimes veering off the trail entirely and getting tangled in the undergrowth. After all, without the light, he had nothing but his bare feet to feel his way along the trail.

As far as productive travel was concerned, Jova found this method doomed. Once when he fell, his hand grasped a loose tree limb. He broke it at a good length, stripped off the little branches, and used it for a walking stick. After that, the going was easier. He stumbled less and was able to feel ahead.

But he knew that for every two steps he managed, Prince Kaboo had probably taken ten with ease. He was falling hopelessly behind.

This discouraging thought had no sooner lodged in his mind when his foot splashed into water. Only his walking stick, which found a deeper bottom ahead, saved him from plunging headlong into some pool, or lake, or—what was it?

Jova stood perfectly still, alert for the sound of a crocodile slipping into the water to come and investigate what tantalizing meal might have graced his table. He heard a quiet gurgling sound several feet ahead of him and jumped back onto the muddy bank. But the gurgling did not seem to come closer.

What could move through the water but not come closer, or, for that matter, not seem to go anywhere? wondered Jova. His heart thumped so loudly it seemed to drown out the other night noises—the thousands of chirping frogs, the whir of bat wings in the trees overhead, even the gurgling in the water. He listened closely, and then the answer came to him with relief: It was not something going *through* the water that was making the sound but water going *around* something. He must be standing before a stream or river that flowed so slowly it was almost silent, except for a spot in front of him where a protruding rock or limb or root disturbed the water enough to make a gurgle.

A chuckle of relief escaped Jova's mouth, then broke into a laugh. As the tension and fear released, he roared so hard that he fell back onto the ground and held his stomach. As he did so, he happened to look up. There were stars in the moonless sky. They extended to the right and to the left, and, as he looked harder, he could see where the stars disappeared out ahead of him. No question about it. He was at the edge of a river that cut its way through the thick jungle—and a fairly large river at that.

But where was Prince Kaboo?

"Kaboo," Jova called hesitantly. "Prince Kaboo."

There was no response, so Jova called more loudly. Finally, he yelled, "Ka-boo-oo-oo," so long and loudly that it echoed through the forest.

Still no answer.

Jova worked his way along the bank, careful not to step on some sleeping crocodile, but the trail seemed to play out at the river's bank. He could not pick it up going right or left. This had to be a crossing. But what kind of a crossing? Could he wade across? Could he swim? He was a good swimmer, but . . . what about crocodiles? He wished there was a canoe pulled up on the bank.

In the dark he had no way of knowing.

Gradually he realized the truth. He had lost Prince Kaboo, and in the dark there was no way to find him.

Jova sat down and began to cry. This whole ordeal had become too much for the young boy. He couldn't continue. He couldn't endure one more trial, one more frightening event. It was just too much.

He cried and cried until he fell asleep there on the cool mud of the riverbank in an unknown jungle far from his home.

The chatter of monkeys and the squawk of birds woke Jova at dawn. They were upset about something, scolding and screaming. Something had invaded the privacy of their forest, and Jova didn't think they were complaining about him. He heard splashing across the river and peered through the morning mist. He saw the problem. The monkeys and birds were protesting the arrival of a half-dozen pygmy hippopotami, wading into the river along the far bank.

The fog swirled and hid them from his view. When it cleared briefly again, he could see that the river was shallow enough to be quickly waded and therefore probably safe from crocodiles, but the coming of the hippos was discouraging. With them munching tender water plants on the other side, he could not cross. An attack by angry hippos could be deadly.

He found some stones on the bank and threw them at the water pigs in an attempt to drive them off, but they did little more than flinch when a rock hit them. Jova yelled and shouted and waved his arms, but his noise disturbed them no more than the monkeys and birds had. The animals' eyesight was so poor that, as long as Jova kept his distance, they took no notice of him. And he wasn't about to get closer.

He waited, finding some grubs to eat under the bark of a rotting, fallen tree.

Finally, when the sun rose over the treetops and burned off the fog, the hippos headed upriver. Jova retrieved his walking stick and waded into the river. If any crocodiles approached, he might be able to scare them off by beating the water with the stick. At least in the daylight he could see them coming.

On the other side, the trail that had led to the river continued on, and, though Jova was not certain that Prince Kaboo had come this way, it was his best choice. Traveling during the day carried the risk of encountering some Grebos on the trail, but by now he was far from the village of the war chief, maybe even out of their part of the jungle. Still, he listened carefully as he went along.

When afternoon arrived, he began to think about catching up with Prince Kaboo. If the prince had traveled all night while Jova was stopped at the river, then pretty soon Jova might come to the place where the prince was hiding for his daytime sleep. But how would he know if he had caught up? What if he passed him by?

Again he began calling Kaboo's name, softly for fear of attracting some distant enemy, but loud enough so his prince could hear if he were holed up just off the trail. But as he walked along, there was no response. *What if he is sleeping soundly and can't hear me?* worried Jova. *Or maybe I passed him much earlier today without realizing it.*

When the forest started to darken with the coming of evening and he still hadn't found Kaboo, Jova gave up. He had not noticed any fork in the path, but his prince had either taken some other trail, or he had passed him while he slept in the woods. Tired and discouraged, Jova turned off the trail and walked a short distance through the jungle to where a small spring trickled cool water down a small cliff.

He drank his fill, then sat down to remove a thorn that had jabbed into his foot as he hurried along earlier that afternoon. He was in complete darkness before the small splinter came free. Then he leaned back against a fallen log to think.

His eyes closed in weariness, and for a few moments he floated free of his problems, dreaming of his home and the pleasant life of his village . . . before the Grebo attacks.

Suddenly a sound startled him. It sounded like someone humming a song. He opened his eyes and blinked as he adjusted to the darkness. There, coming along the trail not more than thirty feet away, was Kaboo in his little circle of light! And Jova's ears hadn't fooled him. Prince Kaboo was humming a familiar childhood song as he swung along the trail. He didn't seem to have a care in the world.

Jova wanted to call out to him, stop him, join him. But

somehow he couldn't. It was as though his voice couldn't make a sound, and yet he knew that he hadn't even tried. Why he didn't try, he didn't know. But he remained silent until Kaboo had passed him by and gone on down the trail, the mysterious pool of light dimly dodging among the trees as it had the first night.

Then, as though he had been released, Jova jumped to his feet and followed along.

The next morning when the dawn began to tease its gray light into the jungle gloom, Jova was watching carefully to see where Kaboo would hide. But instead of turning off the trail to look for refuge in a hollow stump or small cave, Kaboo stepped out of the jungle into an open field.

It was a huge field, larger than any garden Jova had ever seen in his village. And all across the field in orderly rows were small trees, no more than twigs with a few green leaves on them. They were newly planted coffee trees, though Jova had never seen a coffee plantation before.

From the jungle's edge, Jova watched Kaboo as he walked out into the middle of the field. When he headed toward the far corner, Jova followed, but not by walking into the open. He went around the field, keeping himself hidden at the edge of the jungle. He had to move fast in order to get to the other side and see where his prince was going.

Kaboo took a wide path leading from the corner of the field through more jungle. Jova also took this path, staying well back out of Kaboo's sight.

They traveled in this way for about an hour as the road went up one hill and down the next. Always, Jova was ready to duck into the jungle should Kaboo look back. Why he was afraid to be seen, he didn't know. He wished he had contacted Kaboo the first night. Now he felt foolish to have followed so long without revealing himself. So he hung back.

Then, as Jova came to the crest of the final hill, he looked down into a large plain where no jungle grew. There were other roads and houses, and out on the plain stood a huge city, a city of white houses with red roofs. Jova had never seen such a place! But even more amazing, he could see white people walking along the roads and outside the city.

He had heard stories among his tribe about a white man named Doctor Livingston who came through the jungle and traveled on toward the mountains where no Kru or Grebo had ever gone. He talked about a God of love and looked at funny marks in a black book. It was said that he had invited some of the village men to go with him, but none would dare go. That was long ago, when Jova's father was young.

Now Jova could see many white people and black people, too, like himself, walking around the buildings of the city. But the sight of white people scared Jova. Then he noticed that Kaboo was walking down the road into the city. How could he do that? What was he doing?!

Frightened, Jova watched for a long time.

He had heard that white people were devils. Some said they were spirits, but either way, Jova wanted nothing to do with them! He almost ran after Kaboo to beg him not to go into such danger, but his courage failed him. It was as if roots had grown from his feet into the ground. All he could do was watch from the hilltop as his prince drew closer to the white buildings.

Sunshine bathed the top of the low hill where Jova kept his watch, but a great, gray cloud hung low over the white city and seemed to touch the ground just beyond it. Jova remained at the edge of the jungle all day, hoping Kaboo would return. Sometimes the cloud dropped down onto the city and swallowed the houses. Then, a few hours later, it would rise and release them.

When the sun rose the next morning, Jova finally gave up waiting for Kaboo to return. He couldn't stay here; he had to go home. With a sinking heart, he turned back into the jungle. He knew he had been traveling west while following Kaboo, so he headed east. Fear of the big cats and leopard men was his constant companion as he wandered through the jungle. Weak with hunger, on the third day he finally came to a village of Kru people. They were not part of his king's realm, but at least they were not Grebo and did not return him to the Grebos for a reward. He stayed in the village for several weeks until a trading party set out toward his village, and he traveled with them.

When he arrived home, everyone was amazed to see him. His family had given him up for dead! The village had already heard from other escapees about the flash of light and the voice that had freed Kaboo. But why hadn't Kaboo come home? Had their prince been saved from the Grebos just to fall prey to wild animals in the jungle?

Jova was afraid. No one would believe his story of Kaboo following a light through the jungle. But if they *did* believe it and discovered that he had turned back from following his prince out of fear, they would call him a coward.

As the villagers bombarded him with questions, Jova cautiously told about escaping the same day as Prince Kaboo and his adventures in the jungle: tripping and hitting his head on the tree, coming to the river in the dark, having to wait for the hippos to go up river, and finally coming to the friendly village. But he never said a word about following Kaboo to the white city.

For six long years, Jova had kept his secret. But now his tribe needed a new king, and he was the only one who knew where their prince had gone.

CHAPTER 7

JOURNEY TO THE WHITE CITY

Many things had changed in the six years since Jova had followed Prince Kaboo to the white city. He was now fourteen, the same age Kaboo had been when he had walked courageously down into the city. Would Jova be brave enough to do the same on a quest to find his prince?

Jova had graduated from the bush-devil school. He had the tattoo scar on his forehead to prove it. But had it given him courage? He knew much more about the jungle than he had when he had wandered alone in it six years ago. But the jungle was still a dangerous place to travel by oneself.

Nevertheless, this was a quest that he must make alone. Even if he wanted a companion, he doubted whether anyone would believe his story now that it had been held in silence for so long. And even if someone did, that person would mock him for turning back as a coward.

On the other hand, if he brought Prince Kaboo home to

give his people a new king, all would be forgiven and forgotten concerning why he had turned back the first time. No, it was clear. He had to go by himself. No matter what the danger, he would find his prince. It was the opportunity of a lifetime. In finding Prince Kaboo, Jova could save his people, earn a king's fortune, and prove himself to be a great warrior.

All that day as he gathered the things he would need for his journey, Jova thought about his trip through the jungle six years before. In the bush-devil school he had learned about many new plants that could be eaten, how to make a small snare to catch monkeys, what roots made a medicine that would take away the sting of a scorpion. The bush devil claimed powerful magic. But Jova had never seen him do anything as powerful as the flash of light and the voice that had freed Prince Kaboo. The bush devil had never healed anyone so near death as Kaboo had been.

Most important, the bush devil was a cruel god who seldom did anything good for people and never did anything without demanding a high payment. For six years, Jova had thought about Kaboo's release. It must have been the work of some great god, far more powerful than the bush devil.

This god must be very different from the bush devil, too, Jova decided. He had not demanded any payment, and he had acted with unusual love and care in providing the light that had guided Prince Kaboo. Jova had tripped a thousand times over roots and stones as he had trailed along in the dark. But the light had shown Kaboo every step. Jova had not seen him stumble even once. *It must be a very loving god to care for Kaboo like a father,* thought Jova. The bush devil was certainly not loving, nor were any of the other spirits the Kru people worshiped. Usually they just put curses on people.

That night before Jova went to sleep, he prayed quietly,

"Oh, great god of the light, guide me as you did Prince Kaboo so that I may bring back to my people a king who will save them." Then, with an easy feeling in his heart, he went to sleep.

The next morning, Jova simply told his mother that he was leaving to become a warrior. She cried but knew she could not stop him. Her tears made him feel bad. She probably thought he was going off to fight Grebos or hunt leopards, and she feared for his life. Not wanting her to worry, he whispered, "Be easy, Mother, I'm going to find Prince Kaboo. Everything will be fine."

But she cried all the harder. "You go on a fool's errand, my son. After six years, he will not be found."

Jova wanted to tell her that he knew where Kaboo had gone and that the god of the light would be with him, but that would bring up a story much too long for their brief good-byes, even if she could believe it. So he hugged her and said nothing.

After a week of traveling through the jungle using his new survival skills, Jova found the white city. He was encouraged to find it was much as he had remembered. There were hundreds of houses, many with white walls and red-tile roofs. He could see white people going and coming. His memory had not played tricks on him, except for one thing—beyond the city was a huge lake. Water stretched all the way to the afternoon sun, and the shores to the north and south did not even begin to curve to form the ends of the lake.

Could this be the everlasting sea that was mentioned in Kru legends? A great flood must have brought it to the white city since Jova had first seen it. Then he remembered the gray cloud that had hung over the city the first time he saw it. Today there was no cloud. Maybe the sea had driven it away. A question came to Jova's mind: *Is it better to be swallowed by the sea or by a cloud?* He decided that the sea was more dangerous. After all, the gray cloud had been over the city six years ago and the city had still survived. But today the sea threatened; it was very close to the city. He had better find Kaboo soon.

Not having ever seen the sea before, Jova did not realize that the reason he hadn't seen the sea on his first visit was because it was hidden behind a fogbank that drifted in and out over the shoreline. Today, there was no fog, and the sea sparkled clearly beneath the hot sun.

He took a great breath to gather his courage, then marched down the road toward the city. This time he did not turn back but forced himself to continue until he had entered the very streets of the city.

The sights he saw amazed and frightened him. A white man rode on a great beast, larger than a cow, though not as big as an elephant. Strange music and the smell of exotic foods teased his senses. By the white man's calendar, it was the beginning of August, 1892, but this was something Jova was not to learn for some time.

The very day Jova arrived in the city, he set about asking all the people he passed if they had seen Prince Kaboo. It was then that he discovered how many languages humans spoke. Kruan was quite common, and he was able to communicate with many of the black people. But there were others: Mandingo, Kpwesi, Gora, and Bulom. And, of course, there was the white man's language—maybe more than one. Jova couldn't make any sense of its strange sounds.

All afternoon he walked the streets asking anyone who would listen about Kaboo, but people just shrugged or shook their heads.

While traveling through the jungle, Jova had been able to gather berries, pick bananas, or find grubs for food. He even caught some fish in a stream. But in the white city, all the food belonged to other people. It was not like his village where food from each family's hearth was shared with whomever was present at mealtime.

As evening approached, Jova hung around the marketplace until he saw a woman loading her fruits and vegetables into baskets. Two crying children clung to her legs and hindered her work. "Can I help you?" offered Jova. "I will carry your baskets wherever you wish if you will give me one of those yams."

The woman agreed. After carrying the baskets to the woman's hut on the beach, Jova eyed the waves rolling up onto the sand with suspicion. To him, they looked like a snarling cat practicing its pounce on an unsuspecting prey. But the sea seemed to be staying in its bed, so, after he finished helping the woman, he went off to build a small fire and roast his yam. Later, he fell asleep on the sand under an upturned canoe.

He awoke at dawn with the waves lapping at his feet. Not understanding the natural rise and fall of the ocean's tides, Jova jumped up in fear, certain that the sea was rising to flood the white city. At the same time, he noticed that the cloud had returned and covered the sea, the beach, and the city so that he could not see farther than he could throw a stone.

"This is a terrible day," he said to himself. "The white city is doomed, and I have not yet found Prince Kaboo." He hurried off to the marketplace—where he had found the most people the day before—and began again to inquire about Kaboo.

He was so busy with his quest that he did not notice until afternoon that the cloud had disappeared and the sun shone brightly in a blue sky. That evening, having earned some scraps of food by doing odd jobs for the same woman, he returned to the beach to see how much farther the sea had come in its attack on the white city. To his great surprise, the water had retreated. This puzzled him so much that he ran back to the market woman's hut and asked her who had driven the sea back. She laughed at him, explaining the tides. "There is no reason to fear the sea except during great storms," she said. "Even then, it does not invade the city."

This Jova found hard to believe. He promised himself that he would watch the sea carefully from then on to see if it really did go back to its bed twice a day like the woman said.

By the third day, Jova was discouraged. Maybe he wouldn't find Prince Kaboo after all! But in the marketplace he saw an old man sitting in a booth that he had not seen before. The man was carving ivory into beautiful haircombs, knife handles, and amulets. Jova watched in admiration for a few minutes as the man worked.

Then, remembering his purpose, Jova said, "I'm looking for Prince Kaboo. Can you tell me where he is?"

The man worked silently for a few moments as though he hadn't heard Jova, but then he glanced up and responded in a familiar accent, "Prince, you say. Why do you seek this Kaboo?"

"He is to be king," Jova blurted, unthinkingly, "and I must find him and bring him back to our village. Do you know him?"

The man frowned at his work as he made one final gouge to complete the small ivory turtle he was carving. He held it up to admire. "I have heard of a Kaboo," he said slowly. "He is Kru, isn't he?" The man turned to look at Jova. There was a sly grin on his face, and three parallel tribal marks scarred his right cheek.

The old man was a Grebo!

A chill went through Jova. He clapped his hand over his mouth and turned to flee. Even over the noise of the busy marketplace, Jova heard the cackling of the old man's laugh behind him.

What have I done? thought Jova as he darted between booths and carts pulled by bullocks. *Now the Grebos know I'm looking for Kaboo!* But the man had said, "I have heard of him." What did that mean? Had he heard about Kaboo's captivity under the Grebo war chief? Or had he heard of his presence in the white city?

Jova redoubled his efforts. But after that scare, he was much more careful whom he asked. He checked the person's right cheek and asked some other questions first to see if the person spoke with a Grebo accent.

Watching for tribal marks paid off, too. One day Jova saw a boy not much older than himself rolling huge barrels along a dock by the sea. And this young man had a Kru tribal mark between his eyebrows, much like his own.

"I'm looking for a Kru named Kaboo," Jova said after making sure the dock worker spoke his language. "Have you heard of him?"

"Kaboo? Why, yes, I knew him." The dock worker grunted as he rolled a heavy barrel. "We worked together on a coffee plantation north of town, but he's not there now. Last I heard, he lives with white missionaries and paints houses."

Jova could hardly contain his excitement. He listened carefully as the dock worker told him where to find the white missionaries in a far part of town. No wonder he hadn't found Kaboo! Jova had spent all his time looking around the marketplace and along the beach. He had thought those were the logical places to search since that was where the most people gathered each day.

It took a lot of questions to find his way to the mission, which was almost like a small village within the white city. There was a bamboo fence circling several houses inside, which faced a central yard of hard-packed dirt. Jova hesitated. Did he dare go inside? Finally he saw three black men come out of one of the houses, so he found courage to step into the yard.

"Can you tell me where the white missionary is?" he asked them, trying not to let his voice shake.

The men shrugged. There were several at the mission, they said, but they led him to one of the houses.

Jova didn't know how he was going to make a white person understand him. He certainly couldn't speak their language. But when a white woman came to the door and was told by the black men that he wanted to speak to her, she welcomed him in the Kruan language.

Surprised and relieved, Jova spoke boldly. "I am looking for Kaboo. He is a boy from my tribe." He had decided not to say "prince" or speak of the need for a king until he was certain such details wouldn't be carried to Grebo ears.

"Oh, I'm sorry," said the white woman. "Samuel's not here—we call him Samuel Morris now. He changed his name when he became a Christian."

"Became a Christian?" said Jova, not knowing what that meant.

"Oh yes, he had a most dramatic conversion. He was wonderfully changed. I would love to tell you all about it."

Jova was taken aback in confusion. How was Kaboo changed? What did it mean? Had he become white? Jova looked around to see if the Africans who had brought him to the missionary woman's house showed any signs of becoming white. By that time, they were walking away. But they looked just the same as the people in small villages—except for the strange clothes they wore.

Finally he found his voice again. "But where did he go?"

"He took a ship to New York nearly two years ago."

"A ship?"

"Yes. You know, a big boat that goes to sea," said the woman, realizing that the boy from the jungle who stood before her had no idea what a ship was. "New York is far across the sea. It takes a long time to get there."

"Oh," said Jova. His shoulders sagged in despair. Had he come this far only to be stopped by the sea?

He shook his head to clear his thoughts. He was thinking like a child. He must think like a man! After all, he had found someone who not only knew who Kaboo was but knew where he had gone! And if Kaboo had traveled on the sea, why not he?

Jova straightened his shoulders and stood tall. "Well, where do I find this ship-boat?"

CHAPTER 8

ACROSS THE GREAT SEA

The missionary woman stood with open mouth and raised eyebrows, amazed at Jova's question. Finally she managed, "I'm sure I do not know where that ship is . . . but Samuel wouldn't still be on it. He went to New York."

"Yes, I understand that," said Jova. "But I want to go, too."

"Well, it's . . . it's not that easy." She studied Jova for a moment. "Young man, do you have a place to stay? I mean, you don't live here in Monrovia, do you?"

Monrovia! So that was the name of this big village. "No, I don't live in the white city. I was sent by my king." Jova looked around to make sure there were no Africans listening—Africans who might be Grebos. "Our king is dying," he continued in a quiet voice, "and Kaboo is our prince. I must find him and bring him back to our people."

The woman nodded. "Well, you would be welcome to stay here while you look for a boat to New York. We have work you can do, and you can learn English."

Stay with the white devils? Jova quickly shook his head and started to withdraw, but the woman said quickly, "You'll need to learn some English to find a place on any ship to America."

Jova paused. What the white woman said made sense. He knew when he had set out that finding his prince—proving that he was a brave warrior—would take courage. So once again Jova swallowed his fear, agreeing to work at the mission in exchange for English lessons.

The missionary's name was Miss Knoll, and she said he could learn English by attending her daily Bible classes. One day, Miss Knoll's Bible lesson told about a man named Saul to whom God spoke with a loud voice from heaven and a blinding flash of light.

"That's what happened to Prince Kaboo!" said Jova, proud to be able to contribute to the class discussion.

"So he told us," said Miss Knoll with great curiosity. "But how do you know?"

"Oh," said Jova with a big smile, "I was there. I saw it."

This report excited Miss Knoll greatly, and she had Jova go over every detail. As Jova warmed to the story, he even found himself telling about the trip through the jungle where the strange light led Kaboo. By this time, he had grown to trust the other Africans in the class and did not fear that they would laugh at him.

As he talked, Miss Knoll got a faraway look in her eyes, and when he finished, she didn't quiz him about why he had lost courage to follow Kaboo down into the city. Instead, she began to hum a song and then quietly added the words in English,

"Lead, kindly Light, amid th' encircling gloom,
Lead Thou me on;

The night is dark, and I am far from home;
Lead Thou me on:
Keep Thou my feet;
I do not ask to see the distant scene—
One step enough for me."

After a few moments of silence, Jova ventured, "What was that song, Miss Knoll? I did not understand more than a few words."

She smiled shyly, her eyes still glistening with unshed tears. She bit her lip and sighed. "It's a hymn—one that meant a great deal to me when I was in Taylor University. I felt God calling me to follow Him, but I was scared. That hymn helped me follow and obey Him one step at a time. And," she threw her hands up into the air with a tilt of her head, "He brought me here."

She stood up and translated the words for her students. "Maybe together we could come up with a Kruan version of the song. Would you like that?"

Not far from where the mission station was located, it was possible to see any ships that anchored near Monrovia to unload and load their cargoes. Most ships were too large to enter Mesurado Lagoon, which was crowded with smaller boats. But when the weather was calm, larger sailing vessels often lay at anchor offshore for a week or more as longboats and other small craft serviced them.

Whenever a new ship arrived, Jova raced down to the docks to meet the crew, looking for the captain. Whenever he spotted the captain or another well-dressed officer, he ran to the man and said some of the English words he had carefully learned.

"Welcome to Monrovia, Captain. You take me to New York, yes? I work plenty hard."

For weeks he was ignored or, at best, received a scornful laugh, but then one day there were two ships at anchor, one a sleek new schooner and the other a weathered old trader. As soon as Jova identified the crew of the schooner, he approached them. "Are you going to America?" he asked.

"Straight away," answered an officer in a blue uniform.

"You take me to New York, yes? I work plenty hard for you."

The man glanced at him with a sneer. "Passage is one hundred dollars, not a penny less," he barked and walked off.

Discouraged, Jova turned away, but just then he caught sight of the gray-haired captain from the old trading ship. His longboat had just tied up at the dock, so Jova approached him with his question.

"What did you say?" responded the captain as he stretched some of the kinks out of his bones. He had an inquisitive frown on his face and was looking right at Jova.

"I say, welcome to Monrovia, Captain. You take me to New York? I work plenty hard."

The captain stroked his beard slowly as he eyed Jova. "The last time I stopped here a young African said the same thing to me. But he was a little older than you. Tell me, why do you want to go to New York?"

Jova was so excited that anyone had bothered to pay him any attention that he blurted out in a loud voice, "I must find Prince Kaboo. He went to New York."

The captain shook his head and started to move on past several Africans who were working on the dock. One of them was watching Jova closely. "Sorry, lad," said the captain. "I never heard of any 'Prince Kaboo.' Besides, you're a little young to be going to sea."

In desperation, Jova touched the captain's arm to beg a moment more of his time. "Samuel Morris," he blurted. "You know Samuel Morris?"

"Sammy?" said the captain, a broad smile cracking his leathery, old face. "Of course I know Sammy. He changed my life and the life of nearly every man on board my ship. What about him?"

"I go to New York to find Samuel Morris. He is Prince Kaboo."

With his faltering English, Jova finally made his wishes known and discovered that it was on this captain's ship that Kaboo had traveled nearly two years before. The old captain was eager to tell his story, and Jova had such a hard time understanding his fast-spoken English that he finally persuaded the captain to spend the evening at the mission station where he could have help translating.

Around the dinner table, with the aid of Miss Knoll and one of the African pastors, the captain told this story:

When Sammy first asked me to take him to New York—just like young Jova, here—I cursed his brashness and said I would never take someone like him on board.

But he calmly said, "Oh yes, you will. My Father said you would."

"Where's your father?" I asked.

"In heaven," was his answer.

I walked away, disgusted, but the next morning when we brought our longboat ashore, he repeated his request. "Get out of here," I said with a kick to his pants. But that evening when we returned, there he was waiting by the boat. When he made his request for the third time, I finally said, "Well, what can you do?"

"Anything," he said.

So, thinking that he was an able-bodied seaman, I took him on. But once we had lifted anchor and were at sea, I found that he knew nothing. I was angrier than a cat with a knot in its tail, and I took it out on him every day, making him do the dirtiest work. I was a harsh master and angry that I had been fool enough to take on this landlubber. One night I was so drunk when Sammy reported to me, that I slugged him with my fist and knocked him out. But when he came to, he carried on with his work as if nothing had happened. At the time, it made me all the more angry.

Then, during a storm, one of my men fell from the rigging and injured himself severely. He couldn't even rise, but Sammy knelt down and prayed for him. The man immediately got up and carried on as though nothing had happened to him . . . except after that the sailor had the utmost appreciation for Sammy.

This got my attention and everyone else's, too. Sammy was always asking me and the men if we knew Jesus. When we would curse and swear at him for such a question, he would kneel down and pray for us. In time, it got me to thinking about God and the Gospel as I remembered it from my childhood.

Before we got completely away from the African coast, a severe storm damaged the ship beyond seaworthiness. We were lucky to put in behind a small island where, for two weeks, we made repairs. Though Sammy was young and small, he kept at the pumps like my biggest men, all the time claiming that the Holy Spirit gave him the strength.

When repairs were finally completed and we were again under sail, I made the mistake of giving out extra rum to let the men celebrate. Unfortunately, it led to a brawl, mainly led by a big man from Malay who wanted to kill all the whites on board—a regular mutineer. Thinking he had the support of some of his Asian friends and could overpower the rest of us, he grabbed a cutlass and charged us, ready to kill.

Then Sammy stepped in his way and simply said, "Don't kill."

The blade was held high above Sammy's head, and I knew that the Malay hated blacks even more than whites. He had specifically sworn to kill Sammy when I first brought him on board. And to tell the truth, I had expected him to do it long before this because he had killed many other Africans in the past.

But for no reason that any of us could see, the Malay slowly lowered his weapon and went below deck. Every man who saw this happen was impressed. Sammy represented a power stronger than our meanest sailor.

I went to my cabin with Sammy, and he immediately began praying for the men. Before I knew what I was doing, I was praying, too, and confessing my own sins.

That was how I found Jesus as my own Savior. That same day, I vowed never to reward the crew again with rum.

By the next morning, the murderous Malay was dreadfully ill. He was as sick as I've ever seen a man, and I didn't expect him to live out the day. But Sammy was not discouraged. He went to visit and pray for him even though this was the man who hated him and had vowed to kill him. And God answered Sammy's prayer, too. The man recovered immediately and thereafter treated Sammy like a brother.

Sammy started holding church services on deck, and every man participated—not grudgingly, but eagerly. Sammy's faith transformed the whole spirit of my ship, and I'll be forever grateful.

"So," concluded the captain, "if you are a friend of Sammy's, you are a friend of mine. And if you want to go to New York, I'd be more than happy to take you. In fact, I'll pay you for what work you do during the passage. It'll make a man of you."

Jova could hardly believe his ears. Even the missionaries and the African pastors laughed with delight over Jova's good fortune. As the captain put on his hat and stepped to the door, he said, "Be at the dock at dawn tomorrow, Jova, and we'll have a place for you."

Jova was so excited he could hardly sleep that night. When he arrived at the waterfront early the next morning, the sleek schooner had already sailed, but a longboat was waiting to carry him out to the old trading ship.

CHAPTER 9

ASSASSINS

Five months later—in April of 1893—with a little money in the pockets of his white-man's clothes and amazement in his eyes, Jova looked down at the crowded docks along the East River of New York. The captain came alongside and put his hand on Jova's shoulder.

"New York's a big place," he said sympathetically. "But when Sammy left us, he went to Stephen Merritt's gospel mission on Eighth Avenue. We heard some great reports of how he preached to the people at the mission. I don't know if he's still there, but if I were you, that's where I'd start looking. I'll send one of the crew to show you the way."

The captain summoned the ship's carpenter, a friendly New York native who seemed only too glad to leave the unloading to the other crew members. Jova turned and waved goodbye to the captain as he and the carpenter walked down the gangplank.

No sooner had Jova's feet hit the dock than he felt dizzy and had to grab the carpenter's arm to keep from falling. "What's the matter, son?" laughed the old sailor. "You still got your sea legs under you?"

The strange sensation of being on firm ground again passed in a few moments. As they headed up Pike Street away from the docks, Jova saw two black men standing in the shadows of a warehouse door. They turned away when Jova looked at them . . . but not before he saw what looked like three dark scars on their right cheeks.

A wave of terror clutched Jova's chest, as though someone had just hit him in the stomach. Grebos *here*?! What were Grebo warriors doing here in America? Why had they come all the way across the sea?

"Did you see those men?" Jova asked his companion anxiously.

The old carpenter frowned and looked back over his shoulder in the direction Jova had indicated. "You mean the ones back there at the warehouse?"

"Yes. Two black men."

"I saw them," shrugged the carpenter. "What of it? Just a couple dock hands lookin' for a job."

"Did you see them watching me?" asked Jova. "When I look at them, they quickly turn faces away, like trying to hide."

"Hey, what's eatin' you? Probably just talkin' to each other."

"You not see anything strange about them—their faces, I mean?"

Instead of answering, the carpenter turned up his hands in a gesture of helplessness and kept on walking.

But as they worked their way through the streets of New York, Jova couldn't get the experience out of his mind. Jova had let slip the purpose of his search to the Grebo ivory carver in the marketplace in Monrovia. But even if the Grebos wanted to stop him from bringing Prince Kaboo back to the village, how could they have known he was coming to New York? If they had seen him leave Monrovia, how could they have known where he was going? Or how could they have arrived first?

It all seemed too impossible. There couldn't be anything to it. *It must have been the shadows or a smear of dirt on their cheeks,* he told himself. All the same, he looked behind him one more time to see if anyone was following. There was a carriage a block back and some children chasing a hoop, but otherwise the street was empty.

He sighed with relief and hurried on. Soon they were passing through Chinatown; then came a part of town where the white people were all talking a language other than English. It was like visiting many different countries all within walking distance of one another. Jova couldn't believe how big the buildings were, and he had never imagined that so many people existed in the whole world.

The streets were full of carriages pulled by horses. He smiled at how surprised he had been when he first saw a man riding a horse in Monrovia. But then he saw a big carriage going down the middle of the street without any horses or oxen pulling it.

"Where are the horses?" he asked the carpenter.

"That's one of the new horseless carriages," the sailor grinned. "It runs on gasoline and doesn't need any horses. And look at the lights on those poles. They use electricity to shine at night. No one has to go around and light them every night. They just pull a switch at Mr. Edison's light company."

Jova shook his head. He could hardly believe all the new things he was seeing. But he couldn't let himself get distracted. The important thing was finding Prince Kaboo.

When they arrived at Stephen Merritt's gospel mission, the graying Bible teacher welcomed Jova warmly. He was a short, wide man, a little round around the middle, with a big, friendly smile. But Jova waited until the ship's carpenter left to tell him about trying to find Samuel Morris.

"Oh, we certainly remember Sammy," said Stephen Merritt. "Why, that lad brought a great revival to our mission! The first night he gave his testimony, seventeen men gave their hearts to Jesus. The same kind of thing happened in every church he visited around here, too."

"But . . . you mean he isn't here?"

"Oh no. He went out to Taylor University in Indiana to study the Bible. But I'm so excited that you've come all the way from your country to learn about Jesus, too. This is amazing!"

Jova didn't know what to say to the man. He had not come to study the Bible. He had come to America to find Prince Kaboo and bring him home. The Bible study he had attended in Monrovia had been interesting, and Miss Knolls had urged him to give his life to Jesus, but Jova had not understood. Besides, he had another purpose in life. He was on a quest for his prince, and he wasn't going to let anything stop him.

Jova sighed. He was tired from all his travels. He wished he could go back home. "How do I get to this Taylor University?" he said wearily. Would he ever catch up with Prince Kaboo?

"Indiana? Hmm, you're a bit young to go to the university," mused Mr. Merritt, rubbing his chin thoughtfully. "But you seem like a determined young man. The best way to get there is by train. Guess you don't have any trains in your part of Africa—at least, Sammy had never seen one. But a train is a big machine for traveling. . . ." He paused, searching for words.

"Is it a horseless carriage?" asked Jova.

"Why yes. It is something like a horseless carriage. How do you know about those? Do you have automobiles in Africa already?"

"Oh no. But I saw one of yours today, and I would love to ride in it to Taylor University."

"Well, a train is a little different. It has several cars hooked together."

"But it doesn't use any horses, does it?" Jova was excited at the idea of riding on a machine without horses.

Mr. Merritt smiled. "You've got the right idea, but a train is much larger and goes much faster than an automobile. It has a steam engine that pulls it from the front. But it also costs a good deal of money to travel on it."

"I have money," said Jova proudly, pulling out the handful of coins the captain had given him after his voyage.

"That's a nice start," said Mr. Merritt, "but I don't think it will get you to Indiana. However . . ." again he rubbed his chin and studied Jova, "for a young man so interested in Christian education that he would come all the way from Africa, there *may* be another solution."

Jova tried hard to follow the English words, but he wasn't sure exactly what Mr. Merritt was saying. "When Samuel was here," the man went on, "we organized the Samuel Morris Missionary Society to raise money to send him to Taylor University in Indiana. There's still a little more money in that fund." He beamed at Jova with his big smile. "I'm the treasurer and would be glad to use some of that money to help you, too."

The next morning, Stephen Merritt wasted no time in withdrawing some money from the bank. Before Jova really understood what was happening, he was standing in a New York train station with a ticket to Fort Wayne, Indiana.

Jova rode the train all that day, spending much of his time looking out the window at the passing countryside that was bursting with spring flowers and new leaves. Just before dark, he sat up quickly as the ground beside the train dropped away. Then he realized that the train was traveling on a bridge over a large river, but the bridge was so narrow that the train seemed to be flying through the air. When he looked down from the window, all he could see was the water below. What a marvel train travel was! It took his breath away.

After eating some bread and cheese Mr. Merritt had given him in a small bag, he shut his eyes and tried to sleep. But with all the excitement of coming to America and riding this marvelous, strange machine, sleep wouldn't come. After a while he decided to stretch his legs by walking through the cars. Going from one car to the next in the blowing, cold night air was frightening, but he had seen others make it safely. Gripping the handholds tightly, he stepped from one swaying platform to the creaking, groaning platform of the next car. He practically fell against the door and pushed it open. This car was a sleeper and had curtains pulled over each berth with only a narrow aisle to pass through. But the next car forward was a coach like his own.

He walked all the way to the front of the passenger section. "Can't go any farther," said a train man in a dark suit and a little pill cap with a gold band around it. "That up there is the mail car." So Jova returned to his own car. But just as he sat down, he noticed two black men sitting in the last seat at the back. His heart lurched, and he ducked down. Could they be Grebos?

No, that was crazy. There were thousands and thousands of black people in America. Two of them on the train in his car didn't mean anything. But his heart was still pounding. He turned his head to sneak a peek, but the lamps in the coach car had been turned too low for him to get a clear look.

He began to think through his whole quest again. If they were Grebos, how had they known he was coming to America? Then he remembered the afternoon on the dock in Monrovia when he had met the captain of the ship that had brought him over. He had been so excited that he had told him all about Prince Kaboo. Could he have been speaking so loudly that others overheard him?

He squeezed his eyes shut and tried to recall the scene. There had been other Africans working nearby on the dock. Could they have been Grebos? *Oh no. Oh no!* thought Jova as a sweat broke out all over him. *That was it. They heard me, and now they are following me. They've followed me all the way here!* His mind was working fast, and he recalled the speedy clipper ship that had also been anchored offshore that day. The clipper ship's captain had said that it, too, was going to America, only the price had been one hundred dollars. That would be two hundred dollars for two men—a lot of money—if the two at the back of the train were Grebos. But maybe it was not too much to pay if they were being sent by their tribe. There were many Grebos who worked for wages in Monrovia.

Jova sneaked another look toward the back of the train. The men were sleeping, but one of them had turned in his seat so that his face was more fully in the light. Jova froze. There were three dark stripes on his cheek. This was no smear of dirt or trick of the shadows.

He was a Grebo warrior!

Jova sat back in his seat, his heart pounding. He *was* being followed. And the only reason for following him must be that they intended to kill him. He had to come up with a plan for escape—fast.

When the train screeched and wheezed to a stop during the night, Jova slipped quickly off the train and ran through the streets of a small town. He had no idea where he was, but somehow he had to get away.

Finally the whistle blew and he heard the train chug out of town. He breathed deeply of the frosty air and relaxed. His plan was in motion. Slowly he headed back toward the train station. He would catch the next train to Indiana while his enemies traveled on ahead of him. Somewhere down the line they would realize he was gone, but, in this strange land, they would have no idea where he was.

But when he came around the corner of the station, his plan turned into a nightmare. The two Grebo men stood in the moonlight right before him.

Jova froze. An evil grin crossed the face of the shorter warrior. Jova tensed for a blow, sure that they would strike him immediately. But instead, they each stepped aside, bowed, and with their arms motioned Jova to walk between them.

I'm dead, thought Jova as he looked from one to the other. *Together they are planning on killing me, probably by hitting me right in the back.*

Nevertheless, he mustered all his courage. He had known from the beginning that he might lose his life on this quest. He would not turn back in fear as he had done when he was a young boy on the hill overlooking the white city. He stepped forward and walked between them, expecting a knife blade to strike him any moment.

But it did not.

He walked between his enemies without receiving so much as a scratch. As they walked along the deserted station with one warrior on each side, Jova had to resist the overwhelming urge to run. When they came to the door of the train station, the two Grebos ushered him in. Jova sat down on a bench in the dim light and suddenly realized he was alone.

The Grebos had not come into the station with him.

Slowly an even more frightening thought crossed Jova's mind. *If they did not kill me when they had the perfect chance, then they must have some other objective.* His mind raced for an explanation, but when it came, it was no comfort. *They must be following me to get to Prince Kaboo!*

It was the only explanation. They didn't care about him. They wanted to remove the future Kru king.

They were assassins!

CHAPTER 10

A DESPERATE LEAP

Jova sat alone in the train station, knowing that somewhere outside lurked his deadly enemies, the enemies of his people. A large clock on the wall ticked away the minutes that stretched into hours.

For the first time, Jova recalled how the men had looked. One had been tall and thin with a nearly bald head leaving only a rim of hair above his ears and around to the back. He was clean-shaven, with a square jaw and deep-set eyes. His face had seemed chiseled out of ebony—expressionless and cold. But even in the moonlight, Jova had seen the traces of the three scars on his right cheek.

The shorter man had been more muscular, with a round face and a trace of beard. He had been wearing a round-topped hat—a bowler hat, Jova thought it was called. As he thought about this man, Jova remembered that when he had grinned, a couple front teeth were missing. *They were on the opposite side from the cheek scars. So it was his left front teeth that were missing,* Jova thought.

But what difference did it make? He had been told that in America, just like in Monrovia, there were police to protect people from criminals. Maybe he could go to the police, but . . . who would believe his story? "Two assassins have followed me all the way from Africa to find and kill my prince. You must arrest them." Anyone would laugh at such a complaint. So far, the men hadn't committed a crime. They couldn't be arrested solely on the basis of Jova's wild fears.

The clock in the train station ticked on, and Jova got up and walked from window to window. He wiped the fog off the cold panes and looked out to see if the men were lurking outside. There were two gas street lamps burning on either end of the platform beside the train tracks, but Jova couldn't detect anyone in the shadows. It was no comfort. He knew they were still there.

He returned to the bench and lay down. In time, he fell into a fitful sleep. When he awoke, he looked up at the clock. He was glad that he had learned to tell time while living at the mission station in Monrovia. It was 4:25 in the morning. It would be getting light before long, and an eastbound train would soon arrive. Jova could give up and go home. Or he could wait for the next westbound train and continue on to find Prince Kaboo.

If he continued on, he would lead the assassins to his prince—and in so doing, bring death to him. On the other hand, if Jova gave up his quest and headed home, that might draw the Grebos off Kaboo's trail . . . but that was no answer. If he gave up, the Grebos would still win. Kaboo would not return home to reclaim his throne, and his people would be weak and without a leader.

Every way Jova looked at his dilemma, those seemed like his only options. But there had to be another way. He went over each detail again in his mind: His enemies wanted to prevent Kaboo from claiming his throne. Clearly, the Grebos would believe assassinating him was the most certain way to do that; that's why they were following Jova. But the Grebos would also succeed if they kept Jova from finding Kaboo, if they scared him into returning back to Africa without contacting the prince.

Slowly, a new plan took shape in Jova's mind.

He did not wait for the next westbound train. Instead, when morning's first light met the eastbound train as it groaned and screeched and puffed to a stop outside the small train station, Jova walked dejectedly toward it as though he had given up in defeat and was returning to Africa. He got on the last car, paid the conductor some of the money he had earned on the ship, and found a seat near the window where he could watch the station platform. Just as he expected, moments before the train left, his two pursuers jumped on the car ahead.

They were still following him.

Then Jova remembered something: Last night just before it had gotten dark, the train had crossed a trestle spanning a river. How long had that been before he had gotten off in the small town to escape the Grebos? Had it been an hour? Two hours? He couldn't be sure; so much had happened. But the train had crossed a large river on a bridge that was so narrow the train had seemed to be flying across.

If Jova could time it right so that he jumped from the train just as it traveled over the bridge, he could drop into the river, swim to the bank, and escape without the Grebos knowing that he had gotten off the train.

He hoped to trick the Grebos into thinking he was still on the train. It was similar to the plan he had made when he got off the westbound train in the small town the night before. But last night, he had been going west. Now he was going east. If the Grebos continued on, they would not know where he was.

His plan had failed the night before because they had been watching at every stop. When they saw him get off, they, too, got off. But if he leaped from the train while it was speeding down the tracks, no one would think to be watching for him.

Jumping from a fast-moving train onto the hard ground would certainly result in injury, if not death. But Jova was a good swimmer, and he had often dived from the cliffs into the pool at the bottom of the waterfall near his village. If he could time his jump from the train to land in the river, it might result in a neat escape. The best part of the plan was that no one would know that he had left the train, especially not the Grebo warriors.

Twice, as he looked out the window at the lay of the land ahead, it seemed as though they might be approaching some kind of a river. The flat land was replaced by gentle, rolling hills that slowly lost elevation. New spring grass was coming up everywhere, and baby buds put a green mist on all the trees.

The first time it looked as if they might be coming to a river, Jova got up quickly from his seat and walked to the back of the car and opened the door. He stepped out onto the small platform. The crisp morning air buffeted him as he leaned around the back of the train car to watch ahead.

Unfortunately, they were crossing only a small creek.

The second time, Jova didn't even go out into the cold.

He soon saw that it was only a small stream they would be crossing.

But then as he looked out the right windows at the prairie stretching off to the south, broken only by groves of just greening trees, he saw a ribbon of silver snaking off to the south in the brilliant morning sunshine. It was a river. They were coming up on a river.

On the platform at the back of the last train car, Jova made himself ready. He unhooked the small safety chain on the side of the platform and took three steps backward. There was just enough space for him to get a good jump. He peeked around the left side of the train. It was navigating a gentle curve that led onto the trestle. The smoky, churning engine was just venturing out onto the spindly bridge.

I hope it is strong enough to hold the train, thought Jova. Then he reminded himself that he had already ridden a train that had come safely over the trestle from the other direction. Besides, he had more important things to think about. In spite of how narrow the trestle looked, he would have to jump far enough out to miss the timbers that supported the bridge. He tried taking a practice run across the platform. There wasn't much distance to get up his speed.

In addition to clearing the trestle, he would also have to time his jump just right to land in the water below. He could now see that the river was quite wide, but the train was carrying him forward. He would not land directly below the point where he jumped. As he fell the twenty feet or so into the river, he would continue moving in the same direction the train was going. Therefore, he would have to jump before he came to the place where he wanted to land.

But this was it. There was no time to practice.

He was almost there. The sound of the wheels under him

changed as his car—the last car on the train—rolled out onto the trestle. He could see the river. He was almost over the edge of it.

He braced himself.

Then, just as he was ready to go, the back door of the train coach opened and a white woman in a big bonnet stood there with a look of horror on her face. He had to go *now*, before someone stopped him! Jova gave her only a momentary glance before he took three powerful steps right past the surprised woman. She screamed as his foot left the platform, and she kept on screaming as he fell toward the water—and his possible death.

His heart sank. He had not made a clean getaway. She had seen him and had announced his departure to everyone in the train car. Whether he survived or not, he had failed in his purpose of escaping secretly.

Splash!

He hit the water much harder than he had imagined he would—much harder than when he used to land in the pool below the cliffs near his village in Africa. The impact knocked the breath out of him. Dark green water closed over his head, wrapping him in the grip of its icy fingers. *Cold, so cold!* This was not a tropical stream or the waves on a sunny African beach. This was a swift river in North America where the snow and ice of winter had melted only a few weeks before.

CHAPTER 11

RIDING THE RAILS WITH HOBOES

When Jova finally fought his way to the surface of the river, he was gasping and struggling with the swift current that seemed determined to pull him under again.

He fought hard, driving with powerful strokes for the shore. Then his foot hit something, and he recognized it as a submerged log. The log extended from the deep part of the swift river to the shore. There the stump and a large tangle of roots rose above the surface of the water and tucked itself tightly into the muddy bank.

Jova pulled himself along the length of the log until he could grasp the roots and secure some relief from the powerful tug of the current. He rested there, hanging on to the roots with his body still in the water. Taking in great gulps of air, he was conscious that he had come much closer to losing his life than he had expected.

As he regained his breath, the chill of the water began to

have its effect, and he shivered uncontrollably. He had never been in water so cold that it actually hurt, making his arms and legs ache to the bone. Jova started to crawl out of the river when suddenly he heard the mournful whoop of the train whistle, followed by a metallic screeching sound. Cautiously, Jova looked up over the edge of the riverbank. The train had come to a stop a half mile or so down the track. He stood up to his knees in the icy river, his head just over the rim of the bank, as he watched a most disheartening event begin to unfold.

The train engine belched a great billow of black smoke. White steam boiled from its wheels. And then . . . it began to back up ever so slowly. Jova frantically looked around for a better place to hide. On the west side of the river was a forest with plenty of cover, but on the east bank where he had found refuge, it was open prairie. The only tree was the huge fallen log behind which he hid. And the only way he could remain hidden was behind the root mass, which meant continuing to crouch in the icy river.

With more groaning and hissing and clanking, the slowly backing train stopped just before it rolled out onto the trestle that stood on its spindly legs above the river. Jova could hear the engine sighing and grumbling like some enormous, living beast. Mr. Merritt had called it an "iron horse," but it sounded more like an angry, wounded bull elephant to Jova.

Passengers lined the windows on the side of the train that faced Jova. Some had lowered their windows and were leaning out, pointing toward the river. The train cars were close enough that Jova could have thrown a rock and hit one, but he pressed himself against the muddy roots of the fallen log. After a few minutes of confusion, the train conductor and several other men climbed down out of the last car and walked out on the trestle over the middle of the river. A woman—obviously the one who had opened the door just as Jova jumped—stood on the car's platform and yelled directions to the men on the trestle.

"No. Go a little farther . . . a little farther . . . there! He jumped right about there."

"Are you sure, ma'am?"

"Of course I'm sure," she yelled. "I opened the door just as he jumped."

Jova ducked even lower. Two figures had climbed up on top of the last train car and were standing there, shielding their eyes with their hands as they looked down into the water. They were black men—one short and one tall.

"I don't see anyone," yelled the train conductor.

By this time, another train official was standing on the platform beside the woman. He yelled back to the man on the trestle. "If she's right and someone did jump, there's no way he could survive a fall like that."

"Well, I *am* right," snapped the woman indignantly, making sure her voice was loud enough for those out on the trestle to hear. "I saw him with my own eyes!"

"Of course, madam," patiently replied the conductor on the trestle. "But unfortunately, the river has gotten him. It's fast, and it's cold."

"He's dead for sure," said another man out on the trestle.

"Shouldn't we search for the body at least?" demanded the woman.

"Why waste time? You said he was a black boy, didn't you?" said the conductor on the platform.

The woman turned to look at him indignantly. "What's that supposed to mean? What an awful thing to say!"

The conductor shrugged. "Let's get going. We've got a schedule to keep!" he called to the men on the trestle. Then he turned to the woman next to him. "Don't worry about it, ma'am. We'll report it at the next stop. All aboard!" he bellowed.

Jova saw the two black men on the roof of the train turn to each other, then climb down to join the other passengers as they crowded back onto the train.

Soon the whistle blew, and a jolt clanged from car to car as the engine wheezed and puffed and spun its great driver wheels, straining to set the train in motion again. Within a few minutes, the train was out of sight with only a wisp of black smoke drifting away on the wind.

Stiff and aching, Jova climbed out of the water. The river had been so cold that the chilly April air blowing through his wet clothes felt warm by contrast. But it didn't ease his shivering. With his teeth chattering, he climbed back up to the train track and made his way over the trestle, then headed west at a jog. It was half an hour before he could slow down to a walk without starting to shiver again.

But a change of mood had come over him. Instead of fearing that he had failed when the woman noticed him jumping from the train, Jova found himself feeling hopeful. Everyone on the train—including his enemies—seemed to think he was dead. He could continue his quest. It didn't bother him that he was nearly out of money in this strange land and still far from Taylor University. In fact, he had no idea how much farther he had to travel to get to the university, but, one way or another, he was going to find Prince Kaboo.

Late that afternoon, Jova saw a collection of buildings in the distance and gratefully realized that he was approaching a town. The people there could tell him how to get to Taylor University. It wouldn't be long now.

But before he reached the town, he saw several people camping in a little grove of trees beside the train tracks. One man waved him over, inviting him to join him at his small fire.

"Name's Jack," the man said, motioning Jova to sit down on an upturned crate. He plopped some beans on a tin plate and held it out. Jova gratefully took the plate, scooping the beans into his mouth with his fingers just as the man did. The stranger's clothes were so dirty that they all seemed the same color. In fact, the dirt had buried itself so deeply into the pores of his skin that his face was nearly the same shade as his soiled clothes.

"Been ridin' the rails long?" the man asked with the rise of one of his bushy eyebrows.

" 'Riding rails'? I don't know riding rails."

"You know, travelin'. Have you been travelin' long?"

"Oh yes," said Jova. "Many, many months I come . . . riding rails."

"Hey. You talk funny. You're not a regular farmhand, are ya? Where ya from?"

"Africa," said Jova brightly as he licked his lips with the last bite of beans. "I come . . . riding rails . . . from Africa, through jungle and across the sea and behind the iron horse. I'm on a quest."

"Ya don't say. Ridin' the rails across the sea, huh?" grinned Jack as he began to chuckle. "Hey, Daniel," he yelled toward one of the small shacks tucked under a nearby tree. "Get yourself over here and meet a real African."

"A what?" came back the voice of an unseen person.

"A *real* African. He even talks different than you."

"What do you mean? I *am* a real African."

"Not like this, you ain't," chuckled Jack.

Jova jumped with surprise as an old black man in a rolled-brim hat came out from behind the hut and walked toward them on bowed legs.

"Daniel used to be a cowboy," explained Jack, referring to the old man's crippled walk. "Got himself broken up pretty bad when some old longhorn pinned him to a juniper tree out in California."

To Jova's relief, Daniel did not have three scars on his right cheek. Ever since he'd seen the Grebos near the dock in New York, he had checked out every black person very carefully. But this was the first American black person he had met face-to-face.

Daniel rubbed the white stubble growing out of his dark chin and eyed the young traveler sitting on the old crate. "You really from Africa?" he asked.

"Yes, sir. I come riding rails across the sea."

Daniel stared openmouthed for a moment, then broke into a great laugh, holding his sides with his gnarled hands. "Well, if that don't beat all."

Jova looked from one man to the other, not knowing what they found to be so funny. "It was very hard work," he offered, but that made them laugh all the harder.

"Why do you laugh at me?"

"Because," said Jack when he got his laughter under control, "ridin' the rails means travelin' by train. That's what us hoboes do. I don't think there's any train tracks across the ocean."

"No, sir," said Jova, and then he realized his mistake and laughed, too. "No. I go on the ship when it comes across the sea but ride the rails with the train."

"Now you got it," said Daniel as he sat down on a wooden

box. "But what brings you all the way to America? Where ya headin'?"

Realizing that he had to ask directions of someone, and seeing that Daniel wasn't a Grebo warrior, Jova told his story.

When he was finished, Jack said, "Where'd you say this prince of yours was?"

"At Taylor University," said Jova. "Mr. Merritt bought me a ticket, but I got off the train."

"I never heard of Taylor University. Have you?" said Jack, turning to Daniel.

"Nope." The black cowboy pulled a corncob pipe out of his shirt pocket and knocked a few ashes out of it, dug around in the bottom of the bowl, then put it in his mouth. He reached for a twig and held it in the fire to light the pipe with.

Jack pointed a gnarled, dirty finger toward Jova. "You still got the stub of that ticket?" he said.

Jova dug in the pocket of his pants and pulled out the soggy remains of an orange ticket.

Jack shook his head. "That's sure not gonna do you much good now. Leastwise, you couldn't get back on any train with it."

"Do ya even know what town you were headin' toward? Where is this Taylor University?" asked Daniel.

"Yes, sir. Fort Wayne, Indiana," said Jova. That's where Mr. Merritt had told him to go.

"Oh, well, that ain't so hard then," said Daniel, grinning around his pipe. "We can put you on the midnight freight, and you'll be there by noon tomorrow."

Jova enjoyed the rest of the evening with his two new friends and met some of the other hoboes in the camp. Around each campfire, he was offered some small morsel of food—a slice of dried bread, a cup of squirrel stew, a few spoonfuls of creamed corn from a can. As midnight approached, Daniel and Jack walked with him up to the train tracks. Lacy clouds drifted across the moon and painted the landscape in ever-changing patterns of silver and charcoal.

"Now, you see that water tower?" said Daniel, pointing to a huge, dark tank on stilts that stood beside the train track. "When the train stops to take on water, you just run up and climb into one of the open boxcars. Make yourself to home, and you'll be there by noon."

Jova looked up and down the tracks, two lines of shiny cold steel that divided the countryside for as far as one could see. "You mean I don't have to pay? I had to pay when I got on the train before."

"That's 'cause it was a passenger train. This here's a freight. If the car is empty, it's because they're takin' it somewhere to fill it up. Might as well hitch a ride when you can."

"But how will I know when I'm at the right stop?" asked Jova, still concerned about the details of the plan.

Daniel looked at Jack and shrugged. "Well, what do ya say, Jack? How *is* he supposed to know when he's reached Fort Wayne if he ain't never been there before?"

"Ask someone."

"There you go," said Daniel, patting Jova on the shoulder. "You just gotta ask someone."

That idea seemed a little shaky to Jova. "What if no one is around?"

The two hoboes looked at each other. "He's got a point," muttered Jack. "It wouldn't do to ask a trainman. Could get his head cracked that way."

"What do you mean?" asked Jova.

Jack held up his hands as though he were surrendering to the law. "Look, son. Ain't no harm in ridin' in empty boxcars.

They gotta move 'em from one point to another anyway. Don't take nothin' away from nobody. It's not like it was stealin' or nothin' . . . but some train officials don't approve. So we stay clear of 'em best we can, and then there's no trouble."

"Oh, come on, Jack. Why don't you just go with the kid? Keep him company. You could use a change of scene."

"Me? You been in this here hobo camp longer than me. Why don't you go with him?"

Daniel considered. "Why don't we both go?"

"It's a deal." The two men shook hands and slapped Jova on the back.

When the freight arrived and stood idly on the tracks taking on water, Jova's new friends found an empty car with a pile of straw at one end and pulled him on board. When they were settled warmly into the straw, Daniel dug in his pockets and came up with two slightly bruised apples. "Here, rations for the road." He took a bite and passed one to Jova.

The train jerked. It was no sooner rolling at full speed than Jova fell fast asleep.

CHAPTER 12

PRINCE KABOO

Daniel's tattered boot nudged Jova's leg. "Wake up, man."

Bright sunshine silhouetted the old cowboy standing in the open door of the boxcar. He swayed slightly back and forth in time with the clickety-clack of the train wheels. "Time to wake up. We're almost there."

Just then the mournful train whistle sounded from the engine.

"This is Fort Wayne?" asked Jova as he rubbed his eyes and brushed the straw from his hair.

"Be there in about ten minutes. You been sleepin' 'round the clock. Now, you best be gettin' up 'cause we're gonna jump off before this train stops in the train yard."

Jack, who had been standing in the shadows, added, "That way we won't attract the attention of any trainmen."

"I already jumped from a moving train once," said Jova, shaking his head, "and it was no easy thing."

"Don't worry," said Jack. "We'll be goin' slow enough that even old Daniel with his bum legs can make it."

As they stood in the open door of the boxcar watching the countryside race past, Daniel turned to him and said, "Couldn't help noticin' that scar ya have in your forehead running up from your nose. Musta been a pretty nasty injury. What happened?—if ya don't mind me askin'."

Jova touched his fingers to the scar. "Oh, that was no accident. It's a tribal tattoo. It shows I'm from the Kru people. Prince Kaboo will have one, too. But if you see any men with three marks on their right cheek, stay away from them. They are Grebo warriors and not nice."

"Hmm. I knew a feller who had three scars on his left cheek," mused Daniel. "He wasn't very nice neither—'course word was that he got those three scars from a mean old bear he tangled with one night."

The train slowed to enter the town. When it was not going much faster than a person could walk, they dropped to the ground and hurried down the bank into a thicket.

"Now," said Jack once the train had passed, "if you head right along this trail, it will come to a road. Turn left, and you'll be in Fort Wayne in no time."

"Where are you going?" asked Jova.

"Oh, there's a hobo camp back this other way. We'll find some friends there. You'd be welcome to stay with us if you don't find your university."

Jova smiled. "Thank you very much. But I must find Taylor University. I must find Prince Kaboo."

Waving good-bye to his friends, Jova eagerly hiked along the road until he came to the small city of Fort Wayne. Could he really be so close to finding Prince Kaboo? He had never seen a university before, so when he passed a large wooden building on West Main Street, he went to the door and stepped inside. Inside, his eyes widened. He'd never seen such a strange sight.

The building was like a huge barn with a wooden floor, and on the floor several gaily dressed young people were gliding past on strange shoes with small wheels under them. They all seemed to be going around and around in a large oval, accompanied by music being pumped out by a man sitting at a large wooden box in the corner. He was using his hands and feet to make the music change notes.

"Is this Taylor University?" Jova asked a man who was sweeping the floor.

"The university?" laughed the man. "Does this look like a classroom to you?"

"I don't know," said Jova. "I am from Africa, but I am looking for Taylor University."

"Africa? Say, you wouldn't be Sammy Morris, would you?" said the man as he leaned on his broom, eyeing Jova. "No, of course not. You couldn't be. You're too young and much too dirty. Besides he *goes* to Taylor University, so he would know where it is."

"You know him?" said Jova eagerly.

"No. But one night there was a revival service right here in this roller-skating rink, and he was here. People came from all over the county just to be prayed for by him, so I hear. But I didn't come. I had to take care of my sick grandma. Maybe I should have brought her here. There was plenty of talk about him the next day. Some people claimed people got healed when he prayed—"

Eager to be on with his quest now that he was so close to his goal, Jova broke in. "Excuse me, but could you just tell me how to get to the university?"

"Oh, sure," said the talkative janitor. "But you're lucky you got here in time. They're going to move the university to Upland pretty soon. In fact, I heard that for the ground breaking, the railroads are fixin' to send special excursion trains down to Upland. Now, ain't that a kicker, going *down* to *Upland. Down* to *up*—get it?"

Getting more and more impatient with the man's chatter, Jova again broke in. "But where is the university now?"

"Well, if you keep going down this street . . ."

Once Jova had the basic idea of where to go, he excused himself and left before the man got started with another of his stories.

But as he was going out the door, the janitor called after him, "I'd advise you to clean up before you go to a university. You don't look presentable enough to be meeting educated people."

Jova took the man's advice and brushed himself off as well as he could, washing his face and hands in the St. Mary's River, which flowed through the town. When he came to some large buildings, he kept asking questions until he found the main office of the university. The white woman behind the desk smiled and told him that Samuel Morris was indeed a student there.

"However," said the woman briskly, "he's not on campus right now. He has taken ill and is in the hospital."

The woman must have seen the boy's shoulders sag. Her voice softened, and she called to another student and asked if he would show Jova to St. Joseph Hospital.

Jova was trembling as he walked down the long hall to

Kaboo's room. He had come so far . . . could he really have found Prince Kaboo after all this time?

He knocked on the door and heard a soft voice respond in English, "Come in."

There, lying on the white pillow, was the ebony face of an African about twenty years old. He had well-balanced features with strong cheek bones, bright eyes, and a square jaw. His eyes were clear, but he looked thin, and as he rolled his head to see who his guest was, Jova could see that he was weak.

And then Jova had a shock. There was no Kru tattoo on the young man's forehead!

As he stood there uncertainly, the figure in the hospital bed looked at him closely, and then his eyes widened in surprise. "Jova?" the young man said, a great smile splitting his dark face. "How did you get here? I am so glad to see you!"

"Prince Kaboo!" Jova cried. "It is you! But . . . but, you do not have a Kru tattoo on your forehead. I thought . . ." Jova was so overcome with joy and relief that he couldn't continue.

Kaboo smiled weakly. "Do you forget that I was taken by the Grebos as pawn before I went through the bush-devil school, so I never received my tribal mark. But . . . that is a long time ago. How did you get here? Why have you come?"

Jova finally found his voice. "I have come to get you," he said huskily. He had found his prince at last.

With tears, the two embraced and soon began to fire questions back and forth in their native language. Jova explained all about following Kaboo and the strange light through the jungle. He confessed his lack of courage in not going down into the white city the first time. "But I am older and braver now," he said, lifting his chin. "And our tribe is in great need of you. I am sorry to bring you sad news, but the king, your father, is dying. Our people need you to come back and be their king so we will not appear weak to the Grebos."

Kaboo looked out the window of his hospital room with a far-off look in his eyes. "I want to go back," he said finally, "but I have been talking to my Father, and He has not promised me that I will return. I must keep speaking to Him."

Jova was puzzled. "What do you mean? How can you talk to your father? Isn't he still in our village in Africa?"

"If he is still alive, yes. But I was speaking about my heavenly Father, God in heaven. I talk to Him all the time. He helps me in all things. . . . Except," he said after a bewildered pause, "I do not understand why He has not made me well. Last winter when my ears froze—oh, it gets so cold here. You would not believe it, Jova!—but when my ears froze they hurt very much, and when I prayed, my Father made the hurting quit right away. But now I can't seem to get well. I don't understand it."

"You'll be well soon," Jova said confidently. "And then we'll go back to Africa where it is warm and pleasant."

The reunion was interrupted by another visitor, a pleasant-faced middle-aged white man whom Kaboo introduced to Jova as Professor Stemen. "One of my favorite teachers," Kaboo smiled.

After hearing the amazing story of Jova's quest to find his missing prince, the professor immediately invited Jova to stay at his house, which was right across the street from the hospital. When Jova finally left Prince Kaboo's hospital room to get a much-needed meal at the professor's house, Professor Stemen said to Jova, "I'm glad you have come. We are worried about Sammy. He's just not getting well like he should."

Jova looked up from his bowl of hot soup at the professor's grave face. "What do you mean?"

The professor leaned both arms on the table, worry lines

etched in his handsome face. "The doctors think Sammy has dropsy. They say he could be facing heart or kidney failure—probably stemming from the cruelty he suffered years ago when he was a captive. They . . . they fear he may not live."

CHAPTER 13

TAKING HOME A KING

When Jova came to visit Kaboo the next day, the prince was smiling. "Last night," he said, "I talked to my Father, and now I understand why I am not getting better, and I am happy."

"Good," said Jova, remembering that talking to his Father meant that Kaboo had been praying to God. He was becoming more and more impressed with this praying.

The evening before, as Jova had sat at the dinner table, Professor Stemen told him about how Kaboo's faith had virtually saved the university. Just a few months earlier, the university was on the verge of closing. Its money had run out, and the board of trustees had decided to close its doors. They could no longer afford the cost of their buildings in Fort Wayne. "But Sammy," said the professor—Jova still found it hard to think of Kaboo as Sammy—"felt we should pray. And so we did. Then at the next meeting of the board, one of the members suggested that if we couldn't afford to remain in Fort Wayne, we ought to move the school to Upland, Indiana. That seemed impossible, but he said that he would look for a cheaper location and financial support. Within just one day, enough money had been raised to purchase new land and move the school. It was remarkable!"

Jova heard similar stories from other people about how God had answered Kaboo's prayers. So he was eager to hear what Kaboo had heard from "his Father" about his sickness.

Kaboo pulled himself up in his bed until he was in a sitting position with pillows stuffed behind his back. "I am so happy," he said. "I have seen the angels. They are coming for me soon. The light my Father in heaven sent to save me when I was hanging helpless on that cross in Africa was for a purpose. I was saved for a purpose. Now I have fulfilled that purpose. My work here is done."

"That is good!" said Jova. "So now we can go back to Africa?"

Kaboo shook his head, and a slight sadness briefly dimmed his smile. "No. I will not see Africa again. My work here on earth is finished."

Jova stared at him blankly as the meaning of Kaboo's words slowly sank in. Could it be that his prince was going to die? No! Not at a time like this. He was young and his people needed him.

"But what about a king?" pleaded Jova. "I have come all this way on a quest for a new king. What will our people do?"

"Yes," said Prince Kaboo, the old smile returning fully, "they *do* need a new king, and you are just the one to take them one. My Father told me you are to go back and take King Jesus to them. He is the One they really need. I was preparing to do it myself, but . . . I will not be making the journey."

Jova had heard about Jesus from the missionaries in Monrovia. He had heard about Him from the ship captain and Stephen Merritt in New York. And now, here at Taylor University, the name of Jesus came up often. But no one had clearly explained to him who this Jesus was. So how could he take Him back to Africa to be King?

"I have heard of this Jesus, but who is He?" he asked bluntly.

Kaboo nodded his head slowly in understanding. "You have not heard the Good News of the Gospel. Well, I will tell you." The young prince's eyes grew bright.

"God, our Father in heaven, is the Creator of all things. He made the earth, the sky, all life, and every human being. He is only good, but, as you know, people do bad things. They hurt each other. They go to war.

"This makes our Father very sad. He is sad not only because we hurt one another and make our lives miserable but because, in doing bad things, we separate ourselves from Him and His goodness. But our Father loves us so much that He wanted to rescue us from this evil."

Kaboo looked intensely at Jova and continued. "How do we try to make something right when someone has done a very bad thing?" he asked.

Frowning, Jova thought hard. "I don't know. I guess we make them pay for it."

"Give me an example," urged Kaboo.

Jova thought some more. "Well, like the Grebos. When they attack and kill our people, we make them to pay to settle the score . . . if we can."

"Exactly. But does that ever solve anything? Is the score ever really settled?"

"No," admitted Jova. "They get mad and attack us back again."

"But what if someone else paid for their evil, someone who was completely innocent?"

Jova had never thought of that idea. "No one is so good as that. Even we Kru people do evil sometimes."

"You are right. You would need someone perfect. God is perfectly good, and so is His Son, Jesus Christ. God sent Jesus from heaven down to earth to pay the price for all our evil deeds. Jesus came to live on earth long, long ago. But we killed Him and did not want to hear His message of God's love."

"The Kru people killed God's Son?" asked Jova in astonishment. He had never heard such a story.

"It wasn't just the Kru people. All people had a part in killing Him because we are all evil.

"Now this is the great mystery," Kaboo went on, his eyes shining as he leaned forward in his bed. "God said that if we would believe that it was really His Son who came to die in our place, He would forgive us, and the score would be settled. That's the Gospel."

"That's it?" asked Jova, surprised that it was so simple.

"Yes. God has promised that if we believe He sent Jesus to save us from our sins, we will be forgiven. Then we become God's children and He our Father. And Jesus is our Brother and King."

Jova thought for a moment, then cocked his head to the side as he phrased his question. "But how do we know that Jesus was God's Son? That's a big thing to say, but where is the proof?"

"You ask a good question, but there is an even better answer, one that will amaze you as it has amazed people for ages. We know that Jesus was God's Son because God raised Him from the dead. Jesus was buried in the ground for three days, but then God brought Him back to life."

"He was moving around, walking, breathing, speaking?"

"Yes, and hundreds of people saw Him. It says so in the Bible."

"That's . . . that's a real miracle! He must be a wonderful King," Jova said, slowly nodding his head as he accepted his prince's report. Then he asked another question. "But how can making Jesus our King stop the war with the Grebos? What if they don't believe?"

"It would be good," said Kaboo, "if the Grebos believed—and we should tell them about Jesus—but even if they don't believe, we don't have to continue the war. If God has forgiven us because Jesus paid the price for our evil, then we can forgive the Grebos because Jesus paid the price for their evil, too. We don't have to try to get even. Jesus has settled the score."

Jova's head was swimming. "This is all so new," he said faintly.

"I know it is. Just kneel down here by my bed and let me pray for you that God's Spirit would open your mind and help you believe."

Jova knelt down, and Kaboo put his hand on Jova's shoulder and began talking to his Father. As Jova listened, he, too, wanted to be able to call God "Father" and thank Him for sending Jesus.

When he mentioned this desire to Kaboo, Kaboo clapped his hands and said, "Then you *do* believe. Of course you can talk to God. Tell *Him* you believe. Give Him thanks. Say whatever you want to say. He is your Father now, too."

It was so simple . . . but very real.

Some time later, Jova stood up and with a smile of joy on his face said, "Now, together we can go back to our people. You can be their king and we can tell them about Jesus Christ."

Kaboo shook his head. "You do not understand," he explained. "I am dying, so I cannot go with you. I prayed long and hard for our people, and your coming is the answer to my prayer. They do not need me as king. They need Jesus as their King. You must do what I cannot do and go tell them."

"But . . . I cannot. I am too young."

"You came all this way on a quest to become a man. Now is your chance."

"But I do not understand everything about Jesus. I have only just now asked Him to save me. You have been here studying. I will need help."

"Then ask our Father for help, but first promise me that you will go back and take home King Jesus."

Jova felt weak. How could he accomplish such a great task? But as he looked into Kaboo's steady eyes, he nodded. "I promise," he whispered.

The next morning, Jova was helping Professor Stemen mow his front lawn directly across the street from St. Joseph Hospital when they heard a voice calling them. They looked up and saw Kaboo waving from the window of his hospital room. "Don't work him too hard, Professor Stemen!" he called.

Professor Stemen laughed and waved back. "I was just showing Jova how to use this machine," he called up to Kaboo.

"It's better than a dozen goats," called Jova, grinning. "And it leaves no messes."

They all laughed as Kaboo withdrew from the open window.

A few minutes later, one of the nurses hurried out of the hospital and ran over to Jova and Professor Stemen. "You'd better come," she said urgently. "Sammy has just had a sudden relapse."

Jova followed on Professor Stemen's heels as they ran into the hospital and up to Kaboo's room. They stopped at the door. Kaboo lay still on his bed with a peaceful expression on his face. His Bible was open by his side, but he was dead.

On May 12, 1893, at the age of twenty-one, Prince Kaboo, known in America as Samuel Morris, had gone home to his heavenly Father.

The funeral for Samuel Morris was held at the Berry Street Methodist Church, where he had been a member. So many people came that hundreds had to stand out in the street.

During the service, the minister asked Jova to say a few words.

As he stepped forward to speak in his broken English, the number of strange people facing him seemed uncountable, but Jova did not lose courage as he spoke in a clear voice.

"I am going back to my Kru people," he said. "The young man you knew as Samuel Morris was Prince Kaboo to me, the only son of our old and dying king. I came to bring Kaboo back because our people need a new king. Now Kaboo cannot go with me because he has gone to his Father in Heaven."

Jova stopped as a sob gripped his throat. Then he continued.

"So I promised Prince Kaboo that I would take King Jesus back to our people. But I need help. I cannot read the Bible. I do not understand very much about the Gospel. But when I talked to my Father in heaven—to Kaboo's Father and your Father—He told me to ask you. So I am asking: Who will come with me?"

There was a long silence. And then, first one . . . and then another . . . and then another student stood up and said, "I will go with you." Soon, several students had volunteered to go as missionaries to Africa to do the work that their beloved classmate had not been able to finish.

After the funeral, Jova walked near the head of the procession to Lindenwood Cemetery where Kaboo was to be buried. Later, Professor Stemen told him that the long parade of people who followed was the largest the Fort Wayne cemetery had ever seen. And even more people lined the streets through which they moved.

With tears in his eyes and thoughts of Prince Kaboo swirling in his mind, Jova looked up from the cobblestones in the street. Without realizing it, his eyes focused on two African men standing on the curb. One was tall and partially bald. The other was short with a bowler hat. Both had three scars on their right cheeks.

Shock sucked the breath out of Jova, and he felt dizzy. He blinked, hoping his mind was playing a trick on him. But the men didn't go away. They were grinning at him—an evil, triumphant grin. How they had found their way to Fort Wayne, Indiana, Jova could not imagine, but there they were—confident that they had won. Prince Kaboo was dead and would not return to Africa to claim his father's throne.

But had they won?

Jova stared at them as he slowly moved along with the funeral procession. No. A quiet confidence settled on him. His quest was a success. He was returning to his people with a new king. He was bringing them King Jesus!

MORE ABOUT SAMUEL MORRIS

Prince Kaboo, later called Samuel Morris, was born in 1872 in the West African country of Liberia. His father was king of his Kru tribe at a time when there was ongoing warfare with the neighboring Grebos.

Being a king in this part of Africa did not mean being the ruler of a whole country or even of all the people of a specific tribe. Kaboo's father was probably the ruler of a large village or possibly several villages in one region. There were undoubtedly other Kru kings in other parts of Liberia. And no single monarch united all the Kru people.

In the whole country, the Kru people far outnumbered the Grebos, but in the region where Kaboo lived, the Grebos had repeatedly defeated his people.

When a defeated king could not pay the war taxes, it was common to surrender someone the king valued in "pawn" until the debt could be paid. This happened the first time with Kaboo when he was a small child, and his father was able to redeem him rather quickly. However, when he was a young adolescent, war broke out again. His people were defeated, and he was placed in pawn a second time. That provides the occasion for the beginning of this story.

This time, Kaboo's father was unable to pay his ransom, and it appears that the Grebos, intent on crushing the Krus forever, kept raising the price.

Kaboo's imprisonment and miraculous escape—including the blinding light and voice from heaven—are recorded in more than one biographical source. In addition to Kaboo's report to missionaries in Monrovia (and later to Dr. T. C. Reade, president of Taylor University), there was at least one other eyewitness. Another young Kru, later named Henry O'Neil or Henry O. Neil, was a slave in the Grebo village. He also saw the light and heard the voice that freed Kaboo. He did not, however, as this book fictionalizes, follow Kaboo through the jungle and witness the nightly guiding light.

A few years later when Henry O'Neil came to Monrovia, he confirmed to missionaries the miracle of Kaboo's release. And in 1892 when Kaboo was a student at Taylor University, he arranged to raise money to bring Henry O'Neil to the United States to receive ministerial training.

Following Kaboo's arrival at the mission station in Monrovia, there were many witnesses to the remarkable deeds of faith that thereafter accompanied his life.

He talked his way onto a sailing ship bound for New York in order to go to America to study God's Word and learn more about the Holy Spirit. The ship was full of cutthroat sailors who hated him as a black person and were just as eager to do each other in. But Sammy (he had taken on a new name by this time), not only intervened to make peace on board the ship but won their friendship, prayed for healing from their diseases, and led most of the crew to the Lord.

In New York, Sammy brought revival to Stephen Merritt's mission and to various local churches in which he preached.

At Taylor University, he did much the same. Soon the

newspapers were carrying reports of this remarkable African young man who was instigating revival wherever he went—on the campus, in the local churches of Fort Wayne, and even in revival meetings conducted in such public places as a roller-skating rink.

In the winter of 1892–1893, the school was nearly ready to close its doors for lack of funds to pay its bills. But Sammy Morris's example of faith not only made him a leader among his fellow students, but inspired a discouraged faculty and administration. The board of trustees decided to use the Samuel Morris Faith Fund to raise enough money to move the school from Fort Wayne to Upland, Indiana. It was just the thing to preserve the university.

And though Samuel's death seemed like an untimely tragedy, God used it to inspire a substantial number of Taylor students to go to the mission field, many to Africa in Sammy's stead. There was even a Taylor University Bible School established in Africa.

But perhaps the most typical tribute to Prince Kaboo was paid by the captain of the tramp ship on which Sammy came to New York. When he learned that Sammy had died on May 12, 1893, he was so overcome with emotion that he could not speak for some time. Then he said that most of the old crew were still on board and eager to find out about their beloved hero and minister. After all, he had changed life on that ship. Before he came aboard, no one had ever prayed out loud, but after Sammy shared the Gospel with them, they became like one family—a family that could talk to their Father.

FOR FURTHER READING

Baldwin, Lindley. Samuel Morris. Minneapolis: Bethany House Publishers, 1942.

Evans, A. R. Sammy Morris. Grand Rapids, MI: Zondervan Publishing House, 1958.

Konkel, Wilbur. Jungle Gold: The Amazing Story of Sammy Morris. London: Pillar of Fire Press, 1966.

Masa, Jorge O. The Angel in Ebony. Upland, IN: Taylor University Press, 1928.

Reade, Thaddeus C. Samuel Morris. Upland, IN: Taylor University, 1896.

Stocker, Fern Neal. Sammy Morris. Chicago: Moody Press, 1986.

EXILED TO THE RED RIVER

CHIEF SPOKANE GARRY

Authors' Note

We tell the stories in our other thirty-nine TRAILBLAZER BOOKS from the perspective of a young person who encounters the adult hero featured in the book. In this book, however, the main character is the hero of the book because Chief Spokane Garry's incredible ministry and contributions were largely accomplished while he was still a teenager, either sixteen or eighteen years of age.

In addition to dramatizing various details, we have departed from known facts in the following respects: In 1822, Fort Gibraltar's name was changed to Fort Garry. We, however, retained its earlier name to avoid confusion with our hero's name.

Because we do not know the name of the Red River missionary teacher who worked most closely with Garry and Pelly, we have called him Arnold Worthington. Similarly, we gave the man from the Hudson's Bay Company at Fort Assinboine the name of Captain McKay.

Pelly's horse accident did not occur on his trip home but after he arrived back among his people. His injuries were severe, but he still returned with Garry to the Red River Mission in the spring of 1830 to deliver five more young men—all the sons of chiefs—for Christian training. It was while in Red River at the home of Rev. Jones on Easter, 1831, that he succumbed to his injuries.

Finally, Garry learned of his father's death before leaving the Red River Mission, probably in the spring of 1828, by way of trappers returning from the Columbia region, rather than after he arrived home.

CONTENTS

CHAPTER 1

CIRCLING RAVEN'S PROPHECY

Like a dank fog, the sickness crept from lodge to lodge through the whole village. Even in the other villages and other tribes on the Columbia Plateau, which was cupped between the Rocky Mountains and the Cascades, both women and children, old people and great warriors had died from the smallpox in 1782. Those who had recovered displayed rough scars on their faces as though they had done battle with the great porcupine.

But Circling Raven, the shaman, or prophet, among the Spokane people, had faith that *Quilent-sat-men,* the Creator of All, would hear his prayers and send healing. Maybe a few evil people would die, but the great God Most High certainly would save those who worshiped Him and lived a righteous life.

Quiet moaning like the winter wind threading its way through the pines seeped from young Chief Illim-Spokanee's lodge as Circling Raven approached it. The lodge was fifty feet long and fifteen wide, made of limber poles bent in a series of arches and covered with buffalo hides and tightly woven mats of tule reeds.

He tossed back the door flap and stepped in, then stood still for a few moments to allow his eyes to adjust to the dim light coming through the smoke holes in the roof. In the far corner, bending over a sleeping mat, he made out the forms of three women. Suddenly the moaning erupted into a wail of trilling agony that Circling Raven knew was the death cry. Had he come too late? No evil people lived in *this* lodge. The chief and all his relatives were good people, but as he drew nearer, he saw that the sickness had taken the chief's mother.

She was an older woman, about the same age as Circling Raven. Maybe it was her time, but Circling Raven didn't feel like *his* years were over. He tried to comfort the family by praying long and loudly that God would receive the woman's spirit. But even as he prayed, doubts bubbled up inside him like the pungent sulfur water from the hot springs. If God did not hear his prayers and drive away the sickness, how could he believe that God would answer his prayers that the dead would find the path to heaven?

That evening at council, Two Claws, a brash young brave, said, "My woman thinks evil spirits have come to live along the Spokane River and Circling Raven's medicine is not strong enough to drive them away. She says we should move the village."

Circling Raven did not answer. He did not even look up from watching the trail of red ants that marched past his foot. The Spokane people were semi-nomadic, so the idea of moving was not unusual, but this spot along the river, just below the falls, had been a favorite campground year after year. The idea of giving it up because it was unfit would be like abandoning one's mother.

"Where would we go?" asked Chief Illim-Spokanee. "All the tribes have the sickness."

"We could go to the lands of the Blackfeet," said Two Claws. He laughed. "Then we could hunt buffalo whenever we pleased."

"And die at the hands of the Blackfeet," said Chief Illim-Spokanee.

Two Claws snorted. "You sound like a white rabbit. We have at least a thousand people and many braves. We could defend ourselves."

"You are too young to remember anything more than the raiding parties the Blackfeet send to harass us when we enter their lands to hunt the buffalo. But they are a powerful nation."

"Perhaps they have only a few braves, just enough for some raiding parties."

"You are too young," agreed one of the older chiefs.

"And you are old—maybe too old," snorted Two Claws. He kept trying to talk of leaving the camp beside the river, but no one paid attention.

No one, that is, except Circling Raven. The shaman began to wonder whether Two Claws might be right—though not about leaving the Spokane. He knew moving would not protect them, but maybe his medicine was weak. As the days went by, he prayed harder, but the villagers continued to die. Did God no longer care about them?

Then came the day when Circling Raven's own son got sick. Circling Raven prayed all night. He helped his wife nurse the small eight-year-old, cooling the child's fevered brow with a damp deerskin rag and singing softly to him when the boy cried out in his restless sleep. Two days went by, then three, but the fever did not leave the lad until early one morning when it stole the boy's spirit right out of his body, and he was no more.

Circling Raven ripped the flap off the door to his lodge as he ran out. "Why? Why? Why?" He shook his fist at the sky. "If the righteous die while evil men live, why should we continue to follow our laws? Let us live like the animals! Why care about God?" He began tearing down the wooden racks that held the drying salmon over smoking beds of coals. "Here, brother dogs, eat our fish," he yelled, tossing a fish to the dogs that were barking at his wild antics. "And when the winter comes we will eat you. What difference does it make? Or maybe we will eat each other and simply die like dogs!"

Chief Illim-Spokanee came out of his lodge and watched Circling Raven vent his rage and grief until the shaman fell to the ground exhausted and began to weep, not caring whether the other men of the village thought him an old woman. Then the chief came and sat down beside the older prophet. He rocked back and forth like a sapling swaying in the breeze, humming a mournful chant in tune with the shaman's broken heart. The chief stayed with him until the sun was high overhead, and then he said, "My brother, you must not give up your faith. You have just lost your way because of the sickness. It may not be killing your body, but your spirit has the fever."

Circling Raven threw a handful of dust in the air. "I no longer believe in God."

"Then why do you yell at Him? Do you yell at the wind? Do you yell at the trees? No. They cannot hear you. But you yell at God, so I do not think you have lost your faith altogether." The chief put his hand gently on the shaman's shoulder. "Take some time, my older brother; take some time. Climb Mount Spokane and pray and fast. See if you can't revive your spirit before it becomes twisted like the lone pine tree on Pine Bluff."

Circling Raven thought about the chief's words. He could feel his spirit becoming gnarled and ugly like the lightning-blazed pine. He nodded his head. "I will go. I will go to the mountain and pray until God hears me or until I die crying out to Him. For what other reason is there to live if He does not hear our cry and uphold us?"

The next morning, Circling Raven arose before dawn and prepared for his journey to Mount Spokane. His wife handed him a leather pouch of pemmican and smoked salmon, but Circling Raven waved it away and left the village without a word.

He had walked forty-five miles by the time he arrived at the peak of Mount Spokane the next afternoon. He was the only human on the mountain, and even though snow still lay on the ground and he had no buffalo robe, he did not feel the cold as he sat in the mouth of a shallow cave. Instead of seeking his own comfort, he cried out, "O *Quilent-sat-men*, Great God Most High, Creator of All, why have you forsaken your people, the Spokane? If we have displeased you, if we have sinned against you in any way, please forgive us. If I have offended you with my yelling, if I have broken any of your laws, please forgive me."

For four days and four nights, Circling Raven fasted and prayed in this manner. And then . . . God gave him a vision, a vision as big as the sky.

A voice rolled back and forth between the clouds like

thunder. "Why do you cry? Your son is happy here with me, so you should have faith." In the vision, Circling Raven saw his own lodge with smoke coming out of all three roof holes. Healthy children ran around the village without scars on their faces, and in the meadow by the Spokane River, young boys raced their horses and made bets on who could ride faster. And then he saw two men get out of a canoe. They wore strange clothes and had white skin. In their hands they carried a pack of leaves bound together and wrapped in black leather. God's voice crackled: "Pay attention to the marks on those leaves. They are the Leaves of Life."

Circling Raven leaped to his feet and started to run down the mountain, so excited about the vision that he tripped over roots and rocks in his path so many times that his hands and knees were bloody when he arrived at the village. He did not wait to call a council meeting but blurted out his report, describing the vision even though only women and children gathered to hear him. Finally one of the old chiefs interrupted and urged him to come into the council lodge and allow time for the other chiefs and elders to gather.

When all had assembled, they listened to Circling Raven's report and passed the pipe from one to another. But Circling Raven did not tell the last part of his vision, the part about the sad things that would happen later when more white men followed the first few who carried the Leaves of Life. He did not want to frighten his people.

When the prophet finished his report, everyone nodded and passed the pipe around the circle. It went around twice until the oldest chief said, "Could this prophecy be similar to the one given by Shining Shirt to our neighbors, the Salish? They call God *Amotkan,* He Who Lives on Most High. But I think they worship *Quilent-sat-men* just as we do. They just know

Him by a different name. Shining Shirt said to pray to God every day and do only what is right and honest, and someday men with pale skins and long black shirts would come from the East and teach the truth."

There was silence as the pipe went around the circle again. "This is good," some muttered. "We should pray every day, too. We should obey God's instruction." They continued to pass the pipe from one to the other and stared into the fire until only a few glowing coals remained. Then one by one they slipped out of the council lodge and walked to their own homes, careful not to awaken the children as they crawled into their buffalo robes.

The next day they assured their people that Circling Raven had received a true vision. God was good, and He had not forgotten them even though many still suffered from the sickness.

In time, the smallpox epidemic passed, and life in the Spokane nation returned to its normal routine of hunting, fishing, gathering, and horse racing. Even though Circling Raven still missed the son he lost to the sickness, he was able to grow old peacefully and take joy in the healthy children born to his relatives, and in this way his lodge became full again so that smoke rose from all three holes in the roof. Always at the tribal council he urged his people to live righteous lives of honesty and faith in the Creator and to pray daily for His blessing.

And then one day the earth shook and the sky became dark, and dry snow began to fall from the heavens. It covered the grass and the rocks. It caught in the people's noses and made their eyes burn so that they had to sip water continually to keep from coughing, and they had to calm their horses so they would not stampede.

The year was 1800, and the dry snow was ash from the volcanic eruption of the Smoking Mountain (later called Mount St. Helens), hundreds of miles to the west where fire dragons lived. The Spokane people began to cry and tremble. "The world is ending! The world is ending! Everything is lost!"

Circling Raven, however, remembered his vision. "People, people, do not fear. This is not the end," he said as he gathered the people together in the choking cloud of dust. "This cannot be the end because the white men have not come yet."

Slowly they calmed down. He was, after all, a good prophet who had always encouraged them to live a righteous life. Again he reminded them of his vision and pointed out how some of it had already come true. Their tribe had recovered from the sickness and was prospering in every way. God was good!

But he felt badly that he had not had the courage to tell his whole vision. So he cleared his throat and said, "There was one more part to my vision. After the white men come with their Leaves of Life that show us the path to heaven, our lives will change in ways we cannot even imagine. They will show us new ways to make a living, and all wars between us will cease."

A murmur of approval spread through the crowd as various people coughed to clear their throats. Circling Raven held up his hand, indicating he had more to say. "This has not yet happened, so the world cannot be ending. However, after the white men with the Leaves of Life come, other white men will come who will make slaves of us. Then our world will end, but not with ashes. We will simply be overrun by the white men as though by grasshoppers. When this happens, we should not fight, as it would only create unnecessary bloodshed."

The people were silent, except for occasional coughing. Slowly and by family groups, they went back to their lodges. Maybe, thought some, if they could just get the Leaves of Life, they could please God and He would spare them from being overrun by the white men. Maybe they could learn to live together in peace with the white men.

CHAPTER 2

THE SALMON RUN

Eleven winters after the "dry snow," a child was born in the tent of Chief Illim-Spokanee. Later he would be called Spokane Garry. The baby's mother died giving him birth, so even though he had several older brothers and sisters, he would be the last son of the chief, the baby in the family. His siblings cared for him as best they could, but it was never like growing up with a loving mother, dedicated to meeting his every need.

In 1806, five years before the child was born, three Spokane braves had been down the Snake River where they had met white men traveling from the east in large canoes. Their leaders were called Lewis and Clark. So it was true, the braves said when they returned, that such pale-skinned people existed, and there was even a black man among them.

And about the time Garry was born, white men actually came to Spokane country, just as Circling Raven had prophesied, but they had not brought the Leaves of Life. Instead, they built a big log trading post on the flat land just above where the Little Spokane flows into the Spokane River. The white traders were named Finan McDonald—a tall man with blue eyes—and Jacob Finlay, a shorter man who was part Indian.

Could these men with pale faces be the ones to fulfill Circling Raven's prophecy? Just in case, Chief Illim moved his lodge to a site just across the river from the white men's trading post where he could wait and watch, even though he knew that the spring rains sometimes flooded the flats on both sides of the river. Other Indians followed Illim's example until a new village formed on the site. Day after day, as little Garry toddled around the camp, the old chief sat in front of his lodge and watched the white men across the river, but he never saw them pray or worship.

From time to time, Chief Illim went over to the trading post and sat around, asking the white men about what they knew of God, but they only waved a hand in dismissal and changed the subject. "How about trading some of your old dried-out salmon or mangy furs or even a horse for some of these sharp knives and bright beads that we brought? After all, you don't need all those horses." Chief Illim traded when it pleased him and walked away with a grunt when it didn't, but he suspected that the white men knew more about God than they admitted, so he watched.

As the seasons passed into years, young Spokane Garry grew strong and daring, always trying to do whatever his older brothers and sisters were doing. Before he could walk without stumbling, he tried to climb the stately ponderosa pine trees around the village. When other children his age were making mud pies along the riverbank, he waded into the clear pools to chase the elusive trout. When he should have been content to play tag with the dogs in the village, he tried to find a stump to stand on so he could climb onto the back of a pony. And with every new thing, the other children followed. His father nodded in satisfaction. "He will make a great chief someday."

Tribes from around the area called the trading post "Spokane House," and the goods they brought to trade made the Spokane tribe, as well as the white men, rich. But wealth did not satisfy the old chief. He was looking for God, and so in the evenings, around the fire, he told the old stories to keep alive the hope of his people.

Little Garry was always a ready listener. "Father, tell us about the Leaves of Life that the white men were supposed to bring," he often begged. But after Chief Illim recited the old prophecies, the other men around the fire wanted to talk about whether their world would soon come to an end now that the white men had come. Once, an Indian from the great water far to the west, beyond the smoking mountain where the fire dragons lived, stopped at their village. He said he had seen many palefaces. They came from across the sea in great canoes with white wings, but they were only interested in trading for furs and did not build villages or even a log house like the trading post.

Everyone nodded and leaned back in relief. If the white men were not building villages, then they were not planning to stay and therefore couldn't be too dangerous . . . at least not yet.

In 1824, when Garry was thirteen years old, he decided that he definitely wanted to go on the buffalo hunt that fall. The trip east to the land of the Blackfeet was dangerous, and only able-bodied warriors and the strongest women were allowed to go. Garry knew the Blackfeet might attack at any time. But if he could kill a buffalo, that would prove he was a man.

Every day the boy went hunting across the river, climbing the steep crags of Lookout Mountain. Sometimes he stayed out two or three days until he shot a deer to bring back to camp to demonstrate what a good hunter he was becoming.

When Garry was not hunting, he rode one of his father's horses, wheeling it right and left as he raced across the meadow like a hummingbird darting from flower to flower while he clung to its bare back and drove his lance into the rotten stumps in the middle of the field. There was no doubt that he was skilled and strong, but could he kill a buffalo?

One day a new trader arrived at Spokane House, a man named Alexander Ross of the Hudson's Bay Company. In trade for the salmon and furs the Indians brought to him, he offered hunting sticks called rifles that could kill a bear at two hundred paces, steel traps that could catch the beaver in ponds without having to wait and watch, and warm blankets that were lighter and more colorful than the heavy buffalo robes. But the rifles were the prize! They would ensure a successful buffalo hunt and provide certain protection against the Blackfeet.

But in July, all the hunting stopped as the whole tribe prepared for the run of the red sockeye salmon up the Spokane River. The old traps were repaired and new willow baskets were woven. When the fish began fighting their way upstream, young and old went to the falls where the women set up their drying racks, and the men repaired the fishing platforms that stood precariously out over the swirling white water. Then they worked day and night catching, cleaning, and smoking the fish. Salmon were not only a prime source of food for the tribe, but they had become a great trading item with the whites and with other tribes that did not live on a river.

At dusk one evening, when the hills along the river were no more than silhouettes against the twilight glow of the blue-jay sky and the bonfires crackling along the shore, Chief Illim said to Garry, "Take a canoe down to Spokane House and ask Mr. Ross for four new knives. Some of the old ones are wearing out, and women need new ones to clean and cut the fish. Tell him we'll pay him what's fair later."

Garry was grateful to get off the shaky platform where the cold mist from the falls soaked him like a fall rain. He was so tired and his legs so numb that he could hardly keep his footing. It was only a mile to the trading post, but if he took his time, it would be dark before he returned. Maybe by then his father would tell everyone to take a rest. Garry couldn't imagine how such an old man could work day and night without a break.

Once away from the falls, the river smoothed out to reflect the sky. The roll of an occasional salmon disturbed its glassy surface, and sometimes Garry bumped one of the determined submarines with his paddle.

Bullfrogs trumpeted from the tules along the shore, and a muskrat swam to the middle of the river, turned, and drew a V that guided Garry downstream. Once around the gentle bend where the boy could see the white man's smoke thread its way straight up from the stone chimney of Spokane House, he spotted two strange canoes pulled up on the beach near the trading post. They were not Indian canoes.

He wanted to turn around immediately and paddle upriver to tell his father, but he had little to tell—only that strangers had come to the trading post. Drifting with the current, he silently approached the log house, nosing his canoe into a hiding place among some willows above the beach where the strangers' canoes sat, still piled high with supplies.

Garry climbed out and cautiously approached the building. From within he heard uproarious laughter and the strange words of the white man's tongue. At first he was afraid to go in, but his father would be wanting the knives. And he was curious. Who were these strangers? Summoning his courage, he pushed open the door.

"Ah, see here!" shouted Alexander Ross. "I have not scared 'em off. Here's one of the chief's whelps right now. Come in, boy, before a bear follers ya."

Garry stepped in and closed the heavy plank door, thick enough indeed to keep bears out if they caught a whiff of the trader's bacon and maple sugar. In the dim light cast by a small fire and a couple of oil lamps, he saw two dusty trappers, elbows on the table while they shoveled some kind of stew into their mouths. They glanced up at Garry only long enough to note that he was there before holding their bowls out to Ross, who stood to the side ready to serve more of the steaming mix from a large black pot.

"These here men are straight from Hudson's Bay Company," Ross said to Garry. "They tell me that Governor George Simpson of the Northern Division will be coming by here next spring—he's a big chief in the company—and your pa will want to parlay with him. Think you can remember to tell 'im all that?"

"Yes, sir," said Garry.

"Good, 'cause your father keeps pestering me 'bout religion, but Governor Simpson is the man who can tell him everything he'll ever want to know about God. Am I right, Jeb?" One of the trappers grunted as he put down his spoon and raised the stew bowl to his mouth to slurp in the contents faster. "So you tell the chief that," added Mr. Ross.

Garry nodded and backed toward the door. He kept nodding as he opened the door and left. In the gloom of the late twilight, he ran toward his canoe and headed upriver, paddling hard.

It was not until he saw the fires of the salmon camp that he remembered he had not gotten the knives his father had sent him to get.

CHAPTER 3

"TAKE A HUNDRED CHILDREN"

"But, Father, you *can't* say no," moaned Garry as he stood before his father outside their lodge. "I've been counting on this. I'm old enough. I'm ready. I'm a good hunter!"

Chief Illim-Spokanee sat on the old buffalo hide as though he were a stone, the weathered skin on his face sagging like melting beeswax. Even the wisp of smoke that blew into his watery eyes from the ashes of the morning fire did not cause him to blink. Finally he spoke. "You are becoming a good hunter, but I cannot let you go, my son. You are my youngest, my child of promise from the time of the great sickness. I cannot risk the Blackfeet killing you on the buffalo hunt."

"But if that's how you feel, you'll never let me go!"

As a young child, Garry had always loved hearing about the old days, how God had saved their people from being wiped out by the sickness and the prophecies spoken by Circling Raven about the leaves that would tell the way to heaven.

But lately it seemed his father could think of nothing else, as though his only reason for living was to see the fulfillment of the prophecy. "Maybe next spring when the great white chief, George Simpson, comes . . ." he would say, no matter what the subject was, as though the whole world waited on that visit. Garry regretted ever telling his father the news brought by the white trappers during the summer's salmon run.

Now it was time for the tribe to go east on their fall buffalo hunt, and his father wouldn't let him go. Garry crossed his arms and straightened his lean body to its full height. "I will soon be a man, Father, and then you will not be able to stop me!" He cringed at making such a defiant threat, but he didn't care if it angered his father or not. Keeping him home just wasn't fair, especially not after . . . "I've hunted all summer except during the salmon run, and I've probably brought in as much game as any other man. And you know I can ride as well as—"

He talked on, hoping to soften the defiant challenge he had made to his father, but the chief addressed it directly. "I hope it doesn't come to that, my son. I hope you will honor me even when you don't have to."

Garry let out the air he'd sucked into his lungs and dropped his arms, but his lips tightened into a straight line as he turned and stomped away, not caring whether the dust he kicked up drifted back over his father.

It wasn't fair, and he would find some way to show his father how angry he was. It would be childish to simply refuse to speak to his father. On the other hand, what did they have to talk about?—certainly not the buffalo hunt, and Garry was getting so he didn't care anymore about Governor George Simpson's coming.

But as the day approached when the tribe would leave

for the hunt, Garry realized that, for the first time, his father wasn't going, either. Was his father really getting that old? Chief Illim's face was wrinkled and his fingers twisted, but he was still strong, and he could ride like the wind with his long gray hair flying out behind him.

"It is time to attend to other things, like prayer," Garry overheard the chief say to his uncle. "You will do fine without me, especially with those new rifles."

So, thought Garry miserably, *it will be just the chief, the old women and children, and me left back here in the village.* Well, he would just spend more time out hunting so he wouldn't have to be with his father any more than necessary.

On the morning the buffalo hunters rode out of the village, Garry had already hiked high on Lookout Mountain. He blinked back tears of anger and disappointment as he watched the trail of ponies and riders snake across the meadow, still white with the season's first hard frost. He should pray for their success, but he could not bring himself to do so. He didn't want them coming back with great stories from the hunt—the hunt that should have been his first. That would be too much.

When the hunters returned three weeks later, however, they arrived without any glorious hunting stories. Instead, they brought back the bodies of three dead warriors, shot by Blackfeet raiding parties that also had rifles now. As for meat, they had killed only six buffalo, hardly enough to feed the village through the winter, and certainly not enough for new robes to protect them from the cold. "It's a good thing the white traders have blankets," some of the women grumbled.

That night Garry sat on his haunches in the shadows as the council discussed the disheartening hunt. The three dead

Spokane braves had been shot on the same day. Two were killed immediately, and though the other one had clung to life for several days, his life finally drifted away like a wisp of smoke on the morning breeze.

"Our hunting ways must change. We must post lookouts for Blackfeet raiders as well as send out scouts to find the herds."

"The herds we did find seemed smaller and more scattered."

"The Blackfeet are taking more than their share of the buffalo!"

But Garry's uncle disagreed. "A Nez Perce warrior told me that white buffalo hunters have been chasing the herds all summer long and killing far more than they could possibly eat. The Nez Perce had seen piles of rotting carcasses."

Angry murmurs circled the council ring. How would the tribe survive with enemies on every side making it difficult to hunt the buffalo?

Garry crept away before the council broke up. He didn't want to face his father after hearing about the hunters who had been shot. His father would use it to prove he had been right all along and there *had* been good reason to keep him home. "Huh!" Garry muttered to himself. "Just because they were shot doesn't mean that I would have been killed. I would have been more cautious." When he hunted on Lookout Mountain, he sometimes had to climb dangerous cliffs to get into a good position. "Hunting's always dangerous. I could be thrown off a horse and hit my head just riding through camp. Father is too protective! He just won't let me grow up!"

Throughout the winter, Garry held on to his grudge toward his father, talking to him only when necessary just to make sure his father knew how angry he was for not letting him go on the buffalo hunt. From time to time, Garry imagined that his anger might convince his father that he had made a mistake. But he knew he could not manipulate the wise old chief so easily. If Chief Illim still thought it was wrong to let his son go on the hunt, Garry could be as angry as a stirred-up wasps' nest, and though his father would be sad that their relationship was strained, it would not force him to change his mind.

"He is a chief, after all," muttered Garry as he threw a snowball at a squirrel, "not a reed to be swayed by the wind."

Mail traveled remarkably fast in the wilderness, passed from trapper to trapper until Alexander Ross received a letter from Governor George Simpson of the Northern Division of the Hudson's Bay Company. Simpson had spent the winter at Fort George at the mouth of the Columbia River, but he planned to arrive at Spokane House in early April, depending, of course, on the snow in the passes and how high the rivers were. "I would like to speak to the important chiefs in the area if you can arrange for them to meet me at your trading post," the letter said. "The Reverend David T. Jones gave me an assignment that I hope to carry out."

When Ross told Chief Illim of Simpson's request, the old chief nodded solemnly. "I will send word to all the Spokane chiefs and invite our neighboring tribes to attend the powwow, as well," he promised.

When the snow on the mountains began to melt and its gurgling water broke up the ice in the streams, Chief Illim asked Garry to sit with him by his fire in the lodge. It was the first time the chief had asked his son to talk with him in such a formal way.

"I need someone to visit all the Spokane villages to tell

them about the coming of this white man," said the old chief. "Do you want to go?"

Garry hesitated. "Me? At this time of year?" It would take at least three days with the trails still treacherous with ice.

"Choose someone to go with you if you want."

Garry realized the request was a statement of his father's respect for his horsemanship and responsibility, not something he would ask a child to do. But still, clinging to his internal winter, Garry answered coolly, "Why?"

The chief's eyebrows went up, and he stared at his son for a few moments. "Any good brave can hunt buffalo"—he had not forgotten what caused the tension between them—"but this has to do with your purpose in life."

Purpose in life? What did that mean? Did his father really think being an errand boy was more important than proving he was a man? "Send someone else," he said and got up and walked out of the lodge.

To Garry's surprise, his father did not insist, and later that afternoon he saw one of the young braves ride out of the village on the mission his father had offered him.

Three weeks later, the other Spokane chiefs began to gather. In addition, delegations from neighboring tribes arrived, too, especially from the Nez Perce and various Flathead nations. Garry noticed a boy about his age with a Kootenai chief, but since he could not understand the language, he didn't try to make friends. But his father seemed able to communicate adequately with everyone, filling in with sign language when words eluded him.

Then one day, two large wooden boats with several white men pulling on the oars rowed slowly upriver until they beached at Spokane House. The brigade of fur traders had also come to meet Governor George Simpson, who arrived on horseback from the south in the afternoon on April 8, 1825.

Garry feigned only slight interest as the visitors set up their tepees on the meadow between the Spokane village and the river in preparation for the powwow. Eight regal chiefs strutted about in their finest fur-lined ceremonial dress and stately feathered headbands, along with many warriors and leading women. As game roasted over open fires, the white men came across the river, and the festivities began with dancing and feasting and constant displays of horsemanship.

Garry could not resist the horse races. No sooner was one horse race over than someone proposed another. The white men freely bet on who would win each race, putting up a knife or a hatchet or some other valuable item. After winning most of the events he entered, Garry went up behind his father and tapped him on the shoulder. Pointing at Governor Simpson, he said, "Tell the white chief that I can beat anyone in a race to the top of Pine Bluff, around the lone pine, and back down here to the camp if he will put up his rifle as prize." Garry pointed to the gnarled old pine tree on the top of the ridge to the south and then to Simpson's gun so that it was clear what he wanted.

The governor seemed amused. "He wants to race for my rifle?"

Alexander Ross, who knew the Spokane language better, confirmed the challenge. Governor Simpson nodded thoughtfully, looking back and forth between Garry, Chief Illim, and the Kootenai boy, who was obviously interested in participating. Finally he said, "Tell the boy and the chiefs that it's a deal—provided they will let me have those two boys to take to our headquarters in Canada." He pointed directly at Garry and at the Kootenai chief's son.

"What?" roared Garry's father, understanding enough of the white man's speech to get the message. "Do you think we are dogs that we would give up our children for you to take them"—he stuttered, his face getting red—"take them who knows where?" He stood up, whipping his blanket around him like a cocoon.

"Wait! Wait!" said Alexander Ross. "I'm sure the governor did not mean any insult. Now, Chief, you are always asking me about religion, about the Bible . . . you know, the book you call the Leaves of Life. Well, that's all the governor is saying. He's offering to take your son—young Garry here and that Kootenai boy—to study religion at the best Indian school in Canada." Taking a breath, he quickly told Simpson what he had said in Spokane, since the governor's abilities in that language were limited.

"Yes." The governor stood up. "I want to take a couple of your bright young boys to learn how to know and serve God. Then, after four winters, they can come back here and tell all your people what they've learned."

Chief Illim relaxed slightly. "You would teach my boy about *Quilent-sat-men?*"

"Quilent-sat-men?" Simpson frowned at Ross.

"Their word for God. It means *Creator of All.*"

Simpson faced the chief while talking to Ross. "Of course! I would take them to Rev. Jones at the missionary school, and there he would learn about God." Simpson pointed up. "God . . . your *Quil*-something-or-other, whatever you call Him."

The chief's face froze, and then his head nodded ever so slightly. "If you will teach them about God, you can take a hundred of our children." He spoke quickly to the other chiefs in their various languages, and they began nodding vigorously. The Kootenia chief pushed his son forward, and Garry could see that he was even younger than himself.

Chief Illim sat down—as did Simpson and all the other chiefs in a ring around the main fire. Chief Illim drew out his pipe and began to fill it with tobacco.

"What about my horse race?" hissed Garry in his father's ear. "I want to win that rifle!"

"Don't worry about it, son," said the chief over his shoulder. "You will be the greatest chief our people have ever known—not by winning a horse race or killing buffalo, but by bringing home the Leaves of Life!"

CHAPTER 4

EXILED TO THE RED RIVER

Garry stepped back and his mouth went dry. He had been so interested in winning the governor's rifle that he had not paid very close attention to what the men were discussing—something about sending children somewhere . . . to school—whatever that was—in Canada, for four years?

His father had said bringing home the Leaves of Life would make him a great chief, but that didn't make sense. His father had not allowed him to go on the buffalo hunt; then Garry had refused to do his father's errand. Now his father was sending him far away to a place called Red River. It *felt* more like a punishment. He was being exiled, taken away by these white men. And where was Canada? Somewhere north was all he knew.

He looked over at the Kootenai boy. His father was down on his knee in front of the boy talking very earnestly while the boy kept shaking his head like a bear with a salmon in its mouth. Tears were coming into the boy's eyes, and his face was screwing up as though he had eaten green berries.

Garry turned away. Whatever was happening, he would not cry. He walked swiftly to the horse corral, led out his favorite paint horse, and climbed on. Without thinking about what he was doing, he let his horse gallop across the meadow and up the steep hill that bordered it on the southwest and headed toward the twisted figure of the old lightning-blazed tree on the top of Pine Bluff.

Once over the crest of the plateau, he kept on riding, telling himself that the tears streaming back from his eyes were only from the cold wind. He let his horse slow to a walk and find its own way for the next couple miles, weaving around small ponds, following game trails through the underbrush, until he arrived at a burial platform. On top of the platform, Garry knew that the bones of his mother rested, wrapped tightly in old animal skins, maybe little more than dust by now. And yet he felt some comfort in her memory and in what he imagined she would have been like to know.

From time to time, he had asked his older sisters and brothers about Mother. His next oldest brother, Sultz-lee, wouldn't even answer his questions, and the descriptions of his other siblings were short, almost angry, as though he had no right to ask. She had died giving him birth was all they would tell him. Did that mean it was his fault? He sometimes felt like it. But he didn't think she would have blamed him. That's just not what a mother would do.

Garry slid off the paint and sat with his back against one of the poles of the platform, his weight causing it to wiggle and shake some dust down on his head. His mind drifted to what lay ahead—a long trip to a place he didn't know with people who spoke a strange language. He shivered . . . was it a gust of wind off the snow-capped mountains or the draft of cold loneliness swirling in his heart? He tried to think back four years to when he was ten. Being sent away for that much longer seemed like forever. He didn't want to go. And yet, he knew it would happen.

Why was his father sending *him*? Why didn't he go himself if he wanted to learn to know God? And what was all this talk about it making him a great chief? What if he couldn't find the Leaves of Life and bring them back to his people? What if he failed? This wouldn't be like a buffalo hunt where if you didn't kill one of the great beasts one year, you could go back and try again the next.

He looked up at the platform, wishing he could talk to his mother. But of course that wasn't possible. This was something he was going to have to do on his own . . . but he wished he had someone wise to talk to.

A loud cry yanked him from the journey he was imagining in his mind, and he looked up just as a large black bird glided to a perch on top of his mother's burial platform. It cawed as though scolding him. Garry scrambled to his feet. "This is my mother's platform, not yours!" he yelled, tossing a stick at the bird. The large bird swooped off the platform and sailed off between the pines.

"A raven," he muttered—and as soon as he said it, he thought of his long-dead uncle, Circling Raven. *When he felt alone he prayed to God*, thought Garry. *But he was a shaman, a prophet, and I am only a boy.* Garry continued to look through the trees in the direction the raven had flown. Suddenly the bird rose above the treetops and began circling higher and higher on an updraft.

"Oh, God, if you can hear me, if you will listen to a mere

boy, help me to be brave about being sent away! And if you are there, bring me back home safely!"

Garry stood, head back and arms thrown out, as the wind seemed to snatch his words and hurl them upward, like the raven. Then quietness settled back over the forest and, strangely, into his spirit, as well.

Grabbing the reins of his paint, Garry began walking back to the village. Something had changed. Even as he walked, the chill of fear receded like the memory of last night's dream, while eagerness warmed within him to see this Red River—even if he was being exiled. But what had changed? Had his simple prayer made the difference? Had God heard him? The possibility excited him. He vaulted onto his horse and kicked him into a run.

Four days later, Governor Simpson was ready to leave. The water level in the river had dropped because there had been no rain, so it wasn't safe to load the two wooden boats with supplies and passengers; they might smash on underwater rocks. Simpson chose four men to launch each boat and head downriver. The rest of the brigade, along with the two chiefs' sons, would travel by horseback—borrowed from the Spokane tribe—down to the junction of the Spokane with the Columbia. There the water would be deep enough to load passengers and supplies into the boats. The plan, Chief Illim told his son, was to row up the great river to its very head waters, high in the Canadian Rockies. The river journey would be long and hard—and that was only the beginning.

Alexander Ross had decided to make the trip with Simpson to help interpret for Garry. To replace Ross, one of the other Hudson's Bay Company men stayed behind to help manage

Spokane House. But no one in the expedition could speak the Kootenai tongue.

Once the boats had drifted out of sight around the bend in the river, a large crowd of Indians gathered beside the river. Garry carried only a blanket and an extra pair of moccasins. His knife and a tomahawk hung from his belt. He noticed that the other boy—who he'd learned was called Pelly—had a bow and a quiver of arrows.

Garry eyed Governor Simpson's rifle with its long blue barrel and intricately carved stock and wished that he had a fire stick like it. That would be far better than any set of bow and arrows.

Finally the time for departing had come. Chief Illim stepped forward and spoke loudly and fervently to Governor Simpson and Alexander Ross. "You see, we have given you our sons—not our servants or our slaves, but our own children. We have given you our hearts—but bring them back again before they become white men. We wish to see them again as one of our own people. Do not let them get sick or die. If they get sick, we get sick; if they die, we, too, shall die. Take them; they are yours."

Governor Simpson nodded and stepped forward. With equal solemnity, he reached out and shook the hand of the chief. "I will do as you ask."

Then he turned to Garry and Pelly, who were standing side by side at this point. Looking at each of them in turn, he asked a question that Ross quickly interpreted for Garry and then Chief Illim interpreted for Pelly: "We are glad you boys are making this journey to the Red River Mission where you will learn about God so that you can bring the message back to your people. Are you willing?"

Both Garry and Pelly nodded their heads, though Garry's

stomach felt as nervous as a chipmunk at the thought of traveling so far. He glanced at Pelly, who looked terrified. But what else could they do? Their fathers were sending them to the mission.

"Then," said Simpson through his interpreters, "I give you these blankets in solemn pledge to do my best to care for you on this journey." He handed them each a new red blanket.

At this, the women from the two tribes began to moan and cry softly, but Chief Illim raised his hand. "Do not weaken them with your wailing. They are men, being sent out on a man's quest. Make their hearts brave as you would if they were going on a buffalo hunt." Then he stepped forward and grasped the right hand of each boy and put it in the hand of Alexander Ross. The women stopped crying, and the chief said, "It is your task, our sons, to bring back to us the Leaves of Life. Do not fail us! Do not fail the old prophecy!"

Then he turned and walked away, and all the villagers followed him without looking back at the boys as the expedition mounted their horses and headed down the trail that wound its way along the Spokane River. Garry's brother, Sultz-lee, would accompany them as far as the Columbia River in order to return the horses to the village.

Garry, too, did not look back. Nor did he trust himself to say good-bye. All he could think about in that moment was that it would be many years before he saw his father again.

CHAPTER 5

THE EXPEDITION

The mounted brigade of fur traders had no sooner passed Eagle Rock on the shortcut that cut off one of the first large loops of the Spokane River than it began to rain. The white men turned up the collars on their black wool coats and pulled their wide-brimmed hats low over their eyes. Garry rode on until he was shivering from the cold spring rain. Finally he unrolled his new red Hudson's Bay Company blanket and wrapped it around him, pulling it up over his head, leaving only a narrow tunnel to look through over the ears of his paint.

Pelly, who was riding in front of him, turned around and saw that Garry had gotten out his blanket, so he did the same.

Then the chilling rain turned to hail. The stones were no larger than rabbit droppings at first and merely stung Garry's exposed hands, which held the reins. He tried to pull the blanket over them, but the wind shifted around to the west, driving the hail right through the opening in his blanket. Soon the hailstones grew to the size of a bird's egg. They hurt, even through the blanket.

Up ahead, Garry heard a horse whinny and Governor Simpson cry out in angry protest. In spite of the hail, Garry let the blanket slip back so he could see. Simpson's horse had spooked, perhaps from the hail striking it so hard. The animal reared while Simpson clung to its back. Then the animal began to buck while Simpson slowly began to slide to one side in his saddle until he could not keep from falling off. The governor rolled as he hit the ground, luckily avoiding the pounding hooves of his mount.

Relieved of its rider, the horse galloped on up the trail with the stirrups of the white man's saddle flapping like the wings of a goose, nearly igniting other horses it passed into a similar panic.

Garry let his blanket fall to the ground, reined his horse out of line, and urged it into a full gallop up through the woods far enough away from the trail so as not to frighten the other horses. When he came back onto the path, he was in full pursuit of Simpson's runaway. In just a few minutes, he drew alongside, grabbed the reins, and pulled both horses to a trot before he turned around. The runaway's eyes were still wide, showing a rim of white, its ears laid back, and it snorted again and again, trying to pull the reins free as they approached the expedition, but Garry kept it firmly under control until he delivered it to the governor, who had regained his feet.

As Simpson tried to brush the mud off his pants, he said something to Ross—Garry caught the word "Thanks"—who turned to Garry. "Governor Simpson wants to thank you for your quick thinking, Garry. Otherwise, he might have lost his mount."

By then, the hail had melted into a steady, bone-chilling

drizzle that continued for the remainder of the day and on into the night, when it finally ended and the clouds began to break, allowing the moon to peek through.

Mr. Ross rode his horse alongside Garry. "Garry, I wonder if you would take the lead now that it is dark. I think your pony may be the most surefooted, and besides, you are probably more familiar with this country than any of the rest of us."

Garry kicked his paint to the front of the column without comment. He had traveled the forty-five miles down the Spokane River to the mighty Columbia with his father several times, but he had never come this far on this trail. Still, he had no doubt that his little paint could find his way, even when the clouds obscured the moon.

It was well past midnight before they arrived at the Columbia. For some reason the men with the boats had put ashore on the other side of the Spokane, but the fire they had going on the beach certainly looked inviting. Soon they pushed one of the boats out into the water and came over to get the riders.

Governor Simpson and Mr. Ross stripped their saddles off their horses while Sultz-lee tied the horses in a line and prepared to head back to the village. Just as Garry was ready to get into the white man's boat, his brother came up to him and grabbed him in a hard hug. With unshed tears catching the glint of the moon, he slapped Garry on the back one last time and then turned away to head back up the trail.

The slightest glow was emerging along the eastern horizon when Governor Simpson roused the company from their resting places around the fire and said, "It's time to get on the river. We've got many days ahead of us!"

Nevertheless, before the stars winked out in the lightening

sky, the creak of the oars and steady splash of the boat's bow into the waves of the great river had lulled Garry back to sleep on the pile of supplies in the bottom of the boat.

He awoke with the glare of spring sunshine in his eyes, so white it made him squint, but it didn't provide much warmth. He sat up, and it took him several moments before he figured out where he was. He had never traveled up the Columbia River, but to the east he recognized the peaks of the Huckleberry Range—Spokane Mountain, Bear Mountain, Deer Mountain, and Blue Mountain. He had viewed each of them from the other side when hunting on Twin Mountains not far from his village.

He looked north, up the valley down which the Columbia flowed, and felt panic churning in his stomach like salmon trying to jump up the rapids. Soon he would be out of the territory where he could recognize anything, not the mountains or the rivers or familiar trees like Lone Pine. He would soon be a stranger in a strange land. He started looking around for landmarks so he could find his way home—a large meadow by the river, a snow-capped peak to the west, a towering rock formation that looked a little like a horse's head hanging out over the water . . . but would he recognize it coming downstream? They were passing an island with a large pile of snags caught on the upstream edge. But that could all wash away with a heavy spring rain.

Garry could not remember ever being lost. As a child, the Spokane River and the mountains around their village always gave him landmarks that were easy to locate. Even as he got older and went with the women of the village to gather camas roots or pick chokecherries, it was only into the next valley or over a familiar hill—easy to remember and find his way home. And later when he went hunting and fishing with the men, it was the same, adding one or two new mountains or streams each trip to territory he already knew.

But now everything was new, and as the morning passed, he began to fear that he wouldn't be able to find his way back. Loneliness overwhelmed him, as though drowning in deep water with no bottom.

The white man at the oars in front of him, who actually faced the back of the boat so he could pull on the oars, pointed to a leather bag in the bottom of the boat and muttered some instruction. Garry recognized the words "food" and "eat." He opened the bag and found some kind of a biscuit and rancid-smelling jerky. The man indicated that he could have some, so Garry dug out a piece of each and handed the bag to the man, who took his share before passing it to the other men.

Garry began gnawing on the jerky and then noticed the oarsman banging his biscuit on the edge of the boat, knocking out some bugs before taking a bite. Garry did the same, but when he tried to bite into it, the biscuit was nearly as hard as a piece of wood. He had to gnaw at it like a beaver for several minutes before getting a bite.

The oarsman grinned at him and then in a mixture of words and signs asked if he wanted to take his place at the oar. Garry agreed, thinking he ought to do his part.

The two wooden boats traveled continually from before dawn to well after dark. All the men took turns rowing—even Governor Simpson took a turn. At night, everyone was so exhausted that they did little more than build a fire and make coffee before everyone had fallen asleep, sometimes right on the sand.

Occasionally the rapids of the river were so rough that they had to pull into the shallows and get out and wade upstream, pulling the boats along behind them with ropes. This was always agonizing work. The water was so cold that at first Garry's feet throbbed with such pain it was as though he had dropped boulders on them. Soon, however, the pain would mercifully subside as he lost all feeling in his feet and legs, but then it was nearly impossible to find his footing as they struggled forward. Again and again, first one and then another of the travelers fell to his knees, bruising or cutting them on the sharp stones. This sudden shift of weight on the towrope would often cause another person to lose his balance, and sometimes they would all end up facedown in the water before they could regain control against the swift current.

In two weeks, however, the party had traveled 340 miles north to the headwaters of the Columbia River and Kinbasket Lake, deep in the Canadian Rockies. Garry had finally conquered his fear of not knowing where he was. The river and the mountain ranges themselves seemed more recognizable as he traveled along with them each day. And even though he had never been in this part of the north country, he could imagine getting home from where he was . . . if he could build a canoe strong enough to survive some of the rough water of the river.

Garry looked at his hands. His palms were covered with bloody, oozing sores where blisters from rowing had formed, broken, torn off, and then new ones had formed again. He could hardly close his hands, let alone think about building a canoe.

But when he realized that they had pulled their boats up onto a beach at the approach to Athabasca Pass for the final time, he jumped out and fell down on his stomach, kissing the ground. The men near him laughed, and a couple of them did the same, but Pelly just stood watching with a haunted look in his eyes.

Governor Simpson lost no daylight celebrating, however. Each person was outfitted with a pack of the remaining supplies, and they headed up the trail into the mountains. These were mountains like none Garry had ever seen. They soared up into the clouds in great sweeps of treeless granite or fields of crumbling shale, and in many of the valleys between the peaks Garry saw glaciers.

In fact, the next morning, only an hour after they had set out on the trail, it began to snow. The snow fell like the water over Nine Mile Falls, piling up so quickly that it was hard to detect the trail. Finally, when it was two feet deep and clinging to their frozen legs with every step, the clouds began to part and the snow stopped. The mountain was blanketed in silence broken only by the panting of the travelers as they plodded through the snow's depths.

Soon Garry began to hear big sniffs and finally a muffled whimper. He turned and looked back at Pelly, but the other Indian boy had his blanket up over his head, leaving his face unseen. The whimpers became louder, and when Garry looked back, it was obvious that Pelly was staggering. Garry realized that he was crying so hard he couldn't keep his balance.

He stepped aside to walk beside Pelly, though it meant he had to break his own trail, making the going much harder. Even though he couldn't speak Pelly's language, he put his hand on the boy's shoulder. Pelly drew back with a start, letting the blanket fall from his head even though it revealed his tearstained face.

Garry patted him on the shoulder, and then, noticing a robin huddled under an outcropping of rock beside the trail, he pointed the bird out to Pelly and grinned. Robins had barely returned to the Spokane before they had left. What was one doing this far north and this high so early in the spring?

Pelly sniffed hard, but the beginning of a *wow-that's-something* grin tugged at the edge of his mouth. Even without words, Garry and Pelly looked at each other with new understanding. They were brothers here, a long way from home, and they needed to stick together. With Garry's encouragement, the younger boy fell back into line behind him as the expedition wound its way up the snow-bound trail.

CHAPTER 6

DIVING FOR THE FIRE STICK

Coming down into a sweeping valley on the far side of the high pass, the brigade spotted a welcome sight—smoke drifting lazily from the stone chimney of a trading post hugging the shores of Brule Lake, which was just an exceptionally wide and calm section of the Athabasca River. Unlike the white man's squat log house on the Spokane River, Jasper House, as this trading post was called, was made of sawed planks. There was a second story, several windows, and a porch that ran the whole length of the structure.

Garry was curious. He had seen Mr. Ross cut boards from logs at Spokane House. Ross often hired local Indians to do the work, with one man down in a pit operating one end of a saw and another above pulling back and forth on the other end. But it took days to cut up one log. And here was a whole building built of these planks.

That night as they bedded down with their blankets in

one of the upstairs rooms, Pelly gingerly peeled off his damp moccasins. Garry winced. Pelly's feet had several angry blisters and bloody cuts from sharp trail stones. No wonder he had been crying! Garry went downstairs and got a pan of warm water and some rags to bathe and clean the other boy's feet. He was worried. No way could Pelly keep walking on those feet till they healed.

But the next morning, they saw supplies being loaded into six canoes and hurried to help. Garry and Pelly got one of the smaller canoes to themselves, Indian-built, probably traded at Jasper House for some Hudson's Bay supplies. With the sun rising into an azure sky, they dipped their paddles into the emerald waters of Brule Lake. The unusual milky-green color of the water, Mr. Ross told them, came from the minerals scoured by the glaciers that fed the Athabasca River. Along the horizon, the peaks of the Rockies looked like the teeth of the saws the white men used to cut logs.

By midafternoon they had paddled out of the end of Brule Lake and into the Athabasca River, now a clear emerald green, as some of the mineral sediment that had given the water its earlier milky appearance dropped as it passed through the slow-moving lake.

At dusk, the expedition stopped and made camp on a broad sandy beach. Governor Simpson said that even with a moon out that night, it would be too easy to lose a canoe if one struck an underwater rock in the rapids. Before the purple left the sky, Pelly motioned to Garry to follow him into the woods. Once they were out of sight of the white men, Pelly pulled his bow off his back and notched an arrow. He pointed Garry to go in one direction, while he followed a narrower trail through deeper undergrowth.

Garry had gone only a hundred yards when he came to the

edge of a small meadow. He could just make out the shapes of a half dozen deer grazing. He looked back toward the river, which was now out of sight, and wondered how Pelly knew the meadow was there. Obviously Pelly wanted him to move the deer to the other side of the meadow, where he would be waiting to shoot one of them. But he had to give Pelly a few more minutes to get into position.

He was almost within range to try a shot from where he stood . . . if only he had brought his own bow and arrows! But he'd been upset at not getting to race for Governor Simpson's rifle.

Regretting his foolishness, Garry slowly dropped to his knees and crept silently toward the deer just to see if he could get closer. Another mistake. He succeeded in getting closer, but when the deer finally did notice him, they spooked and bolted across the meadow much faster than if they'd seen him at a greater distance and drifted back into the far woods. Now Pelly would have a much harder time hitting his mark.

Nevertheless, Garry heard the telltale twang of Pelly's bow followed instantly by a thump and wild thrashing through the brush instead of the graceful bounds of an escaping deer. "Did you get one?" called Garry quietly, forgetting that Pelly did not speak Spokane. But the other boy understood enough to answer with a muffled, "Yes."

The waning but almost full moon had just risen to stream its ghostly beams through the branches of the fir trees when the boys found the downed deer. Pelly quickly gutted the carcass while Garry cut a pole to make it easier to carry the meat back to camp.

Everyone was grateful for that night's feast, and the boys, whom the trappers had generally ignored before this, became welcome heroes that night. "You can do this every night," said

Mr. Ross, tearing a hunk of roasted venison off a bone with his teeth.

The next morning, Garry and Pelly's canoe led the expedition down the gently curving Athabasca as mist rose from its calm surface like golden smoke in the slanting rays of the morning light. With the sun still at such a low angle, the water looked black, and Garry, who was standing in the front of the canoe, did not notice the huge shape moving below the surface until he hit it with his paddle.

A huge head erupted from the dark water—a moose with antlers large enough to serve a banquet on! The wave created by its sudden upsurge nearly tipped over the canoe, and Garry nearly lost his paddle grabbing the sides. A dripping beard of green river grass hung from the animal's enormous mouth, but Garry shoved the tip of his paddle into the beast's nose and pushed off as hard as he could, sending the canoe skimming down the river out of the animal's reach.

But the boys' canoe wasn't the only intruder on the moose's peaceful breakfast. Five other canoes followed, and the one carrying Governor Simpson was headed right for it. The moose snorted and lunged toward the canoe, soon putting itself into deep water so that it had to swim. But its powerful hooves drove it forward before the governor and his companion could swerve out of the way. The tip of the velvet-covered antlers caught the edge of the canoe and rolled it over in an instant, throwing both men, a bale of furs, a tent, and the governor's beautiful rifle into the icy water.

"Turn around!" Garry yelled. He backstroked with his paddle, and Pelly pulled hard on his paddle to turn their canoe. But the moose wasn't through with his rampage and was heading straight for the governor. "Go! Go! Go!" yelled Garry as Pelly headed the prow of their canoe between the advancing moose head and the governor, who was struggling to keep his head above water.

It was a dangerous move, since the moose could have flipped their canoe as easily as it had the governor's. But the yelling boys, advancing with a frenzy in their canoe, confused the moose, who probably thought he had had enough trouble for one morning. Turning aside, the moose swam back to the shore just as two of the other canoes arrived on the scene.

Quickly Garry and Pelly and the other men maneuvered to rescue the governor and his companion and pick up the floating baggage. The capsized canoe was a little more difficult, as it was nearly submerged and as hard to handle as an old log. Garry grabbed one side and Alexander Ross in another canoe grabbed the other, and together the rescuers managed to pull it to the shore.

"What about your fire stick?" Garry pointed to where he'd seen it splash into the river. Ross translated for the governor.

"It's gone! Gone for good!" said Simpson, struggling out of his wet clothes to wring them out. "Someone get a fire going before we freeze to death!"

Garry ran to collect an armload of driftwood. When he dumped the wood down onto the beach, he said, "If I get it, can I have it?"

Simpson caught the gist of his words and gestures. "What? You think you can dive into that freezing water?"

Garry nodded and pounded his chest with his forefinger. "Can I have it?"

The governor waved a go-ahead but then muttered, "You better not catch your death. I promised your father I'd take good care of you."

Garry peeled off his tunic, kicked off his moccasins, and pulled Pelly toward their canoe. In just a few minutes, they were back upstream at the point where they had met the moose. Without hesitating, Garry was over the side, diving down into the chilling darkness. The water was so cold that he had to try twice before he could even reach the bottom—so full of weeds it would be almost impossible to find anything.

When he broke the surface, Garry knew he had only one more chance. The cold was sapping all his energy, and he was already beginning to shiver uncontrollably. Pelly was saying something to him and pointing out into a little deeper water. Garry turned in the direction Pelly had pointed, took a huge breath, and ducked under one more time. Down . . . down . . . down he went, unable to see a thing in the gloom. Suddenly his hand jammed into a moss-covered boulder on the bottom. His fingers were so cold that they felt like he had dropped the boulder on them rather than just stubbing his fingers.

He flipped over, feet down, when he felt something long and thin scrape along his leg. He reached down, grabbed it, and headed toward the surface. But when he broke into the welcome air and raised his hand in triumph, he discovered he had retrieved only a waterlogged stick. His hands had been so cold he couldn't tell that it wasn't the stock of the rifle. Throwing it aside, he grabbed the side of the canoe to catch his breath, ready to give up.

Only then did he realize that over the three dives, they had drifted downstream from the place where the moose had flipped the governor's canoe. "Back there," he said, pointing upstream a short distance. "Take me back."

Pelly gave a few strong strokes with his paddle, pulling Garry upstream.

"Here," Garry said, his teeth chattering so loudly that Pelly couldn't have understood what he was saying even if he knew Spokane. But that didn't matter, because Garry had ducked underwater one more time. Down he went, his arms and legs barely strong enough to pull him deeper. When he reached the bottom, he felt around among the stones until his lungs felt like they were going to rip open. Suddenly his hand touched something that moved away. He grabbed at it and grabbed again, catching something long and hard. He pulled it close to his face and in the dim light saw that he had finally found the rifle.

But as Garry pushed toward the surface, he could no longer hold his breath. Air exploded from his lungs, and he knew that he couldn't keep from sucking in, but—would it be air or water? He thought he was rising, but it was getting darker as though he were sinking. Just before blacking out, he burst from the surface.

The next thing he knew he was lying on his back on the beach, staring up at lacy clouds floating through a deep blue sky. Garry coughed and sat up. The members of the expedition all stood around him, and there was Pelly, kneeling in front of him and grinning as though his face would split. In his hand, with the butt planted firmly on the sand, was the governor's rifle, still dripping from its bath in the river.

Governor Simpson was true to his word and let Garry keep the rifle. "Here," he said, pointing to the carving on the stock of the rifle, . . . 'Simpson.' My name." He pointed to himself, and at first Garry thought he was asking for it back. But the governor turned to Ross. "Tell him it's just my name. At the mission they'll teach him to read. Then he'll always remember where he got it." The governor also gave Garry a powder horn and shot, and in the evenings before dark, he showed him how to load and shoot.

The rifle had so much more range than a bow and arrow, but it was still hard to hit the center of a stump at two hundred paces. At first, Garry jerked the rifle every time he pulled the trigger. Fire and black smoke exploded with a big bang so close to his face that he couldn't help but flinch. Still, with practice, he got better and couldn't wait to go hunting.

Two more days of easy travel down the Athabasca brought the travelers to flatter country with rolling hills only a couple hundred feet in height on either side of the smooth river. That afternoon as they rounded a bend in the glassy river, Garry saw smoke rising in the distance from some buildings on the bank of the river.

"There's the fort!" shouted one of the trappers as everyone dug in their paddles to cover the last remaining mile to Fort Assiniboine.

Garry and Pelly kept in the lead of the other canoes as they approached the fort until they saw a dozen or more tepees creating a village outside the picket walls of the fort. Then they slowed up to let the other men lead the way. "What tribe are they?" Garry asked Alexander Ross as he passed in his canoe.

Ross shrugged. "Several tribes. They come from all over, but they're all friendly. They just come to trade."

But when the expedition had beached their canoes and walked stiffly through the little village of tepees to the gates of the huge fort, Garry saw the strange Indians and some of the white trappers lounging near the gate eyeing his new rifle as though they didn't think he should have such a fine weapon.

That night, the boys were directed to a hay barn to sleep. With the winter past, it was nearly empty, but there was still enough hay to make comfortable beds for the weary travelers. Garry lay down, pulling his Hudson's Bay blanket over him, and fell instantly asleep, one arm over the rifle that lay beside him like a favorite walking stick.

He slept so soundly that he did not notice when a tall dark shape bent over him, lifted his arm, and drew out the rifle.

CHAPTER 7

THUNDER DRAGONS

As soon as Garry awoke, he knew something was wrong, but it took him a moment to realize what it was.

"My rifle! Pelly, where's my rifle! Pelly!" He shook his companion awake and yanked him to a sitting position. "Where's my rifle?" he yelled.

He motioned wildly with his hands, making up signs, but Pelly had understood the words and was already looking around, bewildered. He began digging in the hay as though he was sure it had to be nearby.

Garry stood up, stomped to the barn door and back, waving his arms and yelling. "Someone stole my rifle. Somebody stole it! Somebody stole it! I'm going to find out who the thief is and take it back!"

"Simpson? Governor Simpson?" Pelly shrugged.

"What?" He stopped pacing. "Governor Simpson? You think he took it back?"

Pelly shrugged again.

Garry went back to the barn door, opened it a crack, and peered out. The fort was coming to life for the day; men drifted past carrying armloads of wood and buckets of water. He looked back at Pelly. "You think Governor Simpson took it back?"

Pelly held his hands out, palms up, shrugged, and raised his eyebrows in a *who-knows?* expression.

Garry opened the barn door and went out, intent on confronting the governor.

"Ah, Spokane Garry," said Alexander Ross when he saw Garry coming. "You look raring to go. Glad to see you up so early. We need to make an early start today."

Ross's jovial manner took some of the steam out of Garry. "Uh, Mr. Ross, does the governor have a rifle?"

"Did he get a rifle? Oh yeah, and he better hang on to it this time! Now, go get Pelly and meet us behind the trading post. There'll be coffee and something to eat. We're going by horse for the next ninety miles, all the way to Fort Edmonton. Now get!"

Garry turned and walked slowly back to the barn, head down, letting his feet drag in the dust. Why would the governor do that? Why would he give him his rifle only to take it back? It didn't make sense! The governor was supposed to know about God, and Garry had already learned that God did not approve of stealing. To Garry, this was the same as stealing.

On the other hand, the rifle did have the governor's name on it in those strange markings white men made. Maybe that meant it would always belong to him and he had only allowed Garry to carry and shoot it for a short while.

When the expedition gathered for departure, Garry watched the governor mount up. Sure enough, the governor tied a long, leather scabbard to his saddle—the kind that held a rifle. He could see it from across the yard; no need to go ask the governor. With head hanging, Garry swung up on the mount that had been assigned to him. It was a bony nag that his Spokane people would have used for bear bait, but none of the other horses were very enviable, either. Garry fell in line near the rear of the column that headed out of the fort. As he rode along, he wondered whether anyone would notice if he ducked into the woods and headed south. If he had a better horse, he might even try it. After all, what could these white men teach their people about God if they didn't even keep their word?

But that evening, when the column of travelers stopped for camp by a small stream, Governor Simpson called Garry over to him. "Son, see if you can shoot us a deer in that meadow downstream."

Garry just stared at him. What an unthinkable request after taking back his gun!

"Well, go on! We could use some fresh meat after such a long ride."

All right. If that's how the governor wanted it. Clenching his teeth, Garry walked over to the governor's horse and reached for the rifle.

"Hey, use your own rifle!" said the governor.

Putting his hands on his hips, Garry turned in appeal to Mr. Ross, who was standing nearby. What was this, some kind of a joke or test? "I don't have it," he said tersely.

"What do you mean, you don't have it?" asked Ross.

Garry pointed toward the governor's horse. "The governor took it back."

"What? You think that's your gun? What makes you think

he'd take it? The governor bought a different rifle back at the fort. Where's the one he gave you?"

Confused, Garry turned and looked more carefully at the gun in the scabbard on the governor's horse. The carving on the stock . . . it . . . it was completely different, without the letters that spelled Simpson! This *was* a different rifle! "I . . . I don't know," he stammered, turning back to Ross. "This morning it was gone. I . . . I thought Governor Simpson took it back. I didn't know—"

"You telling us someone stole your rifle back at the fort?" Ross turned to Simpson and quickly explained in English what Garry had told him.

"What?" said Simpson. "Who?"

Garry shrugged and explained how he had slept with the rifle right by his side but in the morning it was gone. "Pelly even helped me look for it."

"Do you have any idea who else might have taken it?" asked Ross.

Garry was going to say no but then recalled how several Indians and trappers had stared at him when he entered the fort. "Maybe one of them snuck into the barn and—"

"I'll write a letter when we get to Fort Edmonton," said Ross, "and send it with the next travelers west. Maybe someone at Fort Assiniboine will come across it. But don't get your hopes up. A lost rifle could be as hard to retrieve as gossip."

They had no fresh venison that night. Garry went to bed under the stars telling himself he ought to feel better knowing that Governor Simpson hadn't lied to him or taken his rifle. But the fact that he might never get back such a prized possession left him feeling like flint without steel.

The expedition covered the ninety miles from Fort Assiniboine to Fort Edmonton in two days, but once in Edmonton, they had to wait while fourteen flat-bottomed cargo boats were prepared to travel down the Saskatchewan River. Some were still being built. In addition to the furs the governor's expedition had with them, other trappers had sent their bales of furs to Edmonton for sale and shipment.

Garry welcomed the rest from the hard travel, but he found the fort a bewildering marvel of the white man's world. Situated on an eroding bluff above the river, it was as ugly a place to build a village as any place Garry could imagine. "Like an old scab on a bald man's head," he muttered to Mr. Ross.

"Yes," laughed Mr. Ross, "but it is easy to defend. No one can get within a mile without being seen." From the wall of the fort high above the river, Garry thought the boats looked like a swarm of bees moving around on the water below.

Garry and Pelly spent the two-week layover at Fort Edmonton listening to and trying out as much English as they could learn. Garry had learned a little from the traders back at Spokane House, but after spending several weeks with English-speaking people, both boys had picked up quite a lot. Quick to learn, they pitched in to help finish the boats, then helped with the loading of supplies and bundles of winter furs.

On the day of their departure, the Simpson party was down at the riverfront early, finding their places in the boats and getting ready to push off when Garry noticed a trapper on a horse pulling two pack mules that were skidding down the trail to the water's edge. "Hold on! Hold on!" the man hollered. Mr. Ross clambered off the boat to speak to the man. In a few moments he was back.

"Says he just arrived from Fort Assiniboine, hoping to catch our flotilla of boats before it left."

"We're ready to go," Governor Simpson yelled to the man.

"We can't take time to load any more furs. You'll have to wait for the next shipment."

"But I can't wait!" the trapper protested, dismounting from his lathered horse.

"What do you mean, you can't wait?" said Simpson. "They'll pay you the same for your furs up in the fort."

"It's not just my furs. It's me! *I've* got to go with you. Uh—my sister's sick back East, and I've gotta get back to see her . . . 'fore she dies."

The governor frowned and looked around at the boats, as though considering whether he had space for the trapper. As Simpson and Ross conferred, Garry stared hard at the bearded trapper. He'd seen this man before . . . back at Fort Assiniboine.

Scrambling over the side of the flat-bottom boat still beached below the cliff, Garry circled behind the man and casually examined the packs on the mules. On the far side of the second mule, the edge of a rifle butt stuck out from beneath some furs. Reaching beneath the furs, he pulled on the rifle butt just enough till he could see the English letters carved into the wood: SIMPSON.

An iron hand clamped on his wrist. "Hey! What you think you doin'?" snarled the trapper's voice in his ear.

"He's got the rifle!" Garry yelled in Spokane. "The governor's rifle!"

Mr. Ross came running.

"What's he sayin'?" growled the man. "He's a thievin' Indian, that's what."

"Where'd you get that rifle?" Mr. Ross demanded.

The man narrowed his eyes, wary as a cornered wildcat. Then he cracked a wide grin and pulled out the rifle from the mule pack. "This here rifle? Why, I traded three beaver pelts for it back at Fort Assiniboine."

By this time the governor was off the boat and had joined them. "That gun was stolen from us back at Fort Assiniboine." He reached out for the rifle.

"Ah!" said the trapper, pulling back as swiftly as a cat. "If it's this here gun you want, it comes with me and my furs."

"Let me see it first," the governor demanded. Reluctantly the trapper handed it over. The governor examined it a moment. Without doubt it was the stolen rifle.

"Well, now, I can't help it if somebody stole that rifle, then sold it to me, can I?" The trapper waggled his hairy eyebrows. "But I'm a generous man. Might just give it back—even if it did cost me three pelts—but the least you can do is return the favor and let me on one of these here boats."

"All right, all right," snapped the governor. "Find yourself a spot, but make it quick. We're supposed to be casting off right now." Simpson turned and tossed the rifle to Garry. "Keep closer tabs on this from now on."

Garry caught the rifle and climbed into the boat. He was so engrossed in looking it over that he didn't even notice when the boats pushed out into the river. It was his prize rifle, all right, and except for a scratch on the stock, it looked no worse for the wear. Maybe this trip wouldn't turn out so bad, after all, even though his father had sent him away.

But he didn't believe for a minute that the man had paid three beaver pelts for it. Bet he didn't have a sick sister, either.

Travel down the Saskatchewan River was relatively easy. They mostly floated with the current, but the nearly two hundred miles across Cedar Lake and Lake Winnipeg to Norway House, the next trading post, required constant rowing, even though they were able to put up small sails occasionally when the wind was favorable.

The expedition arrived at Norway House on June 14, with the gnats nearly as thick in the air as smoke from a pitch fire. But it wasn't the clouds of insects in the air that were the problem. It was when they bit and got in one's eyes, nose, mouth, and ears. Garry found himself spitting and slapping more than he was rowing, especially when they were anywhere near land.

After a couple days' rest at Norway House, the flotilla set out once more for the three-hundred-mile trip down Lake Winnipeg and up the Red River. Day after day they rowed, the boys' muscles growing firm and strong. As they traveled up the Red River, they began to see more and more of what Alexander Ross explained were farms where white people lived and planted grain and food in the ground and kept their cattle instead of hunting their meat and gathering the nuts and berries that grew wild. Sometimes several farmhouses were built together in a little village. People waved to them from the river's bank, and children would run down to the water's edge to watch them pass.

Garry had lost count of the days. But finally the expedition turned its boats ashore just before reaching old Fort Gibraltar. Its stockade walls were much taller and stronger than Fort Edmonton, and it was positioned more pleasantly, dominating the prairie on the west bank of the river.

Garry and Pelly helped drag their boat ashore and got out stiffly, tired from such a long trip. In seventy-five days, they had traveled 1,850 miles from the Spokane. Garry held tightly to his rifle as he stared up at the fort. It was so strange—and scary—to be this far from home.

Suddenly fire and smoke belched from what looked like the long heads of two black horses peering over the top of the walls on either side of the gate. The explosions were accompanied by a thunderous roar so loud that both boys fell to the mud, hiding between the boats.

Thunder dragons, thought Garry. *They have brought us here to feed us to thunder dragons!*

CHAPTER 8

JUST A LITTLE HORSE RACE

With the thunder still echoing down the river, Mr. Ross said, "Get up, boys," while trying to keep from laughing uproariously like the other men who were bent over and wiping tears from their eyes. "They're only firing the cannons to welcome us. Did you think we were under attack?"

"Attack?" said Garry, rising to his hands and knees while keeping a sharp eye on the black "dragons" peering over the wall of the fort. "Attack by the thunder dragons?"

"Of course not. Those are only cannons, just like your rifle, but much, much larger. What did you think they were?"

Garry eyed the black "heads" on the wall. "Thunder dragons. I thought they were thunder dragons." But just then he saw men pull whatever the black things were back from the edge and ram a stick down their throats, as though feeding the dragons . . . or was it like the ramrod he used to clean and load his rifle? "Cannon? Like my rifle?" he said, looking at Alexander Ross with narrowed eyes.

"Yes, cannons. Just big guns. Very big. Instead of firing shot the size of a chokecherry, they fire a ball as large as two fists together. They're just guns."

Garry and Pelly stood up and hung their heads, letting their long black hair swing forward, half covering their reddening faces. The men's laughter had died to small chuckles as they shook their heads and returned to unloading the boats. "Don't worry about it," said Alexander Ross. "There'll be a lot of new things to see in the next few days. Just stay calm, and . . . and ask questions."

Alexander Ross and Governor Simpson herded the boys up the riverbank and through the huge gates of the stockade into the fort. Garry looked up at the "dragons." Apparently Mr. Ross was right. What had looked like giant horses' heads from a distance were merely black tubes mounted on small wheels. So that was a cannon.

But that wasn't the only strange thing Garry saw at the bustling fort: large wooden boxes that rolled on wheels, pulled by mules; a young girl and her mother with white skin and hair the color of grass at the end of summer; and so many people.

A creeping feeling overcame Garry, similar to what he'd felt when he first learned that his father was exiling him. This place could be a "prison" from which he might never escape!

"Garry . . . Garry." Garry heard Mr. Ross calling his name as Mr. Ross stood before a man with a small beard and a wide-brimmed black hat. "This is Reverend David T. Jones. He's in charge of the Red River Mission, where you'll be going to school. It's run by the Church of England."

Garry had no idea what the Church of England was, but

he reached his hand out in the fashion of white people to greet Rev. Jones with a handshake.

"Glad to have you boys," said Rev. Jones. "I just have a few more items of business to do here, and then we can be on our way to your school."

"Reverend Jones," said Governor Simpson, stepping up. He put his hand over his mouth as though saying something privately, but Garry was close enough and could now understand enough English to catch most of it. "I just want to warn you, Reverend, to take—care of these boys. They are sons of chiefs, chiefs of—influence in the Columbia—. Any accident could stir up warfare with what have been peaceful tribes. You will take care, won't you?"

Rev. Jones looked at the boys and raised his eyebrows as though really seeing them for the first time. "Certainly," he said, giving a slight bow of respect. "I'll see that they are well cared for."

Garry could not have been more relieved than when he walked out of the gates of the huge fort. At least he wasn't being held captive inside its high walls.

The mission school was about a mile north of the fort, back down the river from where they had beached their boats, now fully unloaded. The mission seemed like a small village, for besides the school building—as Rev. Jones explained—there was also a church, a barn, and several homes for missionaries and schoolteachers, all made of logs, not unlike Spokane House near Garry's home.

Rev. Jones guided the boys to one of these log homes where he introduced them to a teacher named Mr. Arnold Worthington. The main room of Mr. Worthington's "lodge," as Garry thought of it, was arranged at one end as a dormitory with bunk beds for six boys. At the other end was a large table built of rough-sawn planks with benches on either side. Beyond the table, the wall was dominated by a huge stone fireplace with its own smoke hole, a chimney similar to the one at Spokane House that let the smoke out before it floated through the room and made your eyes burn.

In the back wall was a doorway that led to Mr. Worthington's private quarters, but the thing that intrigued Garry most were the large square holes in the front wall on either side of the door. He walked over to inspect one, even as Mr. Worthington was explaining that the other boys were out working in the garden. But when Garry got close to the hole, he could see that it was filled with something that he could see right through as though it were clear ice. Except for some cross sticks and wavy lines in the "ice," it was as though it wasn't there. He touched it gently. It was cold, as cold as outside, but not nearly as cold as ice, and it wasn't melting.

Spokane House had had a window but not with "ice" in it. The hole in the wall there was covered with a very thin skin greased with bear grease to let the light through. But it had not let in nearly so much light as this window.

"That's glass," said Mr. Worthington, noticing Garry's interest. "Don't hit it, or it will break."

Garry backed away, still staring through the window, moving his head from side to side and up and down, amazed that it was almost like being outside.

"Now if you boys will help me move these bunks," said Mr. Worthington, "we can make room for a bunk for you boys. I think there is an extra one in the barn."

Pelly waved his hands from side to side. "Sleep on floor.

Good blanket." He held up his new Hudson's Bay blanket that was now rather dusty from the hard use on the trip.

"Oh no, not on the floor. You boys will need a bunk like everyone else. Come on. Help me move this."

What more could they say? *Everything* might be different here in the white man's world.

Class began for Pelly and Garry the next morning. A total of sixteen Indian boys gathered in the schoolhouse, which had four large windows on each side that, to Garry's amazement, made it nearly as bright as outside. He wasn't familiar with any of the tribes from which the other students came, so English became the only common language for communicating, and, of course, it was the language of the white teachers.

When Mr. Worthington began the morning with prayer, Garry began to believe that he might learn something about God that he could take home to his people. And then Mr. Worthington opened a black book and began reading about God. Was it the "Leaves of Life" his people had so eagerly awaited? Garry hardly heard anything else the teacher said that morning—and didn't understand what he was talking about when he did try to listen.

In the middle of the day, everyone was excused from school to get something to eat before going to work on the farm, where the boys were being taught to plant crops and raise animals for food. "It's the way the white man lives," Mr. Worthington had explained. "Some day there will not be room in the land for everyone to get all they need by hunting and fishing and gathering roots and berries. So you will need to learn to farm."

Garry didn't mind the idea of learning a new way to make a living—wasn't that part of Circling Raven's prophecy?—but it sounded crazy to say that someday there wouldn't be enough land.

When the other boys left, Garry hung back and eased his way to the front of the room. The black book was on the corner of Mr. Worthington's table with some papers resting on top of it.

"Yes, Garry?" said Mr. Worthington, glancing up briefly from something he was writing. "Is there something I can do for you? Could you understand what we were doing this morning?"

"Hmm. School okay."

But when Garry remained standing there, Mr. Worthington finally looked up. "Well, what is it?"

"Is that the 'Leaves of Life'?"

"Bible . . . God's Holy Word." The teacher moved the papers out of the way and pointed to the marks on the cover. "See, H-o-l-y B-i-b-l-e, Holy Bible! Here, do you want to look at it?" He handed the precious book to Garry and then went back to writing. A few moments later he stopped and looked up at Garry, who was carefully holding the book as though it might break. "Go ahead, you can open it. It won't be long before you can actually read it. But"—and he raised his left hand to stroke his small beard—"what was that you called it?"

"The Leaves of Life. I think this must be the Leaves of Life. My people have been waiting for it for years."

"Waiting? What do you mean?"

Struggling for words in English, Garry told the white man about the old prophecies. While he was talking, excitement bubbled up in his chest. Maybe . . . maybe his father really *had* sent him to the Red River Mission on a quest rather than just into exile as a punishment.

By the end of summer, Garry's English was good enough that he could carry on a conversation with relative ease. He knew his alphabet and could do simple arithmetic. The Bible and The Book of Common Prayer were the only texts used in the classroom because the object was to learn the Christian faith. However, sometimes Mr. Worthington read stories to them from other books and tried to tell them about the white man's world far to the east and across the Great Sea in Europe. "Someday you might even travel there yourselves," he said.

Farming was hard work, but Garry enjoyed taking care of the animals, especially the horses, which included the horses for the Hudson's Bay Company men who lived in the fort. But what Garry couldn't understand was why white people so seldom took time to have fun. Except for the drinking that many of the trappers did when they were at the fort, it seemed as though work, work, work was all they did.

"How about a little horse race?" Garry said to Pelly and some of the other boys one beautiful September afternoon as they were cleaning out the barn. None of the boys had their own horse at the mission, but there was no rule against them riding the horses that they cared for. In fact, they often hopped on a horse to ride up to the fort on some errand or to deliver the mounts the Hudson's Bay men needed to take a short trip somewhere. So it was not long before six of the boys were sitting bareback on the best horses and ready to race down the road beside the river while several other boys looked on and made bets as to who would win.

"We race all the way to the Chief Peguis Trail and back. Agreed?" said Garry, sitting astride Governor Simpson's prancing black horse that he kept at the mission farm. "The first one back to this point wins!"

"Wait," said one of the other boys. "Do we have to stay on the road?"

"Just make it to the trail," said Garry. "Hiyeeh!" he shouted, and they were off.

All six horses galloped down the road in a pack, turning this way and that as the road hugged the bends in the river. But by the time they approached Chief Peguis Trail, the pack had begun to lengthen, and though Garry and Pelly were running neck and neck, another horse and rider were two lengths ahead.

They skidded to a stop and turned as they crossed the trail, and drove back toward the mission. Garry pulled ahead of Pelly's horse, but he could not urge enough speed out of the governor's horse to gain on the leader. Would the other horse tire? As Garry watched its long, smooth stride eat up the ground, he doubted it. It was a fine buckskin belonging to the quartermaster in the fort.

When the road began to veer left, following a bend in the river, Garry took off across the open field. He would have to dodge occasional willow thickets and ford a small stream, but the shortcut might give him the edge.

The governor's horse leaped over the old trunk of a downed poplar tree with ease. Garry turned it left along the creek bed, galloping hard, looking for a good place to cross. He jumped the horse over a small pile of sticks, and suddenly the horse squealed as it went down, throwing Garry over its head to land on his back in the creek below.

He came up sputtering and turned quickly to make sure his mount did not get away . . . only the horse was still struggling on the bank to regain its feet. Something was wrong. Garry splashed to shore and climbed the bank, only to discover that the horse had stepped into a muskrat hole. He grabbed the reins to help pull the horse to its feet. But every time it lunged, its right leg gave way, and the horse whinnied in pain.

"Easy, easy, boy. Come on. Come on!" He tugged on the reins as the steaming animal balanced on its left front leg and then lunged to get its hindquarters under it.

Garry looked toward the road and groaned. He was not going to win this race, not with the governor's prize horse stumbling on a badly broken leg!

CHAPTER 9

THE EAR BITE

The shot that put down Governor Simpson's horse echoed along the river, momentarily silencing the drone of the mosquitoes as the sun came to rest on the western horizon like a shimmering egg yolk.

"Now," yelled the governor, turning on Garry, "whatever possessed you to race these horses?" Without waiting for an answer, he turned to Rev. Jones. "I want this boy punished. He comes from a people that know horses, and he should have known better than to run a horse right along a creek bank or anywhere else where there might have been holes. He was just asking to break a leg. It's a wonder he didn't kill himself!"

"And what about the other boys?"

"That's your decision, Reverend, but this boy"—he stabbed his finger in Garry's direction—"he should have known better. That was my best horse!" He stomped away toward the road and the buckboard that would carry the men back toward the fort.

Mr. Worthington, however, did not hop on the bed of the buckboard. He silently started walking up the road after the wagon of men. The students, each of them leading a horse except Garry, followed along in silence.

"They just going to leave the horse carcass for wolf bait?" Pelly finally whispered to Garry.

Garry shrugged. What difference did it make? The horse was dead, and the governor was right. He *should* have known better than to be galloping along that creek bank. The pile of sticks he had jumped over just before the horse had gone down had been a muskrat lodge. It was obvious to anyone paying attention! Tunnels and holes were bound to be nearby. He had just been too determined to win the race.

Back at the school, Rev. Jones had all the boys gather outside the barn in the fading light, even those who had not taken part in the race. Corporal discipline was a public matter at the school, intended to instruct everyone about what was right and wrong more than to humiliate the wrongdoer. However, in the few whippings Garry had seen since being at the school, the attention of the other boys was far more on how brave the guilty one was than on what he had done.

Garry pressed his lips in a thin line, determined that he wouldn't cry out.

"Mr. Worthington," instructed Rev. Jones as the boys gathered in a circle around Garry, "since he's your boy, you'll assist on this one. Assume the position, Garry."

Garry approached his teacher warily. Mr. Worthington knelt down on one knee, his back to Garry, and Garry leaned over his shoulder, allowing his teacher to grasp his hands to keep him in position. The old strap whistled through the air as Rev. Jones swung it with all his might, and then it landed with a loud smack across Garry's backside.

Garry jerked involuntarily from the pain, but Mr. Worthington held him firmly.

The strap sailed again and again, landing each time so squarely that Garry feared he would not be able to hold back a cry. In desperation, he bit his lip to keep his mouth shut. He was a Spokane, as brave as any man, and the dim evening light would mask his tears if only he could keep from crying out.

He bit down harder—one, two, three more times—and then the whipping was over. Peeling himself off Mr. Worthington's back, he stood up as straight as he could and looked around at his witnesses. Their images swam from the tears in his eyes, and the lamps shining from the windows of the buildings twinkled. In his mouth he tasted the salty thickness of blood. But like a true Spokane brave, he had uttered not one cry!

Back in his dormitory, Garry went straight to his bunk and flopped down on his stomach—his backside still stinging—and faced toward the wall. The other boys were doing their chores to prepare for supper, and Garry expected any minute for Mr. Worthington to remind him to start the fire, his task for the month. Then he heard the flames beginning to crackle in the large stone fireplace. He turned to see that Pelly had not only done his own job of bringing in the wood but had also built the fire. What a friend to cover for him so he wouldn't have to interact with the other boys until there was no chance of revealing a lingering hitch in his voice or tearstains on his cheeks.

Garry sat up and checked his lower lip with his tongue. It would not do to sport a fat lip before the other boys. But he couldn't find any cuts or sore spots. Funny, where had the blood in his mouth come from if not from his lip that he had bit to keep from crying out? He wiped his face again and breathed deeply, ready at last to face the other students.

Then he noticed Mr. Worthington standing in the corner of the room, holding a white rag to the side of his head. He pulled it away and looked at it. He put it back, but as he did so, Garry noticed that it had a bright red blotch in the center. Garry watched more closely, and every few moments, Mr. Worthington removed the rag to reveal the bright red mark. His ear was bleeding. How could that be?

By the time the boys sat down at the table for their evening's meal of corn cakes and bacon, the bleeding from Mr. Worthington's ear had ceased, apparently without anyone else noticing it. Garry kept glancing at his teacher until the man turned at one point so that the light from the table lamp shown clearly on the side of his head. There, in a hideous crescent on his ear, were red teeth marks.

The horror of what he was seeing trickled down Garry's back like melting snow: He had not bitten his own lip during the whipping. Somehow, he had bitten Mr. Worthington's *ear*!

And yet Mr. Worthington had not said a word . . . at least not yet!

"So what were you racing for so furiously this afternoon?" their teacher asked as he reached for the plate of corn cakes.

No one answered.

"Surely you had some major bet on, or you wouldn't have been running those horses so hard." He looked around the table. "Garry, you seemed to be the organizer; what would you have won if you had come in first?"

Garry swallowed. "Nothing, sir."

"Come now, you mean to tell me you were just racing for the fun of it?"

"Yes, sir." He stopped, unsure of whether to keep quiet or

be more sociable. "I guess we were . . . well, the white man doesn't seem to have much fun, so we made our own fun."

"Trouble is more like it!" snorted the teacher around a mouthful of bacon. "So you organized a race because you were bored? Is that it?" Everyone around the table slowly nodded their heads. Was Mr. Worthington going to pile more work on them? But all he did was growl, "Well, next time, try a foot race; then the only leg you'll break will be your own."

The little moon-shaped scab on Mr. Worthington's ear quickly healed, and as the months went by without anything being said about it, Garry slowly relaxed. It began to dawn on him that Mr. Worthington was not holding the injury against him, and it forged a kind of brotherhood between the two—teacher and student. Garry listened more closely in class and worked extra hard to do well in his lessons.

One morning the next spring, Mr. Worthington began class by reading from Romans 1, beginning with verse 19:

> *"Because that which may be known of God is manifest in [the heavens]; for God hath shewed it unto them. For the invisible things of him from the creation of the world are clearly seen, being understood by the things that are made, even his eternal power and Godhead; so that they are without excuse: Because that, when they knew God, they glorified him not as God, neither were thankful."*

He read on about how wicked people had exchanged the glory of the immortal God for idols they had made with their hands, idols that looked like animals and birds and other created things, rather than worshiping the Creator.

Garry raised his hand. "But what if those people *had*

worshiped the Creator God? What if they *were* thankful? What would God have done to them?"

"Well, I'm not exactly sure, Garry. But I think God would have spoken to them in some way. God is a just God. And the Bible tells us that He is 'not willing that any should perish, but that all should come to repentance.' But why do you ask?"

Garry looked around at the other students. "Because my people have always worshiped the Creator God. We honor His creation because in doing so we honor Him, but we only *worship* the Creator."

"Well, then," said Mr. Worthington, "perhaps that is why you are here."

He closed the Bible and seemed ready to move on to some other subject, but Garry interrupted. "Not perhaps, Mr. Worthington. That's *exactly* why I am here." Why hadn't he seen it clearly before? The bubble of excitement Garry had felt at first seeing the Leaves of Life gave him courage to keep on speaking. "A prophet among our people—Circling Raven—said that white men would come, and we should learn from the Leaves of Life. The marks in them would show us how to go to heaven. I think he was talking about the black book." He pointed at Mr. Worthington's Bible. "My father sent me here to learn everything God says in the black book. It's not just perhaps. That is . . . that *is* why I am here!" When he stopped speaking, he was shaking with excitement.

"I think you may be right," said Mr. Worthington, looking closely at the book he held in his hand. "This passage speaks of God's displeasure at those who ignore His revelation in nature, but it raises the obvious question: What if some people worship God 'in spirit and in truth'? The Gospel of John says that 'the Father seeketh such to worship him . . .' "

The rest of that school day, Mr. Worthington quizzed Garry

about the old prophecy, asking how the Spokane people worshiped and what they had been able to understand about God just by paying attention to His revelation in nature.

"Your story is amazing," said the teacher, genuinely moved. "Here. I want to read another passage to you that talks about this subject. In Psalm 19:

> *"The heavens declare the glory of God;*
> *and the firmament sheweth his handywork.*
> *Day unto day uttereth speech,*
> *and night unto night sheweth knowledge.*
> *There is no speech nor language,*
> *where their voice is not heard.*
> *Their line is gone out through all the earth,*
> *and their words to the end of the world."*

Mr. Worthington turned to the rest of the boys. "Students, do you see what this psalm is saying? The heavens—or all of nature, actually—tell us a great deal about God. But more importantly, there is no place in the whole world—'no speech nor language'—where that message is not heard. That's what Garry has told us, as well; maybe that has been true for some of you who came from other tribes.

"But that is just the beginning. There is so much more. And that is why you are here—to learn the rest of the story, the really good news. Listen what it says beginning in verse 7:

> *"The law of the Lord is perfect,*
> *converting the soul:*
> *the testimony of the Lord is sure,*
> *making wise the simple.*
> *The statutes of the Lord are right,*
> *rejoicing the heart:*

the commandment of the Lord is pure,
enlightening the eyes.
The fear of the Lord is clean,
enduring for ever:
the judgments of the Lord are true
and righteous altogether.
More to be desired are they than gold,
yea, than much fine gold:
sweeter also than honey
and the honeycomb.
Moreover by them is thy servant warned:
and in keeping of them there is great reward."

Mr. Worthington closed the Bible with a thump and held it up. "In this book there is a great reward for you, a great gift! Tomorrow I'll tell you what that gift is. But for now, class is dismissed. Go get some lunch, and then get out there and hoe that corn!"

CHAPTER 10

THE GREAT GIFT

Garry was so eager for class to begin the next morning that after sweeping the floor—his morning duty for the month of May—he helped Pelly with his chore for the month—washing dishes.

When class began, Garry was surprised to see Rev. Jones sitting in the back of the room. But Mr. Worthington rapped for attention as the boys shuffled on their benches.

"We'll continue our study in Romans this morning and discover the great reward I mentioned to you yesterday." The teacher opened his Bible and read verses twelve through sixteen of chapter two. "Here the apostle Paul tells us that those who have never heard of God's written Law will be judged by the law of conscience written on their heart, while those who *have* heard the Law will be judged by the Law. So I have this question: Garry, it sounds like your people learned all they could of God and His character from nature. Is that right?"

Garry nodded.

"And did you try to do what was right according to what you learned?"

"Yes, sir."

"But even by your own standards, did you succeed all the time? Did you ever lie? Was anyone ever cruel to others? Did you sometimes forget to thank God?"

"Well, y-yes," stammered Garry. "But we tried."

"Yes. I have no doubt that you tried. But I have also invited Reverend Jones to join us today because he grew up in the church, learning God's written Law from a very young age. Tell us, Reverend Jones, did knowing the Law keep you or others you knew who were equally aware of its requirements from ever sinning?"

Rev. Jones stood solemnly. "Like Garry here, we tried. But as I look back over my life, I often failed, and so did everyone else I knew."

Mr. Worthington nodded. "Thank you both for your honesty. What I think you both have shown is that whether judged by God's written Law or the law He writes on our hearts—our conscience—we all have sinned. And that's exactly what Paul tells us in Romans 3:23: 'For all have sinned, and come short of the glory of God.' Then later, in Romans 6:23, Paul tells us that 'the wages of sin is death; but the gift of God is eternal life through Jesus Christ our Lord.' 'Death' here means eternal separation from God." Mr. Worthington closed the Bible. "So there you have it. Whether growing up knowing God's laws in this book or without ever hearing the biblical message, we all sin, which separates us from God. But this book tells us about God's great gift. God wants to give you eternal life. Isn't that wonderful?"

The Indian boys just looked at him. No one spoke. Mr. Worthington looked around at his students with a slight, openmouthed grin on his face. "Don't you see?" he asked, but still no one answered.

"Excuse me, Mr. Worthington—" the interruption came from Rev. Jones in the back of the room—"perhaps the boys don't understand how they are supposed to *get* this great gift. Maybe that is why they aren't responding."

"Of course, but it is right here in Romans."

"But you haven't told them yet."

"Indeed." Mr. Worthington looked a little flustered. He opened the Bible again. "Well, Paul says in Romans 3:22 that it comes by faith in Jesus Christ."

"But what does that mean, brother? You still haven't told them."

Mr. Worthington swallowed and looked out the windows as though he had been caught without the proper clothes on for some great festival and was looking for a place to run and hide.

"Hmm." Rev. Jones cleared his throat. "Might I suggest you explain John 1:12 to the boys."

"Of course. Good idea. Thank you, Reverend. Now, students, during the last few weeks we have learned how God sent His only Son to earth to pay the penalty for our sins. You remember that?" There were several murmurs of agreement among the boys. "Well, John writes in his gospel, 'As many as received him, to them gave he power to become the sons of God, even to them that believe on his name . . .' " He glanced at Rev. Jones as though checking whether he was saying it in an understandable way.

Garry turned to look at the preacher in time to see him nodding patiently toward the teacher.

"The way we 'receive' Jesus begins—as John says in this verse—by *believing,* believing that Jesus is truly God's son, that He came to earth to take the penalty for our sins. It's as though . . ." Mr. Worthington cleared his throat. "Remember last summer when Garry got a whipping for breaking the leg of the governor's horse? What if I had stepped in and offered to take that whipping instead? *That's* what Jesus did for us when He died on the cross and rose again."

Garry looked down at the table in front of him. Mr. Worthington hadn't taken his whipping for him, but he had kept quiet when he bit his ear. Garry hadn't meant to bite his ear any more than he intended to sin against God, but it had happened, and Mr. Worthington had covered for him, protecting him from further punishment. Yes, Garry knew what it was like for someone else to take his blame.

"But," the teacher continued, "to 'receive' God's gift also means making Him the center of our lives so that He controls everything. It means giving ourselves completely to Him." His eyes were bright with hope. "Now do you understand?"

Garry kept his eyes on the teacher. He didn't know about Pelly and the other boys, but he nodded his head vigorously. Yes, yes, now he understood.

In the next couple of weeks, Garry talked to Mr. Worthington several times and then went to pray with Rev. Jones, asking God to forgive him of his sins and "receiving" Jesus to be his savior and chief of his life. To Garry's delight, several of the other boys did the same, including Pelly. On June 24, 1827, a procession made its way to the Red River, where Rev. Jones baptized ten boys from the school as new Christians.

After that, Garry's studies took on a different purpose. No longer was he on a quest. He had found the "Leaves of Life," and they had certainly brought him new life and shown him the way to heaven. However, he had much to learn before he was ready to return to his tribe with the prize he had found. Now he had to prepare himself to return to his father and his people.

Garry tried to learn all he could about farming, a skill for improving the daily life of his people. But most of all, he wanted to be able to take back the message of the "Leaves of Life." No longer content to just learn about God from Mr. Worthington and Rev. Jones, Garry learned to read and write. He memorized dozens of Scripture passages and Christian hymns. He learned how to use the Book of Common Prayer for leading daily worship and looked forward to The Day—the day he would be ready to go home.

Three more winters passed. In the spring of 1829, the day finally arrived that Garry and Pelly had worked for so long: graduation day. Each year they had seen other boys graduate and new ones come, but they were still the only ones from the tribes of the Columbia Plateau. Each spring the returning trading brigades had brought reports from the boys' home, but they had been brief and general: "Your father, old Chief Illim, asked about you and said he wants you to study hard and hopes you are well. The salmon run was good this year, but they didn't have so many furs to trade."

Garry was glad for the news, but it didn't tell him much. Mostly he just felt homesick for the next week or two. But now it was graduation time. Soon he and Pelly would be heading home with the outbound brigade.

Mr. Worthington, Rev. Jones, all the students, and even Governor Simpson and a few local families packed into the small schoolhouse for the ceremony on Sunday afternoon, May

10. Rev. Jones opened with a prayer and Scripture reading, followed by a short message. Then Mr. Worthington stood up in a clean white shirt and freshly brushed suit.

"Garry and Pelly, would you please step forward." Awkwardly folding his hands and looking up at the roof as though appealing to God sitting there in the rafters, he said, "This is a momentous day. These young men have come farther than any of our other students. They came to find and study what their people call the 'Leaves of Life' " . . . . He looked at Garry. "And what is it your people call God?"

"Quilent-sat-men," said Garry.

"Yes," nodded Mr. Worthington, "and it means Creator of All—quite appropriate, I think. Their tribes sent them here to discover the path to God. Well, I can testify that they have found that path through Jesus Christ, and they have come to know Him in a deep and personal way. They have found the path to God, and they are prepared now, after four years of study, to tell others about God and the gift of His Son."

He turned to the table beside him and picked up four books, handing two to Garry and two to Pelly. "On behalf of the Red River Mission of the Church of England, I am presenting each of you with a Holy Bible and a Book of Common Prayer. You are both able to read them now and understand the basics of the Christian faith. We here at the Red River Mission charge you to return to your people with the message of the Gospel. May God go with you!"

Garry and Pelly looked at the two prized books in their hands. What a great gift!

More prayers, hearty congratulations, and a special meal followed the brief ceremony. But for the rest of the afternoon, all Garry could do was open the leather-bound "Leaves of Life" again and again. Not only had he found the prize that his father had sent him to seek, not only had he learned how to read its directions, not only had he studied and memorized many of its secrets—but in his hands he had an actual copy of the "Leaves of Life." He would take it back to his people to show them how to receive God's great gift, thereby fulfilling the old prophecy of Circling Raven.

But first he had to get home. Stepping outside, Garry—four years older and several inches taller than when he had first arrived at the Red River Mission—looked toward the far mountains. Between the mission and home lay 1,850 miles of the most desolate wilderness imaginable.

CHAPTER 11

THE HARD ROAD HOME

Traveling with the next season's outward-bound trappers, Garry and Pelly set off on their long journey. They were no longer the children who had come to the Red River Mission four years earlier but strong young men, returning with the treasure their tribes had entrusted them to find. While at the mission, they had cut their hair and worn the white man's clothing, which was easier to obtain than new buckskin. But Garry was looking forward to the looser, more comfortable clothes of his own people. He would shoot his own deer for soft buckskin and kill a buffalo for a new winter robe.

Garry had not had many occasions to use his prized rifle while attending school. Much of the game immediately around the fort had been depleted by the farmers along the river. "That is why you must learn to farm," Mr. Worthington had said. "When so many people live in one area and are hunting all the time, they use up the game, so you must learn to grow your own food and raise your own meat."

"All we have to do," Garry had protested, "is move to a new place where the game is plentiful. Three or four years later, we can come back to the old village, and there will be plenty of animals to hunt again."

"That's good," said his teacher. "But what if some other tribe has moved in while you were gone? In fact, what if in every good location you might move to there's already a village set up there? Then you would have to stay put and make the best of where you are. That's when farming would become very valuable. Some day there will be villages in every good valley and at the fork of every beautiful river."

Garry found that hard to believe, but he had applied himself to learning to farm, and now he had a large pouch with pumpkin, corn, beet, parsnip, and bean seeds. He would show his people how to plant them. These vegetables would add some good variety to their diet. But right now, he was looking forward to hunting as much as he wanted.

Travel up Lake Winnipeg was easier than their trip down had been as the boats were equipped with small sails that eased the rowing when the wind came from the right direction. But they did not go all the way to Norway House. It was faster, said the brigade captain, to cut directly west to Grand Rapids when they were three-fourths of the way up the lake. But once they had traveled through Moon Lake and started up the Saskatchewan River, it was hard work all the way with seldom relief provided by the sails.

In spite of how daily hard work with shovels, hoes, and axes had toughened Garry's and Pelly's hands while at school, rowing the heavy boats upstream from dawn until nearly dark day after day soon rubbed through the calluses on their hands. One after the other they tore loose from the boys' palms, leaving bloody patches like coins at the base of each finger. They wrapped their hands with rags, but still the sores oozed from constant work on the oars that jacked the boats slowly up the mighty Saskatchewan River.

The trappers wisely waited until well after the spring floods had subsided before trying to row upstream, but the summer had its own trials in the form of clouds of little black flies that bit and mosquitoes so desperate for a drink of blood that they would dig right through the bear grease Garry smeared on all exposed skin. Some of the trappers who chewed tobacco joked that they were just getting rid of the mosquitoes that had flown in their mouths if anyone complained about their frequent habit of spitting.

Quite an excuse, thought Garry. He had certainly sucked in enough of the noxious bugs that if he had swallowed them he wouldn't need to hunt for meat.

Fort Edmonton again provided a welcome rest for the weary travelers and additional time for Garry's and Pelly's hands to heal. On the river, the open wounds had finally become thick crusts that had slowly turned back to ugly calluses of sorts, except that they seemed to crack and weep and occasionally even bleed a little.

After four days of rest at the fort, the brigade captain said it was time to leave. All the trappers seemed eager to get to their territories. "Got lots o' traps to repair, and I want to set out a new line in the high country above me," said one of the grizzled men dressed head to toe in buckskin. " 'Sides, if I don't get there purty soon, some interloper is likely to horn in on my region."

Garry and Pelly were just as eager to get home, so, tender hands or not, they were ready to hit the trail. Besides, the next leg of the journey would be on horseback rather than rowing a heavy boat upstream.

As they traveled from Fort Edmonton to Fort Assiniboine, Garry recalled that on the eastward journey four years before, he had been so disheartened over the loss of his rifle that he had paid very little attention to where he was going, just followed the horse in front of him. That kind of carelessness in the wilderness could get a person seriously lost. But even though on his first day out he saw few landmarks that he remembered, the trail between the two forts was so well traveled that no one could lose his way.

Most of the trappers had a packhorse in tow, but the boys had all their belongings in rolls carried on their own horses, so the second day out, Garry and Pelly took the lead as the travelers left camp. Garry slung his rifle proudly across his back the way he had so often carried his bow.

They had drifted almost a half mile ahead of the rest of the party by noon, when the two horses started tossing their heads and prancing sideways. Pelly, followed by Garry, urged the horses forward over a little rise—surprising a huge grizzly bear with two cubs grazing in a huckleberry patch about twenty yards off the trail directly to the right. The bear rose up and grunted while her cubs rambled off away from the travelers.

Pelly tried to keep his frightened horse from bolting as Garry came up behind him. "Just move on slowly," murmured Garry softly. "She's not likely to attack the two of us, especially when we're on horseback."

"Oh, yeah?" muttered Pelly, eyeing the protective mother bear swaying from side to side.

The grizzly roared, dropped to all fours, and suddenly charged the boys. She skidded to a stop in a cloud of dust about ten yards away, proving it was only a bluff, but not before Pelly's horse had bolted up the trail at a full gallop. With all his might, Garry held his horse steady as it pranced and snorted and twisted in place. The bear, however, took off in a full run after Pelly.

Garry let his horse go but had to fight to keep her on the trail. His mare also wanted to run, but in the opposite direction. "Hi-eee! Hi-eee!" yelled Garry, trying to distract the bear as he followed along.

In spite of the fall that had broken the leg of the governor's horse, Garry had always considered himself an excellent horseman, able to control an animal in almost any situation, but getting a shy horse to race after an angry grizzly bear along a rugged, twisting trail was almost impossible. Ahead Garry could see that Pelly wasn't having it any easier even though his horse was fleeing the bear.

Garry saw Pelly yank his horse hard to the left and realized that the trail had come up on a ravine, threading its way along the lip before descending a narrow path to the creek thirty feet below. Garry watched in horror as Pelly's horse slipped and tumbled with him down the bank.

The bear didn't even wait for the dust to settle before it started picking its way down the steep bank. Garry skidded to a stop at the top and hopped off his horse while at the same time pulling his rifle from his back. He took a stance and raised it to his shoulder just as he saw Pelly's horse scramble to its feet and run off down the creek, but the bear was still working her way down to where Pelly lay against a huge boulder.

Should he shoot? Could one shot drop an animal that huge? What if he missed and hit Pelly? But there was no time to waste. He squeezed the trigger and . . . nothing. Frantically he pulled back the hammer and let it fall again. Still nothing, and the bear was getting closer to Pelly!

And then Garry saw the problem. Somehow, his flint had been knocked to the side in the hammer and wasn't striking the frizzen. He adjusted it, pulled the hammer back, aimed, and squeezed the trigger again. The gun roared, and when the smoke cleared, the bear was running up the creek. Had he wounded her? Had he missed? It didn't matter. The old gal was leaving, and Pelly was safe.

Garry hopped and stumbled his way down the bank, kicking up little slides of dust and gravel wherever he landed, until he was at the bottom.

"Pelly! Pelly, are you okay? She didn't get you, did she?"

Pelly groaned and tried to sit up, but with a cry of pain slumped back, his head resting on the boulder. As though pulling his lips to the sides with his fingers, he exposed his gritted teeth and groaned again. Then he coughed.

"Stay still. Let me help you," said Garry as he kneeled beside his friend.

Slowly Garry was able to get Pelly into a sitting position, then standing, then slowly walking down the gully to where the trail crossed. Occasionally Pelly coughed and spat up a little blood, but his shoulder was causing the greatest pain. Garry could hardly touch his friend's arm without him crying out in pain.

In a few minutes the other trappers caught up and were ambling down the steep trail into the ravine. "Where are your horses?" one of them called.

Hearing the story about the bear, the man nodded. "Figures. My horse has been wanting to jump out from under me. Musta smelled that old bruin." He dismounted and came over to Pelly. "Here. Let me see that arm."

He touched it gently, glancing up at Pelly's face when the boy grimaced in pain.

"Hmm. Dislocated your shoulder. Here, Garry, you get around behind him like this, and hold him firmly."

Garry was no sooner in position than the trapper grabbed Pelly's lame arm and gave a yank and twist. Pelly screamed in pain and then let out a sigh of relief. It had worked. Pelly's shoulder was back in place, and though it was still extremely sore, they could tell from his face that the stabbing pain was gone.

The other trappers helped the boys retrieve their runaway horses, and within a half hour, they were on their way again. But as they rode, Pelly continued coughing and spitting up blood. "That don't sound good to me," said the trapper who had popped Pelly's shoulder back in place. "You might have broke a rib and punctured your lung!"

By the time they arrived at Fort Assiniboine that evening, Pelly had such a high fever that he seemed delirious, and he could hardly stay on his horse.

"Take him into my house," ordered Captain McKay, the man in charge of the fort. "There's a little room in the back he can use."

Garry stayed with Pelly every minute during the next three days as his friend slipped in and out of consciousness. The stuffy little room smelled of camphor from some salve Captain McKay said would help him breath. Garry felt he might do better if he got out into some fresh air, but any attempt to move him threw Pelly into a dreadful coughing fit.

Just before dawn on the fourth day, Garry woke from dozing beside Pelly's bed and noticed something funny about Pelly's breathing. The intervals were too long.

"Pelly?" Garry held his own breath, waiting, praying to

see Pelly's chest rise one more time in the dim light of the candle. Seconds dragged into a minute. "Pelly!" He shook his friend, longing to hear the rasping wheeze that had become so frightening during the recent hours. "Pelly, wake up! You can't do this! Breathe! Breathe!"

But Pelly's breath never came again.

Garry's legs felt like angleworms, slowly giving way and sinking to the floor as darkness began to creep in from the sides to choke out his vision. His head and arms draped over the bed like melting wax. Pelly was dead! Dead! Garry couldn't move.

Why! Why had he died? If God had wanted them to bring the Leaves of Life and its message about Jesus back to their people, why had God allowed him to die? Pelly had spent four years studying and learning about God . . . but for what?

Apparently Garry's moans attracted the attention of Captain McKay, who appeared in the doorway. "Is he gone?"

Garry nodded, choking back the tears. But he didn't get up.

"I'm sorry, son. I—I'll get some of the Indian women outside to bury him."

"No." Garry pushed himself to his feet. "He must have a Christian burial. He was a Christian and . . . the best friend I ever had."

"But . . . but we don't have nobody here to pray for him or nothin'," mumbled the deep voice of the captain.

Garry looked at the man who stood there in his worn-out long underwear. What was with these white people who didn't even know Jesus? "Don't need anybody else. I can pray well enough."

McKay nodded, his bushy black beard bobbing like a leaf

in the breeze. "Good enough, then. I'll find someone to dig a grave and fashion a wooden cross for him."

"Thank you," said Garry, numbly turning back to his friend.

Only a half dozen people gathered around the gravesite that afternoon as they lowered Pelly's body, wrapped in his Hudson's Bay Company blanket, into the hole. Captain McKay had suggested that possibly the blanket could be of more value if given to his family, but Garry insisted that his friend's body needed to be treated with some dignity.

It was only after the brief service that Garry discovered why the trappers with whom they had traveled all the way from Fort Gibraltar were not present at the funeral. "Oh, they headed on up country while you were nursing your friend," said the captain. "There was no way to keep them here for long."

It took a moment for his words to sink in. Pelly was dead. His traveling companions were gone. He was alone. Steeling his voice to keep it steady, he said, "Guess I'll be heading out on my own, then. I'll get started in the morning."

"Ah . . . can't let you do that," said the captain.

"Why not? I can find my way up the Athabasca to Jasper House. Maybe I'll meet up with the brigade. If not . . . I know the way over the pass and down the Columbia."

"It's not that," said the captain. "Some of the trappers told me that Governor Simpson is very concerned about the safety and welfare of you boys. Apparently the governor is concerned that if one of you should die, it might start an uprising among the plateau tribes. They said I should keep you here until he comes out himself to escort you home."

A knot formed in Garry's stomach. "When will that be?"

"Well, no way of knowing. If he doesn't travel with the brigade, he sometimes comes in the fall before the snow flies. On the other hand, he doesn't make the trip every year."

"What? I can't stay here indefinitely! That's like keeping me in jail!"

The captain shrugged. "Sorry, son. But I can't go against the governor's wishes."

CHAPTER 12

BACK UP MOUNT SPOKANE

After Pelly's burial, the captain assigned Garry to the bunkhouse where a couple of other men who helped run the fort slept. Garry said nothing, but he wasn't going to remain trapped in Fort Assiniboine—not if he could help it. He had to get home. He had been sent on a mission, and if Pelly couldn't return with him to complete it, he would have to do it by himself. He certainly wasn't going to wait months or a year for the governor to arrive. The sooner he could get home, the better.

That night, Garry waited until all was quiet and the fires had burned low before he slipped out of his bunk. Stuffing the hard bread and dried meat he'd saved from his supper into the bag containing his books, seeds, and blanket, he slung the bag over his shoulders and let himself quietly out of the bunkhouse, careful not to wake the other men.

He was heading for the gate of the fort when he remembered his rifle. He had been in school so long that he had gotten out of the habit of keeping his weapons near him at all times. How foolish! He had left his rifle in the little room in the captain's house next to the bed where Pelly died. Worse, he had since learned that it had been the captain's bed, which he had graciously loaned to the injured Pelly.

Making his way by nothing but the light of the stars, Garry diverted his path to the captain's house and gently tried the door. But it was bolted from the inside. He went around to the side and was ready to slit the greased window skin when he heard the captain cough and get up out of bed. Garry waited, but then he saw a light flare up from a lamp or candle.

There was no retrieving his gun now. Who knew how long the captain would remain awake. It was either wait for some other night to escape or go without his rifle.

That rifle meant so much to him—a prize in itself and earned the hard way—but he decided that his freedom and completing his mission meant more than the gun. He turned away and headed toward the gates.

Once outside, he could not replace the pole that bolted the gates closed from the inside, so he propped a large rock against them to prevent them from swinging open with the wind and possibly making enough noise to set off an alarm before he escaped.

As he headed down to the river's edge, a dog began barking from one of the tepees outside the fort. The mutt came racing toward him, yapping all the while but remaining just far enough away that Garry could not catch it and calm it.

Garry continued down the path, hoping the dog would give up and go home, but apparently it considered this whole area its territory and Garry an intruder. At the water's edge Garry found only two canoes—a large one that would require two or three people to paddle it against the current and a small one, old and half full of water. He emptied the water while the dog continued to bark and was about to push it out into the current when someone began calling for the dog. Soon a light flared near the tepees. Garry could see an old woman had ignited a grass torch from the dying coals of the evening's fire.

She stumbled toward the river, calling and scolding the dog. A layer of clouds hid the moon; Garry hoped that the old woman couldn't see him with her own eyes dimmed by the brilliance of the torch light, but he didn't want to take any chances. He tossed a stick at the dog, hoping to chase it away, and stepped into the large canoe, where he lay down on the bottom, out of sight.

Unsure whether to return to the woman or continue chasing off "the intruder," the dog ran toward the woman and then back to the canoes, then back to the woman. Garry peeked over the gunwale of the canoe and sighed with relief when he saw her reach down quicker than any old woman should move and grab the dog by the scruff of the neck as it came close to her.

The dog let out one yelp, then followed her obediently up toward the tepees.

A few moments later, Garry was on his way upriver in the smaller, leaky canoe. But at least he was no longer trapped in the fort!

The hardest part of the canoe trip was passing the place where he had dived for his rifle, where Pelly had hauled him from the water. A deep sense of loss threatened to overwhelm him. He was returning home without his rifle . . . and without Pelly. He coasted on the dark water, almost tempted to dive in again as though he might find what he had lost in those cold depths. But he knew that wasn't true. And he did have the Leaves of Life and Good News for his people.

That would have to be enough.

Late that night he beached the canoe some distance from Jasper House and hiked around it, keeping hidden in the woods lest some Hudson's Bay Company men see him and try to detain him. He slept in the hollow of an immense rotting pine near the point where the trail began to ascend toward Athabasca Pass.

The next morning it wasn't hard to follow the trail on foot, and soon fresh footprints in the snow proved that the trappers had gone that way within the last few days. The bread and dried meat were gone; all Garry could do was quench his thirst with snow.

He hadn't thought about how he would navigate the Columbia. When he reached the river on the other side of the pass, he realized no riverboats were waiting for him. Upset with himself for not having foreseen this, Garry began hiking, unwilling to let anything stop him.

At the end of one day's hiking, he had traveled south, west, and then had to loop back east without finding any way to hike down the Columbia. What he had failed to realize was that at that point the Columbia River, its tributaries, and Kinbasket Lake created a tangle of waterways that were impossible to cross without a boat of some kind.

With great relief he finally stumbled upon a tribe of Indians he did not recognize. They were camped on the banks of the big river, and he gratefully accepted their offer of food. As he filled his belly with hot venison stew, Garry listened carefully but couldn't understand a word of their language. He tried sign language, but it took over an hour of bartering before he finally reached a deal to trade his Hudson's Bay blanket for an old canoe.

Again he was on his journey.

The long summer days provided sixteen hours of daylight, and Garry took advantage of every one of them to paddle down the mighty Columbia, sometimes plowing through its smooth waters, amazed at the towering saw-toothed mountains rising to the sky, and sometimes bobbing like a leaf over the rough rapids and huge waves, never sure whether the next toss of the boiling water would capsize him or not.

Four exhausting days later, with nothing to eat but some of the pumpkin seeds he had intended for planting, Garry paddled his leaky canoe ashore along the Spokane River, with the lodges of his village in sight across the green meadow where horses grazed peacefully in the late afternoon. Across the river, Spokane House looked abandoned, its door hanging open and blackberry bushes growing all around.

The children playing at the water's edge did not recognize him. And it was only after staring at him for several moments that his sister, Qunit-qua-apee, who was washing clothes in the river, squealed and ran toward him with her arms wide. "Garry! Garry is back! Garry is finally back!" Then to one of the children, who were now staring open-mouthed at Garry, she said, "Go tell your Uncle Sultz-lee that his brother is here. Go on! Hurry up! And tell everyone," she called after the naked child who was running across the grass toward the village.

Soon a stream of people were running from the village to meet him as he walked beside his sister through the meadow in the lengthening shadows. He spotted his brother and other familiar faces. "But where is my father? I don't see Chief Illim."

His sister dropped her head. "You didn't hear? He died winter before last. But his passing was peaceful."

Garry felt as if one of the snowfields clinging to the sides of the Rocky Mountains had just avalanched down on him. He nearly crumbled to his knees and couldn't catch his breath. After all the miles . . . the long, dark winters . . . the hard study . . . and the death of Pelly . . . this was too much. His father had sent him to bring back the Leaves of Life, but he was too late. He would not be able to tell his father about God's gift of His Son, Jesus. What would happen to the old chief in the afterlife?

The images of his brother and the other villagers coming toward him across the meadow swirled before his eyes. Soon they were all around him, slapping him on the back, pulling at his short hair, and laughing good-naturedly about his strange clothes. The old women were looking up at him and marveling at how tall and strong he had grown. But Garry felt as though he were inside a cocoon with the hubbub spinning around him on the other side of a thin shell.

No one understood. He had failed his mission. His father was dead. He was alone.

Garry let the crowd move him along toward the village, like a log floating down the river when the ice breaks up in the spring, being jostled this way and that but unable to affect his destination.

When the sun had set and he was seated with his brother and some of the tribal elders around the fire as the women stood behind them whispering in little huddles, his brother Sultz-lee said, "Did the white men freeze your tongue? You've hardly said a handful of words since you got home. What's the matter? Did you get the Leaves of Life? Father always wanted to know."

Garry nodded. "Yes, I got them."

"Well, then! Tomorrow we will send out messengers to all the Spokane villages and to the Nez Perce and the Flathead—to everyone!—and invite them all to a great potlatch."

"A potlatch?" said Garry, realizing for the first time what his brother was saying. "I have nothing to give them. Why would we have a potlatch?"

Sultz-lee frowned, confused. "You said you brought back the Leaves of Life. You can give them the words from it. What could be more valuable to give away than the secret path to heaven? It will be the greatest potlatch ever."

Garry said nothing. Why did his heart feel so heavy?

Garry arose early the next morning and left the village before dawn. He took the Leaves of Life bound in brown leather and climbed the rocky paths of Mount Spokane to one of his old favorite spots overlooking the valley. He tried to pray as the rising sun awoke the valleys below to dazzling color. Why had God brought him all this way if his father was not here to receive the Bible and recommend his message to the tribe? Even worse, what joy could he convey in telling the Gospel if his father had gone to the place of separation and suffering rather than to God's side in heaven?

Desperate for answers, he opened his Bible and began reading the same passage in Romans 1 that Mr. Worthington taught from: "Because that which may be known of God is manifest in them; for God hath shewed it unto them. For the invisible things of him from the creation of the world are clearly seen, being understood by the things that are made, even his eternal power and Godhead."

If his father had worshiped the true God from what he

learned in nature as Garry knew he had, and if God had sent his people the prophecy about the Leaves of Life, why hadn't God kept his father alive long enough to receive the gift of Jesus Christ?

How unfair to take him just before the message arrived! It seemed unjust!

Just? Unjust? From somewhere Garry remembered verses about God being just. But where? He turned to the back of the Bible, knowing that the Book of Revelation spoke of final judgments and how everything would end. Though he had not been able to understand what he read there, this time as he thumbed through the pages, his eyes fell on verse 3 of chapter 15: "Great and marvellous are thy works, Lord God Almighty; just and true are thy ways, thou King of saints."

Just and true are thy ways. Just and true are thy ways. Just and true are thy ways . . . Garry kept saying it over and over. His father had longed to know about the true God. If God was indeed just, then He would deal fairly with his father.

But how could he know? How could he know exactly what his father faced in the afterlife?

Slowly a peace settled on him and lifted the heaviness in his heart. Just like everything else he had learned about Quilent-sat-men—Creator of All—Garry would have to practice faith by trusting that God would deal justly with his father, whatever that meant. Yes. He could do that. If he could trust God with his own future, he could trust God with his father's life in the afterlife.

A large black raven landed on a boulder behind Garry and began cawing in its irritating voice as though trying to chase him away. Garry smiled, recalling the vision Circling Raven had received on that very mountain and God's instruction to pay attention to the marks on the Leaves of Life.

He stood up and waved his arm to scare away the black bird cawing off-key, which sailed off over the valley below. Then in a clear voice that floated after the bird, Garry began to sing his favorite song he had learned at the mission:

> *"I am so glad that our Father in heaven*
> *Tells of His love in the book he has given*
> *Wonderful things in the Bible I see*
> *This is the dearest that Jesus loves me.*
> *Jesus loves me*
> *O Jesus loves me*
> *Jesus loves even me."*

When the echo of soft notes had floated away after the receding raven, Garry sighed and started down the mountain. He had indeed brought home Good News for his people.

MORE ABOUT CHIEF SPOKANE GARRY

Spokane Garry became a great evangelist, and in years to follow, his people honored him as an important chief. Hundreds traveled from all over the region to hear him preach from the Leaves of Life about the path to heaven through Jesus Christ. He taught them songs of worship and instructed them to pray morning and evening and observe the Ten Commandments. He taught the people to set aside Sunday for worship and learning about God. He also instructed them in basic farming techniques.

Within four years, the impact of his preaching had spread throughout the whole region, even as far as Fort Alexandria, British Columbia, over four hundred miles to the northwest in Canada.

But perhaps the greatest testimony to the effectiveness of this revival occurred the year after Garry's return, when five regional chiefs brought their sons and asked Garry to take them to the mission school so they could learn the Good News, as well. The Nez Perce tribe also sent a delegation down to St. Louis, asking for a missionary. In 1836, Marcus and Narcissa

Whitman and Henry and Eliza Spalding responded to that call . . . with mixed results. But that's another story that can be read in the TRAILBLAZER BOOK *Attack in the Rye Grass.*

In the village across the river from the abandoned Spokane House, Garry built a small church, complete with a bell, where he called his tribe together on Sundays for worship. On weekdays Garry held school in the little building, where he taught English, simple agriculture (growing potatoes and vegetables), and the Christian life. During the winter, when the tribe was not busy hunting and gathering, he had as many as a hundred adults and children in attendance at his school.

By the fall of 1833, all but one of the other students Garry had sent to the Red River Mission had graduated and returned to teach Christianity to their people.

In the summer of 1834, Captain Bonneville made a trip through the region and recorded the following in Washington Irving's 1837 book, *Adventures of Captain Bonneville*:

> *Sunday is invariably kept sacred among these tribes. They will not raise [move] their camp on that day unless in extreme cases of danger or hunger; neither will they hunt, nor fish, nor trade, nor perform any kind of labor on that day. A part of it is passed in prayer and religious ceremonies. Some chief . . . assembles the community. After invoking blessings from the Deity, he addresses the assemblage, exhorting them to good conduct, to be diligent in providing for their families, to abstain from lying and stealing, to avoid quarreling or cheating in their play, to be just and hospitable to all strangers who may be among them. Prayers and exhortations are also made early in the morning on weekdays.*

Undoubtedly, by the time these religious practices had spread from village to village and tribe to tribe, they lacked some of the essential content of the Gospel, but they nevertheless reflected a people eager to know and serve God.

On this foundation, Garry and the other students from the Red River Mission begged the Church of England to send them missionaries who could build a strong, sound church among them. But for a variety of reasons, years passed without a missionary.

Finally, in 1835, the American Board of Foreign Missions sent Rev. Samuel Parker to survey the region. Upon arriving in a Nez Perce village, the chief agreed to assemble all the people for worship the next day, which was Sunday, September 6.

Parker was amazed when four to five hundred men, women, and children gathered in a carefully prepared lodge about a hundred feet long and twenty feet wide. He reported, "The whole sight affected me, and filled me with admiration, and I felt as though it was the house of God and the gate of heaven." They sang and prayed and listened to Parker's sermon, translated by an interpreter from Fort Hall, at the end of which they said in unison their equivalent of *amen*.

The next summer, Henry and Eliza Spalding came as missionaries to the Nez Perce while Marcus and Narcissa Whitman went to the neighboring Cayuse.

Soon, however, large numbers of white settlers began to arrive, aided considerably by the Whitmans' efforts in "opening" the Oregon Trail. From then on, friction with white settlers hindered the establishment of a solid church.

The massacre at the Whitman mission in 1847 sealed in the minds of many white settlers that Native Americans were their enemies—or at the very least obstacles to their desire for land—and so increasing pressure was mounted to remove the Indians to reservations.

Bloody skirmishes and all-out war ensued for years. In 1855,

Chief Garry met with white representatives in an appeal for understanding and peace. That same year, Old Joseph, chief of the Nez Perce, signed a treaty with the U.S. that allowed his people to retain much of their traditional lands. However, eight years later, another treaty was drafted that severely reduced the amount of land, but Old Joseph maintained that this second treaty was never agreed to by his people. And so it went.

By 1870, Chief Garry realized that all the tension and lack of receiving missionaries to build a church for the Spokane had left his people in moral decay—marriages failing when white husbands deserted Indian wives, alcoholism from the whiskey introduced by the whites, and a general disinterest in the things of God.

Along with two assistants, Chief Garry launched a revival among his people in 1871 and experienced substantial success, so much so that he wrote to Henry Spalding, asking him if he would come and help. Accompanied by fourteen Nez Perce believers, Spalding held three weeks of services in May 1873 and then two additional evangelistic trips later that summer. At the end of the revival, heralded by the theme, "What shall we do to be saved?" 334 people on examination gave satisfactory evidence of conversion and were baptized, including eighty-one children, according to Thomas Jessett in his book, *Chief Spokane Garry: Christian, Statesman and Friend of the Whiteman*.

But still no permanent minister was assigned to minister among the Spokane. Not until 1884, fifty-five years after Garry returned from the Red River Mission to plant the seed, was Rev. J. Compton Burnett sent by the Episcopal Church (as the Church of England was called in the United States) to Spokane Falls. Unfortunately he proved to be an unscrupulous man, who swindled the tribe out of land for his own farming ambitions.

After this, Chief Garry never again asked the Episcopal Church for assistance.

Chief Garry recalled the last half of old Circling Raven's prophecy: "After the white men with the Leaves of Life come, other white men will come who will make slaves of us. Then our world will end. . . . We will simply be overrun by the white men as though by grasshoppers. When this happens, we should not fight, as it would only create unnecessary bloodshed." Certainly this tragedy was coming true for all Indian peoples. Garry could not stop it! On three occasions, he applied for a reservation along the Spokane River where his people could "work the land and practice the teachings of Jesus Christ." But the land was too valuable to the white settlers, and each time the U.S. government denied his request, saying the Spokane would have to remove themselves to the Colville, Coeur d'Alene, or Jacko Reservations.

Finally Garry himself was swindled out of his little farm. In 1891, he became too ill to work, and when a deceitful white man promised that if Garry would pay five dollars and sign some papers, he could get Garry's farm back for him, Garry said, "I am dying, and all I am thinking of is God. Soon I'll have nothing more to do with this world."

With his well-worn Bible and prayer book in his hands, Chief Spokane Garry died in his sleep on January 14, 1892.

A note from the authors:

Such sad conduct on the part of our government and even the church begs for some kind of a response. Fortunately the Bible gives us four steps for dealing with such sweeping historical wrongs as the ill-treatment of Native Americans or the enslavement of Africans. (1) Acknowledge it was wrong. (2) Clearly ask for forgiveness. (3) Do no further wrong. (4) Be prepared to do whatever you can to make it right.

The Bible says, "Confess your sins" (James 5:16). Too often we are tempted to excuse or explain away past wrongs by saying things like, "Well, the other side wasn't perfect, either," or "That's just the way it was back then." Perhaps we make these excuses because we find the burden of guilt too heavy. It is hard to say that in the process of building this great country, our forebears did wrong. It makes us feel like we don't deserve our current privileges and wealth. And on one hand, we don't. Everything we have has come from someone else, even our most prized possession, eternal life.

But God doesn't leave us feeling guilty. We can ask forgiveness. "But," you may say, "why should *I* ask forgiveness? I didn't do the wrong." Hopefully not, but if you consider yourself an American, then you identify with and benefit from this country's history. The Bible includes examples of "innocent" people asking forgiveness on behalf of the guilty. Jesus Christ prayed on the cross, "Father, forgive them, for they know not what they do." But long before that Nehemiah prayed, "[I] confess the sins of the children of Israel, which we have sinned against thee: both I and my father's house have sinned" (Nehemiah 1:6), even though it was unlikely that he personally committed the sins he then lists. So we *can* and *should* ask God's forgiveness for past wrongs even if we didn't personally commit them. And if we are ever in a position where it is appropriate, we can ask individuals for forgiveness for how our ancestors treated them or their ancestors.

Doing no further wrong is self-explanatory, but the fourth step may be more challenging. There may come times and ways when we can and should make restitution for those wrongs, even the wrongs done by our ancestors. After all, most of us are still enjoying land that was obtained unfairly from the Indians and wealth that came from the unpaid efforts of slaves. We owe a lot. How to repay what was unfairly taken is a complicated issue, but the *willingness* to "make it right" is a godly attitude.

FOR FURTHER READING

Jessett, Thomas E. *Chief Spokane Garry*. Minneapolis: T. S. Denison & Company, Inc., 1960.

Twiss, Richard. *One Church, Many Tribes.* Ventura, CA: Regal, 2000.

ASSASSINS IN THE CATHEDRAL

FESTO KIVENGERE

Authors' Note

All the background events and many of the people in this story whose names are already known are historically true. The reign of terror by General Idi Amin; the worldwide ministry of evangelist Festo Kivengere; Archbishop Janini Luwum's arrest and death; a play reenacting the story of the early martyrs for the Church of Uganda's Centennial; the disappearance of six young actors . . . all are true.

However, the Kabaza family (Theo, Eunika, Faisi, Yacobo, and Blasio), their relationship to Bishop Kivengere, and their involvement in Archbishop Luwum's household is fictional. We tell the story through their eyes only to help tell the other events and their impact on ordinary Christians like the Kabaza family. In this way we hope to protect the privacy of the real parents, probably still living, of the six young actors who suffered the terrible events in the spring of 1977, Kampala, Uganda.

Special thanks to Jackie Nalule and her family from Uganda, who gave us invaluable help about Ugandan life and culture. Any inaccuracies are our fault alone.

CONTENTS

CHAPTER 1

THE GOOD FRIDAY PARADE

Yacobo Kabaza pushed his way through the crowd that was slowly winding its way like a lazy snake through the streets of Kabale. The fourteen-year-old looked this way and that in growing frustration. It was just like his little brother to disappear in the middle of the Good Friday parade! Always goofing off—even on a solemn occasion like today! And where was he supposed to look for him? Yacobo didn't know whether ten-year-old Blasio had dropped back to be with some of his friends or had run ahead.

Yacobo did know one thing: His mother would give him a piece of her mind if he showed up back at the house without Blasio. Why did he always get stuck looking after his little brother? Yacobo hadn't even wanted to come to the parade today; he'd wanted to stay home and work on the ending of the story he was writing. After all, if he got the story finished, he could show it to Bishop Kivengere when the bishop and his wife came over to see his parents this evening.

But, no, the whole family had to come to the parade, and he was supposed to keep track of Blasio.

"This is important, Yacobo," his mother had said firmly. "We promised Bishop Kivengere we would all be at the parade again this year as a witness of Christian unity."

Bishop Festo Kivengere sure wasn't afraid to speak his mind, Yacobo thought with grudging admiration as he pushed and shoved his way through the parade marchers, trying to keep an eye out for Blasio. The dynamic evangelist was the Anglican bishop of the Kigezi district, nestled in the southwestern corner of Uganda in East Africa. His sermons in St. Peter's Cathedral here in Kabale, the largest town in the district, tended to be unforgettable.

"If Christ tells us to love even our enemies," the bishop had preached two years ago, *"how can we have hatred in our hearts for fellow Christians? There is already too much political violence and tribal hatred in Uganda today. What must the Muslims and unbelievers think when they see us Christians fighting about our differences? Only the love of Christ—for one another and for our enemies—can overcome the violence and divisions in our land."*

That woke people up! So here they were on Good Friday, 1976, joining hands with Kabale's Catholics for only the second time in Uganda's history. As it had turned out, the people who were most affected by last year's parade were the Protestants and Catholics who had marched in it. Yacobo had been startled when both his father and mother had confessed wrong attitudes in their hearts and asked forgiveness of their Catholic neighbors. They were eager to march in the parade again this year.

But not Yacobo. If he didn't get back home soon, he'd never

get his story done in time to give it to the bishop that evening. And now Blasio was missing!

For weeks Yacobo had been writing a story for English class at Kigezi High School—a story he wanted to show Bishop Kivengere because it was partly about him. Once Yacobo had started writing, the story seemed to grow on him like a second skin. Walking to and from school, in bed at night, sometimes even when his mother was talking to him!—the story kept turning over and over in his mind. Even now, halfheartedly looking for Blasio among the parade marchers, Yacobo kept thinking of ways to write the final paragraphs. Should he stop when the firing squad fired their rifles? Or should he—

"Eh! Yacobo! You should see the big cross and gold statues they're carrying at the front of the parade!" a voice giggled at his elbow. "And the Catholic fellow walking with Bishop Kivengere sure is wearing a funny hat!"

"Blasio!" Yacobo snapped, grabbing his little brother's arm. "Didn't Mama tell you to stay with me during the parade?"

Blasio's mischievous grin faded. "No," he pouted, jerking his arm away. "She told *you* to stick with *me*. Besides, I came back, didn't I?"

Yacobo pressed his lips tightly together. If he told Mama that Blasio had run off, she would probably be upset with *him* for not keeping a sharp eye on his little brother—and then there would be a big upset. It would probably be best to say nothing.

To Yacobo's relief, Blasio didn't say anything, either, when they got home. It would have been just one more worry for their parents. Their beloved country, Uganda, "the pearl of Africa," seemed on the brink of ruin after six years of President

Idi Amin's terrorist rule. And now they'd heard rumors about violence at Makerere University, where Yacobo's older sister, Faisi, was a first-year student. Just rumors so far—nothing on the radio or in the newspapers. But Kampala, the capital of Uganda, where the university was, was only 260 miles from Kabale, and news had a way of trickling to the outlying towns.

It was these rumors that had prompted Yacobo's parents to invite Bishop Kivengere and his wife to come and pray with them for Faisi's safety that evening after the Good Friday parade. Tea was at six; that meant he still had three hours till they arrived, Yacobo thought gratefully, slipping out into the tiny garden in back of the house with the notebook that contained his story. It was the only place he had any real privacy.

He opened the notebook and skimmed back over what he'd already written. The story was about three young men who had been executed by Idi Amin's soldiers right here in Kabale's stadium four years earlier when Yacobo was only ten years old. Bishop Kivengere had been there; the Kabaza family had been there—they knew the families of the three young men who had faced the firing squad. Yacobo had not really understood what crime the three young men had committed. But two years after General Idi Amin had staged a military coup and named himself "President for Life" of Uganda, the young men had been accused of treason and ordered to be killed in a public execution as a warning to others. There had been no trial. Just accusations, the arrests . . . then the firing squad.

Yacobo hadn't wanted to go to the stadium. How terrible to go see people be executed! But Eunika Kabaza, his mother, had said, *"We can't let those young men die alone with no one to be their witnesses! I could never face their parents again!"*

And so they had gone to the stadium that day with three thousand other Kabale residents. The crowd was silent and grieving. It should have been a terrible day—except for the strange and wonderful thing that had happened. Bishop Kivengere had asked for permission from the army captain in charge to speak with the prisoners before the execution. But as the bishop stepped forward to speak to the condemned men, all three had turned to face him with smiles of joy. "Oh, bishop!" one cried. "The day I was arrested, in my cell, I asked the Lord Jesus to come into my heart. Tell my wife not to worry. I am going to heaven to be with Jesus!"

The other two told similar stories, raising their handcuffed hands upward in praise. The youngest one said, "Please warn my younger brothers never to go away from the Lord Jesus!"

Moments later shots rang out, and all three fell to the ground.

Everyone was stunned. Most of the witnesses had not been able to hear what the prisoners had said to Bishop Kivengere; they could only see the smiling faces and hear the joyful shouts. What had happened to make them so unafraid? Later, preaching at St. Peter's Cathedral, Bishop Kivengere had told their story as they'd related it in the few moments before they died. What Idi Amin had meant for evil, God had used for good.

It was a powerful story—but Yacobo worried whether he had written it well enough. Had he shown what it felt like for a ten-year-old boy to stand in the stadium under the warm East African sun, waiting for three young men barely in their twenties to die by firing squad? Could the reader *feel* his amazement when the young men—

"Welcome! Welcome!" His father's voice from inside the house broke into Yacobo's thoughts. Bishop Kivengere and his wife, Mera, must have arrived. Yacobo closed the notebook carefully. It would have to do. He slipped into the house, where his father, Theo Kabaza, was escorting their guests to the table in the small room that was used for both sitting and eating. Theo Kabaza was a tall, sturdy man who looked more like a farmer or cattleman than a city taxi driver, though he'd driven a taxi as long as Yacobo could remember. "We are so concerned about Faisi at the university," he said. "We don't know what to believe about the rumors we hear."

Yacobo sat on the floor near the four adults and glared a warning at his brother, not wanting Blasio's usual antics to get them sent outside. He carefully held the notebook containing his story, waiting for a chance to show it to the bishop. But not yet . . .

Eunika Kabaza offered milk and sugar to go with the tea and passed plates of bread and butter. "Have you heard anything from Charity about that Kenyan girl who disappeared?" she asked anxiously. Charity Kivengere, Festo and Mera's youngest daughter, was also a student at the university.

Festo Kivengere shook his head. He was not a large man, but his outgoing personality and warm nature seemed to fill the room. "Not from Charity, no," he said. "She doesn't want to worry us. But I'm afraid some of the rumors are true. The Kenyan student was trying to get out of the country, was stopped for questioning at the airport, and has simply disappeared. And, unfortunately, just last week we heard that another student was shot by soldiers off campus."

Yacobo saw the look of alarm on his mother's face.

"But"—the bishop held up his hands soothingly—"that doesn't mean the students are in danger. We don't know why the Kenyan girl was arrested, but the Kenyan government has been very critical of President Amin recently, and so the president may be playing some kind of political game. As for the shooting, we don't know if it was political or just a drunken brawl with police."

"Oh, we never should have let Faisi go to the university," said Yacobo's mother, wringing her hands.

Mera Kivengere laid her hand on the other woman's arm. "Sister Eunika, doesn't Faisi's name mean 'faith'? You must trust our Lord to care for your daughter. We cannot hide our children beneath our skirts forever." Her voice was gentle, but it had strength in it. Years ago she and Festo had lost a daughter to a childhood illness.

"Yes," the bishop agreed, "we, too, are concerned. But Faisi and Charity are brilliant young women. If our country is ever to come out of these dark days, our children must be educated and prepared to function in the worldwide community. If we give up, we have already let Idi Amin win his war of destruction."

The four adults continued to talk, sharing verses of comfort from the Bible, and then the praying began. Yacobo's mother cried, and the bishop prayed for God's peace to replace "the spirit of fear." Then they prayed some more.

Yacobo squirmed. If the bishop thought his sister was all right, that was good enough for him. How long was this prayer meeting going to go on?

Suddenly the Kivengeres were rising and saying they must be going. Yacobo leaped to his feet.

"B-bishop—sir," he stuttered. "May I speak to you?" He dropped to his knees in the traditional Ugandan greeting of respect.

"Yacobo!" said Festo Kivengere warmly. "You boys were so quiet, I forgot you were here. How is school going? You started high school this year, am I right? And keeping up with your studies, I hope!"

Festo Kivengere had been a teacher for twenty years, while preaching and going on evangelistic missions in the evenings, on weekends, and on school holidays. He always asked Yacobo about his studies.

"Oh yes, sir!" said Yacobo. "In fact, that's what I wanted to talk to you about." He thrust the notebook into Bishop Kivengere's hands. "I . . . I've written a story for English class, and I wondered if you would read it and give me your opinion. Because—well, I'd like to be a writer someday, and I wonder if you think . . . well . . ." Yacobo didn't know what to say next.

"Yacobo, the bishop is a busy man," scolded his father. "He doesn't have time to correct school papers anymore. Festo, I apologize for my son—"

"No, no, it's all right," said the bishop graciously. "I will read it when I get a chance and let you know what I think. All right?" He smiled at Yacobo, bid Theo, Eunika, and Blasio good-night, and walked with his wife into the sweet springtime evening with Yacobo's story under his arm.

The messenger arrived just as the Kabazas were sitting down to their dinner after the joyous Easter worship service at St. Peter's Cathedral two days later.

"Bishop Kivengere asks if we can come to their home for tea this evening," said Yacobo's father, reading the message. He looked up at his wife. "All of us—the whole family."

Eunika's eyes widened. "Do . . . do you think it's bad news? Maybe he has heard something from the university! Oh, Theo—"

"Now, Eunika, have you forgotten how we prayed the other night? Faisi is in God's hands. We must trust in Him. Let's eat this excellent *luwombo* you have prepared"—Theo eyed the steaming bowl of green bananas boiled and mashed in banana leaves, as well as the fried beef and *lumonde,* or boiled sweet potatoes, and rubbed his hands together—"and then we will pay a visit to the Kivengeres."

A few hours later Theo drove the family in his taxi through the empty streets of Kabale and pulled up at the bishop's home. Festo Kivengere greeted them wearing a casual shirt and slacks. It was one of the few times Yacobo had seen him without his clergy collar and black suit coat.

"I will come right to the point," said the bishop when they were seated and Mera was serving the tea. "I read Yacobo's story yesterday, and one thing is very clear to me—this boy has great potential to be a talented writer. He should be given the best education possible to prepare him for university. There is a school in Kampala that has a strong writing program for students his age and—"

"Festo!" cried Eunika. "What are you saying? It is hard enough to let Faisi go so far away to school, especially to the capital, where there is so much violence these days. But like you have said, she is almost a grown woman. But Yacobo is only fourteen, and I could never . . ."

Yacobo's ears were burning. Had he heard right? The bishop had said, *"This boy has great potential to be a talented writer."* A talented writer!

"Let me finish, dear Eunika," said the bishop. "I know your concern. But as I was thinking and praying about this, I remembered that Archbishop Janini Luwum in Kampala has asked me to recommend some trustworthy people for his household staff. Theo, you used to drive taxi in Kampala for a few years, did you not? And, Eunika, you are not only a worthy woman of God, but you also are an excellent cook. I know! Every time we break bread at your house, I have to go on a diet!" Festo laughed and patted his stomach. Then he got serious again. "The archbishop needs a cook and a personal driver. Would you consider making such a change—your whole family? That way Yacobo could begin his education in earnest and you would be able to see Faisi frequently and satisfy your concern that she is all right. What do you say?"

A stunned silence filled the bishop's sitting room as Theo and Eunika looked with round eyes and open mouths at Festo and Mera.

Yacobo heard all the words the bishop had said, but only one phrase stuck in his head: *great potential to be a talented writer . . . great potential to be a talented writer . . .*

CHAPTER 2

THE HIJACKED AIRLINER

Archbishop Janini Luwum and his wife, Mary, were pleased with Festo Kivengere's recommendation of the Kabazas for their household staff. By the time the boys' schools let out for summer holiday in early April, the plan was settled. The Kabazas sold their small house, packed up their belongings, and set out in Theo's taxi for Kampala.

It was Uganda's rainy season, and the squeaky windshield wipers kept up a steady beat mile after mile. The car seemed to crawl along the wet, tarred road, which had turned muddy red from the rich red earth along its shoulders. Twice they were stopped at roadblocks by soldiers who demanded to know who they were, where they were going, and why. The boys watched, wide-eyed, as Theo got out of the car and stood in the rain while the soldiers looked at the letter from the archbishop. Both times they were finally waved on.

Yacobo had never been to Uganda's capital city. From a distance he could see tall, modern buildings and red-tiled roofs nestled among Kampala's seven hills. But as the taxi threaded its way through the city's nearly deserted streets late that evening, he saw soldiers on many street corners, stores boarded up, and windows and walls pock-marked with bullet holes—grim reminders of Uganda's ongoing civil war.

The taxi climbed Namirembe Hill, and the boys stared as St. Paul's Church—Namirembe Cathedral—loomed into view. "The Protestant church in Uganda will be celebrating its Centennial next year," Theo told his sons as they passed the beautiful cathedral.

"What's centennial?" Blasio asked.

"It means a hundred years, empty-headed boy," Yacobo muttered.

"That's right," their father said. "One hundred years ago the first Protestant missionaries came to Uganda and presented the Gospel to King Kabaka Mutesa. He was eager to know more, but his Muslim son, Kabaka Mwanga, who later became king, hated Christianity and killed three of his own servant boys who had become Christians."

"Boys?" said Blasio in disbelief.

"Theo . . ." cautioned Eunika, frowning.

But Theo was enjoying his role of teacher. "That's right. They were the first Ugandan Christian martyrs."

Yacobo was silent. Uganda's tribal kingdoms were supposedly united under a president now. But from the little he knew about the former president, Milton Obote, and the current president, Idi Amin, presidents weren't much improvement over kings. If the president didn't like you, you died.

The taxi slowed, then turned into a large, open gate. The archbishop's residence was large and roomy without being lavish or showy. Even though it was late, the Kabazas were welcomed graciously by Mrs. Luwum and shown to the staff living quarters behind the house. They had a few days to get settled and get the boys enrolled in school before Theo and Eunika started their new duties as driver and cook.

"Oh, Theo, let's go see Faisi at the university tomorrow," Eunika said after the car was unloaded. "I just want to know that she's all right."

Faisi Kabaza poked her brothers playfully as she led her family down the hall to her student room on the campus of Makerere University. "Boys aren't usually allowed in the women's residence hall, you know," she teased. "But since you're family . . ."

Faisi was petite, like her mother. She had dancing brown eyes and a lilting voice. She spoke excellent English and already seemed so much more wise and grown-up in Yacobo's eyes.

He tried to look interested as the family crowded into his sister's room. The room was small and shared by several other young women. Bunk beds and chests of drawers seemed to fill every inch of space. He wondered if the men's residence hall was like this one. Where could a person study in such a small, crowded room?

"So what's it like living at the archbishop's residence?" Faisi asked.

"A lot bigger than this!" Blasio piped up.

Faisi laughed. "And Bishop Kivengere really thinks you have writing talent?" she said, eyeing Yacobo in a half-mocking, half-admiring way.

Yacobo blushed. He was just going to tell his sister what the bishop had said when Blasio crowed, "Hey, Faisi, look at me!" The ten-year-old had put both feet in a wastebasket and was hopping around the small room like a one-legged toad.

"Blasio!" scolded Eunika, impatiently hauling her youngest son out of the wastebasket.

Yacobo rolled his eyes. They should have left this clown back at the archbishop's house. "Where do you study?" he asked his sister, trying to sound grown-up and serious.

"At the library," she said. "Come on, I'll show you."

"Uh, maybe another time," said Theo Kabaza quickly. He looked uncomfortable in his suit and tie. "Are you sure you're all right, Faisi? We heard that there have been demonstrations on campus against the government—you know, after that Kenyan girl disappeared and the other student was killed. Why don't you come live with us for this next school term? At least until things settle down and are safe again."

Faisi looked upset. "No, please, Papa. I don't want to interrupt my studies. I've only just started! Don't worry; I'll be fine. I'm not political. I just mind my own business and do my schoolwork."

Theo and Eunika looked at each other. "All right," Theo sighed. "But . . . please be careful."

Yacobo was disappointed not to see the library. He'd read practically all the books in his school library back in Kabale and would love to see a really big library. But surely they would visit Faisi again soon.

Yacobo had not seen Festo Kivengere since they'd moved to Kampala. His parents said the Kivengeres were traveling in Europe for a series of evangelistic meetings. At a youth convention in Germany, Festo was scheduled to share the preaching with his friend Billy Graham, the American evangelist.

But before he left Uganda, the bishop had put in a good word for Yacobo at the Senior School for Arts and Science, and

Yacobo had been placed in an advanced writing class, even if he was only a Senior 1 student.

Once the school term started again in June, Yacobo settled into a familiar routine. Dressed in his school uniform—white shirt, khaki shorts, and gray knee socks with a red band around the top—he quickly ate his breakfast of millet boiled into a mush and walked Blasio to his primary school. Then he caught a *matatus*, a small bus that took him to the senior school. Yacobo got out of school later than Blasio, so his mother usually picked up his little brother in the afternoon.

Yacobo felt strange at first in his new school. Back at Kigezi High School, many of the students—like himself—were from the Bahororo tribe, and they spoke the familiar Ruhororo language on the playground. School classes were taught in English, and most students also had to study Swahili, Africa's trade language. But here in Kampala, the students came from many different tribal backgrounds—Kakwa, Langi, Acholi, Iteso, Banyankole, and others—and each one had its own dialect. So even on the playground the students had to use English.

It was also the first time Yacobo realized that a person's tribal background could get him in trouble.

During his first week at the new school, one of the Senior 4 boys backed him up against a wall and looked him up and down. "Your name—Yacobo—is that a Christian name?" the boy demanded.

Slowly Yacobo nodded. Like many Christian parents in Uganda, his parents had christened him with a name from the Bible: Jacob, or Yacobo.

"You're Langi, then? Or Acholi?"

Yacobo shook his head. "Bahororo. Does it matter?"

The boy sneered. "You're lucky you're not Langi. Langi

are traitors. *Ex*-President Obote was Langi." He put a lot of emphasis on "ex."

The older boy started to walk away. But Yacobo didn't like being pushed around. "You are . . . ?" he called after him boldly.

"Byensii. Kakwa tribe," the boy said proudly. "Same as President Idi Amin. The Muslims are running the country now. So watch yourself, Christian boy."

Yacobo watched the boy swagger away. Now he understood why his sister, Faisi, said, "I'm not political." He didn't care what tribe someone belonged to. He just wanted to make some new friends and get a good education.

There had been another terrible incident at the university. The warden in charge of the women's residence where the Kenyan girl had lived had been scheduled to give her testimony at court. But the day before the hearing, the warden had been arrested in broad daylight, taken away, and killed. Now Yacobo's parents were *really* worried about Faisi; he didn't want them to worry about him, too, so he didn't tell them about what had happened at his own school.

Besides, they were busy with their new jobs. Theo drove the archbishop on official business, picked up visitors at the international airport in nearby Entebbe, about thirty miles from Kampala, and kept the cars running. Eunika was often called on to cook for the archbishop's many guests. It seemed that every Christian mission worker or evangelist or church official was hosted by the archbishop and his wife at one time or another.

One Sunday in late June, Theo came home from the airport looking flustered and upset. "Have you heard the news?" he asked, turning on the kitchen radio and trying to find a station amid all the static.

Yacobo looked up from his homework that he was doing at the kitchen table.

"Theo, what—?" Eunika began. She was chopping vegetables for that night's supper.

"A group of Arab terrorists hijacked a plane full of Israeli passengers and forced it down at Entebbe airport! I was supposed to pick up one of the archbishop's guests at Entebbe, but they've diverted all planes to other countries." Theo gave up on the fickle radio.

"Why, Taata?" Yacobo asked, using the childhood name for his father.

Theo shrugged. "From what I heard, they're demanding the release of political prisoners." The big man shook his head. "Israel won't do it. They never cooperate with terrorists. But . . . the hijackers said they'd start shooting hostages if they didn't."

"O Lord, have mercy," said Eunika, putting down her chopping knife. "Let's pray for the hostages right now."

The next day, the hijacking was all anyone at school could talk about. Byensii, the Senior 4 student, was talking loudly to a wide-eyed group of boys. "Those hijackers were smart landing at Entebbe," he smirked. "They knew Idi Amin would protect them."

"Why would the president protect a bunch of foreign terrorists?" Yacobo spoke up. Immediately he was sorry he'd said anything.

Byensii turned on him. "What do *you* know, Christian boy?" he sneered. "Because he's a Muslim and all Muslims stick together. And *nobody* stands in Idi Amin's way . . . nobody." He jabbed a finger at Yacobo's chest just as the school bell rang to call them inside.

Three days . . . four days . . . five days went by, and still the hijacked plane sat on the ground at Entebbe airport. The Israelis seemed willing to talk to the terrorists, and so the deadline for shooting hostages was extended. Archbishop Luwum called for national prayer. News on the radio and in the newspapers gave lots of coverage to the terrorists' demands.

But after a few days Yacobo quit caring about it and tried to concentrate on his new classes. He had a full schedule—geography, Ugandan history, English, Swahili, general science, algebra, and advanced writing, as well as soccer. It was tempting to spend extra time on his writing assignments, but he knew he had to keep up in his other subjects if he wanted to stay in this school.

After attending worship at the Namirembe Cathedral on Sunday, July 4, Eunika Kabaza served a light lunch for Archbishop and Mrs. Luwum and several visiting district bishops. When Yacobo's mother came back to the Kabaza apartment, she said, "Yacobo, the archbishop would like you to come see him in his study." She looked at him suspiciously. "You haven't been fooling around and getting into trouble, have you?"

"No, Mama!" he protested.

Why does the archbishop want to see me? Yacobo wondered anxiously, tucking in his shirttail as he hurried into the main part of the house. The house was cool and quiet. At the study door he stopped. He could hear voices inside. Taking a breath for courage, he knocked.

"Come in," said a pleasant voice.

Archbishop Luwum and several other men in clergy collars were sitting in comfortable chairs, leaning slightly toward one another as if they had been having a lively discussion that Yacobo had interrupted.

"Ah, it's Yacobo Kabaza," the archbishop said to the other men. "Sit down, young man."

Yacobo sat, wondering nervously what he was doing here.

"I understand you have a serious interest in writing."

Yacobo nodded. "Yes, sir."

"My fellow bishops and I have been discussing plans for the Centennial," the archbishop explained kindly. Janini Luwum was a short, stocky man, dark skinned like the tribes in the north, with a wide, flat nose. "Of course, each bishop will plan special events for his own district, but many believers plan to come to Kampala for the main celebrations—"

"And we are eager to tell the history of the church in Uganda in a way that will be interesting to young and old alike," interrupted one of the other bishops.

Again Yacobo nodded, feeling puzzled. Why were they telling him these things?

Janini Luwum seemed to sense the boy's bewilderment. "Yacobo, have you heard about the boy martyrs in King Mwanga's court?"

Yacobo found his voice. "Yes, sir, a little." He tried to remember what his father had told them in the car on the way to Kampala about the three servant boys who had been killed for becoming Christians.

"Bishop Wani here has an idea of presenting a play at the Centennial celebrations about these young martyrs who gave their lives for Christ, to be performed by our youth. We have enjoyed much religious freedom in this country up to the present, but dark storm clouds are gathering over Uganda. Tensions are growing, both politically and religiously. Some people are already suffering; many more may suffer in the future. We must encourage one another to have the faith that these young martyrs had."

Yacobo thought he should nod again, but his bewilderment was growing. What did this have to do with him?

"We need someone to write this play," the archbishop said. "Festo Kivengere seems to think highly of your writing potential. Would you be willing to take on this task?"

Yacobo's eyes widened in astonishment. He opened his mouth, but no words came out.

"It would mean doing a lot of research," the archbishop cautioned. "Possibly we could arrange for you to use the university library to find resources. Your writing teacher could supervise your progress. It would be a lot of work. But it would also be a great contribution to our Centennial celebration. What do you think?"

"Oh yes, sir! I mean . . . I would like to try," he heard himself saying. "It would be an honor." No sooner had he opened his mouth than Yacobo felt a rush of fear. Could he write a play? To be performed before thousands of people? What if he failed? What if—

There was a knock on the study door. All eyes turned as an excited Theo Kabaza stuck his head in the door. "Please excuse me for interrupting, Archbishop Luwum," said Theo. His eyes blinked with surprise at seeing Yacobo sitting in the archbishop's study. "We just heard news—last night a band of Israeli commandos landed at Entebbe airport in a surprise attack and freed all the hostages from the hijacked plane! All the terrorists were killed, as well as the Israeli commander."

There was a stunned silence in the room. Bishop Wani murmured, "Praise God the ordeal is over."

Someone else said, "But how did the Israelis get into Uganda? This is going to be very embarrassing for Idi Amin."

Archbishop Luwum interrupted. "One moment, gentlemen. Yacobo, you may go now. Talk to your parents and give me an answer soon."

Yacobo rose and walked to the door, where his father waited. As father and son shut the door behind them, Yacobo heard the archbishop say in a sober voice, "Brothers, I smell trouble."

CHAPTER 3

ARRESTED!

Yacobo couldn't get a word in edgewise that night as the family first gathered for tea at six o'clock, then supper at nine. Talk, talk, talk about the Israeli commando raid on Entebbe airport. Apparently the Israeli commandos had flown four Hercules transport planes undetected at low altitude into Entebbe, unloaded a black Mercedes identical to President Amin's personal car, and used an Idi Amin lookalike as a decoy to approach the plane. Taken by surprise, all the terrorists were killed and the hostages loaded quickly into the transport planes. The entire rescue had taken less than an hour.

Blasio was excited by the rescue. Jumping up from his chair, he held an imaginary machine gun and "blasted away" at imaginary terrorists.

"Stop it, Blasio," said his mother sharply. "Christians cannot be happy when anyone is killed, not even our enemies. The hijackers were bad men; what they did was wrong. But

I wish . . . I am sorry they lost their lives. We must pray for their families."

"The trouble is not over," warned Theo. "I heard the bishops say that this raid is very embarrassing for President Amin. To have Israeli commandos use a car like his and a lookalike of himself as a decoy—he is probably furious. There may be trouble."

"What kind of trouble?" asked Blasio eagerly, still making shooting noises with his mouth.

Eunika and Theo Kabaza exchanged a look. "I don't know," Theo said. "But I want you children to stay close to home."

Yacobo groaned. How could he do research on the boy martyrs if he had to stay close to home? The archbishop had even suggested the university library. This would be the perfect excuse to go there!

"Yacobo! Are you asleep?" asked his mother. "I asked what the archbishop wanted to see you about."

Yacobo looked around the table. His father, mother, and brother were all looking at him curiously. He took a deep breath. "Oh. I almost forgot in all the excitement," he said casually. "Archbishop Luwum asked me if I would write a play for the Centennial celebrations next year—about the boy martyrs in King Mwanga's court. You know, the servant boys you were telling us about, Taata."

"A play? For the Centennial?" said his father, astonished. "But you've never written a play before."

"Well, now," said his mother, beaming, "that doesn't mean he can't. The archbishop must have faith in his ability. But, son, we really don't know much about that story. How will you learn all you need to know to write a whole play?"

"You are right, Mama!" Yacobo saw his opportunity. "The archbishop says I need to do a lot of research—probably at the university library. That way I can find out all I need to know about the Kabaka kings and what happened when the first missionaries came to Uganda and—"

Eunika Kabaza shook her head. "No, no. Not the university library. It is too dangerous. Didn't you hear what your father just said? There could be trouble in the city."

"But, Mama—!"

Theo Kabaza put up his hand. "No more, Yacobo. We will talk about it later."

Yacobo's writing teacher, Mr. Wabaki, readily agreed to supervise the play project. He, too, recommended that Yacobo do research at the university library as part of the learning experience. But Yacobo's parents hesitated. It seemed too dangerous. Idi Amin was blustering again, condemning the Israelis on the radio; the number of soldiers on street corners increased, and so did random searches of cars and homes. Rumors of arrests and missing persons continued to surface. Festo Kivengere arrived back in the country just in time to be ordered, along with the archbishop and many other religious leaders in Kampala, to the conference centre to hear Idi Amin's outraged version of the "raid on Entebbe."

Whether Bishop Kivengere spoke to Yacobo's parents while he was in town, or whether it was just a gradual sense that "life must go on," Yacobo wasn't sure. But in August, Theo and Eunika reluctantly agreed to let him take the matatus from his school to Makerere University twice a week to use the library. But because he was only a high school student, he was not allowed to check out any books; he had to use them at the library.

Yacobo didn't mind. That meant he had to go more often

in order to read and take notes for the play project. Sometimes he did his other homework there; it was quiet and peaceful and he didn't have to put up with his annoying little brother.

One afternoon after Yacobo had been coming to the library for a couple of weeks, he was struggling through a big book on the history of the kings of Uganda when he heard a teasing voice at his elbow. "Hey, big boy. At this rate, you're going to graduate from the university before I do."

Yacobo looked up into the grinning face of his sister. "Faisi!" he said. His parents had forbidden him to just wander around the university campus looking for his sister, so he was glad she had found him in the library. Her hair was cut short in the boyish style popular on campus, and her warm brown skin seemed to glow with good health and laughter. Today she wore a white skirt and red blouse with no jewelry, and her arms cradled a stack of textbooks.

"How's the play going?" she asked, flopping down beside him and dumping her books on the table.

He shrugged. "Haven't started writing the play yet. I'm still trying to get background on the story about the boy martyrs."

"So what have you found out so far?" Faisi asked.

Yacobo looked at his sister in surprise. She actually sounded interested. At home his mother and father mostly seemed relieved when he got home safely from the library, and only as an afterthought asked, "How's the project going?" When he said, "Fine," they'd say, "Good, good."

But Faisi was actually asking. Eagerly Yacobo scanned the notes he'd written down. "It's a lot more interesting than I thought," he said. "A hundred years ago, Uganda was still ruled by the Kabaka kings. In 1896, Uganda became a British protectorate, and then we got independence back in the 1950s—but you know all that stuff."

He scanned his notes. "Oh, here's something interesting. In 1877, two English missionaries—one was named Wilson, the other Shergold-Smith—walked nine hundred miles from the Indian Ocean until they reached Lake Victoria. Then they sailed two hundred miles on Lake Victoria and landed on the northern shore at Entebbe. They were welcomed with a great ceremony by King Kabaka Mutesa, who had become a follower of the Christian faith from talking to Henry Stanley, the English journalist—"

"You mean the newspaper writer who came to Africa looking for David Livingstone? He was a Christian?" asked Faisi. "I mean, I know that David Livingstone was a great missionary explorer. But I didn't know that Stanley was a Christian or that he converted King Mutesa."

"I guess so," Yacobo said. His eyes were bright with excitement. He had never really liked history before in school, but it was fun finding things out for himself and piecing bits of things together to discover a story. "Anyway, Mutesa wanted to learn more about the Christian religion from the missionaries," Yacobo grinned slyly, "and he was also hoping he would learn how to make guns and gunpowder from these Englishmen."

Now it was Faisi's turn to roll her eyes. "Oh, thank you very much. Uganda is in great shape today because we have guns and gunpowder." A bitter edge crept into her voice.

"Anyway," continued Yacobo, "that meeting of King Mutesa and the English missionaries is considered the beginning of the Christian church in Uganda. That's why we're celebrating the Centennial next year in '77."

"But . . . if King Mutesa was a Christian, why did he kill his servant boys for becoming Christians?" Faisi asked.

"Wrong king," Yacobo smirked. "King Mutesa died, and his son, Kabaka Mwanga, became king. Mwanga followed the Muslim faith, and when his father died, he decided he would squash this new religion. So when he discovered that three of his own servant boys were Christians, he decided to torture and kill them as a lesson to anyone else who was thinking about becoming a Christian."

"Gruesome. How old were they?"

"I'm not sure about the middle one. But the oldest was fifteen, and the youngest was only eleven."

"Fifteen and eleven!" Faisi said, looking a little sick. "That's just a year older than you and Blasio."

Yacobo stared at her. He hadn't thought of it like that. Suddenly the story he was writing about felt a lot more real.

"I have to go," Faisi said suddenly, collecting her books. "There's a student meeting about recent government actions and I—what? What's the matter?"

Yacobo stared at his sister. "But you told our parents that you aren't political," he said accusingly. "They worry about you all the time."

Faisi looked uncomfortable. "Well, I'm really *not* political. But Charity Kivengere says we Christian students can't close our eyes to what's happening in our country." She leaned closer to Yacobo and lowered her voice. "It's getting really bad, Yacobo. Idi Amin is wrecking Uganda, and nobody's stopping him! His soldiers arrest people who disagree with him, but they never get a trial; they just disappear. Hundreds of Asian business people have been kicked out of the country, and their businesses have been given to people who don't know how to run them. It's crazy! Idi Amin acts like Uganda is just a bunch of warring tribes instead of a modern democratic country. He's putting our progress back a hundred years!"

Yacobo stared openmouthed at his sister. He'd never heard her talk like this.

"Anyway, I've got to go," Faisi said. "And maybe you should go home, too, Yacobo. But . . . don't say anything to Mama and Taata, all right?"

Yacobo watched his sister walk out of the library, then he turned back to his book. He hadn't gotten a chance to finish telling Faisi what he'd learned about the boy martyrs. There was more—a lot more. *Well,* he thought, *she can go to her dumb old meeting.* He'd go home when he was good and ready.

Yacobo finally put the book back on the shelf and gathered up his own schoolbooks. His stomach growled, and for the first time he realized he had stayed later than usual and had better hurry if he was going to be on time for tea. He noticed that no one else seemed to be in the library.

Hurrying out of the library, Yacobo headed across campus for the front gate of the university, where he could catch a matatu. But before he reached the gate, he heard a loud noise and the squeal of tires. Suddenly several army trucks roared through the front gate and sped past him. Yacobo stared after them. What were army trucks doing on the university campus? And why were they in such a hurry? With a sick feeling, he realized the trucks were heading in the direction of the residence halls where the students lived!

Without thinking, Yacobo ran after the trucks. By the time he caught up with them, soldiers were running into the residence halls and dragging students out. Screams and shouts filled the air.

Badly frightened, Yacobo ducked behind the corner of a building out of sight. Peering around the corner, he saw many students trying to run away, but the soldiers hit them with the butts of their guns and made them crawl over the rough gravel toward the trucks. Cries and screams mingled with the harsh shouts of the soldiers.

The soldiers were rounding up both young men and young women and making them climb in the back of the open trucks. How many? One hundred? Two? Suddenly he saw a girl wearing a red blouse being pushed and shoved onto a truck. Right behind her was another girl in a blue blouse, a few years older, who looked familiar.

It was Faisi! And Charity Kivengere!

In horror, Yacobo watched as the rear gates of the trucks were slammed shut, each one full of frightened students packed together like livestock. Yacobo kept his eyes on the red and blue blouses as the idling engines were gunned and the trucks spun out toward the front gate of the university and were gone.

Stunned, Yacobo didn't know what to do. People were running this way and that, shouting to one another and crying. Where were they taking his sister and Charity? What was going to happen to them?

A cold knot of fear in Yacobo's chest made it difficult to breathe. He had to get home. He had to tell his mother and father!

CHAPTER 4

LAW AND DISORDER

"Oh, Lord, not Faisi!" cried Eunika Kabaza, crumpling to a heap on the ground when she heard that her daughter had been arrested.

Yacobo could hardly remember how he got home. Somehow word had already reached the archbishop's residence that a large number of students at the university had been arrested, and when Yacobo stumbled into the courtyard, he was greeted with cries of relief. But as he gasped out his story of soldiers dragging students out of their residences and hauling them away by the truckloads—including his sister and Charity Kivengere—relief turned to shock and alarm.

"Theo, let my wife stay with Eunika," said Archbishop Luwum, taking charge of the situation. "Will you drive me to the university? I must find out for myself what has happened. We must send an advocate to the prison to speak on behalf of the students who have been arrested. And the students and professors whose friends and classmates were taken away need pastoral care. Oh—" he turned to his assistant—"get word right away to Festo and Mera Kivengere about Charity."

Yacobo watched his father drive off with the archbishop and several others from his pastoral staff. Going back to his family's apartment, he saw that his mother had stopped her tears and was down on her knees, her Bible open on a chair before her. She and Mary Luwum read Scripture, prayed, and cried together. Then Eunika got up, fed the boys their supper, helped Blasio with his homework, and put him to bed. Even after Yacobo went to bed, he could hear her reading the Bible and praying far into the night.

When Yacobo woke up the next morning, he had a terrible feeling inside, like someone had died, but at first he couldn't remember who or why. Then he remembered: Faisi had been arrested yesterday and taken to Idi Amin's prison. Icy fingers of fear gripped his heart. He had never heard of anyone actually leaving that prison alive.

Yacobo pulled on the clothes he'd worn the day before. There was no way he could go to school today, not with his sister in danger. He was prepared to fight his mother on this point, but she said nothing about school as he came into the tiny kitchen of their apartment. Eunika's eyes were puffy and her face strained, as if she had not slept all night.

"Sit down and have some breakfast, Yacobo," she said, putting a bowl of cornmeal on the table, along with some goat's milk and honey.

"Not hungry," he mumbled.

Eunika stopped what she was doing, took Yacobo by the shoulders, and looked into his eyes. "Whatever happens, Yacobo," she said gently, "we must remember that there is nothing—nothing!—that can happen that will separate our Faisi from the love of God."

Yacobo looked away, a lump tight in his throat. He knew those verses—Romans 8:38 and 39. They were easy verses to say when he was learning them in Bible class, but it wasn't easy now that his sister was in Idi Amin's death prison.

All that morning they waited. And then when they thought they couldn't stand not knowing what was happening one more minute, the archbishop's car turned in at the gate and pulled up in front of the house.

"Mama, Mama!" yelled Blasio, dancing up and down. "Taata's back!"

Eunika Kabaza, Yacobo, Mary Luwum, and others who had gathered to wait with them came running. Car doors opened. And then Blasio screamed, "They've got Faisi!"

Yacobo could hardly believe his eyes, but it was true! Theo got out of the driver's seat, then helped his daughter out of the backseat. Eunika and the boys rushed toward her, then stopped.

Faisi's face was bruised, one eye was swollen, and cuts were all over her head and shoulders.

"Oh, Faisi," wailed Eunika and burst into tears.

"I'm all right, Mama—really I am," said Faisi softly. A strange smile was on her face. "Let's go inside, and I will tell you all about it."

"No, first we must attend to those cuts," Theo said firmly, putting a protective arm around his daughter and guiding her inside.

When Faisi's cuts had been cleaned and the worst ones bandaged, Mrs. Luwum brought tea for everyone, and they all gathered in the Kabazas' small sitting room to hear Faisi's story.

"We were all terribly frightened," she said, her voice soft. Yacobo had to strain to hear. "The soldiers kept hitting us and pushing us around. One student asked, 'Why are we being arrested? What did we do?' And the soldier in charge—a captain, I think—spit and said something about the students at the university going on strike and plotting to overthrow the government."

"What?" said her mother, shocked.

"It's not true, Mama," said Faisi. "I mean, it *is* true that many of the students got very upset when the lady warden—who is . . . who was . . . very popular with students—was arrested and killed just because she was going to testify on behalf of that Kenyan girl! We were so upset that sometimes we didn't go to our classes, and instead we met together in small groups to talk and support one another. But we weren't causing a disruption, and we certainly weren't plotting to overthrow the government!" Faisi's eyes flashed.

"That's all right, sugar," said Theo. "Go on and tell your mother what happened at the prison."

Faisi took a breath. "They made us line up and . . . and the soldier at the gate was beating the students with a spiked club as they entered. There were over two hundred of us, and they crowded us into a locked room. All of us were frightened, some were crying. And many were hurt or bleeding in some way. We gave each other first aid as best we could."

Faisi looked at the archbishop. "Charity was wonderful—Festo and Mera Kivengere would have been proud of her. Many of the students were Christians, and Charity gathered us together and we all started praying quietly. We knew we were in serious danger, but as we prayed, the terror left us, and we began to feel calm and unafraid. Someone said Jesus would want us to forgive our enemies. So we prayed that God would forgive the soldiers who had hurt us, because they didn't know what they were doing!"

The light returned to Faisi's face. "And then another student reminded us that nothing in this world can separate us from the love of God—not even death. And if we died, we would go to heaven to be with Jesus, our Savior. And suddenly our spirits felt . . . lighter, and we even began to laugh with relief and joy."

Yacobo looked with astonishment from his sister to his mother. That was the same verse his mother had quoted that morning!

"But how did you get out, Faisi?" asked Blasio, crowding close to his big sister. "Did you escape?" His eyes glowed with high hopes for a jail-break story.

"We got out by . . . prayer." She looked around the room. "I know you all were praying. There's no other way to explain it. The military chief-of-staff came into the room where we were being kept, and he seemed surprised to see us sitting so peacefully. We greeted him respectfully, and he even ordered tea for all of us! He gave us a long lecture on patriotism and being good citizens, then he ordered us to go back to the university and attend our classes and not cause any trouble! The same trucks that brought us to the prison took us back . . . and there was Taata and Archbishop Luwum and the Catholic cardinal holding prayer meetings on campus for us!"

"Glory!" cried Eunika and spontaneously burst into a song of praise. The others joined in, even Yacobo and Blasio. But even as they sang, Yacobo had a feeling of unreality. Had this really happened to his own sister? They'd been so terrified they'd never see her again, and now here she was telling this incredible story. As the singing and thanksgiving continued, Yacobo slipped into the bedroom he shared with Blasio, took out a sheet of school paper, and began to write down the story Faisi had told.

Faisi insisted on going back to school after a few days of recovery with her family, but there were no more trips to the university library for Yacobo. Idi Amin's soldiers now seemed completely out of control. There was another attack on the university—this time on just the men's residence hall. No students were arrested but many were badly beaten and injured. "President Amin is afraid of a coup," said Theo grimly. "He's trying to make the students too frightened to organize any protests."

Both soldiers and ordinary criminals felt free to loot stores and homes and beat up on citizens. Law and order was breaking down everywhere. Even though the Kabazas and other families tried to go about their daily tasks, Theo drove Yacobo and Blasio to and from school each day in his old taxi, just to be safe.

Yacobo was frustrated. He still needed more information before he could begin writing the Centennial play. His writing teacher refused to supply the information he needed. "Knowing how to get information is a critical tool if you want to be a writer, Yacobo," Mr. Wabaki said. "You will find a way. In the meantime, you can organize the material you do have and begin writing a rough outline of your story, scene by scene."

Yacobo didn't want to do it that way. How would he know where to begin his story if he didn't have all the facts yet? Would he begin with the Kabaka kings? Or with the English missionaries? Or maybe with the boys themselves.

Trouble at school was another problem. The high school headmaster and teachers kept strict order, but whenever they were out of sight, Byensii, the Senior 4 Kakwa boy, and a gang of other Kakwa students lost no time bullying Yacobo and other students they disliked. Every time Yacobo was tempted to tell his parents about it, he clamped his mouth shut. He knew they wouldn't need much of an excuse to pull him from the school, writing class or no writing class.

And then, in November, Yacobo found a way to continue his writing.

According to Archbishop Luwum, there was a new openness to spiritual things on the campus of Makerere University ever since the arrests and beatings of students last August. He asked Festo Kivengere to come to Kampala and lead a "mission" on campus for the university students. It would be a joint mission along with an evangelistic Catholic bishop, lasting a week.

Faisi Kabaza and Charity Kivengere were excited about the mission. They'd been witnessing to the other young women in their dorm, who had come to respect these Christians who'd been arrested and beaten but didn't react with hatred or anger.

Yacobo had his own reason for being glad to see Festo Kivengere. As he lay in bed at night he hatched his plan: Bishop Kivengere would be staying at the Anglican guest house during the mission and going to the university each day. If Yacobo chose the right moment to ask, surely his parents would allow him to ride along with their very own bishop and use the university library during the preaching services. No soldiers would dare attack the university while both the Protestants and the Catholics were holding evangelistic services on campus.

The plan worked. Yacobo asked his parents when Festo Kivengere stopped in briefly to visit them, and the bishop immediately said, "Why, I'd be more than happy to take Yacobo with me to the university and return him safely to you. Anything to help this play project along—it's a wonderful opportunity for him." What could Theo and Eunika say?

In the library on the first night of the mission, Yacobo read some more about the Kabaka kings and what happened when King Mwanga had the three servant boys killed by fire. People had been weeping and their parents were pleading with them to give up their Christian faith. But they would not. They even sent a message to the king: "Tell His Majesty that he has put our bodies in the fire, but we won't be long in the fire. Soon we shall be with Jesus, which is much better. But ask him to repent . . . or he will land in a place of eternal fire."

Then the boys sang a song that later became known as the "Martyrs' Song" in all the Christian churches in Uganda. Yacobo remembered hearing the song, though he hadn't known the story behind it. He sang to himself the little bit that he could remember: " 'O that I had wings like the angels. I would fly away and be with Jesus!' "

Yacobo kept reading. King Mwanga became angry because he couldn't frighten the boys into denying their faith. He ordered his warriors to chop off their arms and then throw them alive into the fire. The youngest boy, named Yusufu, pleaded, "Please don't cut off my arms. I will not struggle in the fire that takes me to Jesus!"

The people watching were shaken by such heroic strength in such young boys. What kind of faith was this that could not be controlled by torture and death? That very day, forty adults put their faith in Jesus.

Yacobo slowly closed the book. Did he have that kind of faith in Jesus? Oh yes, he believed in Jesus and wanted to be a good Christian. But . . . would he not be afraid? Would he cling to his faith if he were faced with torture and death?

A hard little seed of doubt, like a cherry pit stuck in his

throat, began to worry him. If he couldn't imagine having that kind of faith, how could he write about it in a believable way?

Walking slowly, Yacobo left the library and went over to the building where the two bishops—one Anglican, one Catholic—were holding their mission. Festo Kivengere was standing in front of a group of students who were listening attentively. He was not preaching to them, just talking.

" . . . knew I could no longer keep on hating my stepfather with Christ in my heart," the bishop was saying. "But the only way to quit hating my stepfather was to forgive him. I didn't want to do that! He had mistreated my mother! But the Bible tells us to 'walk in the light,' and that meant I had to confess my hatred and forgive him. My knees were shaking as I walked up the path to my stepfather's house. He was surprised to see me, and when he heard why I had come, he was very quiet. Then he put his arms around me. As he did so, I realized the hatred was gone. I was able to love him with God's love."

The students were very quiet.

"But if you think that was hard," Festo Kivengere joked, "it was easy compared to the time I had to forgive a white man!" The students laughed.

Bishop Kivengere went on to tell a story about how he had held resentment for many years against an English missionary who had acted superior toward him. The white man did not treat the Ugandans as equals. Instead, he made Festo feel like a child, even though he was a grown man. "But when I went to him and asked him to forgive me for my resentment toward him, it was as if a wall came down between us." The bishop looked around at the students. "Many times since then I have proved that the Cross of Jesus is the end of racial prejudice and separating walls of all kinds."

Yacobo thought about what Bishop Kivengere was saying. He knew the Bible said a person should ask for forgiveness if he does something wrong to someone—but weren't the stepfather and the white missionary in the bishop's story the ones who were wrong? Why did Festo ask their forgiveness?

As if reading his mind, Bishop Kivengere said to the students, "I could forgive them because Christ died for me and forgave me *even while I was still a sinner*. And even though their actions were wrong, so was my hatred and resentment."

A young man put his hand in the air. "This 'walking in the light'—I don't understand what it means."

The bishop smiled his winning smile. "Jesus said, 'I am the light of the world.' When we let His light into our lives, His Word shines on things that are not like Jesus so they can be cleansed. And His light shines on our brother or sister, making them precious." He paused and grinned. "I said precious, not perfect." Laughter again rippled around the room.

Then he was serious again. "Some of you have heard the story of the students who were arrested and beaten last August. My daughter Charity was among them. She tells me that the Christian students prayed for the soldiers who abused them and forgave them. How is that possible? Because those students knew that their own salvation is only possible because of Christ's love, grace, and forgiveness—when He covered their sins with His own blood on the cross. If God can love and forgive us like that, can we do any less toward our fellow sinners?"

It was quite late when the bishop was finally free to leave. Students were still praying in small groups. All the way home in Bishop Kivengere's car, Yacobo was quiet. His thoughts skittered around uncomfortably, like drops of water on a hot skillet. The boy Yusufu, only eleven years old, had been willing to die by fire rather than give up his faith. . . . Festo Kivengere asked his mean stepfather to forgive him for his hatred. . . . Faisi and Charity forgave the soldiers who hurt them. . . .

He felt a growing uneasiness about agreeing to write the play. It was beginning to feel too close and personal.

CHAPTER 5

KING HEROD

The mission at the university was over. "God did a mighty work among the students!" Festo Kivengere reported to the archbishop and others who had gathered around to see him off. His trim moustache only accented the wide grin on his face. "The tragic events of this year created an eagerness to hear about spiritual things. Lukewarm Christians have received a new fire to live their faith. Other students put their trust in Christ for the first time. It was a great day for the Gospel! And," he winked at Yacobo, who was hanging around the edge of the send-off, "I think many of the students were astonished when the Catholic bishop gave me a big hug in front of everyone and said, 'I love you, Festo!' Right, Yacobo?"

Yacobo grinned, too. He'd been amazed himself.

"Festo, are you sure you can't stay for the meeting with the cardinal and the grand mufti?" said Archbishop Luwum, shaking the bishop's hand in a reluctant good-bye. "It could be very important."

Festo shook his head. "I must get back to my district. I have been gone too long this year. But I will notify all the churches in the Kigezi district. We will be praying for you."

Bishop Kivengere said good-byes all around. When he came to Blasio, he punched the youngster playfully on the shoulder and said, "I hear you volunteered to be King Herod in the Christmas pageant at the cathedral. Is that so?"

Blasio giggled. "Yes! He's the big bad king who kills all the babies, trying to get rid of Jesus." He made his face look fierce.

"Hush, Blasio!" scolded Eunika Kabaza. "You don't have to be so gruesome."

"But he was really bad, Mama!" Blasio protested.

"He was definitely a wicked king," Bishop Kivengere agreed. "Well, Blasio, I know you'll do a good job. You have, shall we say, a natural acting talent."

The adults laughed. Blasio's antics were becoming well known around the archbishop's household.

Yacobo rolled his eyes. He felt a little jealous hearing Festo Kivengere praise Blasio's "talent." *He* was the one who had the talent. Hadn't the bishop said so himself? *"Great potential to be a writer,"* he'd said. In fact, Yacobo couldn't imagine Blasio doing a serious job in a play. His brother was just a clown.

As Bishop Kivengere's car turned out of the gate and disappeared into traffic for the long ride back to Kabale, the rest of the household went back inside. Yacobo tugged at his father's sleeve. "Taata, what did the archbishop mean when he talked about the cardinal and the grand mufti? What is a grand mufti, anyway?"

Theo Kabaza scratched his chin thoughtfully. "He's the

head of the Muslim religion here in Uganda. If the Catholic cardinal, the Protestant archbishop, and the Grand Mufti are planning a meeting, why, that represents nearly the whole of Uganda. I wonder . . ." Theo did not finish his sentence. But Yacobo thought his father looked a little worried.

School was out the month of December for the "winter holiday." Faisi came home from the university to spend the holidays with her family. Soon Christmas celebrations were in full swing. Advent services each Sunday at the cathedral—celebrating the "advent" or "coming near" of the Christ—were full of joyful worship. Christmastime had always been special back home in Kabale, but there was a special excitement here at the big cathedral in Kampala. Colorful banners were added and new candles lit each week in anticipation of Christ's birth. But the really big celebration, they'd heard, would be Christmas Eve, when the children and young people would put on their Christmas pageant and the archbishop would deliver his annual Christmas sermon, which was broadcast on radio to the whole country.

Before school let out, Yacobo's writing teacher had suggested that he use the winter holiday to begin writing the first draft of the Centennial play. But where was he going to find a quiet place to write? Faisi was now using the family sitting room as her bedroom. Blasio was always running in and out of the boys' sleeping room or practicing his King Herod lines in a loud, pompous voice. Finally Yacobo took his problem to the archbishop.

Janini Luwum was more than gracious. "Let's see . . . you may use my study, Yacobo. In fact, tomorrow I will be at a meeting all day. No one will disturb you. You should get a lot of writing done, eh?"

The next morning Theo Kabaza brought the archbishop's official car to the front door. Several other district bishops—Yacobo recognized Silvanus Wani—who had come to Kampala for this meeting got into the car with the archbishop. Before he got back into the driver's seat, Theo Kabaza mouthed the words "grand mufti" to his son, who was watching from the front steps. "Pray."

Yacobo gave a slight nod. So this was the big meeting with the Catholic cardinal and the grand mufti. He went back inside the house and, feeling a little out of place, headed for the archbishop's study. He wondered what they were going to talk about. Maybe they were going to argue religion. But . . . it was one thing to talk about cooperation and brotherhood between Protestants and Catholics. After all, Catholics were Christians, too. But the Muslims—why, they didn't even believe Jesus was God's Son!

But Yacobo soon forgot about the archbishop's meeting as he concentrated on his story. He would do as his teacher had suggested and write a summary of the whole story, scene by scene. Once that was done, he would go back and work each scene into a script for a play, using dialogue to tell the story.

"I'll probably have to have a narrator between scenes," he mused to himself, spreading out his notes on the table the archbishop had said he could use. "But . . . maybe not." He felt a little thrill of excitement. He had never tried using just dialogue, the things people say, to tell a story. But that was the way a play was written. Just using dialogue. Nothing else.

Yacobo worked all morning, and he was surprised when his mother brought him some plantains, bread, and tea with milk and sugar for his noon meal. All afternoon he kept working, telling the story of King Kabaka Mutesa gladly greeting the English missionaries in 1877 in one scene. The next scene was the death of King Mutesa and the new king's vow to purge Christianity from Uganda. Scene by scene, Yacobo summarized the story, reviewing his notes from time to time to make sure he was getting everything in. After he had made martyrs out of his three servant boys, King Mwanga sent his warriors from village to village to kill any Christians they found. But for every Christian they killed, it seemed ten more declared they wanted to become Christians. Yacobo chuckled to himself. That would be a good scene. Christians popping up all over the place.

Voices outside the archbishop's study made Yacobo realize he'd lost all track of time. He heard the archbishop saying, "Yes, yes, Mary, it was a good meeting. We agreed on many resolutions protesting what is happening in the government.... Specifically? Why, the president's intelligence officers have been given power to arrest and execute people with no trial! Soldiers and common criminals alike are looting and killing... ordinary citizens are being harassed and searched in their own homes." The door opened and the voices continued. "We've sent a message to the president, asking for a personal meeting with him to present these—oh, Yacobo!" The archbishop, with Mrs. Luwum at his side, stopped in surprise at seeing Yacobo in the room. "I forgot you were using my study today. Did you get a lot of writing done?"

"Oh yes, sir," said Yacobo, quickly standing up and gathering his pages together.

"No, no, just leave them," said the archbishop. "I have no visitors scheduled tomorrow, do I, dear? I may do some reading and sermon preparation. We can work quietly together, eh?" He smiled warmly at Yacobo.

The next day, Yacobo felt strange doing his writing in the same room with the archbishop. He wished he could work alone, but it was the archbishop's study, after all. Soon, however, he forgot the man on the other side of the room and began to fill out some of the scenes he'd sketched the day before.

The telephone rang. The archbishop answered and Yacobo wondered if he should leave the room. "Yes, I'll hold," said the archbishop. He didn't say anything to Yacobo, so the boy shrugged and went back to his writing. Then he heard, "Good morning, Mr. President."

Yacobo was startled. President Idi Amin?

"Yes," said the archbishop, "the cardinal and the grand mufti and I did make a request to meet with you personally." Long pause. "Why did we have a meeting without your permission? I'm sorry, Mr. President, but we have never needed per—. . . Of course. We would gladly have asked for permission if we had known. . . . I see. Yes, of course you may have a copy of the minutes of our meeting. In fact, that's why we requested a meeting with you, to tell you personally about our meeting and—. . . All right. We will send the document to you by personal carrier today. . . . Yes, Mr. President. Good-bye."

Yacobo sat frozen at the table in the archbishop's study. The archbishop seemed to have forgotten that the boy was in the room. He just sat at his desk, his hand still resting on the telephone receiver, frowning in thought. After what seemed like a long time to Yacobo, who scarcely dared to breathe, the archbishop abruptly got up and left the room.

Quickly Yacobo gathered up his papers and left the study. He didn't feel like writing anymore. He didn't understand what was going on, but he knew one thing: The archbishop was worried about something.

A few days later, fifty delegates from the Church of Uganda—including Archbishop Luwum and Festo Kivengere—boarded a bus bound for Nairobi, Kenya, for the Pan African Christian Leadership Assembly, or PACLA, as it was called. Christian leaders from many African countries met together to encourage and support one another. Billy Graham, the American evangelist, was going to be there, and Festo Kivengere was going to translate for him. The next night, Festo—Uganda's own evangelist—was going to preach.

Yacobo overheard his father tell his mother that he was surprised Idi Amin had given permission for the delegates to leave the country. "That man is so unpredictable," Theo had muttered, shaking his head. "Furious with religious leaders one day, agreeable the next."

Before he left, the archbishop gave Yacobo permission to use his study while he was gone as a quiet place to work on the Centennial play. All week long Yacobo worked on it. But it was slow going. He had come across some new information he wanted to work into the plot. There was another martyr the same year the boy martyrs were killed—Bishop Hannington. Hannington had been sent by the Church of England to be bishop of East and Central Africa, and his caravan entered Uganda from the east.

But there was an old Ugandan tradition that said, "Beware the stranger who enters the country from the direction of the rising sun. He is dangerous and plans to take over the country!" King Mwanga, not knowing Hannington's purpose, sent warriors to murder the "stranger" before he crossed the Nile River. As the warriors speared him, the dying bishop had said, "I am now going to die at your hands, but I want you to tell your king that my blood has bought this way into the country."

Yacobo had been excited when he discovered this part of

the story. The book he read had said the bishop's words came true, because the main roads and railways into Uganda today come from the east.

But telling a story using only dialogue was a lot harder than Yacobo thought it was going to be. Sometimes in a fit of frustration he threw out what he'd written and started over again. And sometimes he just felt stuck.

"Why don't you put it aside for a few days," his sister, Faisi, suggested when he complained to her. "Sometimes when I get stuck writing a paper for one of my classes, if I give it a rest my mind often comes up with fresh ideas when I'm ready to work on it again. Besides, I think Mama can use some extra help. The archbishop has a lot of guests coming into town for the Christmas Eve celebration tonight, and I'm trying to finish Blasio's King Herod costume."

Yacobo was only too glad to put his writing aside. It was almost a relief to run errands for his mother and help serve some of the meals for the archbishop's guests. He helped his father wash the old taxi and the archbishop's official car. Before he knew it, it was Christmas Eve.

Theo drove Blasio to the cathedral early to get ready for the pageant; then he came back and picked up the archbishop and Mrs. Luwum and the rest of his family. The cathedral was packed not only with people who lived in Kampala but with people who lived in the outlying towns. Beautiful Christmas music swelled from the organ. The choir sang some traditional Ugandan hymns. Then it was time for the pageant.

Yacobo poked Faisi. "I hope Blasio doesn't goof up his lines or make faces trying to make people laugh," he whispered. Faisi rolled her eyes in agreement.

It turned out to be a wonderful pageant. The power of the Christmas story held everyone in awe, even though there were the usual childish flubs as an angel's "halo" fell off and Mary the Mother of Jesus tripped over her robe. But even Yacobo had to grudgingly admit that his brother did a powerful performance as King Herod. The ten-year-old acted with mock delight when the wise men told him about the star, his voice dripping with honey when he said he wanted to worship the new king, too. Then his voice changed to cold cunning as he hatched his evil plot to destroy the baby king.

Then Archbishop Luwum preached his annual Christmas sermon. His theme was the birth of the Prince of Peace and the factors in their homes and in their nation that destroy peace. He warned the people not to give in to the tribal jealousies that were tearing the government apart. He pled with the people to speak out against violence and bloodshed, but to do it in the love of Christ. Finally, he called on all Christians and people in government to obey the "laws of God."

Yacobo felt uneasy. He remembered that the archbishop's message was being broadcast on the radio. What if Idi Amin was listening? Would it make him mad?

When the Kabaza family came outside after the Christmas Eve service into the sweet, warm evening, they noticed more than the usual number of soldiers standing on the street corners and army trucks cruising slowly past the cathedral. Instead of waiting to greet people as they normally did, Theo herded his family into the car and took them home, then went back to wait for the archbishop.

While they were waiting for their father to return home, Yacobo idly fiddled with the dial of the radio in the kitchen. Suddenly it crackled to life with the angry voice of Idi Amin.

". . . some bishops do not support their government," the radio sputtered, "but are preaching rebellion over these very airwaves! Do not listen to their treason! This government deals harshly with anyone who speaks treason!"

Eunika, Faisi, and Yacobo looked at one another in dismay. Blasio, letting off steam by turning somersaults on Faisi's bedroll in the sitting area, was blissfully unaware of the president's speech. No one spoke, but the question was in all their eyes: Was the president publicly threatening the archbishop?

As Yacobo turned off the radio, he heard Faisi mutter, "Uganda's got its own King Herod."

For Christmas, Archbishop Luwum and his wife gave small gifts to their household staff. For the Kabazas, this meant a bonus for Theo and Eunika, a book for Faisi, and American baseball caps for Yacobo and Blasio. The children knelt in traditional Ugandan fashion to express their thanks to the archbishop.

"This boy is to be congratulated," said the archbishop jovially, pumping Blasio's hand as the children got to their feet again. "Young man, you make a *mean* King Herod!"

Everyone laughed.

"You know, Yacobo," said the archbishop, turning to the older boy, "Blasio's performance set me to thinking. Wasn't one of the boy martyrs about Blasio's age?"

Yacobo hesitated. What was the archbishop driving at? "Yes," he admitted. "Yusufu, the youngest, was eleven years old."

The archbishop beamed. "I'm thinking maybe we have found one of our actors for the Centennial play." He patted Blasio on the shoulder. "That would make this play a real family affair!"

All around him, Yacobo's mother, father, and sister nodded and smiled and agreed that it would be a wonderful thing. But

Yacobo felt a rush of anger and protest. He didn't want Blasio to play Yusufu! He turned away. Why not? Was he jealous of all the attention Blasio was getting? Yes, a little, he admitted to himself, but it wasn't really that. He couldn't put a finger on it. But it was . . . something else.

CHAPTER 6

KNOCK IN THE NIGHT

New Year's Day, 1977, came and went, and it was time for Faisi and the boys to go back to school. Yacobo was now starting his Senior 2 year. But as he looked at his new class schedule, Yacobo realized his mistake in not finishing the first draft of the Centennial play during the December holiday. He would now have to write the play on top of all his other schoolwork! But, he thought, at least his old enemy, the Kakwa boy, wouldn't be around this term.

But to his dismay, Byensii was leaning against the wall of the school, surrounded by a small gang of admirers, the same old smirk on his face. Yacobo groaned inside. But he shouldn't be surprised, he thought. Many students were kept back until they met the strict educational standards.

"Hey, Christian boy," sneered Byensii, "if you're smart, maybe it's time to change your religion."

A warning flag went up in Yacobo's mind. "What do you mean?"

"Don't you listen to the news? The president is kicking out the Christians in his government and replacing them with good Muslims. Pretty soon Uganda will be a Muslim country . . . and then we're going to walk on you." He laughed.

Yacobo walked into the school without answering. He hated that boy! . . . No, he shouldn't even let that thought into his head. He knew what Bishop Kivengere would say: "You shouldn't judge a whole group of people by the actions of a few." After all, hadn't the grand mufti, the leader of the Muslims, cooperated with the archbishop and the Catholic cardinal in denouncing the violence? And two years ago in Kabale, hadn't the Muslim governor—hostile at first, until Bishop Kivengere reached out to him in friendship—ended up providing government trucks to bring food for the people who attended the forty-year anniversary of the East African Revival?

Still, Yacobo decided to avoid Byensii as much as possible.

Yacobo stayed after school to show his writing teacher the work he'd done on the Centennial play so far. Mr. Wabaki seemed pleased with the scene summaries but challenged Yacobo to finish the first draft of the actual script. "You've got a good grasp of the story," he said, "and a good start on the dialogue in the first scene. But when you finish the first draft, then we can work on the pacing and dramatic tension."

That night after Blasio had fallen asleep, Yacobo sat on his bed and got out his writing tablet. He was working on the second scene, where King Mwanga ties up the three boy servants and threatens to throw them in the fire if they don't give up their faith. But the image of his sister and Charity Kivengere being thrown in the army trucks by the soldiers kept pushing into Yacobo's mind. He shook his head, trying to get rid of the memory. But as he wrote down the brave words spoken by little Yusufu, the youngest of the martyrs, Yacobo suddenly looked over at his little brother, sprawled peacefully in his sleep. In his mind he could almost hear the words spoken in his brother's dramatic voice: *"Please don't cut off my arms!"*

Yacobo threw down his pencil. No! He didn't want Blasio to play the part of Yusufu. How could he write a part for a boy *just like his little brother*? It made the story feel too frightening, too real.

Yacobo let the comings and goings of the archbishop's household that January of 1977 swirl around him without really noticing. He had enough on his mind with homework, working on the play, and trying to avoid Byensii at school.

His father was gone for several days, driving Archbishop Luwum to two different conventions in northern and western Uganda. When they returned, his father reported that the archbishop was really excited about what God had done at these conventions. In northern Gulu, the churches had suffered twenty years of tribal tension and unrest, but at the convention the Holy Spirit had begun healing and reconciliation. In the west, in the shadow of the Ruwenzori Mountains, right in the middle of the archbishop's sermons, people began to sing and weep and come forward to accept Christ! "No one was more amazed than the archbishop himself," said Yacobo's father. "It was truly a work of the Holy Spirit!"

Yacobo also got to see Festo and Mera Kivengere when they came to Kampala and stayed in the Namirembe Guest House after the Kivengeres and Luwums had consecrated a new bishop the last weekend in January. "What an occasion!" Festo exclaimed, beaming, as he sat at the festive table prepared by

Eunika Kabaza for the archbishop and his guests. "Sitting in the front were rows of military men, policemen, government officials, clergymen, bishops, Catholic dignitaries, my friend the Muslim governor, and even some of Idi Amin's intelligence officers!"

"You preached a very brave sermon," said Archbishop Luwum somewhat gravely.

"From Acts 20 . . . yes, Paul's charge to church leaders to shepherd their flocks in perilous times," Festo chuckled.

"You didn't stop with a charge to church leaders," Mera Kivengere chided her husband gently. "You talked about government officials who abuse their authority, and challenged those present to use their authority to heal, not hurt."

"But what could I do?" her husband teased. "That was the text for the day on the church calendar!"

Later, Yacobo heard his father and mother talking quietly in the Kabaza kitchen. "I had a strange feeling listening to the sermons preached by Archbishop Luwum and Bishop Kivengere," Theo said in a low voice. "It was almost like . . . like they were saying good-bye."

"Hush, now, don't talk like that," scolded Yacobo's mother. "But we must remember to pray for our spiritual leaders every day. These are difficult times."

The next day when Yacobo arrived home after school, no one was in the apartment. He peeked in the pot simmering on the electric stove and sniffed the delicious smell of goat's meat and vegetables. Grabbing a piece of melon from the refrigerator, he went wandering into the main part of the archbishop's house looking for one of his parents.

As he neared the first-floor entryway, he heard Festo Kivengere's voice, excited and talking faster than usual.

" . . . I didn't recognize the man," he was saying. "Mera and

I just heard the gunshots out in the street—in broad daylight! When we looked out the window, children were screaming and women were running every which way. Then the men who were shooting went into a building and dragged out this man, tied him up, and took him away."

Yacobo saw his father and Archbishop Luwum standing in the entryway with Bishop Kivengere. What was going on?

"They weren't ordinary soldiers, you say?" said the archbishop.

"No, the gunmen were dressed in street clothes—colorful shirts, sunglasses—the 'uniform' of the so-called 'Research Unit' or intelligence officers of Idi Amin's Special Forces. From what I've heard, they are the most cruel of all."

"We appreciate your telling us, Festo," said Archbishop Luwum. "But . . . why are you so concerned about this incident in particular? Unfortunately, thousands of people have disappeared since Idi Amin took control of the country."

"Yes, disappeared—usually under cover of night. But this was broad daylight. They didn't care who saw them. In fact, maybe they wanted people to see and be afraid. Amin is angry . . . and I think I know why." Bishop Kivengere frowned. "It may be just a rumor, but I heard from a reliable source that some army officers attempted a coup last Tuesday. It was squashed right away, and the government is pretending it never happened."

Yacobo sucked in his breath. A coup!

"Last Tuesday?" Theo spoke up. "What's today—February first? That makes last Tuesday . . . January twenty-fifth." He raised his eyebrows. "Oh."

Bishop Kivengere managed a wry grin. "Exactly, Theo. The attempted coup was on January twenty-fifth—the anniversary of Idi Amin's own coup back in '71! I'm sure Amin got the message. But now he'll be more determined to squash anyone he thinks is plotting against him. We . . . well, we must all be 'wise as serpents and harmless as doves,' as the Bible says."

"Thank you, Festo," said the archbishop, clasping his friend's hand. "Don't worry; we'll be careful. God bless you as you and Mera drive back to Kabale."

As the door closed behind Festo Kivengere, Theo took his son aside. "No need to mention this to your mother."

Yacobo nodded, but he wasn't surprised the next morning when his father drove him and Blasio to school and picked them up in the afternoon . . . not only that day but for the rest of the week.

Friday evening Yacobo asked Janini Luwum if he could work awhile on the Centennial play in the archbishop's study. Blasio usually stayed up later on Friday nights, and it was hard to get any studying done in the boys' room. But if Yacobo worked really hard this weekend, he might actually get the first draft done. He'd be glad to get it finished.

The dialogue was coming a little more easily now, and Yacobo wrote page after page. It was after midnight when he laid his head down on his arms and closed his eyes to rest them—just for a minute, he told himself. Somewhere outside he heard a dog start barking, then another one. Then . . . it sounded like someone pounding on a door and shouting.

Yacobo sat bolt upright. That pounding and shouting sounded close—too close.

Suddenly he heard someone hurry past the study door and down the stairs to the front hallway. Opening the study door, Yacobo made his way to the top of the stairs. He could hear the pounding clearly now on the front door below and shouts of "Archbishop! Archbishop! Open! We have come!"

Peering down into the hallway from the top of the stairs,

Yacobo saw the archbishop in his bathrobe reach the first floor, just as his father rushed into the hallway from the back entrance. Yacobo crept halfway down the stairs and watched as Archbishop Luwum pulled back the curtain on one side of the front door and peered out.

"Oh, I know this man—name's Ben Ongam," the archbishop said. "Looks like he's hurt. Open the door, Theo. Maybe he needs help."

Yacobo watched as his father unlocked the front door and opened it. Suddenly several big men waving pistols pushed a badly frightened man in handcuffs into the entryway and began yelling at the archbishop. "Where are the guns? Show us the guns!"

"What guns?" protested Archbishop Luwum. "There are no guns here."

Yacobo shrank back into the shadows, but where he could still see what was happening. The man the archbishop called Ben Ongam had many cuts and bruises on his face and arms. The other intruders wore colorful casual shirts and carried pistols and rifles. One of the brawny men held a pistol to Theo Kabaza's neck. Another held his rifle on the archbishop while a third searched them both from head to foot.

"We know there are guns here," snapped the leader. "Ongom here confessed that you are fronting for the rebels." The man sneered. "Very smart. No one would think of looking in the archbishop's house, right?" Then he pushed the archbishop so hard that Janini Luwum nearly fell down. "Walk! Run! Show us the house. We'll find the guns if it takes all night."

Just then one of the armed men saw Yacobo behind the plants. "You!" he yelled, taking three big strides to where Yacobo was crouched. He was a big, muscular man with a flat nose and small eyes. Grabbing Yacobo's arm, he snarled, "Take us to the staff quarters. We'll search there."

Yacobo's legs felt like two wooden sticks, hardly able to obey him. But somehow he led two of the armed men out the back door to the staff quarters.

In the Kabaza apartment, Eunika was anxiously clutching her nightclothes around her. The men ignored her but turned pillows and bedding upside down. In the boys' room, they dumped a startled Blasio out of bed and turned the mattress over. Wide awake now, Blasio watched with wide eyes and open mouth as the armed men searched the room.

The search went on for almost two hours—bedrooms, study, chapel, storerooms, kitchen, courtyard, inside the cars. The men found nothing.

By this time the intruders had rounded up everyone in the main house and staff quarters.

Ben Ongam looked terrified. "Please, Archbishop," he begged, "give me some names of Langi or Acholi families so that these men may search for guns." He didn't say it, but the look in his eyes seemed to say, "It's the only way I know to stay alive."

Yacobo was startled at the mention of the tribal names. Was that what this was all about? He remembered the Kakwa boy at school saying that ex-President Obote, living in exile in Tanzania, was Langi. Maybe Ben Ongam was Langi, too. Langi and Acholi—the Kakwas hated those tribes. Was President Amin afraid some people from those tribes were plotting against him so Obote could regain power?

Yacobo felt a little wave of relief that his family was Bahororo, like the Kivengeres.

"Mr. Ongam," the archbishop was saying, "I am archbishop for all people in Uganda, not just for one or two tribes. This is

God's house. There are no guns here. We pray for the president. We pray for the soldiers. We preach the Gospel. We help the poor. That is our work, not smuggling guns."

Janini Luwum turned to the armed men, and his voice changed to steel. "This search of my house in the middle of the night is outrageous! Why not come during the day, with a search warrant in your hand? We have nothing to hide. I am going to tell President Amin of your conduct immediately."

The men simply hardened their faces, pushed Ben Ongam out the door in front of them, and were gone.

No one got any sleep the rest of the night. They put bedding back on the beds, picked up dresser drawers that had been dumped out, straightened up closets and chairs that had been overturned. Finally Eunika made some tea, and the Kabazas sat around their kitchen table sipping the hot drink silently. Even Blasio had no smart remarks to make.

Suddenly Yacobo wondered something. Turning to his father he said, "Papa, what tribe does Archbishop Luwum come from?"

Theo pursed his lips. "Acholi. Why do you ask?"

CHAPTER 7

SUMMONED

Yacobo had a hard time concentrating on his lessons at school on Monday. The search of the archbishop's house at gunpoint in the middle of the night had left him shaken and jumpy. Several times his teachers called on him to recite in class, and he stumbled over the answers. Some of the other students snickered. In writing class, Mr. Wabaki said, "You are not paying attention, Yacobo. Is something wrong?" Yacobo just looked at the floor and shook his head.

If only his father would be waiting for him right after school so he could hop in the car and not run into Byensii. But his father's old taxi was not in the school driveway, and Byensii was.

The Kakwa boy held a small transistor radio turned up at its highest volume, and a small crowd of boys was listening intently. Byensii's eyes locked on Yacobo, and he held out the radio. "Listen to this, Christian boy." It was a command, not an invitation.

It took several moments before Yacobo could make out the words on the scratchy transistor radio. Then the announcer's voice became clear. " . . . discovered near the archbishop's house. The schoolchildren alerted the authorities, who quickly confiscated the stash of foreign-made guns. We repeat, several schoolchildren today accidentally discovered a stockpile of weapons near the home of Janini Luwum, the Anglican archbishop. The authorities—"

Yacobo felt a rush of anger flood through him. The so-called "authorities" couldn't find anything during their illegal search in the middle of the night, so now they were making up a story about finding guns *near* the archbishop's house! He felt like yelling, "Lies! Lies! It's all lies!" at the triumphant sneer on Byensii's face. But just then he saw the familiar old taxi pull into the school drive.

Jumping into the front seat, he blurted out to his father what he had just heard. Grim-faced, Theo Kabaza quickly drove back to the archbishop's house. Yacobo was surprised to see several bishops from districts all over Uganda standing in the courtyard, talking in twos and threes. One small group was listening to a transistor radio and calling out the news to the others.

"The archbishop has called an emergency council of the bishops to discuss how to respond to the attack on his home," Theo told Yacobo as he parked the old taxi behind the house. "If they just let it pass, none of the religious leaders in Uganda will be safe from harassment."

All week long the council of bishops met to discuss what to do about this latest outrage by Idi Amin's Special Forces. On Saturday, February 12, most of the bishops returned home, but eight stayed, including Festo Kivengere and Silvanus

Wani. Looking tired, but still wearing his warm smile, Bishop Kivengere dropped in to see his friends the Kabazas.

"Mmm, Eunika, you're still one of the best cooks in Uganda," he said, patting his stomach after two generous helpings of her chicken stew. "Yacobo, how is the writing of the play going?"

Yacobo had hoped the bishop might forget to ask. "All right," he said vaguely. "I got the first draft done . . . now my writing teacher will critique it and help me with the second draft."

"Wonderful!" said Bishop Kivengere. "I cannot wait to read it!"

Yacobo squirmed uncomfortably. He wasn't happy with the play. Something was missing . . . yet he didn't know what. But he had to finish the play soon. The Centennial celebration was scheduled for June 1977, less than four months away. Actors had to be chosen, rehearsals gotten underway . . .

The table conversation turned to the week-long council of bishops. "Yes, we prepared another document to present personally to the president, but so far he has refused to see us," sighed Festo. "We reminded the president that many people around the world know me and Archbishop Luwum and are watching Uganda. He cannot abuse our archbishop without reaping worldwide condemnation.

"But the outrageous search of the archbishop's home last weekend is only one of our many concerns. Many of Uganda's best and brightest are fleeing the country, creating a 'brain drain.' Government agents continue to arrest and kill, leaving a distressing number of widows and orphans. Private property and cars are being taken away for military use. The list goes on and on. We will try again early next week to get an appointment with the president to present these concerns in a respectful way, but someone needs to speak up!"

Wasn't it dangerous to speak up? Yacobo thought uneasily. He shivered at what might happen if he challenged Byensii's menacing attitude—and Byensii was only a schoolyard bully, not the president of Uganda.

———

Someone was knocking on the door. Knocking, knocking . . .

Yacobo sat bolt upright in his bed. A pale gray light coming through his window told him it was early morning. He'd been dreaming about Ben Ongam and the dreaded Special Forces knocking on the archbishop's door. But it wasn't a dream. Someone *was* knocking on the door! His heart seemed to stop. Had Idi Amin's gunmen come back?

But as he listened, he realized the knocking was not at the main house, but on the door of his family's apartment. A familiar voice was calling, "Theo! Theo Kabaza! Are you awake? The archbishop needs you!"

Yacobo could feel his heart begin beating normally again. It was only the archbishop's assistant calling for his father. But what did he want at such an early hour? Yacobo got out of bed and came into the sitting room just as his father, sleepy eyed and unshaven, opened the door.

"Oh, Theo. Sorry to bother you, but the archbishop needs you to drive him and Mary to Entebbe. He needs to be there by nine o'clock this morning."

"Nine o'clock!" Theo said. "We will have to leave right away. What—has something happened?"

The assistant shrugged. "We're not sure. The archbishop got a call late last night from the president . . . very angry, making all sorts of accusations. But the archbishop was able to speak in a firm, loving way, refuting his charges. Then, early this morning, he received another call from the president's office, summoning him to the State House in Entebbe by nine o'clock! Mary is insisting on going with her husband."

"I'll be out front in ten minutes," Theo said as he pulled out a clean shirt. "Yacobo, you will have to take Blasio to school today. Just . . . be careful, son."

Blasio grumbled about not getting a ride, but otherwise seemed oblivious to the general tension in the household caused by the events of the past week. Yacobo knew his mother was anxious about the boys' having to walk to school, but all she said as she handed them their lunches was, "Blasio, you stay with Yacobo, you hear? I'll pick you up after school. And, Yacobo, you be sure to come straight home."

Yacobo intended to duck out of school the moment the school day ended, but Mr. Wabaki asked him to stay after class to talk about his play. The writing teacher had finished his critique and wanted to go over his suggestions with Yacobo.

At least Byensii was nowhere to be seen when Yacobo finally scurried out the door and ran two blocks to catch a matatu. All the way home he wondered what had happened at the State House in Entebbe that day. Would the Luwums and his father be home yet?

To his relief, the official black car was sitting in the driveway when he walked through the gate, along with the Kivengeres' car. Inside the main house, his mother was serving an early tea in the sitting room to everyone, but she grabbed him as he came in. "Where have you been?" she hissed. "I don't need to be worrying about you, too."

"I'm sorry, Mama. I couldn't help it," he whispered back defensively, showing the play with the teacher's handwriting all over it. He pulled away from her and walked over to where his father, the Luwums, and the Kivengeres were just sitting down with their tea and sandwiches. Blasio, as usual, escaping the watchful eye of his mother, was already wolfing down slices of sweet bread.

"It was the strangest thing, Festo," Janini Luwum was saying. "After the president's angry midnight call, I have to admit I was worried what this 'summons' was about. I didn't want Mary to go with me, but she insisted. But when we got there, Idi Amin was laughing and smiling and welcomed us like old friends! He introduced us to his other guest, a Major Greene from England, who had trained Amin as a young army officer. Newspaper reporters were there and took our pictures all together."

Festo Kivengere frowned. "Ah. Now it all makes sense. A friend of mine in London called over the weekend to see if we were all right. It seems British newspapers had published a story that Archbishop Luwum had been arrested and beaten."

Mary Luwum gasped. "You mean, this was just a big show to prove the rumors are false?"

"Yes. But that's not all bad." Bishop Kivengere smiled encouragingly. "Now Amin knows the world is watching."

"Well, I'm afraid I could not let my opportunity go by," said the archbishop. "After Major Greene left, I spoke to the president and protested the search of my house—not the search itself, but *how* it was done, at midnight, at gunpoint. I told the president I had nothing to hide and would gladly cooperate with authorities when done in the proper manner. Then I told Amin that the bishops had been wanting to speak with him all week."

Festo Kivengere lifted his eyebrows. "How did he respond?"

"He laughed loudly and said in his booming voice, 'Don't

worry about a thing! I'm going to invite all the bishops to come, and put them up in a hotel at my expense, and we'll talk it all over!' So," the archbishop said with a slight smile, "I left him a copy of our document of concerns. Festo, did you—?"

Bishop Kivengere nodded. "Yes. Bishop Wani and I delivered copies to the cabinet ministers and the secretary of the Defense Council today. In person."

Yacobo saw the adults look at one another with glances that were both wary and cautiously optimistic. "Now we must pray," said the archbishop.

"It looks like the president is being true to his word," Theo Kabaza reported to the family Tuesday evening. "All the religious leaders—Protestant, Catholic, and Muslim—have been summoned to the conference center here in Kampala tomorrow morning. Yacobo, you must walk Blasio to school again, as I am needed to drive the archbishop. I will be gone all day."

"Mm-hmm," Yacobo said absently. He chewed on his pencil and frowned at Mr. Wabaki's comments written in the margins of his play. WHY would they choose death rather than their own safety? the teacher had scrawled. You haven't shown me WHY their faith is that important. Convince me!

What does he want? Yacobo thought in frustration. *I wrote what the martyrs said. Isn't that enough?*

He read and reread what he'd written and mulled it over in his mind all the next day. Once or twice on Wednesday he wondered what was happening at the meeting with the president that day, but he wasn't too concerned. His father and the Luwums had come home safely from the State House on Monday. Surely nothing would happen today with so many religious leaders present.

After school, he and Blasio settled down to doing their homework in the archbishop's kitchen while Eunika prepared the evening meal for the Luwums and their guests. Mera Kivengere, who was sick with bronchitis, was resting in one of the guest rooms while they waited for the bishops to return.

About five-thirty, Theo Kabaza rushed into the kitchen, his tie loosened, his face damp with sweat. "Eunika, come quickly," he said. "You must go to Mrs. Luwum. The archbishop has been arrested!"

Yacobo followed as his parents rushed to the little chapel where Festo Kivengere and the other seven bishops who had accompanied the archbishop that day were gathered around Mary Luwum. Yacobo caught bits and pieces of the story as Bishop Kivengere tried to tell the archbishop's wife what had happened that day.

They were made to stand outside in the hot sun all day, he said, while the vice-president made angry speeches to a large crowd of army personnel and diplomats. "He accused us of hiding behind our clergy collars and prayer books while plotting against the president," said Festo. On cue the soldiers yelled, "Kill them! Kill them!" Finally, at two o'clock the religious leaders and diplomats were told to go into the conference center, where they would meet with the president. But the bishops were led into a separate room and kept there while the president addressed everyone else.

"We did not know what was happening in the other room, though we could hear clapping and shouts," said Festo wearily. "Then about three-thirty the meeting was over, and we were bluntly told we could all go home. We were disappointed that we had not been able to meet with the president as expected, but were relieved to go home. As we started to leave, a guard said, 'Not you, Archbishop. The president wants to see you. . . .' "

The other bishops protested. They did not want to leave without their archbishop. They tried to wait but were ordered outside. They waited outside by the car, but still the archbishop did not come out. "Theo here got very stubborn," said Festo. "He said he was the archbishop's driver and would not leave without him. But the guards said they would bring the archbishop home in another car and ordered us at gunpoint to leave. That . . ." his voice nearly broke. "That was when we knew in our hearts that our archbishop had been arrested."

Mary Luwum was weeping. "I must go to the conference center and find out what has happened to my husband," she said suddenly. "Theo, will you please drive me?"

"No, Mrs. Luwum!" said Eunika, holding the other woman. "It is too dangerous."

Bishop Kivengere and the other bishops also tried to discourage her, but Mary Luwum was determined to go. Theo Kabaza said nothing, but put on his hat and went to get the car.

Yacobo knew his father, too, wanted to go back to the conference center. He would not rest until he had done his duty and brought the archbishop back home.

All thoughts of supper and homework were forgotten as everyone stayed in the chapel and prayed. A few hours later, Mary Luwum and Theo Kabaza returned home, their strained faces telling the story. No word about the archbishop.

It was late. Eunika told Yacobo to take Blasio back to their apartment and put him to bed. "I will come get you if we hear anything," she promised.

Yacobo nodded and herded Blasio outside. Once in bed,

the younger boy fell asleep right away, but Yacobo lay awake for a long time, listening to the loud silence.

The morning sun was streaming through the bedroom window when Yacobo awoke. At first he was confused. Why had no one awakened him for school? And then he remembered. The archbishop.

Blasio was still sleeping, but his parents' bed had not been slept in. Yacobo pulled on his clothes and went into the back door of the main house in his bare feet. The smell of coffee filled the house. As he passed the open front door, he saw his mother outside in her apron picking up the morning newspaper. He had the eerie feeling that it was just another morning. Maybe the archbishop had been released in the night and everything was all right. But, no, his mother had said she would come tell him if they heard any news.

He cracked the door to the chapel and slipped inside. The bishops were still on their knees, praying. He could see his father among them, his head in his hands. A cough caught his ear. Mera Kivengere was up and dressed, sitting with Mary Luwum, a raspy cough from her chest punctuating the murmured prayers from time to time. But her lips were moving, too, in silent prayer.

Just then a cry of agony tore the quiet fabric of the morning, and Eunika Kabaza ran into the chapel holding the morning newspaper in front of her. The bishops scrambled to their feet as the bold headline leaped out at them:

ARCHBISHOP KILLED IN CAR CRASH

A picture of a wrecked automobile was splashed across the front page.

A moan like a wounded cat escaped the lips of Mary Luwum, and she slumped against Mera Kivengere. But Theo Kabaza took several long strides and snatched the newspaper from his wife. "Let me see that picture." His eyes narrowed. "I recognize that car. It was totaled in a wreck two weeks ago. If our archbishop is dead, he did not die in that car accident."

CHAPTER 8

FLIGHT

"They have murdered him," said Festo Kivengere quietly, speaking all their thoughts aloud, "and now they are trying to cover it up."

Mary Luwum had slumped to the floor, and Mera Kivengere and Eunika Kabaza were kneeling with her, holding her, and crying with her. Even the grown men were fighting back tears of grief and anger.

Yacobo sank into one of the small pews of the chapel. His eyes burned, and a lump filled his throat. What was happening? Why would anyone kill the kind archbishop? This was crazy! The whole world seemed to be spinning out of control, like a tornado that only looks threatening from a distance, and then suddenly is upon you, tearing everything up by its roots.

Suddenly Bishop Kivengere began to sing, a song of hope and trust in Jesus. One by one several of the others joined him, their voices weak, almost whispering. But gradually the voices grew stronger until the last verse faded away.

"Brothers and sisters," said Bishop Kivengere, his own voice husky and breaking with grief, "this is a moment of severe testing. We will be tempted to hate, to want revenge. We may want to fight with whatever power we have available to us to bring this evil man down. But let us remember, the only place of power is down low, at the feet of Jesus. Let us never take our eyes off Him and the reconciling work of the Cross, or we will sink into the waves of destruction that are all around us."

Together the little group cried and prayed. Then they pulled themselves together and tried to decide what to do.

"We must go to the government and ask for Janini's body."

"We must notify the bishops in every district in Uganda—"

"—and friends and officials worldwide."

"We must make arrangements for an official funeral at the Namirembe Cathedral. What day is today? Thursday? Sunday is three days away—February twentieth. Can we do that?"

It was decided that Theo would drive Mrs. Luwum, Bishop Kivengere, and Bishop Wani—who was from the Kakwa tribe, which might be useful—to obtain the body, while others began making the necessary funeral arrangements. Mera Kivengere, who was coughing badly, went to bed, and Eunika Kabaza began cooking pots of food to feed the constant stream of guests that were expected.

Faisi got word at the university, and she and Charity Kivengere came as quickly as they could to help out. Yacobo was saddled with keeping an eye on Blasio, running errands, and taking messages back and forth in the big house.

It was good to keep busy, to put off having to think about what was going to happen after Sunday. But when Theo Kabaza came home that evening, he shook his head in discouragement when his wife asked what happened. "We kept getting the runaround. The minister of health told Mrs. Luwum the matter had been turned over to the minister of defense, and the body would be released after they finished their investigation."

But on Friday, after being sent from official to official, Mrs. Luwum was finally told that her husband's body had already been taken to the archbishop's "home village" in the north and buried. There would be no official funeral in Kampala.

Frustration spilled over as the bishops and staff gathered together Friday night around Mary Luwum. "It's obvious what has happened," Yacobo's father was saying bitterly as the boy slipped into the room. "They do not dare release the body for public burial because he was shot, and that would make a lie out of the car accident story."

"What about the funeral?" Bishop Wani asked.

All looked at Mary Luwum. Tears shone in her eyes as she said bravely, "What is to stop us from celebrating the life of Janini Luwum on Sunday morning at the cathedral—with or without my husband's body?"

Just then Faisi stuck her head in the door. "There are some people at the door. They say they are a delegation from the archbishop's home district and have come to escort Mrs. Luwum home to attend her husband's funeral there."

All eyes looked at Mary Luwum. "I will not go!" she cried. "The government is trying to hush this up, to keep it quiet and private."

"She is right," said Festo Kivengere. "I fear for Mary's safety on the road." Everyone agreed. Bishop Kivengere went out to meet with the delegation and express Mrs. Luwum's regrets.

While he was out of the room, Theo spoke up. "Mrs. Luwum is not the only one whose safety we should be concerned about. While we were out today, we met more than one person who was shocked to see Bishop Kivengere alive and well. There are rumors going around that he, too, has been killed."

"Of course, Festo just smiles and says, 'Well, as you can see, I am quite well, thank you . . .' " said Bishop Wani. Everyone laughed nervously.

Talk turned once more to plans for the memorial on Sunday. Wandering back to the Kabaza apartment, Yacobo flopped down on his bed, resting his hands behind his head and staring into the darkness outside the small window.

In the quietness, Yacobo let his mind drift beyond the memorial service on Sunday. Who would be the new archbishop? The thought startled Yacobo. What if the new archbishop didn't want his father to be his personal driver? Or his mother to be the cook?

For the first time since the archbishop had been killed, Yacobo suddenly realized his parents' jobs, their home here in Kampala, and his schooling could be gone in a matter of days.

But just as quickly, a comforting idea calmed his anxious thoughts. The new archbishop might be Festo Kivengere. Why not? He was even better known than Janini Luwum had been. Wasn't he an international evangelist? He'd been a close friend and adviser of Archbishop Luwum. They often shared the platform at conventions—two popular preachers. Of course! It made perfect sense. And if Festo Kivengere became archbishop, of course he would want the Kabazas to continue on as part of his household staff. Coming here had been his idea in the first place! And Bishop Kivengere was strong and confident. As long as their bishop friend was there to lead, Yacobo felt safe.

Comforted by these thoughts, Yacobo let his heavy eyelids droop and soon fell into a dreamless sleep.

As Yacobo was getting dressed the next morning—Saturday—he noticed the Centennial play and the rest of his school books sitting on the little desk in the bedroom, untouched since Wednesday night when they first got the news that the archbishop had been arrested. He and Blasio had missed two days of school, and his parents had said nothing about it. Yacobo shrugged. Surely his parents would write an excuse and he could catch up next week.

Blasio, tired of being ignored in the crisis, put salt in Faisi's morning tea and giggled with delight when she gagged and spit it out. He kept bugging his mother until finally she ordered Yacobo to take his brother outside and kick a soccer ball in the driveway until lunch was ready.

People were coming and going all morning. Yacobo sensed something was up. Everyone was talking in low voices, looking worried, and shaking their heads. His mother had left lunch on the table in their apartment for him and Blasio, but the apartment was empty. Then Faisi came in. "Come on over to the chapel right away. Bishop Kivengere wants to talk to everybody."

Curious, Yacobo dragged a reluctant Blasio with him over to the chapel in the main house and made him sit. Seeing that everyone had gathered, Festo Kivengere said, "I have asked you all here to pray with Mera and me as we make a difficult decision. We have received a strong warning that my name is now at the top of Idi Amin's hit list. Several of my brother bishops feel that we need to leave Kampala immediately—maybe even leave the country."

Yacobo sucked in his breath. Leave Uganda?

"I am not inclined to run," Festo continued. "I love my country and am not afraid to die for it. But I must consider seriously what my brothers are saying. They have reminded me of the apostle Paul, who was warned of danger by his friends and let down the city wall so he could get away."

Bishop Kivengere's sober words were interrupted by his wife's raspy cough. He laid a tender hand on her shoulder. "As you can hear, Mera is not well. She is running a fever. We are not sure what to do. We need you to pray with us."

There were murmurs around the room. "God help us." "Have mercy, O God." The murmurs swelled into prayers. Some people knelt; others wept. Even Blasio sat quietly as though pinned to his seat by the urgency of the situation.

And then there was a stillness, and in the stillness Yacobo heard his father say in a voice thick with emotion, "Brother Festo, hear me as one of the people. We have already lost one bishop this week. We cannot afford to lose another one. Please, leave Kampala *now.*"

The prayer meeting was interrupted by a phone call for Bishop Kivengere. It was Leighton Ford, American evangelist and son-in-law of Billy Graham, calling to say that many people around the world were concerned about his safety. Another call was put through from Stanley Mooneyham from World Vision with the same concern.

Bishop Silvanus Wani spoke up. "I think God is making it clear. You and Mera must leave right away—at least get out of Kampala and go home to Kabale."

And so it was decided. Festo and Mera would drive home immediately to Kabale. They would test the situation there as to whether they should stay or keep going. Theo and Eunika Kabaza offered to drive behind them so they wouldn't be making the six-hour trip alone.

And then they were gone.

The entire household waited anxiously for news all that afternoon and evening. It was late when the telephone rang.

Bishop Wani answered it in the archbishop's study. "That was Theo," he reported. "He said it was not safe in Kabale. They are gone."

Gone! That meant Festo and Mera Kivengere were fleeing the country.

As the household finally retired, Yacobo retreated to the bedroom he shared with Blasio in the staff quarters. His younger brother was already asleep in sprawled innocence. Yacobo shook his head. Life swirled around Blasio without seeming to affect him. Yacobo, on the other hand, did not understand all the feelings that churned inside him. Of course he didn't want anything to happen to Bishop Kivengere. Maybe fleeing was the right thing. But stabs of resentment poked holes in those logical thoughts. *What about the rest of us?* Now that Archbishop Luwum was dead, who was going to stand up against the violence and terror if Bishop Kivengere wasn't even in the country? And if Bishop Kivengere wasn't there to be archbishop, who cared whether his parents had a job or Yacobo continued with his writing?

He felt abandoned. Suddenly his eyes fell on the pages of the play script. In one vicious motion, he ripped the pages from top to bottom. Then he wadded them up and threw them in the wastebasket.

Why not? he thought angrily. How could he write now with his world falling apart? Besides, with the archbishop dead and Festo Kivengere fleeing the country, surely there would be no Centennial celebration now.

CHAPTER 9

KIDNAPPED

Sometime during the night, Theo and Eunika Kabaza arrived home. After a few hours' sleep, they got washed and dressed and together with Faisi, Yacobo, and Blasio drove to Namirembe Cathedral for the memorial service for Janini Luwum.

The government had announced there would be no official funeral, only "private services." Foreign dignitaries who had wanted to come were refused entrance into the country "for reasons of national security," so the government said. But over 4,500 Ugandans showed up at the Cathedral anyway, and there was nothing the soldiers could do about it.

The former archbishop of Uganda, Erica Sabiti, who had retired, read the Resurrection story from the New Testament: " 'He is not here; he is risen!' All glory to Christ!" The choir started singing, "Glory, glory to the Lamb . . ." The people joined in, and the song swelled in the Cathedral. Yacobo's neck prickled. They were singing, "Tukutendereza Yesu!"—the "Martyrs' Song."

Back home over a simple lunch, Theo and Eunika Kabaza finally had a chance to tell their children what had happened when they got to Kabale. "Neighbors met us at the Kivengeres' house," Theo said, "to tell us that soldiers had come knocking on the door three times that day to see if Festo was home. 'You must go—now!' they said." Mera was still running a fever, but after a brief time of prayer together, Festo and Mera put their suitcases back in the car and, without stopping to take any of their personal things from the house, drove toward the Rwandan border.

"So we don't know if they are safe yet?" Faisi said.

Eunika shook her head. "No. We must keep them in our prayers." She looked anxiously at her daughter. "What about you—are you going back to the university?"

Faisi nodded. "Charity Kivengere will be taking final exams soon. We both want to keep attending classes as long as possible."

To Yacobo's surprise, his father agreed. "You are right. We must keep our chins up and go forward."

A week went by with no news. But rumors were flying of new killings, especially among the Acholi and Langi tribes. Several more bishops fled the country. And then one day Bishop Wani came to the archbishop's residence with news: Festo and Mera had arrived safely in Nairobi, Kenya!

"The night they left Kabale was very harrowing," said Bishop Wani to the small group who gathered in the little chapel. "People on the road warned them of a roadblock up ahead, so they drove the car through the forest with the headlights off until they got around it. A while later they had to abandon the car and go the last distance into Rwanda by foot, up the mountains. It was very difficult for Mera, who was still feverish and wearing a long skirt. But just at sunrise on Sunday, February twentieth, the day of the archbishop's memorial service, they crossed the border into Rwanda, singing praises to God."

Yacobo felt something in his chest relax, like a tightly wound spring unwinding. He was glad the Kivengeres were safe. But the fact that they left at all was still a sore point.

Bishop Wani had other news. "I had a long talk with Festo," he said. "He encouraged us—and I agree—to continue with the plans for the Centennial celebration in June." The bishop put up his hand as several people started to protest. "If we don't, brothers and sisters, then 'Big Daddy' Amin has already won. But as our brother Festo said, the celebration of God's work in Uganda must go on!"

Yacobo felt a stab of panic. If the Centennial celebration was still going to happen, that meant—

Bishop Wani was speaking directly to him. "Bishop Kivengere asked how your script was coming along, Yacobo. He said when you have finished, he would like to see a copy!"

Yacobo swallowed. He thought of the script, torn in two and thrown into the wastebasket. Was it even still there? Or had it been taken out to the dustbin?

Guiltily he slipped out of the chapel and ran back to his apartment. The wastebasket in the boys' bedroom was overflowing. Dumping it upside down, he pawed through the scrunched-up school papers, rotting melon rinds, banana peels, and pencil shavings.

The script was still there—ripped, wadded up, and dirty. Yacobo let out a long breath of relief.

Yacobo stayed up most of that night taping together the damaged script and then recopying it onto clean paper. As he recopied, he started rewriting, working on the second draft.

Day after day, he worked on rewriting the play. He focused on the notes his teacher had written in the margins. Too stiff. Would someone really talk this way? or More feeling! The king is really angry! He felt driven to get it done. Bishop Wani had said rehearsals would begin as soon as school break began. At the same time, Yacobo felt as though he was forcing his writing, like rolling rocks uphill.

It didn't help that the rumors of more arrests and killings were growing. What kind of country makes war on its own people! The whole world seemed crazy. Yacobo shut his ears and tried to block it all out.

It might have worked—except for Byensii. The first week Yacobo returned to school after the archbishop's murder, Byensii backed him up against a wall and sneered, "That traitor Luwum had it coming!"

"You don't know what you're talking about!" Yacobo screamed and pushed himself past Byensii, hearing the other boy's laughter behind him.

As the body count on the radio and in the newspapers grew, the Kakwa boy strutted and crowed about "rooting out the rebels." Fistfights in the hallways and athletic field became common, usually Kakwa boys picking fights with Acholi or Langi students. Yacobo did his best to steer clear of Byensii, but his anger at the other boy grew hard and bitter. "One of these days . . ." he muttered to himself, relishing fantasies of making Byensii eat his words.

Finally he finished his rewrite of the play. With a few corrections here and there, Mr. Wabaki pronounced it "Good," and said he looked forward to seeing it performed at the Centennial celebration in June.

Good? Yacobo thought as he walked out of the school. He had hoped his writing teacher would be impressed, that he'd say, "Excellent!" or "Wonderful!" But Yacobo had to admit to himself that even he wasn't totally satisfied with the job he'd done on the play. Maybe "Good" was a fair evaluation.

"What's this?" said a dreaded voice. Yacobo felt the play script being snatched from his hand.

"Give that back!" yelled Yacobo, grabbing for the papers that Byensii was now holding.

. . . "Martyrs' Song," by Yacobo Kabaza,' " Byensii read in a mocking voice. He scanned through several pages, jerking them out of reach as Yacobo tried to get them back. "What is this? A crybaby tale of boys like you, too stupid to know they've been duped by white people's religion? This is just a bunch of trash!"

Panic rushed through Yacobo's veins. That was the only copy of the play he had! He could never write it again! Pushing and punching, he grabbed wildly for the papers in the older boy's hands, but Byensii just laughed and dangled them out of reach. Finally, with a desperate leap, Yacobo grabbed the papers and took off running, Byensii's mocking laughter chasing after him.

He apologized to Bishop Wani for the wrinkled pages, but the bishop told him he would have his assistant type up the script and make several copies.

Bishop Wani was filling in for the archbishop until a new one was appointed. Mrs. Luwum was getting ready to move, but the Kabazas had been asked to stay on to help in the transition.

"I'm glad Blasio has something to do during the school holiday," Eunika Kabaza said when Bishop Wani told her rehearsals for the Centennial play would be held at the cathedral twice a week for six weeks during April and May. "That boy has more energy than a wind-up toy!"

It became Yacobo's job to take Blasio to and from the cathedral for rehearsals. But Eunika was very worried about the boys' safety. "Keep to the main street," she told Yacobo. "Don't take any shortcuts. Avoid attracting the attention of any soldiers. And don't let Blasio out of your sight!"

Five boys of different ages had been selected to complete the acting troupe for a total of six, some playing more than one role. The director spent the first few rehearsals assigning roles and hearing the boys read through their lines. Yacobo quickly became bored. After all, he knew the script backward and forward. He might as well do something else until it was time to pick Blasio up and take him home.

After wandering the streets around the cathedral during a few rehearsals, Yacobo tried something a little more daring: He caught a matatu to the university, slipped into the library, and browsed the books and magazines before catching another matatu back to Namirembe Hill. By timing how long it took to travel to and from the university, Yacobo discovered he had about one hour free to read in the library in order to get back to the cathedral in time to pick up his younger brother.

Only one hour was like biting into a juicy mango and having to stop at one bite. Yacobo found himself devouring travel books on South Africa, Nigeria, Australia, Russia. References in these books sent him looking for other books on other subjects: the Boer War in South Africa; the practice of banishing English criminals to Botany Bay, the prison colony in Australia; stories by the Russian writer Leo Tolstoy . . . He was frustrated at not being able to check out any books to read at home and eagerly looked forward to his private journeys into other times and places.

One day his mother received a letter from Mera Kivengere in Pasadena, California, which Eunika read aloud to the family at the supper table. "She says Festo travels a good deal, preaching and trying to arouse concern about the situation here in Uganda. He is also trying to organize something to help the thousands of refugees fleeing into other African countries. . . . Oh, she is very frightened for Charity at the university and wants us to beg her to leave and go stay with her sister Peace." Eunika looked up. "Theo, do you think we should insist that Faisi leave, too, before something terrible happens?"

Yacobo had heard this conversation a dozen times.

In spite of the growing tensions in the capital city, plans for the Centennial celebration marched forward. To no one's surprise, Bishop Silvanus Wani was appointed the next archbishop of the Church of Uganda. Yacobo shrugged off his disappointment. He had hoped it would be Festo Kivengere, but it served him right for leaving the country.

Dress rehearsals for the Centennial play loomed the last week of May. "Please stay and watch the dress rehearsals!" Blasio begged Yacobo. "I've got my lines all memorized, and you can see what a good job I'm doing as Yusufu."

"Why would I want to see the dress rehearsals?" Yacobo said crossly. Seeing the disappointed look on Blasio's face, he softened a little. "I'm sure you're doing a good job, Blasio. But

I want to see the real performance, kind of like for the first time."

Riding the matatu to the university, Yacobo realized he was feeling more and more anxious about seeing the play. Why? It made him feel naked having his writing be exhibited to a lot of people in this way. What if they thought the writing wasn't very good? And then there was the whole thing about Blasio playing the part of Yusufu. He wished it were a stranger, somebody he didn't know.

Yacobo shrugged off the feeling and enjoyed the extra time he got to spend in the university library. Dress rehearsals were longer than usual; he had plenty of time to get back and pick up Blasio. By the time the matatu dropped him off near Namirembe Cathedral, his stomach was complaining, and he hurried to get Blasio so they could go home for supper.

But as he turned the corner, he stopped. One . . . no, two black Mercedes were pulled up in front of the cathedral. They were the kind of cars government men rode in. In spite of the mild seventy-degree weather, chills ran up Yacobo's back. Was something wrong? Should he run in to see if something was the matter? Should he—

Just then the door of the cathedral burst open, and a man in sunglasses and a brightly colored shirt stepped outside. He was holding an automatic weapon and stood guard right outside the door. Yacobo ducked down behind a parked car and peeked around the taillight. Right behind the guard, more men wearing sunglasses and carrying pistols hustled down the steps, pushing several boys ahead of them toward the black cars. The boys said nothing, but the terrified looks on their faces said everything.

Blasio! Those men had Blasio! Why were Idi Amin's henchmen taking the boys from the acting troupe? Yacobo wanted to scream for help, but his whole body felt paralyzed as he watched the men push all six boys into two of the cars. Car doors slammed, tires squealed, and the black cars roared down the hill and out of sight.

CHAPTER 10

WINDS OF FIRE

Afterward, Yacobo couldn't even remember how he got back home, or what he said when he stumbled, gasping for breath, into the apartment. But he would never forget the look of fear on his mother's face, like that of an antelope cornered by hungry lions.

"Blasio!" she whispered in a strangled voice. "They took Blasio?" And then her voice became louder and louder, until it was almost a scream. "Why did they take my baby? Where is he? *I've got to find him!* I've got to find—"

Suddenly she turned on Yacobo. "Where were you, boy?" she demanded. "You were supposed to take care of Blasio! Where were you?"

Yacobo tried to swallow, but his mouth was as dry as week-old bread. "I . . . I was just coming back to pick him up," he said miserably.

"Back from where?" his mother screamed.

"Eunika! Not now, not now," Theo Kabaza interrupted,

taking his wife by the shoulders and turning her face to look at him. "Yacobo could not have stopped those men. They might have taken him, too! We've got to pull ourselves together and find Blasio. I'm going to go get help. You must contact Faisi at the university, tell her to come home. Pray! We must pray."

Theo jammed his cap on his head and rushed out.

Yacobo's mother just sat in a chair and rocked herself, moaning, "Oh, God, they've taken my baby. Oh, God . . ."

Not knowing what else to do, Yacobo used the archbishop's phone to call Faisi at the residence hall at Makerere University. She wasn't there, so he left a message at the front desk.

Waiting was hard. Too much time to think. Why would Idi Amin's Special Forces kidnap six boys? Surely the president didn't think they were plotting to overthrow the government! Ridiculous!

Faisi flew into the staff quarters about ten o'clock that night. She made Yacobo tell what happened. When Yacobo confessed that he'd been at the university library reading, he saw his mother's eyes flash anger again, but she turned away and didn't say anything.

"Come on, now, Mama," Faisi said in a steady voice, "let's pray. We must pray. God is bigger than this. Come on, now . . ."

They prayed—or rather, Faisi did. All Yacobo could manage was a desperate silent plea. O *Jesus, please help Taata find Blasio, and make him be all right.*

They waited all through the night with no word. Morning came, and Faisi fixed tea for everyone and buttered some bread. Then they heard slow footsteps coming up to the door. The door opened and Theo Kabaza just stood there, looking from one to the other and opening his mouth, as though searching for the right words.

Eunika half rose from the kitchen table. "Blasio," she whispered. "Did you find . . . ?"

Theo's shoulders heaved. "Dead," he said in a hollow voice. "The local police found . . . found all six boys dead in a vacant lot."

Dead? Not dead! The words screamed silently inside Yacobo's mind as he lay on his bed, hot tears streaming down his face. In a sudden fit of rage, he beat on his pillow again and again, until he finally fell back in exhaustion.

Why? Why kill six innocent boys? Archbishop Wani said there was only one reason: Idi Amin wanted to stop the church's Centennial celebration. The president felt threatened by the idea of thousands of Christians gathering in Kampala in joyful worship. *He* was master of Uganda. He didn't want anything going on he couldn't control.

In the next room, Yacobo could hear his mother weeping. She'd been crying for hours. He could hear Faisi's voice, alternately crying with her, praying with her, making soothing murmurs.

His mother blamed him. Yacobo knew she did. Why not? He blamed himself. *If only I hadn't gone to the library!* his mind accused. Would Blasio be alive and well right now? Would it have made any difference? He remembered how helpless they had all been the night Amin's gunmen had pushed their way into the archbishop's house. What could he have done against men with guns?

As Yacobo lay on the rumpled bed, the pillow wet with his tears, the "if onlys" kept coming. If only Blasio hadn't been acting in the Centennial play. . . . If only Yacobo hadn't agreed to write the play in the first place! . . . If only plans for the

Centennial celebration had been dropped after the archbishop was killed—

Suddenly Yacobo sat up in his bed as a fierce, hot resentment seemed to bore a hole in his gut. If Bishop Kivengere hadn't encouraged them to go ahead with the Centennial play anyway, even after the archbishop had been murdered, Blasio would be alive today.

The next few days felt unreal. Like watching terrible things happen on a movie screen, Yacobo felt distant, detached. His father and Archbishop Wani retrieved Blasio's body from the police. The small coffin sat in the intimate chapel of the archbishop's residence like a stark exhibit in a museum. The family gathered in the chapel with the new archbishop to discuss what should happen next.

"Maybe we should leave Uganda," Theo said, his voice still husky with grief. "My family is too high a price to pay for Amin's madness."

"I just want to bury my boy back home in Kabale," Eunika said dully, her eyes on the coffin.

"There will be a memorial service for all six boys at the cathedral in a few days," said the archbishop kindly.

"I just want to bury my boy back home in Kabale," she repeated.

Theo Kabaza laid an arm around his wife's sagging shoulders and nodded. "She is right. We will go home to Kabale right away—tomorrow."

Faisi nodded slowly. "Yes. I will come, too. But I worry about Charity . . ."

"She is already gone," Archbishop Wani said reassuringly. "Strangers have been reported on campus, asking where she stays, what her schedule is. We all agreed she is not safe at the university. She has gone to stay with her sister Peace, whose married name gives some safety."

School was just about to start after the two-month holiday, but no one said anything about Yacobo's school. He shrugged to himself. What did he care? It didn't matter. Nothing really mattered anymore.

They buried Blasio next to his grandfather in a Bahororo graveyard on the outskirts of Kabale. "Children shouldn't go before their mothers and grandmothers," wailed Eunika as dirt was shoveled in on top of her son's coffin.

"Do not forget," Theo said gently to his wife, "Blasio is with Jesus. He, too, is a martyr in the kingdom of God."

"Thank you, Jesus!" whispered Faisi fervently.

Yacobo clenched his teeth. A martyr? More like a victim. Where was the triumph, the so-called "ringing testimony" in his brother's death? Slaughtered, that's all. Slaughtered like goats on butchering day.

Maybe all those martyr stories were just myths—made-up stories to give some "meaning" to senseless, tragic deaths like Blasio's. What a fool he'd been to try to write up the martyr stories! No wonder he couldn't make them sound believable.

The Kabazas stayed with Eunika's mother until they found a small bungalow of their own to rent. As the rainy season ended and the June sun warmed the air and kissed the tops of the Bufumbira Mountains in the west, gradually they tried to put their lives back together. Theo got his job back as a taxi driver, and Faisi got a job as a secretary at the Kigezi district church office, which was trying to hold things together in Bishop Kivengere's absence.

But even though it was the middle of the school year, Yacobo refused to attend the high school. "I won't go," he told his parents flatly. "I'm fifteen, and I don't have to finish. I'll get a job."

Later he heard his parents talking about him—or rather, he heard his father talking to his mother about him. His mother rarely said anything to or about Yacobo anymore. She seemed sunk in her grief, doing household chores mechanically. When Yacobo did catch his mother's eye, he looked away quickly to avoid the blame he saw there.

"I have a friend—Michael Barongo, remember him?—who farms not far from town," said Theo to his wife. "He said he'd take Yacobo on. It's a hard time for the boy. Some physical labor will probably be good for him." But there was sadness in his voice.

Fine, thought Yacobo. *That's exactly what I want.*

Theo fixed up an old bicycle for Yacobo to use to get back and forth to work on Mr. Barongo's farm. Yacobo went early and came home late, eating the cold supper his mother left for him. And soon it became easier to just stay overnight most nights during the week and come home only on weekends.

Yacobo liked the hard work—once the blisters on his hands healed and formed calluses. He hoed potatoes, yams, carrots, onions, and cabbage. He fed goats and mucked out sheds. He learned how to milk the Longhorn cows, leaning into their soft, warm sides and hearing the milk *swish, swish* into the metal bucket. Mr. Barongo, silver-haired, with smile wrinkles around his eyes, told Yacobo that their tribespeople, the Bahororos, traditionally were cow herders. Cows were valued and respected, and the rhythms of the day revolved around milking and herding. As a child in his family kraal, the farmer told Yacobo, he drank nothing but milk mixed with cow's blood until the age of fourteen.

Yacobo wasn't sure about milk and cow's blood, but he was glad to be on Mr. Barongo's farm. It was hard work, but he liked it that way. It made him tired—too tired to think at night when he fell into bed.

One weekend when he was home, Faisi said, "We got a letter from Bishop Kivengere—there on the table if you want to read it."

Yacobo ignored it. But as he was about to leave for work early Monday morning, he casually picked up the letter and skimmed through it. News of the tragic deaths of the young actors had reached them in America, the bishop wrote, and he and Mera grieved deeply with their friends. *Please, dear friends,* the letter said, *do not let the terrible loss of your beloved son keep you from receiving the deep love of* Christ *and giving that love to others. It is the love of* Christ *that heals wounded hearts. Love is a language anyone can understand.*

A fresh flood of resentment broke through the wall of apathy Yacobo had built over the last few months. He threw the letter aside. Love! Could love bring Blasio back? Could love fill his mother's empty arms again? He slammed the door of the bungalow, hopped on his bicycle, and pedaled furiously toward Mr. Barongo's farm.

———

The new school year rolled around in January of 1978, and still Yacobo refused to go to school. But since he was still willing to work on Mr. Barongo's farm, his parents let him continue. Eunika gradually came out of her shell, but still she and Yacobo talked very little, and they never talked about Blasio.

In June, a year after he started working for Mr. Barongo,

the aging farmer gave Yacobo a small, unused garden plot of his own to plant, and said he could take home or sell all the produce. Yacobo, now sixteen, worked feverishly, tilling the ground behind a plodding cow, planting seeds, chopping out weeds, watching with satisfaction as the little shoots of yams and potatoes and corn pushed up through the rich red earth. He daydreamed about taking home the first bushel of vegetables that he'd grown himself and imagined a big smile on his mother's face.

At home he said nothing about the garden plot Mr. Barongo had given him. Faisi was enjoying her job at the district church office and often brought home reports of Bishop Kivengere's travels. He had set up an organization to help Ugandan refugees and get them resettled in Tanzania, Kenya, Rwanda, and Burundi, with aid from Christians around the world. "He hasn't lost his sense of humor," Faisi laughed once, reading a news report from England. "Some reporter asked him if Idi Amin refused to let him back in the country. 'No,' Festo grinned, 'he just couldn't guarantee my safety!' "

Yacobo did not join in the general laughter.

In October, the newspapers trumpeted that General Amin was taking a "bold new offensive" against Tanzania, where Milton Obote was living in exile. But the invasion fizzled out, and the *Monitor* and other newspapers skillfully refocused the public's attention on the fires sweeping across African grasslands, threatening wildlife and farmers' crops.

Pedaling his bicycle along the tarred road toward the farm, Yacobo shut out the news of an invasion, just like he shut out the reports of continued slaughter among the northern tribes of Uganda. All he cared about right now was doing his work for Mr. Barongo and harvesting the vegetables he'd planted before the fall rainy season set in. He pushed hard against the pedals as the road eased up a long, low hill. He was not really thinking, not really seeing the gray-black haze that was boiling up over the horizon.

But as he crested the hill and started to coast down toward the farm, he was startled to see smoke like boiling clouds rolling along the ground under a clear blue sky. He pulled up on his bicycle and stared for a moment. Then he realized what he was looking at: *grass fire!* And it was sweeping straight toward Mr. Barongo's farm!

CHAPTER 11

STRONGER THAN HATE

Yacobo stood at the edge of the garden he'd planted and nudged a charred cornstalk with his boot. The entire plot was still smoking from the fire that had raged two days earlier. In fact, as far as his eye could see, the land was scorched and blackened.

Mr. Barongo's house and outbuildings had been spared, thanks to a muddy irrigation ditch he had dug years earlier to catch the rains during the rainy seasons. But the crops were gone. The grasslands were gone. Alive, green, and thriving one day, holding so much promise . . . and the next gone, just like that.

Suddenly Yacobo's chest began to heave, and a loud cry of protest sprang from somewhere deep inside him. Dropping to his knees, he put his face in his hands as sobs shook his whole body. The garden—gone. Blasio—gone. Archbishop Luwum—gone. Bishop Kivengere—gone. His writing—gone. Everything—gone, gone, gone.

After losing his fall crops, Mr. Barongo could not afford to pay Yacobo to work for him anymore. Yacobo shrugged. What did it matter? Nothing much mattered anymore. Using his bicycle, he managed to find several odd jobs running errands and making deliveries for Kabale shop owners—anything to help bring some money *into* the house and keep him *out of* the house as much as possible.

The New Year of 1979 was heralded in the newspapers as "the eighth year of President Amin's 'Life Presidency.' " Yacobo tried not to think about the future. What kind of future could it be with Idi Amin as "president for life"? It was still too dangerous in Kampala for Faisi to return to Makerere University. Why should he bother even going to high school if there was no hope of completing his education? Idi Amin had already ruined their lives and was going to ruin the whole country, just like the grass fire had destroyed all the land in its path.

In February, the newspapers reported that Ugandan "rebels" were joining up with the Tanzanian army to invade Uganda. But Idi Amin's government didn't seem too worried. Hadn't they already crushed an earlier attempt by Tanzania to invade Uganda?

Even though his father and sister tried to keep up with the news, Yacobo let it all go in one ear and out the other. The biggest problem he let his mind consider was how to do his delivery job. The spring rains had started early, making it difficult for Yacobo to be out on his bicycle.

One late afternoon, soaked to the skin, he leaned his bicycle against the bungalow and ducked into the house to get dry clothes and a slicker before going back out again. To his surprise, his mother was curled up against some cushions, reading a small blue book. She didn't even look up when he came in, but he noticed a strange, hungry look on her face, as if she was devouring the words on the page. Strange. It had been a long time since his mother had done any reading, not even the Bible.

The next day he saw her reading again, and this time she was crying. Yacobo felt uneasy. What kind of book would make his mother cry? He hadn't seen her cry since Blasio was killed. In fact, all her emotions had seemed to dry up. She looked up and saw him looking at her, and for a moment he thought she was going to speak to him. But her eyes filled with tears again, and she looked away.

Curious, Yacobo waited till his mother left the house to go to market, then he stole a look at the book title: *I Love Idi Amin*. A jolt of anger surged through him. What was this trash? He snatched up the book and looked at the author's name: *Bishop Festo Kivengere.*

Yacobo threw the book across the room. How *dare* Bishop Kivengere write such a book? How could he write about *loving* the man who was responsible for killing his brother? And why would his mother—his *mother*, of all people!—read it?

At supper, Yacobo had to practically bite his tongue to keep from demanding where the book had come from. But he didn't dare lash out in anger at Bishop Kivengere in front of his mother. Didn't she still blame *him* for not staying with Blasio at the cathedral that terrible day?

The tense suppertime was finally over, and Faisi started to clear the dishes from the table. To Yacobo's surprise, his mother said, "Yacobo, could . . . could I talk with you?"

Yacobo stiffened. Talk to him? He and his mother hadn't really talked in almost a year and a half. Was she going to dump all her feelings of blame on him again? Didn't she know nothing could be worse than the blame he already felt for Blasio's death?

The rain had stopped, and Eunika Kabaza walked outside into the damp evening. Yacobo followed obediently, wishing desperately he was someplace else. Standing beside her, Yacobo realized he had grown taller than his mother.

"Yacobo," Eunika said slowly, "this is very hard to say. Because I know you have felt blamed by me for Blasio's death . . ."

Yacobo sucked in his breath painfully. Yes, he had sensed it, felt it. But it was like a sharp knife in his gut to hear her actually say the words.

"But I want you to know that Christ has taken away all blame from my heart. In fact . . ." His mother paused and turned to Yacobo, lifting her eyes to meet his. They were brimming with tears. "In fact, *I was wrong* to blame you, my son. Will you—can you—forgive me for holding you so far away from my heart?"

Yacobo blinked rapidly and tried to swallow the lump in his throat. *No, no!* his mind cried out. *It is* I *who needs to be forgiven for leaving Blasio at the cathedral without your permission!* But the words would not come out.

As if reading his mind, she said gently, "You were wrong to leave Blasio during the play rehearsals without telling us . . . but your father is right. You could not have stopped those gunmen even if you had been there. *It is not your fault, Yacobo!* I forgive you, and God forgives you. Now . . . you must forgive yourself."

"Oh, Mama," Yacobo whispered, his voice choked. She put her arms around him as mother and son cried together.

After a few minutes, Eunika said softly, "You see, Yacobo, Bishop Kivengere has reminded me that God's love is stronger than hate. If we don't forgive those who have hurt us, we allow them to continue to hurt us every time we think about the evil they have done. But if we forgive others like God forgives us, we break the power of evil in the world. We are free! Free to love again, free to live again." She kissed him and went inside.

Yacobo could hardly sleep that night. What had happened to bring about such a change in his mother? And yet something . . . no, everything seemed different. In the morning he heard her singing and praising God in the kitchen, just like she always used to. And the walls between them had just . . . disappeared. She smiled at him and touched him gently on the shoulder as he sat down to eat his breakfast of boiled millet and mashed bananas.

The rain had started again, heavy now, and Yacobo could not do his deliveries. Picking up the book by Festo Kivengere, he started to read. It was like walking a familiar road after a long, long time of being away. The little book started by telling the story of the arrest and death of Archbishop Janini Luwum at the beginning of the Centennial year of the Church of Uganda. *How like the beginning of our church this was! Festo wrote, when our church started with shed blood. But,* he wrote, *a living church cannot be destroyed by fire or guns.*

Yacobo could not put the little book down. Chapter by chapter Festo Kivengere told the story of Idi Amin's ruthless grasp for power and the events of the past eight years. Each event, so familiar to Yacobo, right up to Festo and Mera Kivengere's flight out of Uganda. But then Bishop Kivengere shared his own struggle in exile, of his heart becoming hard and bitter toward this man, Idi Amin, who had murdered his friend, threatened his daughter, spied on his home, and made it necessary to live in exile apart from his beloved country.

So, Yacobo thought. Festo Kivengere also knew anger and hate.

He kept reading. On Good Friday of that first year in exile, as Bishop Kivengere meditated on the Crucifixion story, he was struck by Jesus' words, "Father, forgive them, for they do not know what they are doing." The bishop asked himself: Could he forgive Idi Amin? The Lord seemed to be saying to him, "You owe Amin the debt of love, for he is one of those for whom Christ shed His precious blood."

Yacobo put the book down. He mulled over Bishop Kivengere's words. God forgave us while we were still sinners . . . Christ forgave people who tortured Him . . . Bishop Kivengere said God wanted him to love Idi Amin . . . his own mother forgave him. . . .

The thoughts overwhelmed him. He had to think.

The April rain had eased to a light mist. Shrugging into a light slicker and hopping onto his bicycle, Yacobo began to ride out of the town, out into the countryside. He hadn't been out to Mr. Barongo's farm for several months. It had been too depressing to see the ruined fields. But maybe he should say hello to the old fellow. The fresh air felt good in his lungs, and pedaling the bicycle up and over the gentle hills sent blood surging through his body.

As he neared the farm and came over a small rise, something seemed different. At first Yacobo didn't know what it was. Then suddenly he braked and stood staring at the fields all around him.

Every single field had burst into bloom, lush and green in the gray mist. The charred ground had all but disappeared under new green shoots poking up through the ashes, even thicker than the year before.

Yacobo grinned, then began to laugh. All around him nature was confirming what Bishop Kivengere had been writing about: The fires of destruction may destroy for a time, but God's power is stronger than evil and hate and feeds new life even in the middle of devastation.

When Yacobo finally rode his bicycle back into town, he thought he heard the sound of drums, music, and shouting. *What could that be?* he wondered. It wasn't a holiday, was it? It had started to drizzle again, but everywhere he looked, people were out in the street, dancing in the rain, hugging each other, laughing and shouting.

Quickly riding home, he let the bicycle drop to the ground as he rushed inside. The bungalow was full of neighbors, talking and laughing. "What has happened?" he asked. "Why are people out in the street?"

"What?" Faisi cried. "You haven't heard? The Tanzanian army has entered the city of Kampala, and Idi Amin's own soldiers have turned against him. He has fled the country!"

Finally the last neighbor had gone home and the rest of the family was in bed. But Yacobo sat on his bed, leaning against the wall. Something new was stirring inside him. He kept thinking about Bishop Kivengere's little book. Just words on paper, but they had wakened his mother's sleeping spirit and put things into a new light for him, as well.

Words on paper . . .

With sudden determination, Yacobo reached over to the little table beside his bed, pulled out paper and pencil, and began to write.

CHAPTER 12

MY WEAPON IS LOVE

The streets of Kabale were full of people in a holiday mood. Drums and flutes added to the merriment as people sang and danced. Today was Saturday, May 12, 1979, and their very own bishop was coming home from exile!

Theo and Eunika Kabaza, followed by Faisi and Yacobo, pushed their way into St. Peter's Cathedral. Kabale's modest cathedral was already packed with men, women, and children eager to see Bishop Kivengere. Everyone was by now familiar with the news: After the Tanzanian army had helped liberate Kampala, Yusufu Lule had been named "interim president"; Idi Amin had fled Uganda and asked for sanctuary in Libya; the so-called "State Research Bureau" had been opened, revealing stockpiles of weapons, torture chambers, and hundreds of rotting corpses.

But Bishop Festo Kivengere's return to the Kigezi district in the southwestern corner of Uganda had become their symbol that Idi Amin's reign of terror was truly broken.

From the cheers of the hundreds outside, Yacobo guessed that the Kivengeres had finally arrived. Soon the beaming bishop and his wife were led into the church, their necks adorned with garlands of flowers. Hands from all sides stretched out toward them as they slowly made their way to the front of the church. Along with the cheers and singing, the whole congregation was clapping. Faîsi and Yacobo grinned at each other. They had never heard anyone clap for someone in an Anglican church!

Finally the congregation quieted down so the bishop could speak. His voice choked with emotion, Bishop Kivengere said, "It is a great, great joy—I can't put it into words!—to feel in Uganda the fresh air of liberty, to look around, no guns at one's back." He opened his Bible and read Psalm 126, the psalm of hope that had sustained him all during his exile. . . .

> *"When the Lord turned again the captivity of Zion, we were like them that dream. Then was our mouth filled with laughter, and our tongue with singing: then said they among the heathen, The Lord hath done great things for them. The Lord hath done great things for us; whereof we are glad."*

". . . The Lord hath done great things for us, whereof we are glad! . . ." the bishop repeated. His voice broke and he could hardly continue. But at the end of his greeting, he said, "Uganda has suffered deeply. There are gaping wounds that must be healed. But we cannot afford retaliation and revenge. We cannot reconstruct without reconciliation. The healing love of Jesus Christ is the only antidote to the terror that has poisoned our country. Uganda is not destroyed! Uganda is the land of resurrection!"

Eunika reached over and squeezed Yacobo's hand. He gave

his mother a quick smile. It was true. The reconciling love of Jesus had healed his relationship with his mother. But there was still something else he had to do before he was free.

The Kabaza family attended the big feast in Festo and Mera's honor at Kigezi High School that evening. Theo and Eunika Kabaza then went home to bed, but Yacobo and Faisi joined a crowd of neighbors and friends who built a bonfire under the canopy of African stars, and spent the night singing and praying with joy outside the Kivengere home.

Yacobo tried not to be impatient as he watched the sparks from the fire dance and snap. But the way things were going, it might be days before he could speak to Bishop Kivengere alone!

The next day, Sunday, St. Peter's Cathedral was again crowded with well-wishers. Bishop Kivengere addressed the congregation, again encouraging his fellow Ugandans to not give in to bitterness and hate. "While I was in exile," he said, "I was asked how I would react if I were handed a gun and President Amin were sitting opposite me. The only reply that I could give was that I would hand the gun to the president and say: 'I think this is your weapon. It is not mine. My weapon is love.' "

There was a shuffling and murmuring throughout the congregation. Yacobo thought he knew what most people were thinking: *Do I have that kind of love?*

On the way home from the cathedral in the old taxi, Theo Kabaza said thoughtfully, "We must pray that Uganda heeds the words of Bishop Kivengere. Already I have heard people talking about making the Kakwa tribespeople pay for the sins of Idi Amin."

Take revenge on the Kakwas? For the first time in almost two years, Yacobo thought of Byensii, his old enemy at school in Kampala. Was Byensii afraid now? A slight flicker of satisfaction made him want to smile. But then he thought of the bishop's final words that morning: *"I don't believe the church can ever take up the sword to fight and still have a ministry of healing."*

Help me, Jesus! he prayed silently. *Help me love Byensii in my heart.*

The weekend of celebration was over, and the next week Yacobo finally rode his bicycle over to the Kivengere home. He wore a pouch slung across his shoulder.

"Yacobo!" said Bishop Kivengere, greeting him with a big smile. "You have grown into a young man since I last saw you."

Mera Kivengere greeted him with a sad smile. "We were devastated to hear about . . . about Blasio and the other boys."

The bishop and his wife wanted to hear all about his family, but Yacobo finally was able to say, "Bishop Kivengere, I . . . I have something I need to say to you."

Gracefully, Mera Kivengere suddenly thought of something she had to do and excused herself.

Yacobo had thought about this moment for weeks, but now that it was here, he was having a hard time finding the words. Finally he said, "Bishop Kivengere, I need to ask you to forgive me. I . . . I was angry when you left the country after Archbishop Luwum's death. And after Blasio and the other boys acting in the Centennial play were killed, I blamed you for encouraging the bishops to go ahead with the Centennial celebration in spite of the political climate."

Yacobo paused. Festo Kivengere was listening intently, but he did not say a word.

The boy took a deep breath. "But I was wrong in my heart. I know that now. Can you . . . can you forgive me for holding these things against you?"

There. It was out. But what would Bishop Kivengere think? Would he think this was a backhanded way of trying to accuse him?

"Oh, Yacobo," said the bishop kindly. "You and your family have suffered so much. I am so sorry. And I am sorry that I was not there for you—your own bishop. Of course I forgive you. How can I not? So many times I have failed my wife, my friends . . . and God has forgiven me. We will talk no more about it. It is completely covered by the blood of Jesus."

Yacobo nodded, for a moment speechless in the big bear hug the bishop gave him. Now he was free.

As he turned to go, he said, "Oh, I almost forgot." Reaching into the pouch, he drew out a handful of papers, which he handed to the bishop. "This is something I've written—after not being able to write anything for almost two years. It is called 'Martyrs' Song,' the same title as the play. In fact, it covers some of the same stories as the other things I've written. But this time it is *my* testimony, how the deaths of the martyrs of Uganda, including the archbishop and my brother, Blasio, have helped me understand freedom in Christ."

The bishop took the manuscript. "Thank you, Yacobo. I will gladly read it." He laughed. "You will be published yet, young man!"

Yacobo grinned. "No, thank *you*, Bishop Kivengere. It was your little book, *I Love Idi Amin,* that showed me the power of a testimony—words on paper—to change people's lives."

MORE ABOUT FESTO KIVENGERE

He was born in a traditional "kraal" of the Bahima or cattle herders of the Bahororo tribe in Uganda, probably in 1919 or 1920. Kivengere, as he was named, was a grandson of the last great chief of the Bahororo tribe. But just before the turn of the century, Uganda had become a British protectorate that linked the various tribes into a coalition, using tribal chiefs as local government officials.

Formal education was primarily provided by "mission schools." At the age of eleven, Kivengere was designated a "reader" and eligible to receive Christian baptism. It was the custom for Christian godparents to choose a biblical name at baptism, so young Kivengere was christened "Festus" (or Festo) after the Roman governor in Acts.

His conversion was genuine in the sense that he left the religion of pagan spirits behind, but it was a conversion based on law, not grace, and by the time he went to university, he had become a cynical agnostic. At the age of nineteen, he was horrified to return to his hometown of Rukungiri and find newly converted Christians praising the Lord in the street, returning stolen goods, asking forgiveness of people they had wronged. This was sheer fanaticism!

The East African Revival, as it came to be known, swept across Kenya, Uganda, and other East African countries. His younger sister, his niece, even his best friend were all praying for Festo. Finally he fell to his knees and committed his life to following Jesus with his whole heart.

What a transformation! The sacrificial love of Jesus filled his heart and began to change him. He asked his abusive stepfather, whom he had hated for many years, to forgive him for his hatred. He was also convicted to ask the forgiveness of a white missionary whom he had resented and had spoken against behind his back. The words "Please forgive me" broke down walls of separation between these men and resulted in reconciliation. Festo was amazed at the power of Christ's revolutionary love.

Although trained as a teacher, his real passion became evangelism. In 1945, he and his wife, Mera, went as "missionary teachers" to Dodoma, Tanzania, where Festo spent every available weekend and holiday on preaching missions to the surrounding villages and towns. Their family was growing, and by the time they returned to Uganda in 1956, they had four girls: Peace, Joy, Hope, and Charity. But they left behind a little grave: Lydia, their second child, had died in Dodoma the same day Joy was born.

The reconciling love of Christ became a major theme in Festo's preaching. A dynamic preacher, he was invited to speak in Australia and Britain. He also translated for the American evangelist Billy Graham when he came to Africa in 1960, eventually giving up teaching for full-time evangelism both at home and abroad. Teaming up with South Africa's Michael Cassidy, Festo Kivengere helped the evangelistic and relief organization known as African Enterprise spread over many African countries, eventually reaching around the world.

Uganda, meanwhile, was marching toward independence from Britain, which she obtained in 1962. Kabaka, king of Baganda, the largest Ugandan province, became the president of this new independent nation, and Milton Obote was its prime minister. But in a swift military coup, Obote unseated Kabaka, who ended his days in exile in London. Less than ten years later, Obote's army chief of staff, Idi Amin, staged a military coup of his own and took over as "president for life."

Uganda, the "pearl of Africa," with its rich resources, mild climate, and fertile farmland, was rapidly being torn apart by tribal rivalries and civil war. Against this backdrop, Festo became ordained in the Anglican Church, then was appointed bishop of the Kigezi district in southwestern Uganda. His message of the reconciling love of Christ and forgiving one's enemies faced its greatest challenge during the reign of terror of the 1970s, when thousands of Ugandans died at the hands of Idi Amin's military rule.

After the death of Anglican Archbishop Janini Luwum, Festo and Mera fled for their lives. But Festo had to bring his hard and bitter attitude toward Amin to the foot of the Cross. "I had to ask for forgiveness from the Lord," he wrote, "and the grace to love President Amin more." The years in exile were fruitful ones, as Festo continued his evangelistic missions, pled the plight of Uganda before foreign governments, and established a relief organization to help resettled Ugandan refugees. But at the news that Idi Amin had been driven from Uganda, Festo canceled all his scheduled meetings and went home as quickly as possible. Uganda was hurting and needed the healing message of Christ's love.

Milton Obote returned and won a popular election but

turned around and retaliated against the northern tribes that were considered loyal to Amin. Hundreds of thousands more died before he was overthrown by Yoweri Museveni at the end of 1985. Museveni is still president of a Uganda that is gradually reclaiming its stability and prosperity.

All through those years, Festo not only continued the work of African Enterprise and evangelistic tours around the world but was deeply concerned for the children of Uganda, who had grown up only knowing terror. He also started an immunization program against the numerous epidemics that were taking many lives, as well.

In 1988, Festo Kivengere succumbed to leukemia, but the "Billy Graham of Africa," as he was sometimes called, had touched the lives of millions with his message of revolutionary love.

FOR FURTHER READING

Coomes, Anne. *Festo Kivengere: A Biography*. Eastbourne, East Sussex: Monarch Publications, 1990.

Kivengere, Bishop Festo, with Dorothy Smoker. *Revolutionary Love*. Fort Washington, PA: Christian Literature Crusade, 1983.

Kivengere, Bishop Festo, with Dorothy Smoker. *I Love Idi Amin*. Old Tappan, NJ: Fleming H. Revell Company, 1977. Subtitle: *The Story of Triumph Under Fire in the Midst of Suffering and Persecution in Uganda*.